Pure Pressure

To Nigel   3/8/14

Hope you enjoy
the read

Best wishes

Louis Julienne

5/4/2013

ljulienne@btinternet.com

Pure Pressure

Louis Julienne

AuthorHouse™
1663 Liberty Drive
Bloomington, IN 47403
www.authorhouse.com
Phone: 1-800-839-8640

© 2011 by Louis Julienne. All rights reserved.

No part of this book may be reproduced, stored in a retrieval system, or transmitted by any means without the written permission of the author.

First published by AuthorHouse   06/28/2011

ISBN: 978-1-4567-8509-3 (sc)
ISBN: 978-1-4567-8508-6 (dj)
ISBN: 978-1-4567-8507-9 (ebk)

Printed in the United States of America

Any people depicted in stock imagery provided by Thinkstock are models, and such images are being used for illustrative purposes only.
Certain stock imagery © Thinkstock.

This book is printed on acid-free paper.

Because of the dynamic nature of the Internet, any web addresses or links contained in this book may have changed since publication and may no longer be valid. The views expressed in this work are solely those of the author and do not necessarily reflect the views of the publisher, and the publisher hereby disclaims any responsibility for them.

Acknowledgements

There are many people I want to thank for their support in getting this book finished, including people who have inspired me and those who have nagged me over the years to get the darn thing done. They shall remain anonymous but most will know who they are. Special thanks to Sharon Parkinson-Burgan for her encouragement and Heather Sunley for her eagle eye in proofreading. Finally, thank you Henrietta Mary Weaver and Robert Armand Julienne for your silent guidance.

Chapter 1

Crisis

5pm Friday 3rd July 1981

Googie bounded up the concrete staircase two steps at a time like a man in a hurry. Although Googie could be described as cool, laid back, a phlegmatic sort of man, a man who is never rushed, today he was in a hurry. He had been in a hurry all week, waiting for today to happen. Today was a hot and sunny day, as it had been yesterday and the day before going back to weeks, it seemed. Googie liked hot and sunny days; they gave him a feeling of freedom and goodwill. One day Googie intends to emigrate to somewhere hot. Sweat was pouring from him as he stopped at the top of the stairs. Sweat, the payback for hot sunny days. Gallons of the stuff poured out of his lithe body. He was taking two tee shirts into work because by early afternoon large dark patches appeared under the armpits. The fact that there was no air-conditioning where Googie works did not help his condition. He had to nag the management for days before they agreed to buy an electric fan.

Googie took a deep breath and walked purposely along the concrete open walkway. On one side, thin-walled magenta painted maisonettes and the other side afforded a panoramic view of the large expanse of grass that fronted the Englefield Green estate. Although still relatively new being less than ten years old, the estate was already in neglect. The green grass in the middle of the estate, from which its name derived, was littered with paper wrappers, abandoned toys, broken glass, spent condoms and soiled nappies—'the detritus of poverty', Lenny Roberts, Googie's Uncle, called it.

He was like that Googie, a bit of a snob, a blamer of victims for being victims.

"I and I nah riff-raff an' I and I nah mix wid no riff-raff," he would say as a badge of defiance and contempt in avoiding the rude boys.

Every other Friday, Googie took his four-year old daughter Michelle for the weekend and today was the right Friday.

Googie's small, not-quite-reaching-his-neck, locks were dancing, just above the said neck, like little ballerinas as he strode along the corridor his heart beating with anticipation. He hesitated a few moments before knocking on the door, readying himself for what he was going to say. It was always Molly, Michelle's grandmother, who was there at the handover. Molly hardly went out of the door. Elsie had said her mother was agoraphobic. Googie always arranged to pick up Michelle when Elsie was at work.

This was no routine access for the weekend visit. After today, Michelle would not be coming back. That was Googie's plan on this hot sunny afternoon. Take Michelle away from this septic household living on a septic estate. Michelle was going to live with him. Googie had been increasingly convinced over the months that Michelle was brought up wrong with the wrong kind of people around her. Molly, who supposedly babysat her all day and every day, when Elsie was at work, was an irresponsible alcoholic who smoked cigarettes all day long, polluting Michelle's little lungs. Googie wanted better for his daughter. He wanted her to be an Ital child.

"Hello, how are, you Michelle been alright," was Googie's usual gambit and he would stick to the same script so as not to arouse suspicion. He was going to say it in the same smiley and polite way he always did, everything as normal.

Googie had been planning this day for weeks. He would ring the duty officer at Social Services late in the evening, so they would not be too pleased about coming out. He would tell them that he took his daughter from the house because he felt she was at risk. Molly, her Grandmother was if not always drunk at least always tipsy. For Jah's sake, where was the dignity in these people.

Bonny, Googie's first cousin had spoken to Jamal in the off-licence and he confirmed Molly bought alcohol every single day, the cheapest whisky usually. Elsie worked in the bookies on Upper Stanhope Street in the daytime and behind the bar in the Alex on Upper Hill Street in the evenings. Both these jobs, Googie knew, were illegal. Elsie received Benefits on the condition that she was unemployed, and Elsie had two jobs. One job would have been bad enough but TWO. Elsie had always been the breadwinner in the Wright household from the time she was fifteen, including for her older brother Peebo who died of a heroin overdose two months ago, on May 11th the same day Bob Marley passed away.

Googie knew that most evenings Elsie went straight from the bookies to the Alex without going home to check if his daughter was okay. He had watched her, so he knew. He also knew she fiddled some of customers at the bookies taking out a few pounds from large winnings; Elsie told him herself when they were still talking. He could get her the sack if he informed her employers; he would not do that of course, and drew some credit from not doing something he would never do. If he were really nasty he would shop her, blow her up, pure and simple.

Googie's justification bowl was overflowing: Michelle was left alone, all day and most evenings, except for nursery in the mornings, which, he will remind the Court, he pays for out of his meagre salary from the John Archer Youth and Community Centre, where he holds a poorly paid but highly responsible position.

Senior Administrative Officer, he would tell the Court proudly. It sounded so much more impressive than Administrative Assistant, his real title, but one that did not convey his full responsibilities.

It was he, Googie Roberts, who took the minutes of all the Management Committee meetings, which were known to last for hour after hour. He typed them up, collated them and distributed them. It was he, Googie Roberts the Rastaman, who introduced an Actions column to the Minutes. It was to him, Googie Roberts, committed man, peaceful man, who de yout dem in the Centre related to, more than the staff whose job it was to actually engage the youths. Moreover, (Googie liked that word), he always had to correct his boss, Treasa, whenever she gave him a letter or report to type. The woman only had the faintest of acquaintance with orthography and her vocabulary was barely functional. However, she was Irish. Not that Googie had anything against Irish people. Hell, he had Irish blood coursing through his veins. However (another word Googie liked using when he was being pedantic), Treasa was foreign, Irish, and English was her second language so he corrected her grammar with good grace. Googie was tolerant in that way. After all, Googie considered his written English as good as any he had read. Googie's day-to-day language was very different of course, he spoke like a Rasta but could switch at will of course and talk as he wrote—the Queen's English but with a Scouse accent. He was versatile that way.

"You should have been a writer," Treasa said to him once.

"I am a bloody writer," Googie replied, "it's just that I haven't been published yet, but that time will come."

She never made that remark to him again.

It was he, Googie Roberts, who trained the Youth Opportunities Programme placements to become Administrative Assistants. It was he, Googie Roberts, who drove the minibus and took kids on outings, drove the football teams and sometimes the basketball teams to their away games. It was he, Googie Roberts, Administrative Officer for the John Archer Youth and Community Centre, who advised some of de yout dem to claim benefits, and how to treat a sistah, where to get forms to join college—all dose tings dem 'im 'ave t'do.

Googie would speak to the Court in proper English, of course, and tell them he had four GCSEs and two RSA certificates at advanced level, one in typing and one in office practice and that he was doing day release in accounting at Colquitt College in town. He would tell them all that in slow, properly enunciated English, like his Mam wanted him to speak when he was speaking to white people in authority. He had it all figured out. Nobody knew about his plans, not his Mother, not his best friends, nobody except Maureen Ajayi. She had advised him, she knew all about that stuff on the law and the procedures. He would get custody of Michelle. His brother Alan could speak up for him; Alan was a big wheel at Middlesbrough Council and the Chairman of the John Archer Youth and Community Centre. He would tell the Court that Michelle would live in a big house with him and his Mother and that they had a large extended family. Googie was sure he would win the case.

It might not even come to court. Elsie might give up the case when he threatens to blow her up to the Benefits people. He could be ruthless when he had to be.

Elsie was a mistake, a big mistake, Googie always said; but she was pretty back then and still innocent; at least she acted innocent but that soon stopped. Googie was a wise man about women now. He could suss the serious ones from the frivolous just out for a good time. Eventually, he knew, he would need to get a mother for Louise. Elsie would still be her mother and he would provide Elsie with ample access. Lizzie, his Mum would be her Mother as she was his. Lizzie was good at being a Mother; it was what she did best.

Googie rattled the letterbox twice as he knew the bell did not work. Molly answered the door dressed in a yellow tracksuit with the zip low enough that you could almost see her nipples, and they were way down, almost parallel with her belly button.

"Hello Mrs Wright, how are you, how's Michelle?" he asked politely.

"Come in lad, want yer t'meet 'Ank says he knows yer," Molly slurred.

Wonderful, thought Googie, Molly was pissed, more grist to the mill.

Molly grabbed Googie's hand and dragged him into the hallway. Googie had not been inside the house since just after Michelle was born when they broke up, he always waited by the door.

Molly was once a stout woman, but now was painfully thin. She had but two teeth, both of them standing guard on both sides of her lower jaw, an elastic band pulled her dark hair back tightly. She was in her mid-thirties but looked a weary 55. Every time that Googie had seen her she had a lit cigarette dangling from her dry lips, the smoke curling up towards her half closed eyes and today was no exception with the long ash tipping inside her vertiginous cleavage.

The heat inside the flat was more oppressive than outside. Googie blew into his tee-shirt to get a cool breeze down there but it made little difference.

"Come in, me son," Molly said. "'E's come t'see ar' M'chelle, 'Ank, haven't yer lad? Aaar, she's lovely is ar' M'chelle, isn't she 'Ank?"

Googie walked into the living room dominated by the largest television set he had ever seen in his life, a gigantic affair that took up a quarter of the small living room.

"I've come to take her for the week-end. I arranged it with Elsie," said Googie trying hard to breathe through his mouth to avoid the unpleasant odours that were floating around the room. "Nice telly," he said with a polite smile.

"Ar' Elsie bought it me for me on Mother's day. She got it off the ticket man."

"Awrrright' cuz, wha' 'appen' man. Lion, respect," said Hank Crawley, Molly's incredibly tattooed boyfriend.

Hank's ear lobes were covered with red tattoo ink, but more startling was the thin navy-blue line that ran straight from the centre of his forehead to his chin. The line traced the length of his nose interrupted only by a brown bushy moustache, then down the middle of his chin along his throat disappearing behind an incongruously pristine white tee-shirt.

Hank was lounging on the brightly coloured carpeted floor, his back propped up against a shiny mauve-coloured sofa that would take a forensic scientist to uncover its original colour/s. Hank was throwing a plastic ball across the room for a small energetic black and white dog with Welsh Collie origins to chase the ball wherever it landed.

"Awrrright cuz," Hank repeated.

The word cuz was short for cousin and routinely used between black Liverpooleighters to denote tribal closeness, whether related or not. Cuz was also used when somebody you had seen around the neighbourhood for years but didn't know his or her first name although you invariably knew their second name if the person had siblings. Some white guys used the term to black Liverpooleighters as a form of insult, Implying, and that goes deep, that all black Liverpooleighters are related because they've fucked each other for generations. A second category of white Liverpooleighters were those who had hung around with black Liverpooleighters from childhood to adulthood and had earned the right to use the greeting and be called it back. Hank was none of these. Hank called himself a weirdo, a wino, a druggie from Speke and nobody disagreed with him. He had moved into the area a few years back and could regularly be found cadging drinks in the African clubs when he was not in prison. Hank said 'cuz' ingratiatingly so that Googie would treat him as one of the boys. Some hope.

Hank was perfect for Googie's scenario, a real bonus; that startling tattoo alone should gain him custody of Michelle. Social Services will be begging on their knees for him to take her.

Hank held out his hand, Googie proffered his hand instinctively and Hank gave it a most elaborate ghetto handshake to prove his credentials as an adopted 'bro'.

"You okay Rasta man," Hank said.

Michelle rushed into the room and into Googie's arms and he swung her around in the air and plonked her on his shoulders. Michelle was pleased to see him, she always was.

Googie had tried to get custody of Michelle but Social Services were never going to agree to that, not give custody of a young child to a black man, a Rasta man, working or not. Nevertheless, the courts granted him regular access and, for the past fifteen months, he had been collecting Michelle every fortnight.

The tattoo would swing it. How Googie loved Hank's tattoo.

They left immediately. When they got in the minibus, Googie took the large brown envelopes from the front passenger seat, shoved them under his seat whilst making a mental note not to forget to post the minutes of the committee to the members at the main post office before seven o'clock. He placed some cushions on the seat and gently sat Michelle on top of them and locked the seat belt around her.

With the windows wound down and the sun shining on his bare arm sticking out of the window, Googie felt like a king, the Rasta king, ridin' wid 'im picknee dem, cruising in the mini-bus, cutting a fine figure up Princes Road singing along and gently swaying his locks to the taped music.

Michelle, ma belle, sont des noms qui vont très bien ensemble.

Très bien ensemble.

Me luv you, me luv you, me looooooove you

Dat's all me want to saaeeeaaeeeaay . . .

Michelle laughed at him singing her name, and started imitating her Dad's head movement, swaying her auburn little pigtail as her slim shoulders punctuated the reggae beat.

"Mich-elle, ma belle," Michelle sang word perfect, "son day mow qui vun tray bienne ensemble, tray bienne ensemble."

Googie always played the same tune every other Friday when he picked her up. She was word perfect.

"Wow, yes," Googie shouted, "youze a French gal now!"

"Do you want to come and live with me?" he asked her turning the volume of the music down.

She looked at him and blinked.

"Forever you mean?"

"Yes, forever. You would still see your mother and your grand mother and Hank. Do you like Hank?"

"No, because he doesn't smell nice. Would we live in Nanny Lizzie's house because she doesn't like me"

"Of course she does, darling, Nanny loves you."

"I don't think so, sometimes she shouts at me."

"She shouts at me too," he answered. "She doesn't mean harm by it princess; she loves you. Anyway, I would get our own place, a nice little house where there's other little girls you can play with."

"What if Mummy says no."

"I'll take it through the courts and win, but in the meantime you'll stay with me."

Googie stopped off at Ali's, the grocery store on Upper Stanhope Street to buy cigarette papers and a chocolate bar for Michelle.

They had a race back to the minibus and he let her win.

Michelle strapped herself in to show how clever she was and he clapped her for her dexterity then fired up the engine.

"Where we goin' Daddy?"

"To your Nanny's; she's got a nice dinner waiting for you."

"I don't like spicy food, Daddy," she said pulling a face.

"Nanny'll do a special dinner juss for you," he reassured her.

"Will there be lots of people there?" she asked her eyes shining in the sunlight.

"Lots and lots," he replied. "Your cousins will be there, your aunties from London and America, and your uncles."

"Goodie, goodie," Michelle sang clapping her hands.

The bus beamed bright blue in the sunlight as it took a right turn into Berkeley Street. He drove past St Nicholas the Greek Orthodox Church set back from the road on his right and strangely anonymous until you looked up and your eyes were drawn to the dark red brick building's arched white framed windows and the four large round cupolas crowning its roof that suggested Byzantine architecture.

Googie was into architecture. He had done a project in school on the buildings in Liverpool 8. He got top marks for it and used it for his art portfolio.

Googie drew up to the traffic light, next to the drive-in bank that took up the whole of the corner of Princes Road and Upper Parliament Street. He saw Slim with his head stuck under the bonnet of his car. Although Googie could not see Slim's face he recognised him by his legs, no one in Liverpool 8 had longer or skinnier legs than Slim

Googie lowered his window and shouted: "Wha' 'appen', Slim?"

Slim looked up resignation stamped indelibly in his eyes, as if his mother had died or he was about to commit suicide. When Slim recognised Googie as the younger brother of Paul Leung, the car mechanic, hope gleamed instantly in his eyes and the broad grin that spread over his face. Slim's shirt collar was three sizes too big for him and drew attention to an Adam's apple almost the size of an apple that bobbled up and down his elongated throat as he spoke like a busy elevator.

"Wapn' Ras," Delroy known as Slim why-use-eight-syllables-when-two-can-do-except-when-telling-a-joke Branker beamed in reply, translated as *'What is happening, Rastafarian man, are you well?'*

"How's Paul?" he continued, the apple shooting up to his neck like a rocket. Any second now and Googie expected mini passengers to disembark from Slim Branker's mouth.

Quoting Paul Leung's name was Slim's way of putting up his credentials as a friend of Googie's brother and thus worthy of rescue.

Googie parked the van in front of the Vauxhall and stepped out after reassuring Michelle he would not be long.

"Eez wha' de problem, star," Googie asked, joining Slim under the raised car bonnet.

"De ting nah work," Slim replied in his high-pitched Guyanese accent.

"Go turn de key in de ignishun dem," said Googie looking at the greasy engine.

Slim went swiftly and did as he was instructed; Googie liked the idea of telling an older man what to do as it made him feel important. There was no engine noise just a click.

Googie gave his prognosis.

"Eez de startin' mota, star. Gorra 'ammer or 'eavy spanner wid you brodder-man?" involuntarily mixing Jamaican patois and Scouse.

"Me fetch f'yu."

Slim brought back a heavy spanner from the boot of his car.

Pure Pressure

"Y'know de difference between man and wooman," Slim said to Googie when he returned with a spanner.

Googie shook his head, wondering what it had to do with anything. Then he remembered that it was Slim why-use-eight-syllables-when-two-can-do-except-when-telling-a-joke Branker he was talking to, so he knew a joke was coming

"Man ee drivin' up a steep, narrow mountain road. A wooman she drivin' down de same road. As dem pass each udder de wooman lean out she window and shout: 'PIG!' De man lean outa he window and shout: 'BITCH!' Dem each continue on dem way, and as de man go round de nex' corner, he crash into a big pig standing in de middle o' de road."

They both laughed.

"You can't park there, Sunshine," said an unfamiliar voice.

Googie recognised the tone as a white voice, a Police voice.

He looked up and was not pleased to have guessed right. For a brief second before looking up he hoped it was one of the boys trying to put the shits up him.

There were two of them; white, tall, big black boots, brutally dark uniforms, shiny buttons and unsmiling helmeted heads. One had a podgy beetroot for a nose that intimated, quite falsely as it turned out, bonhomie and graciousness; the second had a thin, spiteful line where his lips should have been.

"Pressure me brethren," Googie whispered to Slim.

"Me jussa fix me brethren's car, offissa, Good Samaritan" said Googie to the grim faces as he took the spanner from Slim's hand and leant into the engine's bowels. He then gave the engine a firm knock with the spanner.

"Try it now," he said to Slim.

"Did you hear what I said, Sunshine, you can't park dere?" said Beetroot Nose pointing at the van, his voice totally deprived of charm or accommodation

"Yes offissa, dem fix now," said Googie patiently.

Slim's engine started almost immediately as if on command.

"'Oy, leekle Paul," shouted Slim through the open window of his car as he revved the engine. "Grab 'ola dis, nuh," he added as he proffered his closed hand towards Googie.

One pound, Googie noticed as he stuffed the note inside the palm of his hand.

"Safe man, safe," Googie thanked him.

"An' leave de man alone, you bumba-cloth bully" Slim shouted to the uniforms as he roared through the lights and turned left into Upper Parliament Street in a screech of tyres with a big grin on his face.

"Who's your comedian friend?" asked No Lips. "Whatsis name?"

"I only know him as Tiny, offissa," replied Googie with great sincerity.

"Where d'ya cum from?"

"Jamaica, offissa."

"Jamaica?" grinned Beetroot Nose. "Got ya passport?"

"Look, no, I'm not Jamaican," said Googie thinking the situation was getting out of hand. "Me Dad's Jamaican, I'm British, I'm born here. I'm a yer-no-warramean-like Scouser. I don't need no papers, officer."

"What's ya name?" said Beetroot Nose moving up real close to Googie as if he was going to embrace him or something. But Beetroot Nose did not embrace Googie, instead he jabbed a finger half an inch from his face and repeated "what's ya name".

Googie shook the unwelcome hand off and slipped into the front seat of the minibus. "I'm leavin' now, okay?" he said as he quickly closed the minibus door behind him.

"Are the bizzies gonna arrest you?" Michelle asked.

Googie thought he must do something about Michelle's language and locked the door.

"Open dat door," shouted No Lips.

Googie started the engine, suddenly feeling the heat of the sun peeping through the clouds as beads of sweat wet his brow and trickled down his temples.

No-Lips and Beetroot Nose placed themselves in front of the car, blocking his way.

Googie turned the engine off. Michelle kept on singing oblivious to a situation that was palpably turning ugly. No Lips was on his radio summoning support, whilst Beetroot Nose banged his fists on the window shouting at Googie to open the door.

Michelle stopped singing and began crying.

"It's okay, sweetheart," he said to her, smiling without conviction.

Before long, a van full of uniforms drew alongside Googie's car. One of the uniforms with a fleshy face had his baton out and threatened to smash the driver's side window.

Googie unfastened Michelle's seat belt, took her in his arms, unlocked the transit door and made to step out but he was grabbed and felt a dozen hands pulling him by his locks, at his limbs, tearing his shirt, punching his face. Michelle fell to the floor with him on top of her, and then he felt himself being lifted, carried away and thrown on the metal floor of the police van all the time trying to struggle free. He protected his head from the blows and shouted for his daughter but they were in no mood to listen they just wanted to hurt him.

Taken to Admiral Street Police Station, Googie submitted to a search and was locked up in a cool cell where the sun had never shone.

This was his first time in a police cell. It was as not as medieval as some of de yout dem had described. It was half tiled and an oasis of cool after the glaring heat of the day and the airless police van.

Googie hoped and then prayed to his God that someone had seen what had happened and taken Michelle somewhere safe. Maybe Slim came back. Surely, someone who knew the family had taken her to her house. This was a small community where everybody knew everybody. Michelle only lived around the corner, she may have walked home of her own volition. She was surely safe now. If this had happened anywhere else in Liverpool, Googie would be truly worried, because anything could have happened, but in the middle of Liverpool 8, you could not get a more central point than the Rialto. People met outside the Rio, stopped and talked outside the Rio, caught a bus to town outside the Rio. There were food shops and hairdressers, off-license, Nat West bank (the first drive in bank in the country Uncle Lenny said) around the Rio. There were probably some witnesses without a criminal record hanging around the Rio who would testify that he did nothing wrong. His brothers Alan and Paul, would know what to do to get him out. They were probably on the phone now, demanding his immediate release. They would get him out in no time.

Googie had lost track of the time because the police had taken his "gold metal watch" and his money, and cigarette papers, matches, and the bar of chocolate he had bought for Michelle but did not want her eating before he dinner. They had put all his belongings in a cardboard box and made him sign for them. He wished he could give her the bar of chocolate now. They found his herbs also, not much, just enough for a few spliffs. The gloat in the desk sergeant's voice was disquieting.

"And what we got dere, sunshine? Cannabis! That'll go on your charge sheet."

They questioned him about the cannabis; Googie swearing he smoked it for religious purposes, the police accusing him of being a pusher.

If someone had not taken Michelle to his mother's house, Googie was sure that they would have taken her to the Johnny Archer because of the van. Everybody knew the Jacy bus with the name and address prominently stencilled on the sides and the back of the vehicle. Everybody knew the blue John Archer Youth and Community Centre van. A lot of people, the type who walk past the Rio, even knew where the Jaycee was on Park Way, and they would take Michelle there, and she would be safe. Caroline would be there in the office, getting ready for when the kids came in after school at five, doing her nails and listening to funky music stuff on the radio. She would know to phone the house to inform the family about his situation.

The mail, Googie remembered, the minutes of the Committee meeting would still be in the minibus. He was always prompt in sending out minutes. He typed them up the next day, had them checked by Treasa (mostly he had to chase her—she was always so 'busy') and in the post the same day. He prided himself on his efficiency. Bobo Jones, the youth worker would be sorting out papers or doing funding applications because that's what he liked to do. Juss gi' me de paper work. Joe, the caretaker, should be there playing table tennis should be there also if he had not sloped off to get drunk somewhere, and he would know what to do. You could tell when Treasa, the boss, was away, everybody slacked. Including Googie, who would never have taken the bus to pick Michelle up, and in work time, if Treasa had been in the office. She was away at a conference for the weekend leaving Caroline, in charge but Caroline could not tell Googie what to do; he had put her right months ago when she tried pulling rank over him over making tea.

"I'm nobody's Skivvy," he had told her with dignity.

That had shut her up. Besides, Googie was Treasa's brown-eyed boy. They both adored Bob Marley. He was sure Treasa also fancied him but she was much too old for him. She was nearly old enough for him to call her Aunty if she were black.

What if he was found guilty of breaking the peace and supplying cannabis? Would he lose his job and go on the Dole forever because he had a criminal record? What if he went to jail? There would be no women there so he might even turn battyman. What if a pervert took Michelle with him; he could be abusing her this very minute, then killing her, choking the life out of her little body.

Googie pressed the bell on the cell wall. He waited a few seconds for a response. He could hear the bell ringing, so they could hear him. He rang again and kept his finger pressed firmly on the button. He then began banging the cell door furiously with his fists, his elbows, his knees, his feet, shouting at the top of his voice.

"I want to know me daughter's safe! Open the door!"

Finally, he heard the sound of the key turning in the cell lock. A large policeman in shirt sleeves with menace written all over his face asked him what the problem was. Googie told him he was worried about his daughter. Menace told him his daughter was back home and fine but warned him not to ring that bell or to bang on the door or he will start banging him.

Michelle was safe. His daughter was safe., that's what the man said. Googie was so relieved; it was as if he had suddenly lost 10lb of surplus fat. She was back home. Googie had forgotten about his plan to take Michelle off Elsie. He would have to postpone that plan for a few months, when all this was sorted. He needed to get out of here, out in the sunshine.

He wanted to sleep and lay on the wooden bench fixed to the back wall but it stunk of piss and tears. He shut his eyes but in the darkness, he could see himself dragged away from the car, Michelle screaming and then the kicks in the van, so he opened them again but still the images kept flashing in front of him as if they were happening again. They cannot get away with this, he told himself. There were bound to be loads of witnesses; people in their cars, on the buses. Slim maybe, no, Slim could not wait to get away. Wait until he tells Paul about him, running off like that when Slim knew Googie was in lumber.

He opened his eyes to the stone walls around him and the metal door, closed his eyes back tight again and prayed.

Princes and princesses shall come forth out of Egypt, Ethiopia now stretch forth her hands before Jah. O Thou God of Ethiopia, Thou God of Thy Divine Majesty, Thy Spirit come into our hearts, to dwell in the paths of righteousness. Lead and help I and I to forgive, that I and I may be forgiven. Teach I and I Love and loyalty on earth as it is in Zion, Endow us with Thy wisemind, knowledge and overstanding to do thy will, thy blessings to us, that the hungry might be fed, the sick nourished, the aged protected, the naked clothed and the infants cared for. Deliver I and I from the hands of our enemy, that I and I may prove fruitful in these Last Days, when our enemy have passed and decayed in the depths of the sea, in the depths of the earth, or in the belly of a beast. O give us a place in Thy Kingdom forever and ever, so we hail our God JAH. Who sitteth and reigneth in the heart of man and woman, hear us and bless us and sanctify us, and cause Thy loving Face to shine upon us thy children, that we may be saved, Selah.

Some time later, the door was unlocked.

"Get off yer arse, yer bein' transferred to Cheapside," Menace growled.

Menace led him down the corridor, unlocked another door leading to a courtyard and then into a windowless prisoners' van. Googie was surprised it was still daylight. Maybe it was morning, Googie thought, or even late evening. He asked one of the policemen, a wiry man with wistful eyes, what time it was, but all he got for an answer was a grunt.

Animal noises, that's all you could get from Babylon; grunt like a pig and bark like a dog.

Both wrists tightly handcuffed, Googie was led away in a van to the main Bridewell in Cheapside, an old and narrow street. At reception, two of the policemen that arrested him took his photograph and his fingerprints, made him empty his pockets and searched him. They placed him in front of a jovial sergeant with bushy eyebrows and a round, well-padded belly who charged him with assault occasioning actual bodily harm on four policemen, causing an affray and being in possession of illegal substances. Bushy eyebrows warned Googie was better equipped for dealing with police procedures than police actions.

"I have nothing to say until I see a solicitor," he said firmly.

Googie had given that advice to dozen of yout dem.

"Don' say noffin until you see a solicitor, no statement, no noffin."

The two policemen, No Lips and Beetroot Nose, stood close by his side as if he was going to run away and Beetroot Nose was grinning at him the whole time. He was marched to another windowless airless disinfectant-smelling cell with the de rigueur stained wooden bench and a toilet bowl that Googie dare not use for fear that thousands of unseen malevolent germs would feast on his delicate parts. One distant voice appealed for some tobacco, another pleaded his innocence and another predicted a revolution.

"I'm dyin' for a ciggie." White voice.

"I shouldn't be 'ere. I didn't do nuttin'." Black voice.

"Shut yer cake-hole, dick-head. Everybody's innocent 'ere!" replied the tobacco-less smoker.

"We're gonna cane the pigs." Second black voice.

"I swear on me Mam's life! I didn't do noffin'!" First black voice.

"Neither did I, but where was it going to end," thought Googie.

Was this the worst situation in his short life, he asked himself. Worse than shitting his pants in class and Gracie Martins loudly leading the chorus of fellow pupils as they pinched their noses and mocked him? Worse than the time his mother walked in on him just as he was bringing himself to climax? No. Nothing compared, not even close. Maybe this was going to be the worst moment of his life even if he lived to a biblical 175.

Googie Roberts spent a restless night trying to get comfortable. There was no room to toss and turn on the narrow bench and there were constant noisy goings on outside his cell door.

Someone in a neighbouring cell was singing repeatedly a lament to a Beach Boys tune.

I wanna go home, I wanna go home. Oh, I feel so fucked up, I wanna go home.

The song went on for an age, who knows how long as time had lost its rhythm in this timeless place. He found himself singing along unconsciously at some stage with the 'I wanna go home' ditty. Then the singing stopped followed by an eerie silence; he could hear his heart beating and his belly grumble. A whole night to go, then the Magistrates, then jail, for sure. Might get bail; should get bail, no question. Might lose the job; Googie liked his job. Dread was filling his soul but he found a diversion, a piece of paper wrapped up small in his back pocket that had evaded the search. He carefully unfolded the A4 sheet of white paper that had gone undetected through two searches. It was hand-written; he recognised his pointed and elaborate handwriting. It was the agenda he was meant to type up and distribute with the Minutes for the next meeting of the Management Committee. He read it out loud:

John Archer Centre Management Committee
Agenda

Apologies

1) MINUTES OF THE MEETING HELD ON WEDNESDAY 13th MAY 1981:
1.1 Accuracy
1.2 Matters Arising
2) CORRESPONDENCE
3) Manager's Report
3.1 Existing Projects
3.1.2 Table-tennis tournament
3.1.3 Basketball Club
3.1.4 Preparatory classes
3.2 Proposed Projects
3.2.1 1982 Carnival float
4) FINANCE REPORT
4.1 Quarter 1 Accounts (1 April-30 June 1981)
4.2 Fundraising
4.3 Draft Audited Accounts
5) ANY OTHER BUSINESS
5.1 Change of name
6) DATES OF NEXT MEETINGS

He remembered that he had typed up nonsense Minutes for Gary Clarke to show him the layout for Minutes. He smiled when he thought about the character assassination of each member of the Jaycee management committee depicted in the mock up. Pity they would not get to see those Minutes, that would have got some tempers to rise. Googie's smile turned into giggles and then outright laughter, uncontrollable laughter to the point it had him gasping for breath. Then the hilarity suddenly disappeared as quickly as it had arrived and disintegrated into body-shaking sobs.

Nobody came and he tried desperately to go to sleep, to get away from this bad dream. He forced his eyes shut but he did not like what he saw in the darkness that he had imposed, so he sat up on the wooden bench and took out the agenda again and read the note eight times before he could memorise it, and then he tried to recite it from memory. He did it at the second attempt having forgotten *Change of name*. How could he forget that entry, it was the only constant among sub-headings under Any Other Business. *Change of name* was Norris Nobleman and Nat Ajayi's perennial agenda item and everybody else's bête noire. According to paragraph 43.7 sub-paragraph iv: *any two members of the management committee can include an item under Any Other Business so long as it is provided at least three clear days before the meeting is scheduled to the Secretary of the Management Committee, and without regard to the chair of the management committee.*

Ben Miller, who prided himself on being able to write like a lawyer, drafted that last sentence. The name change they persisted with and which they tried to speak at length about at each meeting was to change the name of the Centre from Alan Archer to the Liverpool 8 Centre, but they were flogging a dead horse. Googie began reciting the agenda from memory backwards.

Meetings Next of Dates
Name of Change
Business Other Any
Accounts Audited Draft
Fundraising
1981 June 30 April 1 Accounts 2 Quarter
Finance Report
Float Carnival

He cursed. Shit, the Carnival Float or rather the Float Carnival comes after the Women's' keep fit . . . He tried it eleven times before he got it absolutely right, then he recited out as loud as he could.

"ACCOUNTS AUDITED DRAFT! FUNDRAISING! 1981 JUNE 30 APRIL WEDNESDAY! ACCOUNTS! ONE QUARTER! FINANCE REPORT!"

He heard some banging in the distance, protest banging no doubt against his nonsensical declarations.

"Shut yer fuckin' face, dick-head!" shouted one voice.

"I wanna go home!" sang another.

Googie tried to count the number of letters contained in the agenda without looking at the note. Eventually thinking he had it right with 446 letters. Then he counted the number of times the letter 'a' came up, then 'b' and right through the alphabet. There were no 'k', 'q', 'v' or 'z'.

"I wanna go home," Distant Voice wailed, reprising his refrain.

Googie's mind wandered some more. He had thought long and hard about keeping his name. George was his official name, but Googie was what everyone had called him all his life. He had been tempted to call himself Benjamin. Benjamin after all was Jacob's twelfth and youngest son and he was Lizzie Leung's youngest child, so there was a connection.

Googie was a cool name; even his mother, who was never one for nicknames, called him Googie, although that was probably because she detested his real name, George, because it was also his father's name. His mother always mentioned his father's name with curses. She never had a good word to say about the man. His sister Doreen hated his father also, for no reason or none that made much sense.

GOOGIE, a unique name shared by no one else. When you said 'Googie', you did not have to say which Googie or big Googie or fat Googie or African Googie or Lanky Googie, because there was only one Googie in Liverpool 8. He knew three Benjamins: Benji Farrell, Ben Miller and Benny Ankrah. However, Googie was surely tempted when Jimbo, Victor, Harry and Maurice (some of his main men), also became Rastas and changed their names, respectively to Agu, Gad, Reuben and Niya short for Nyahbinghi, the oldest Rastafarian sect, and the one to which I and I and I posse belong. Nyah-bin-ghi, after Queen Nyahbinghi of Uganda; Googie loved that name it made a nice sound.

He stood firm, no name change and Googie he remained, with a sort of defiant pride, like he was holding a tiny little bit back from the olden days, from pre-Rasta bald-head days; the same with his accent which had generally become Anglo-Jamaican but occasionally slipped back to South-end-Scouse depending on circumstances and who he was speaking to.

Googie also thought of William Huskisson, an 18th Century Liverpool MP who had become a big noise in the government of that era. Or rather, he thought of William Huskisson's statue on the corner where Princes Road and Princes Avenue meet at the entrance to the BOULEVARD. The best spot in Liverpool 8 to have a 15-foot statue. There haughtily stands William Huskisson MP (1770-1830), dressed in a Toga, one hand slightly raised, staring towards the Rialto, the best dance hall in Liverpool 8 or rather towards what used to be the best dance hall in Liverpool and was now Swainbanks, the ever-growing second-hand furniture store.

After Bob Marley died—a bad, bad day (Gad himself was crying tears and nobody had ever seen Gad cry before or since)—they, Googie and some of his Rasta and non-Rasta brethren and sistren developed some projects to honour Bob's memory. One of these projects was to dismantle the statue of William Huskisson MP (1770-1830) and replace it with a statue of Bob Marley AS (Artist Supreme 1945-1981). Kipper Bailey was working on a bust in plaster already.

Trying to bring a 550-pound bronze statue down with some ropes and a sledgehammer surreptitiously at three o'clock in the morning in one of the brightest-lit street in the city is no easy task. On the third night, the statue of William Huskisson MP (1770-1830) fell but the police came and they all scattered.

The Council took the statue away it was presumed, but maybe an opportunistic passer by took advantage of all that precious metal lying around doing nothing except littering the place.

Googie only fell asleep for a few minutes before being woken up by the sound of his cell door being slammed open in the morning.

The sergeant who opened the door had a round, humane face, like he was someone's father rather than the thug-like demeanour Googie had come to expect from Babylon. The sergeant brought in what passed as breakfast on a metal tray.

"When can I go home?" Googie asked him.

"You're goin' to the Magistrates in a coupla hours' time, sunshine," humane-face answered. "Here, eat this."

Googie shook his head. "No thanks, I'm not hungry. Can I see a solicitor and ring home?" he pleaded.

"Sure, mate, when the day shift comes on."

Human-face gave the tray to Googie.

"Take it, you might feel hungry later on."

Human-face was turning away and slamming the door shut behind him before Googie had finished saying: "Nobody knows I'm here, I need to make a phone call."

Pure Pressure

Googie finally got his wish for a phone call but his mother's phone was constantly engaged and neither Norris Nobleman nor Agu's phones were answering; Reuben and Niya did not have a phone. It was one of those days. Everybody is out on a Saturday morning with football, shopping, leading normal lives while he is stuck in there, unknown to the outside world.

Googie eventually saw a very young looking duty solicitor who told him an application for bail will be made and Googie made him promise to ring his Mother and made him write her number down. He was taken to a large cell with 18 other prisoners. Most of them were black. Most of them Googie knew by sight and others by name, including Nello from Ponsonby Street, Twinny from the Lane and Bomb-Head and Peter Lee from the Falkner Estate.

Googie was told to sit in a small room and wait for his solicitor. The middle-aged solicitor, Mr. Reed from Frombisher and Elliot, had seen and done it all before and mostly failed, BUT HE STILL MADE A DECENT LIVING. It was a different solicitor from the one who promised to ring home on Googie's behalf.

Mr. Reed, said he will try and get "us" out on bail.

Googie was perplexed at first before he realised that the "us" was purely metaphoric, Mr. Solicitor Reed from Frombisher and Elliot meant he was trying to get HIM, Googie Roberts, out on bail, not HIM, Mr. Solicitor Reed from Frombisher and Elliot.

Googie was not convinced Mr. Solicitor would fight for Googie's liberty as if it were his own; it was more a way of speaking, if you like.

'If you like' was a favourite saying of Mr. Solicitor Reed from Frombisher and Elliot, it crept in at least half a dozen times in their conversation.

Googie hoped his Mother and perhaps one of his brothers were upstairs in the courtroom waiting to take him home to his daughter, to his music, to his bath so he could soak away this episode from his life and eat a nice Ital breakfast and change into fresh clothes and get to his job and just return to normality. Ital food for Googie was vital (from which the word derives). It meant food that was natural, organic, pure and from the earth (no colourings or preservatives for Googie Roberts) to increase his Livity, his life energy.

By the time he reached the dock, Googie's stomach had knitted so tightly it made it difficult for him to breathe, he had to swallow greedily for air and his eyes were that of a trapped animal. He was accompanied by two policemen who waved for him to sit down on a chair. Three magistrates sat elevated ten yards away from him and, apart from the Court Clerk in a black cloak fussily checking sheets of paper and a bored-looking journalist, the court was deserted. There was nobody in the gallery, no family, no friends, nobody. Googie's mother certainly was not there; neither were his brothers or sisters or even Norris Nobleman who was always around the courts to offer support to *members of the community*'s accused.

Googie's lawyer nodded at him. The clerk of the court asked him to state his full name and address.

Googie's lawyer asked for bail with the conviction of a man reciting a train timetable aloud to no one in particular.

"Mr. Roberts," he droned, "is in fulltime employment and lives with his Mother in Liverpool. He has joint custody of his young daughter aged four and he will strenuously deny the charges set before the court this morning."

The severe-looking prosecutor opposed Bail because of the gravity of the offence.

The magistrates whispered to each other for a few seconds, stared at him with what seriously looked to Googie like contempt, then one of the magistrates said in a voice that suggested he was passing a death sentence.

"In view of the events in the Liverpool 8 area where very serious civil order disturbances have developed and many police officers have been injured, some quite seriously, you will be remanded into custody until Friday the tenth of July."

Googie's vision blurred with tears and he felt a violent throbbing in his temples. TENTH of July, that's a whole week!

Googie shouted that they had made a mistake but no sound came out. His head and shoulders slumped, even his locks seemed limp, as he was led away back down the stone steps, barely noticing Nello brushing past him as he too went to face his fate anything but reassured by Googie's demeanour.

Fourteen of the eighteen prisoners that morning, including all the black ones, were remanded in custody in the specially convened Saturday Court. This was not a day for cautions or for giving bail; the message was clear, the courts were cracking down on this mayhem that had descended on the streets of Liverpool and they were gonna whup arse, particularly black arse.

Six hours later Googie Roberts, shivering despite the heat of the day, was locked in a cell at Risley Remand Centre near Warrington. He shared the cell with a middle-aged white guy from Page Moss who spoke in hoarse whispers as if he was sharing precious secrets.

Googie lay on the top bunk face down, his head buried in his hand. He was so desperate to let the tears stream out but he felt he could not in front of a total stranger. He could not imagine spending one night in this place let alone seven.

The lawyer had guaranteed him he would get bail next week and not to worry. These are exceptional times, the lawyer added gravely.

Googie did not get to see his Mother or Alan or Paul, his brothers or even pass on a message to find out about what had happened to little Michelle ma belle. He was not really listening to Page Moss's stories of mishap and misfortune; they all seemed like so much bad gas in the air, polluting his thoughts, increasing his depression, aggravating his situation.

Chapter 2

High Tide Or Low Tide

5:45pm Friday 3rd July 1981

Lizzie Leung was in a queasy mood on the eve of her sixty-fifth birthday. The idea of becoming an old person, the moment when the line between late middle age and old age is forever breached. This was not a problem to her at this moment but something else, something she could not put her finger on. She was in good health apart from a persistent smoker's cough and there was no reason why she should not go on to live another ten, even twenty years she often told herself whenever longevity doubts crept up in her mind, which was increasingly often these past few years. Old age was a phenomenon Lizzie had not taken lightly. Why should she when she felt no different from when she was 15. For sure, her body had taken some battering in the intervening years. The marks, the sags, the wear, but her mind had expanded and been enriched. Yet, deep down, in fact not that deep at all, she was still Lizzie Roberts, the effervescent teenager who was madly in love with Clarke Gable and Paul Robeson, and kidded herself that she not only looked just like Dorothy Van Engle, the black American movie star, but she was Dorothy Van Engle whenever she looked in the mirror.

Lizzie could not give an answer as to her uneasiness, but something was pulling at her mind. Maybe it was because she was too happy, and Lizzie knew that tragedy often followed happiness. She could write a book on the tragedies in her life if she were that way inclined. She sat facing the television in her armchair, glasses on the end of her nose, her eyes alternating between her long fingers switching the knitting needles into closely interweaved rows of bluish purple wool and the evening news on the television, with her mind fixed on neither.

" . . . *The Irish National Liberation Army has issued a statement claiming responsibility for the attempted assassination of Protestant leader Ian Paisley . . .*

The British government is said to be considering increased Irish participation in home rule..."

"They should have killed that loud mouthed fingy," said her son Paul, "a bloody trouble maker, always whippin' up the Proddies," lounging on the dining room chair.

"That's not a nice thing to say about anybody," Lizzie said without taking her eyes off her knitting. "I don't like him either, but I wouldn't wish him dead, him or anybody. Stop rocking on that chair, you're gonna break it."

"You don't hate anybody, Mam? There muss be someone you hate, maybe not to want to fingy, them but you know . . ."

"I don't hate anybody," she replied simply.

Lizzie had started on the sleeve of one of the cardigans she was going to do for the twins. They will be ready before the end of the summer. She will get Martine Goolsby to put the trimmings on. That is what Martine was good at, putting trimmings on, trimmings like ribbons for the girls and elbow patches for the boys, and pockets and collars and cuffs that turned a garment from nice to really nice. If it was gaudy you were after Martine Goolsby could do that in spades and sometimes she could do the sublime as well. Lizzie's forte was the durable; her cardies could withstand the fiercest hand washing without losing their shape. The art had passed down her female line and she had kitted out three generations with her handiwork.

" . . . The families of IRA hunger strikers met with the Prime Minister Garret Fitzgerald today to . . ."

All should be well. Food was cooking, Beryl's twin, Doreen was up from London, Alan, her middle son, down from Middlesbrough, and Googie, Googie, her baby, was on his way. Before six he had promised, with his little girl Michelle. She loved children; all children were God's children, although she had particular concern about Michelle who had a mouth like an alley cat; the Roberts gene of decorum had seem to by-pass the poor child.

The Roberts did decorum very well or at least most of them did, as her mind went directly to her sister Esmee. Decorum and Esmee did not go well together, admittedly, but Esmee was an exception. Sure, Esmee could sing like an angel but her mind was gone, if it had ever been there in the first place.

Yet she felt like there was a pulling movement going on inside her chest. Like something was not right.

" . . . There were riots between skinheads who had been stoning and burning shops in the area and Asian residents in the predominantly Indian neighbourhood

of Southall in West London . . . Our reporter Percy Woodbridge sends this report from a troubled Southall . . ."

Lizzie had no reason to be anything other than happy; all her children were with her.

Beryl was here with her twin girls. Beryl was her favourite child . . . no! Lizzie had no favourites, all her children were equally important to her, she reminded herself. However, if Lizzie had a long train journey to go on she would rather have Beryl for company than any of her other children, because Beryl was an entertaining and knowledgeable conversationalist, she could also listen and not be intimidated by silence.

Beryl had flown in all the way from Atlanta Georgia two days earlier with Alice and Alma, to be there for her birthday. Beryl was a loyal daughter and she thanked God every day for blessing her with Beryl. She was the lightest of Lizzie's children. Her complexion was not pinkie white like a Berkshire rose, more light honey; her complexion suggested overseas, yes, but the Mediterranean or perhaps a distant Moorish past—and her eyes shone fiercely Irish green, directly from Lizzie's grand mother. Beryl could easily have passed as white to the uninitiated, but she was fiercely proud of her blackness, her Africaness, although her features had nothing left of Africa. Beryl was an African woman as militant as any Mau-Mau warrior; a little too militant sometimes for Lizzie's taste, to the point of bigotry. To say that Beryl did not like white people was to understate her feelings. She had the reasons, of course, and everybody had heard them all—slavery, colonialism, neo-colonialism, apartheid, racism.

Beryl had a bruise on her left temple that she tried to hide by rearranging her hair, but it did not escape Lizzie's eyes for one moment, glasses or no glasses. At first Beryl said it was an accidental trip; but when Alma told Lizzie '*Marmy and Daddy*' had been fighting she confronted Beryl and got the truth from her.

Beryl confided in Lizzie that she had decided to return to England to live, finally giving up on her American dream.

" . . . Typhoon Kelly caused massive destruction in the Philippines. Hundreds of people are feared to have died in the most sustained storm season the region has known in generations. The storms have been raging since March this year and show no signs of abating. . . ."

That's all the news were, thought Lizzie, bad news and more bad news, riots, hunger strikes, assassinations, disasters killing thousands. God was not doing His work either. He was sleeping or He just could not be arsed.

Greg Carter, Beryl's estranged husband, had beaten Beryl up because she was finally divorcing him. Beryl made her mother swear she would not repeat this to anyone.

"May God strike me dead as I speak, girl. I wouldn't tell a soul," Lizzie promised.

Beryl said Greg changed after getting a head wound in Cambodia, but Lizzie never liked Greg from the first day she met him. He had a good job in the American Air Force, based at Upper Heyford near Oxford and, as a quartermaster aged only 26, he had prospects. But that was not enough for Lizzie, not only because she considered Greg shifty and ugly, bad enough sins in themselves, but also because he never had a word to say for himself and the few times he did speak he never looked you in the eye.

Doreen, Beryl's twin, had come up by train from London yesterday afternoon. She planned to return to London on Sunday morning. Doreen could not be apart from her husband Evelyn and six children for too long. Fourteen years since Doreen left for London. She did not struggle for long. Walked into a Nursery job and got a flat in no time. Shortly afterwards she met Evelyn and within three months they were married and she was expecting the first of the six kids she produced in seven years.

Doreen only came for set pieces—birthdays, weddings and the like. Doreen was a good girl, a good daughter. She paid Lizzie's phone and electric bills directly from her bank by standing order. Doreen got her money's worth you have to say, and Lizzie said it often to herself; always on the phone to London whenever she visited, talking or rather listening to Evelyn because Evelyn could talk for the whole of Christianity.

A long train journey with Doreen would be silent throughout except for the one word answer to any question, her head stuck into a book, any book to save having to converse.

Lizzie thought that Doreen's horrific scars would ruin her life, would prevent her getting a decent man, and would undermine her confidence and her chance to make something of herself.

Lizzie had tried so hard to make Doreen her special child, her mission, but she did not, she could not. Doreen was quiet by nature, but the fire, Lizzie was convinced, had made her deeply introverted, right up to the time she left for London. It became harder to communicate with her. It seemed the event had permanently traumatised her. Doreen did not do well at school; Lizzie suspected she could not do well if she tried. Maybe the fumes damaged parts of Doreen's brain Lizzie often thought but never said. Maybe Doreen took her reserved ways from her father and that is who she was regardless of the fire. The scars were still visible down the left side of Doreen's face. She missed a lot of schooling through the operations, so Lizzie was so pleased when she got a responsible job. Doreen is the manager of a children's nursery. She manages other people and is in charge of the finance and everything.

Lizzie had other reasons to feel guilty towards Doreen, apart from the burns, a guilt that was harder to shift because Doreen had never let her forget it. Not that she ever spoke about it to Lizzie, apart from the first year; it was the looks, and the silences that spoke louder than words. So although never spoken about or referred to, even when they were alone, every so often Doreen would go moody on her, antagonistically silent even, for no apparent reason, and only Lizzie knew why. The one time Lizzie did say to her: "What's the matter, love, you okay," (and that was a long time ago) Doreen spat out "You know what the matter is!"

"I did it for your own good, love," Lizzie croaked back.

That was the end of that conversation. The next day Doreen was her normal silent and polite self again as if the incident had not happened.

Lizzie was contented and proud having them all here, celebrating her birthday, so why the queasiness that was nagging away in the background?

Lizzie was in reasonably good health. Her left knee had reduced her mobility, stiffening up periodically for no apparent reason, but she still did all her own shopping on foot: Harold's on Granby Street for her fish every other day, they closed on Mondays so that was always a meat day, a fry up of Sunday's dinner when all the kids were with her. Every Tuesdays and Thursdays, she still walked the three miles, in all weathers, to St John's market in town for her meat and vegetables and around town to just browse around.

Esther, an old school friend, had started a weekly keep-fit class for the old girls. Esther would pick her up in her car, but she could have taken the 80 bus and got off at a stop not far from Netherley Church Hall where the sessions took place, but Esther loved a jangle.

Only Lizzie's hair, as white as clean snow, hinted at her age. Her tawny coloured complexion skin was unblemished. Her slim figure, her height, and her posture—shoulders and head always held well back—took years off her appearance. Her high forehead and her large round sparkling black-brown eyes, gave her an air of fearless intelligence.

Lizzie's mother, Elizabeth Simmons, was black and local as had been Elizabeth's mother and grandmother before her, and her father was a very tall light-skinned Bajan. Lizzie was born Elizabeth Roberts and married Kai Leung. It took a while for Lizzie to get used to having a Chinese name. She suggested to

Pure Pressure

Kai to change the name Leung to Lee, as it would be easier for the kids when they grew up. Kai exploded, the second time in their lives together that Lizzie had seen him angry. She never brought up the subject again.

She shared the same birth date (4th July) as Paul her eldest, seated at the table eyes fixed on the television, his long legs stretched right across the room like extended ladders so that you had to jump over them or say 'scuse please' to get passed him. Using the long train journey test, Paul would chatter non-stop, repeating himself several times. He would invent stuff to try to keep you interested; and Paul never listened. He looked just like his father, but it was not always so. Paul was very dark when he was born and the crinkly black hair and round eyes did not suggest China by any stretch, as the looks from neighbours and even family and people she called friends implied. This child's father was black and Kai had nothing to do with it was the verdict of many. Kai was away at sea for months on end, giving her plenty of time and opportunity to dally, wagging tongues said. Of course, these comments hurt her. She knew Paul was Kai's child and she was so pleased he was so dark and so like the Roberts. Kai was in Caracas when Paul was born. He did not set eyes on his first child until the baby was in his seventh month. Paul had been a difficult breached birth and breached babies often made difficult toddlers. Paul would not let any other human being near him; he just wanted his Mum. It was a lovely moment for Lizzie when Kai took Paul from her arms the first time he saw him and, expecting the usual whinge followed by the nerve shattering, screams, Paul settled immediately, as if he knew it was his Dad. The enchantment of seeing Paul's head nestled on Kai's shoulder has always stayed with her.

When Lizzie told Kai that people were saying he was not Paul's father, Kai told her not to worry. These people had three or four kids to three or four different men, he told her, and that is what they expect. Pay them no mind, he advised, they like gossiping, even when there is nothing to gossip about.

In his later years, Paul had physically metamorphosed into Kai, especially now that he had started wearing glasses. Paul was much taller and meatier than his father but the face, the walk, the talk and the build were Kai all over. Paul Leung was a big man; six feet tall and over 16 stone, but more bouncy-castle than trampoline. He wore baggy dark blue jeans held up with braces over a black tee shirt that strained around his rotund belly like a second skin and sported a slim expensive gold watch on his thick wrist and a chunky gold ring on each of his small fingers. His hair, cut short against his skull, had much grey at the sides. He had the Leung high cheekbones and hooded eyes; the large forehead, fleshy nose and the height came from the Roberts. After Paul's birth Lizzie never wanted any more children. It had been so painful. Twenty-six hours in labour, when she wanted to die and really thought she would. However, Kai was an only child and had longed for a large family.

She had Lillian twelve years later and Elizabeth a year after that. They were 5 and 4 years old when they died, they would be 38 and 37 come March the 10th and the 20th if they were still alive, and March would come soon enough to remind her, it always did. The twins, Doreen and Beryl, her youngest daughters, were toddlers when Lillian and Elizabeth died and Alan came a year later.

Alan came in the house. "It's only me," he shouted. Alan still had a front door key. He walked in the room and made straight for Lizzie, kissing her warmly on both cheeks. He was like that Alan, very affectionate, kissing and hugging her a few times.

Alan, long tall Alan at six foot two and barely ten stone, was 32 or was it 31, no, 32 next May. Lizzie always got mixed up trying to remember her children's birthdays. Alan was the intellectual of the family, as was Lenny, Lizzie's brother. Lenny was not here because Lizzie had barred him from the party for causing trouble.

"Lenny Roberts would cause trouble in heaven, he could not help himself," Lizzie always said about him.

Lenny was a trained nurse. *"The most well-read nurse in the whole of the National Health Service"* he boasted, but he did not go to University and get a Degree with Honours as Alan did.

Alan had just gained promotion at work; he was a Senior Policy Adviser with Middlesbrough Council. He had driven down the 160 odd miles yesterday in a brand-new company car just to be there for his mother's special day. He had brought Eiddwen, a fair-haired, good looking Welsh girl, who he lived with and her ten year old son Cardew. Lizzie had only met Eiddwen twice and liked her but did not like her son principally because, even at that tender age, she thought he acted like he was superior to everybody.

Despite disliking Cardew, which she hid very well she thought, ("the type of child only a mother could love," she had confided to Beryl), Lizzie had expected to accommodate them in the attic rooms but they had made arrangements to stay with Eiddwen's sister in an even larger house than hers by Sefton Park, as Cardew had cheekily remarked. Just as well in the end, as Beryl told her two days later that she and the twins were coming after all. She could have still made room for Alan, Eiddwen and the brat by shuffling people around a little. She had done it many times before, like when her sister Maggie and her Welsh tribe came for a few days unexpectedly. There is always room in the Roberts household, and if we haven't we'll make room.

The house was getting too big for her now with only Googie staying there regularly and even he often went away for whole weekends at a time without telling anyone. Googie did not start well, after college (from which he dropped out because of the "*Babylonian*" curricula); he spent years on the dole not doing much except sleeping most of the day and playing thumping music and entertaining friends at night. Then he met that Elsie Wright and she got pregnant, deliberately thought Lizzie. Then he became a Rasta. He finally got himself a job in the community centre through Alan being a big cheese in the place and that seemed to have sorted him out. Googie would be a good companion on that long train journey. He would talk a little, listen a little, read a little and sleep a little; Googie liked to sleep.

Lizzie loved her home, a double fronted terraced house on Kingsley Road. They were the first black family to live at the Princess Park end of Kingsley Road opposite the police station and Lizzie was particularly proud of that. The police station was gone now and the area was becoming wild with the drug dealers and the junkies haunting Granby Street corners at all hours like the plague, and feral kids racing around in stolen cars. Not that she should complain about kids who steal cars, her Paul must have stolen dozens from in his early teens and she always found excuses for him. Schools did not engage him and there were no youth clubs. At least Paul did not race them up and down the neighbourhood; he would race his stolen cars in someone else's neighbourhood.

Lizzie liked living where she did despite its faults and would live nowhere else but Liverpool 8. Lizzie could have gone to live in one of the white areas, she often said, she could have afforded it and Kai was all for it, but he always left the main decisions to her and she did not feel she would be happier elsewhere. Liverpool 8 was where she was born and brought up and that is where she would probably die. You never had to wait long for a bus and there were bus stops everywhere and Churches if you liked that sort of thing. The area was yards away from the two of the best city parks in Liverpool. It was a fifteen minute walk to town, and she knew everybody, well, every adult. These kids all looked alike and dressed alike, you could not tell one from the other unless you had actually given birth to it.

Kai had bought and paid for the house in full after the fire, even before the insurance money came through; she did not realise how much he had saved over the years. Kai was always a saver. Such a spacious home, luxurious even, compared to where they lived before, crammed into a two up three down house on High Park Street, with the outside toilet and a tiny kitchen and having to go to the wash-house off Lodge Lane to wash the clothes. Nevertheless, it was the first house they owned after years in rented accommodation. Now Lizzie had a washing machine. Although she still did much of her washing in the sink, delicates and that. Lizzie was convinced she had the best house of all the Liverpool 8 girls she grew up with, except for Gwen Davies, of course, who had married well and lived in Woolton Village and who now behaved as if she was a white woman. She only ever came back for funerals to show off her expensive clothes and her car; she was always flash from young. Gwen however, did start coming to Rachel's fitness sessions; she had no option because she had no friends where she lived, she was too dark for them.

It was not easy buying the property, she remembered. When she went to view the house the haughty white woman who answered the door barely hid her contempt for Lizzie and would not let her in the house, although Lizzie explained in her in her politest English voice that she had made the appointment through the estate agent and showed her the estate agent's letter.

Lizzie waited until Kai came home from sea months later to pursue her dream house. Kai went to the house and negotiated the price with the woman. Lizzie guessed that a Chinese man would be a more acceptable buyer for her precious home than a black woman would, and she was right, the sale went through smoothly once Lizzie removed herself from the proceedings.

"Israel's Prime Minister Menachem Begin defended the bombing of a French-built nuclear plant near Iraq's capital, Baghdad, saying they believed it was designed to make nuclear weapons to destroy Israel . . . Chris Evert Lloyd defeated Hana Mandlikova in the Wimbledon final today in straight sets 6-2, 6-2 . . ."

Lizzie who was half listening to the television instantly thought of Althea Gibson, the first black woman to win Wimbledon. How they celebrated the event. They could not afford to go of course; in fact, they had never travelled further south than Birmingham. Kai had travelled the world as a seaman, but not his own country. They played tennis in Princes Park for the rest of that glorious summer.

During school holidays, Lizzie used to sneak over the fence at the posh school in Belvedere Road and play tennis there with her best mate. That is how she met Kai, well she knew him by sight of course because he lived in the neighbourhood, but that was the first time they had ever spoken. Kai was cleaning the school windows in his spare time after school. Kai told her that he was a qualified window-cleaner and he was going to make a lot of money. They used to wave whenever they passed each other for years without talking other than "you alright" "yeah and you".

Pure Pressure

They really got together as a couple at one of Lenny's birthday parties. It was not really Kai's scene, full of middle-class people and you could not dance to the music he played, all this avant-garde Louis Armstrong stuff. They left early and Kai took her for a meal in Chinatown and that was that, they were hooked to each other until death do us part as indeed it did.

Those were high moments in Lizzie's life and she treasured those parcels of memories, opened them and often lived them all over again. There should be no more low points for her, God willing, she had had more than her fair share of those.

Lizzie was getting concerned; it was gone six o'clock and still no sign of Googie. Something must have happened to him, an accident maybe. She had always worried about Googie.

George Small was Googie's father; a butcher by trade and a swine of a man he turned out to be. Googie was born less than two years after Kai died at work when the forklift truck toppled over him. Googie was born three months prematurely, incredibly tiny and quite dark; much darker than he should have been as George was lighter than Lizzie was, but these things happen. Throwbacks have a mind of their own; they come and go as they please.

Googie never grew as big as his brothers did and he was much more sensitive and vulnerable than her other children. He was so loving and caring, always had been even now, she thought, and he still lived at home, as all good boys should. He was a Rastafarian and that meant him talking like a Jamaican, not combing or cutting his hair and being particular about his Ital food—no pork, no seafood, and fairly recently no meat at all. The boy was fading before her eyes bless him. Googie's room always smelt of burning bushes, his '*sacred herb*'. Lizzie pretended she could not smell it to save causing a scene. The last time she lectured him about the evil of the weed, about how it makes you lazy and sends you crazy, Googie got stroppy. He lectured her back about her drinking and cigarette smoking, that they were even worse drugs than weed which was natural and wasn't addictive. Lizzie mocked him saying why he was always smoking the damned stuff if it was not addictive.

It was the biggest row she had ever had with him since he had cut up her favourite black dress to make Zorro masks when he was ten years old.

Lizzie and Googie came to an unspoken agreement that he would smoke only in his own room, he was to keep his door shut and the windows open to get the fumes out.

The day had swept into Lizzie's room beautifully warm and sunny with a seagull symphony playing outside her bedroom window, a day full of promise.

Alma, the more expressive of Beryl's twins—greased plaits, white ankle socks and an Atlanta twang—had woken her twelve hours earlier with a piping hot cup of coffee, prepared just the way Lizzie liked it—black and fierce (unlike her men who had both been light-skinned and mild mannered).

"Wake up Granma; it's me Alma, yaw very fayvrit granchile. Yaw wan' me fix ya sump'n teet, Granma? I can fix yaw some fried taters and eggs. Marmy taught me."

Lizzie put her knitting down next to her glasses on the side table and walked into the kitchen. Like a conductor synchronising an orchestra, Lizzie had timed all her dishes to be ready at precisely the right time. She took out of the hot oven a large brown, shiny and steaming roasted chicken. Then a salmon swathed in shiny metal. The treacle coloured almost black, soya sauce based gravy was bubbling merrily, the steam from the vegetables had stopped hissing out steam from below the lid, and the salads were ready to be tossed.

Lizzie never let the kids forget their Chinese origins. She had put the dim sum, ordered earlier from Chinatown, in the steamer and they were three minutes away from being ready.

Googie did not care for Chinese food much, but then he was not Chinese; but all the others did including Beryl's twins. She had prepared Ital food for Googie, fried red cabbage, crushed chickpeas with coriander and mashed potatoes.

Lizzie could hear the twins singing in the backyard. Eiddwen was playing chess with Cardew at one end of the table and Doreen was telephoning home.

Lizzie was pleased that Doreen had found someone to love her despite all the scarring. Not that Evelyn was any oil painting with his huge pockmarked nose, those funny teeth and the turn in his eye, but they were happy. Doreen seldom visited Lizzie; in fact, she had seen more of Beryl since she went to the States than she had Doreen who only lived in 200 miles away.

Lizzie had visited them twice in London in the ten years since Doreen went to live in London and twice she cut her visit short because she felt she was in the way of their perfect family in their perfect home. And the rules: not allowed to smoke, not allowed to drink alcohol, no television before the kids went to bed and then it was never anything frivolous and Lizzie loved frivolous television. Doreen had done well considering that Lizzie always thought her the slowest of her children. She managed the nursery and Evelyn ran a mini-cab business as well as preaching at their local church and beyond. Their kids went to their church's fee paying school; they were well behaved and bright and disappointingly called her Grandma Leung but Evelyn's mother Nanny without any qualifying and demeaning additions; just like the Queen is THE Queen Nanny should mean HER to all her grand children; little details like these got to Lizzie. To her other grand children she was simply Nan, Nanny or Granma, but Doreen's kids had been trained, Lizzie was convinced, to give her less respect, less love than to Evelyn's mother. Sometimes Lizzie thought that Doreen was ashamed of her, because she was too much of a Liverpooleighter for Evelyn (what a name to curse your male child with) and their Southern-happy-clappy-privately-educated set.

As Lizzie walked towards the kitchen Paul, Beryl and Alan came into the back room.

"I'm tellin' you it could never fingy in Liverpool," said Paul opening the cupboard door.

"If you carry on saying fingy," said Beryl, "you'll be known as *Fingy*."

"He already is," said Alan.

"Got any booze, Mam?" Paul asked Lizzie through the open kitchen door, ignoring the remark.

"There's no way," he continued, "that kids 'round 'ere'd fight the police; no way, they're too fingy, too fuck . . ." Paul checked himself. "They're too fingy scared of the police. This new generation are scared of their own fuck . . . fingy shadows. Not like us, we used to fight all the time. I've got the thingies to prove it."

"The scars?" asked Beryl.

"No," he boasted, "the convictions."

"It's nothing to be proud of," Lizzie rebuked him softly: "And all you ever got done for was stealing cars. Car mad, still are."

"I disagree," said Alan, anxious to prove he had his finger on the street pulses. "It's happening now. Look what happened to Boysie Harris the day before yesterday on Selbourne Street. The police tried to arrest Boysie and dozens of kids battled the police. So don't tell me it won't happen here cos it's happening right now and has always happened in Liverpool, more than anywhere."

Alan was a passionate Liverpooleighter. Some of that passion, no doubt, was because he had spent so much of his later life away from the area so that "the community" had become an idealised anchor from all his wanderings. He had helped found the John Archer Youth Centre five years previously to get kids from the area off the streets and try to provide them with positive outlets.

"Remember Myrtle Gardens, remember the 1978 'Listener' demo, remember the riots in 1948, and in 1919, remember Charlie Wootton," Alan recited rhythmically to Paul quoting previous noted confrontations between Liverpool's black and white communities.

"Mam, tell our Paul about the 1919 riots; tell him about black people fighting for their lives; tell him," Alan implored.

Lizzie shook her head and grinned walking into the back parlour.

"Yes, he's right you know," she confirmed. "We had to barricade ourselves in our own homes, black men getting beat up and being locked by the police for their own protection. I was only a small child then but they talked about it for years."

"What do you know about the kids around here, *Geordie*," said Paul.

"I don't have to live here to find out what's going on in my community; don't forget I run the Johnny Archer Centre. You got your finger on the pulse have you?" added Alan showing his metaphoric medals.

"Bloody right I have. I know what's goin' on 'round 'ere, let me tell ya, lah. I know all about that Boysie business as well; it's fingy . . . it's common knowledge. Anyway all the noises the kids made didn't stop Boysie getting arrested and getting fingyied, though, did it?"

"You know nothing about the kids around here, you live in a separate world," said Alan.

"He knows the kids alright," Beryl interjected with a bitter laugh. "He buys stolen motor parts off them, doesn't he?"

"That's a fuck'n lie. Watch yer fuckin' mouth you, Yankee Doodle," Paul warned raising his voice.

"Language Paul; there's no need for it. Can't you take a joke?" Lizzie rebuked him.

"Sorry Mam, but it's not a joke. Dat Beryl, she doesn't know how to fingy. She's been in the States too long."

"Who do you fink you're talkin' to telling me to watch me mouth? I'm not one of your little silly white girls who you can easily shut up. This woman's got a goddamn mouth and a brain and I'll goddamn well use them whenever I like."

"You're juss as bad, Beryl," said Lizzie peeping out of the kitchen door, her reproachful eyes going from Paul to Beryl and back again. "Turning the Lord's name into a swear word. Neither of you were brought up that way,"

"Oh, we know you've got a mouth," Paul reposted, "it runs like a sick nigger's arse. Silly little white girls, what are you on about, I don't know any silly little fingies, white or black except you."

Beryl gave him a withering look that annoyed Paul more than Beryl's words.

"You've got a real problem with white people you have," Paul said to her. "What you gonna do when one of the twins comes home with a white guy."

"If she loves him and he's a good man, noffin', but I hope it never gets to that and that they learn from me to keep their distances from white men"

"When's dinner ready Mam?" Alan asked to change the conversation, concerned about Eiddwen's sensibilities

"How long we gorra wait for Googie, Mam?" asked Paul.

"Not long, a few more minutes," Lizzie answered.

"Tell you what, Mam," said Paul, "I'll go de offy on Granby t'get some Champagne and we'll fingy in real family styleeee."

"Get me ciggies while you're there, Paul, and go round to that woman's house to see if your brother's there," Lizzie said before he left the room. "Don't forget," she shouted after him.

Doreen and Beryl went into the kitchen to carve meat while Lizzie laid out cutlery and crockery on the table, noticing that Eiddwen had not offered to help.

"What's up with you shitty arse," Lizzie thought without looking at Eiddwen. "Don't want to help in black people's house but you eat black people's food; stuck up bitch."

"Who's winning?" she asked Eiddwen sweetly.

"He is," Eiddwen replied without looking up, "he always wins."

"How's the nursery Doreen?" Beryl asked her sister.

"Fine, you know the usual," Doreen replied.

"And the family," Beryl persisted.

"The same," said Doreen without passion, and then realising that Beryl wanted to strike up a conversation she added recklessly, "Mam said you're down for a few weeks. Why don't you and the twins come down to London and stay with us for a few days."

"Yeah, that would be great," replied Beryl with a broad smile.

Beryl was the senior of the two and not only because she was born two hours earlier but Doreen and Beryl were as unlike as sisters could be. Beryl was gregarious, pushy and she liked to speak her mind, like her mother, but more so. Doreen was shy, quiet and avoided confrontation.

Doreen and Beryl loved and cared about each other's welfare as sisters do but they did not like each other very much.

There was no chance of Beryl going to stay with Doreen. Both of them knew that but they played the game of keeping face, of keeping family solidarity. The Leungs were a happy family, a close family; that was Lizzie's unbreakable edict.

Lizzie walked into the kitchen, resigned now that the food would be overcooked. She put the meats back in the oven to keep warm and turned the bumbling gravy off.

The doorbell rang in the distance.

"Googie," Lizzie sighed with relief. "He must have mislaid his key, he was always doing it; this would be his third set."

"Hello Uncle Lenny," said Doreen when she opened the front door.

It was Doreen's handed down duty to answer the door as the youngest adult in the house.

"Hello Doreen, is the birthday girl in?"

Lenny Roberts had come with his latest sequacious squeeze Rita. She was white, freakishly tall, (certainly taller than Lenny and he was nearly six foot), unhealthily skinny, half his age with wide heavily mascaraed eyes and large teeth unevenly scattered round her mouth like tombstones.

Cardew said Lenny looked like Jesus. Lenny accepted the remark like a man well used to superlative compliments. He had a trimmed black beard and moustache streaked with grey and frizzy silver hair tumbling down to his shoulders. Lenny was dressed in a crumpled dusty pink linen suit, the jacket sleeves folded to just below the elbow, and a bright orange tee shirt with matching socks and brown plimsolls.

"He looks more like Santa Claus," said Alma.

Cardew laughed loudly at the description.

Lizzie lit a cigarette and discretely blew the smoke downwards in Cardew's direction.

Lenny was two years younger than Lizzie was but looked fifteen years younger despite the puffed up bags around the eyes. His skin was like Lizzie's, smooth and dark brown; his nose (the meeting of two continents—sharp European angle and broad African box) looked like it had been broken and made him look tougher than he was or wanted to be. His full lips when he smiled, which was often, showed two rows of movie star teeth.

Lenny smiled and rushed to hug Lizzie warmly as soon as he walked into the kitchen.

"Can't call you middle-aged anymore, Lizzie-baby, you're an old lady now," he said planting a noisy kiss on each of her cheeks.

"We're all old now, lad," she answered warily pulling gently away from him and barely acknowledging Rita's feeble hello as Lizzie always did with Lenny's floozies

Lizzie had not seen Lenny for four years after a huge row they had over their sister Esmee at Mrs. Harrow's funeral.

There was a congregation of over 200 hundred people there, going back to infanthood some of them, people you had not seen for thirty, forty years and more, since before the war even.

Lenny has the most vicious mouth in the world. He could not fight or run to save his life but no one had a more fearsome weapon than Lenny Roberts' tongue when it was on fire.

In front of everyone, Lenny with his well-pronounced vowels, called Lizzie a fucking bitch. Lenny only ever swore when he had drunk too much alcohol. He called her an evil, selfish, stuck up bitch who thought she was better than everyone because she had a few bob. He accused her of ruining Esmee's life, of sending her crazy, almost sending her to the nut house over the fire by torturing her year after year with guilt, and driving their mother to an early grave because of her selfishness. Pretty strong stuff but par for the course for Lenny Roberts. He was born to regale and insult people. Paul uncerermoniously knocked his Uncle Lenny out with one punch to the head. End of argument.

When Lenny came to, he was sitting on the late Mrs. Beckles' front steps on Montpelier Terrace. How he got there, he did not know, his dark green velvet trousers ripped at the crutch and stained with blood from his head wound. His escort of the moment, a plump platinum-haired woman young enough to be his grand daughter, bathed his bloody brow with her snot-stained handkerchief.

"Hello Lenny," Lizzie said, metaphorically shaking her head at Lenny's effrontery for turning up but acting as if nothing had happened between them.

"Happy birthday girl," he answered and thrust the clinking carrier bag onto her lap.

Lizzie peeped inside the bag and saw a bottle of cheap vodka and a bottle of fresh milk.

"You sure know how to make a woman smile," Lizzie said not smiling. "Get your lady friend a chair, there's enough food for everyone."

There was an awkward silence whist Lizzie went back into the kitchen to put the bottles in the fridge. However, silence and Lenny were enemies.

"It's nice to see you there surrounded by all your family," he said following her. "All it needs is Kai and everything would be perfect."

"Have you come here to upset me Lenny Roberts, cos if you have you'd best get on your bloody bike straight away out of me house," Lizzie said sternly.

"Come on sis, I was only trying to cheer you up, that's all."

"Don't 'come-on-sis me, Lenny Roberts."

"Do you want a cup of coffee, Uncle Lenny?" Doreen asked quickly.

"Full teaspoon of coffee, hot milk no water, and four sugars; same for Rita with two sugars, there's a good girl. Still a creationist or have you moved on now my happy-slappy-singing-dancing-up-yer-bum-not-quite-a-nun favourite niece?"

Doreen pointedly ignored him.

"If all you've come here for is to insult my kids, you'd best leave right now, Lenny, I'm not having it," said Lizzie rapidly losing her patience.

"Sorry sis, Doreen knows I'm only teasing, honest."

"Final warning, Lenny, I'm not joking, another snide remark from you and that's your lot, you're out of my house forever."

Lenny bowed his head, joined his hands together as if in prayer, and gladly offered to get himself hung and quartered if he so much as said another untoward word this evening.

Paul returned from the off-license also clutching a clinking carrier bag. It was the night of noisy carrier bags. He gave Lenny a sour look but Lenny smiled at him.

"How's my big and strong nephew," Lenny said smiling grandly.

"Did you find out about Googie?" Lizzie asked Paul.

"Yeah," he replied, "I fink they've gone out with the baby somewhere. I got the fingy he won't be back tonight, might even have gone off for the week-end."

"Where have they gone then, he knows it's my birthday," Lizzie persisted.

"Probably over the water somewhere; she's got family there I fink."

The Wirral, as 'over the water', as if it was overseas, almost a foreign country, yet it was separated by less than a few hundred feet of the River Mersey at its narrowest.

"But why didn't he ring then?"

"Googie's a big lad now, Mam. Stop fingyin' about him; he probably did ring and it was engaged or somefin," he said glancing at Doreen, the telephone queen.

"Hello, Uncle Lenny," Paul said as they hugged each other without passion. "Hope you're fingyin' yerself, behavin' yerself."

"Don't worry," Lenny replied almost sheepishly, though Lenny Roberts did not do sheepish very well, "I'm behaving myself alright."

They all sat around the table as Doreen and Beryl brought in the food from the kitchen.

"I've just seen Greg; I thought you two weren't together?" Paul said to Beryl as he grabbed a shu mai with his fingers from the steamer.

"Greg! Where?" blurted Beryl and Lizzie in perfect unison, as if they had rehearsed.

"I'm tellin' ya. He was driving an A reg' Simca going down Parly; JD was with him."

"He was driving?" said Beryl scrunching her face in disbelief. "Where would he get a car from, that's impossible? It doesn't make sense; and with Jimmy Duncan, the boxer?"

Paul nodded.

"Greg doesn't even know Jimmy Duncan, I'm sure; and driving a car," contended Beryl.

"Lissen," said Paul sure of his ground. "My eyesight might be fingyin' but I've just seen your Greg driving a beat up Simca down Parliament Street by Lodge Lane with JD in the fingy seat."

"What's goin' on?" asked Alan.

"Noffin'," said Lizzie.

"Noffin'," repeated Beryl.

"Am I missing something or what?" asked Lenny his mouth already full.

Paul and Alan pushed for an explanation until Lizzie reached out and grabbed Beryl by the head.

"That's why! She's terrified of that bloody monster!" she shouted jerking Beryl's jaw forward to show her bruise as if she was displaying a nasty stain on her pristine carpet. "That's what that animal did to my daughter," she said before bursting into tears and ignoring Beryl's betrayed look.

"Mam!" said Beryl accusingly. "That was between me and you, you promised."

"Yer lie," said Alan astonished.

"I'm gonna find that little low down Yankee bastard," spat Paul through pursed lips. "Who does he fink he is?"

"Is there anything I can do?" asked Lenny hoping not to be asked.

"I'll come with you," offered Alan.

"Mind him," Beryl warned. "He's unstable, and probably on cocaine; sniffs it all day long if he can get it."

Paul shrugged the shrug of Alpha-man, fearless man.

"Where you gonna go looking for him?" asked Alan.

"Fingy's gambling house," said Paul helping himself to the dim sum tray. "It's juss round the corner," he added his mouth full.

"Turkey's gambling house?" asked Alan.

"No, Freddie Robinson's; JD practically lives there. It's only round the corner, this end of Jermyn Street."

"I didn't know Robbo had a gambling house," said Alan.

"Told yer, yer oura touch ar' kid. I'm happy to show my fingies as being street savvy, an' that I'm a got-my-ears-to-the-ground type of guy."

"Watch that Freddie Robinson, he's a hatchet man," said Lenny solemnly.

"How would you know Uncle Lenny?" asked Paul mockingly.

"I'm telling you he is. He chopped up one of my members, nearly killed him and got away with it."

Lizzie knew, as big sisters always seem to know, when he was telling lies so she told him to shut up and stop exaggerating.

"Anyway," said Paul heading for the hallway, "I'm goin' to sort him out."

Lizzie, however, talked him out of it.

"Leave it for now Paul, there's a good lad. God is slow but sure, he'll get his come-uppance, mark my words," she said.

Paul sat down and everyone was silent for a moment until Cardew spoke.

"Mrs. Leung," said Cardew, "why are you wearing a scarf when the weather's so warm?"

Lizzie instinctively put her hand to her throat.

"Nanny Leung, please young man," Lizzie reposted, a little too sharpish thought Alan, but he let it pass.

"Nanny Leung, why do you wear a scarf for dinner, are you cold?"

Eiddwen swiftly but discreetly kicked her son under the table.

Instantly Cardew screamed holding his leg and staring incredulously at his mother as if she had just stabbed him with a seven-inch knife.

"To hide my sagging neck," Lizzie replied calmly as she slowly removed the diaphanous scarf.

"There," she said unwrapping the scarf and pointing to her neck with a grin. "It looks like the Himalayas Mountains hanging upside down, doesn't it?"

Doreen tapped her fork against the plate to attract everyone's attention. She cleared her throat, lowered her head and intoned in a low voice:

"Bless O Lord this food for our use," she began, eyes closed and palms together. "And bless us to your loving service. For food in a world where many walk in hunger; for friends in a world where many walk alone; for faith in a world where many walk in fear; we give you thanks, O Lord. Bless us all and keep us from harm. Guide and direct us through all our days and keep us ever mindful of the needs of others. Amen."

"For food and family we give thanks . . ." began Beryl, her face a mixture of bitterness and fear. "And may our enemies perish and our friends flourish."

"I'll eat to that," said Paul as he deftly lifted a shu mai with his chopsticks.

"Bravo," said Lenny with a hint of irony clapping his hands with great enthusiasm to remove any doubts. "What marvellous blessings from blessed nieces"

Lizzie gave him a sharp look.

Everybody ate except Cardew who was just playing with his food.

"What do you think the odds are for Newcastle to get back in the first division?" Cardew said in his loud, ringing, can't-be-ignored voice.

"We don't want any football talk around the table," Lizzie said sharply. "Go make yourself useful, get the hot pepper sauce in the kitchen. You could do with rinsing your mouth out with it; that might keep you quiet for a few minutes."

"There's no need for that, Mam," pleaded Alan catching Eiddwen's exasperated look from the corner of his eye. "Stop picking on him."

"He's too damn hard-faced," she muttered. "Children shouldn't butt into big people's conversations."

"I beg your pardon," Eiddwen protested looking to Alan for support.

This was the first time Eiddwen had spoken all evening.

"My son's been very well brought up Mrs. Leung. I make sure of that. He's a bright lad and he likes to talk and I encourage him to express himself."

Lenny raised his brow and pursed his lips in sympathy with Eiddwen. He had been there before. He tried a joke he had used a few times in tense situations. Lenny had a joke for every situation.

"The King said to the Jester: 'My Queen is dying, my coffers are empty, my army is losing the war against my worst enemies and the people are in revolt. Make me laugh.'"

Nobody laughed except the children.

Beryl could normally be relied on to break any silence but she was sullen and just picked at her meal despite Lizzie's gentle promptings.

Beryl kept asking herself what Greg wanted coming to Liverpool. She did not believe Greg had come all the way to England for the twins because he had never shown any lasting interest in them in the past. He must have realised they were going to England and followed them, or rather followed her. What did he hope to achieve, she wondered, win her back? There was no chance of that. No, it was to kill her; that's why Greg had come to England, she was convinced of that now, it was to kill her.

"I'm going to call the police," Beryl said suddenly.

She got up and grabbed the phone and asked: "I was going to dial 911. What shall I dial for the police?"

"What you ringing the police for?" asked Alan.

"For Greg; he's crazy. I know what he can do."

"You can't dial 999 because it's not a fingy, an emergency," said Paul. "Anyway, you don't need the police, I'll deal with him, believe me; as soon as the meal's over I'm goin' over to Robbo's. If he is there I'll sort him out, don't worry 'bout dat," he assured her.

"It is an emergency," retorted Lizzie. "Dial 999, luv; tell them what he's done to you."

The police, when she finally got through and tried to explain her predicament, told her this was a domestic matter and they were too busy to come because of a large number of emergencies tonight, but she was free to make a formal complaint at the station.

With everybody preoccupied with a problem that escaped Lenny completely, he sought to strike up conversation or better still a debate with the only adult who seemed distractible.

"Doreen, do you really believe that religion is the only salvation for mankind?" he said in the most matter-of-fact-how's-the-weather voice he could muster.

"Yes I do, Uncle Lenny," she answered turning away to avoid carrying the conversation on any further.

"But you never used to believe that when you were younger, don't you fink you may have been brainwashed," Lenny persisted.

"Listen to who's talking," countered Alan. "I remember when you said you were a Marxist and now you're a right wing Daily Mail reader."

"The Daily Telegraph, if you please. Any way, to paraphrase Winston Churchill, you're idealistic and a socialist in your youth but if you remain a socialist in your old age then you're a fool. Put another way by Muhammad Ali, **if a man sees the world the same at fifty as he did at twenty he has wasted thirty years of his life'.** I'm not just talking politics here I'm talking about personal relationships as well as how you relate to and interpret events and systems."

"Alleluia," said Alan sarcastically.

It was nearly eight o'clock when Paul and Alan decided to go out for a few games of snooker at Cliffie's place off Berry Street after dropping Cardew and Eiddwen off at her sister's house.

Doreen had been on the phone to Evelyn and the kids for most of the time and then she went to bed early with the good book. Beryl also went to bed early with the kids because she felt light-headed with that Champagne and she was taking the kids out early for a walk in the park.

The front door finally closed behind Lenny who was the last to leave. Lizzie had to tell him to stop tormenting her with his giddy talk and go home. Lizzie went to the kitchen and poured herself a cocktail with the most expensive Vodka she could buy, her birthday treat, the real Russian McCoy, none of that Warrington muck that Lenny had brought. When the mixture glided past her throat she felt the sparks flying from her stomach to the furthest reaches of her body just like Chekhov had described.

Lizzie liked her own company. She knew how to pass the time alone having had plenty of practice in these latter years. She took out her knitting from the side table, sat down, adjusted her glasses and began knitting, a cigarette dangling from her mouth with the smoke clinging around her head like early morning mist on the river Mersey.

Chapter 3

Bad Card

7:45 pm Friday 3rd JULY 1981

On this hot summer's evening, the yellow sun was playing hide and seek behind fluffy white clouds as it descended slowly towards the horizon behind the stretch of the river. While Liverpool had finished its tea and was watching telly, Bonny Roberts was walking up Upper Duke Street, quick-step as always, like he was in a hurry, skilfully dodging occasional piles of dog shit without losing his gait. He was on his way to Robbo's gambling house, the usual, but he had a lot on his mind this evening, plenty of pain in his head.

His partner of seven years, Valerie, had left him. He had come home at 8.30 this morning after baby-sitting his sister Gloria's demanding son Eric Junior, to find the flat he shared with Valerie and their two children completely bare. Everything had disappeared as if by magic.

Valerie had managed to take away everything they ever possessed in less than 12 hours; all the furniture, the sofas, the table, the wardrobes, the curtains, the light bulbs even for goodness sake! The photograph albums that chronicled every major event in their life, his sound system, his record collection, his whole life had gone. She had left his clothes behind thankfully, piled up in a corner.

Appearances were important to Bonny. Long before black is beautiful became a popular cry, Bonny had always thought he was beautiful. His body was well proportioned, he carried no excess fat, his eyes were too wide apart and his face too round to be handsome but he kept it scrupulously hairless and cologned, and his hair natural and combed forward to make a little peak above his broad forehead; his clothes always neatly pressed and his shoes polished. Bonny was probably the fastest runner of his generation in the neighbourhood, well, except perhaps for Joe Bassey who would have run him close.

Bonny found his soiled football kit and football boots in the bath, thrown there with vengeance no doubt, Valerie hated the time he devoted to playing the game.

"Gambl'n an' football is all you care about," he could hear her voice reverberating around the empty walls.

He could always get another sound system, he mused, but his cherished record collection, the envy of everyone from his generation. From Lloyd Price's *Stagger Lee and Billy* (the first record he had ever acquired, stolen from some GI party in Heman Street back in the early sixties), right through to the Motown era, including the Temptations and the Four Tops' entire repertoire and including the Stax and disco eras. There were priceless gems amongst these—Frankie Lymons' greatest tunes on 78 and all of Otis Redding's records including his Little Richard period. He was not into all this new funky music stuff, all rhythms and no melody or meaningful lyrics.

The mirrors had gone too, so he could only guess at the incredulous and miserable expressions etched starkly on his face. He punched a bare wall with his fist a few times in pure frustration and cursed loudly.

This was a moment to listen to a lament by Ben E King, say *There Goes My Baby* or Otis Redding's *Sad Song*. However, it was not to be, not now, not until he found her and his record collection. Then, he would play her these songs, and she would cry with him and they would make it all up.

Not even a note of explanation.

He sat cross-legged on the living room's carpeted floor all morning (at least she had left the carpets) occasionally talking to himself, his voice echoing eerily. If he had a voice like his mother he would have sang some appropriate blues numbers, but he did not so he just moaned, crying without tears.

He was homeless now, as the flat had been in Valerie's name so she could claim benefits for her and their two kids, Mark and Melody, as a single parent. That was another irking situation for Valerie, having to hide from the authorities and snooping neighbours the fact that Bonny lived there with them.

He tried to recall any recent sign in Valerie's behaviour or words that could have led to this catastrophe. For sure, she nagged him all the time but then she nagged him on their second date when he took her to see a Mafia film that she thought was lousy. Valerie was born to nag and scarcely needed ammunition.

He remembered that only four days earlier he had introduced her to an old school friend as his wife and that had not gone down too well.

"Don't you ever introduce me as your wife again; we're not married, I don't wear a frigging wedding ring." Valerie spat at him when they got home.

The venom in her voice startled him at the time but he just put it down to it being the wrong time of the month or something. Bonny was convinced that incident in itself would not have made her pack up everything and disappear; Valerie was not impulsive, she must have planned this weeks ago.

"I am not your wife, we're not married, I'm not evun your partner or evun your best friend. You don't put food on the table, you're out every night gambl'n an' don't come in till morn'n. You see the kids for maybe one hour a day if they're lucky. You kip all day, and play football every week-end, we don't go anywhere and we never do anything. Why don't you just go and let us lead our own lives, a better one than the one you're given us."

Maybe that was her final straw. Not that he didn't want to marry her, he loved the bones of that woman, it was just that he dreamt of a big wedding and never quite managed to raise that kind of money in one go and he didn't know how to save.

Bonny was walking on the left hand side of street, up the hill with the garish neon lights and sweet and sour scents of Chinatown behind him. He was about to cross the street when a car beeped him. The driver, a white guy, wound down his window and shouted Bonny's name. At first Bonny thought it was the Busies, but Busies always travel in twos.

It was Alan Marsh.

Bonny had not seen him for maybe twenty years.

Bonny did not have many white friends; all the white people he knew he had known more or less all his life, like Alan Marsh, or they were Valerie's relatives from Huyton. He never really socialised with white people; he kept well away from them, they only brought trouble.

"What's happenin Bonny, long time no see. Jump in; I'll give yer a lift."

Bonny approached Alan smiling and they shook hand through the open window.

Bonny had liked Alan Marsh back then in the old school-yard days and he did not seem to have changed much. He was bald but he looked prosperous in his flashy motor.

"I'm only going round the corner," said Bonny who really was overawed by the car and would feel uncomfortable being driven in it in the area. People would think Alan Marsh was a Busy and he was a grass.

They chatted for over half an hour through the open window, Bonny leaning his elbow on the roof of the car in the middle of the road. Traffic was light or there could have been congestion. Alan Marsh did most of the chatting; he was always like that Alan Marsh, full-a-chat.

"Wharrabout Zacky, you two still spars?" Alan Marsh finally asked him after talking about his life, his wife, his affairs, his kids, his businesses, cursing in his reminisces about school kids he used to hate and exaggerating the virtues of those he liked; he seemed to remember everyone.

"Yeah, me n' him are still tight. He's working on the rigs in Scotland," Bonny replied by then sitting in the front seat of the car, the engine still running, wasting petrol, another sign of Alan's wealth, thought Bonny.

Alan Marsh was living in Crosby now and was opening a club on the Dock Road in November. Bonny asked if he was looking for security, because he had experience. Alan Marsh could see that Bonny was in shape so he gave him his card and told him to ring him nearer the time to make arrangements.

Alan asked Bonny what he was up to these days and Bonny told him a little bit of this and a little bit of that, but mainly security work.

Bonny's little bit of this and little bit of that was essentially gambling. An inveterate gambler, Bonny Roberts would and had gambled on which of two pigeons ambling on the street searching for crumbs would fly away first. His working life revolved around gambling, and playing football, he was the team captain, a box-to-box midfielder for the John Archer Youth Centre Football Club.

Now that Valerie had left him destitute and homeless he had to think quickly what to do next; Bonny was not a long-term planner. Things eventually took care of themselves, whatever will be will be was his motto.

Bonny would live mainly at home in his mother's flat on the Thackeray estate or maybe his sister's flat in Chinatown. He was always welcome at his sister's home, but Bonny did not like her boyfriend Eric, the baby's father, a flash bastard drug dealer, lived with his wife and kids over the water, and stayed a couple of days a week at Gloria's house. Sometimes she did not see him for weeks at a time. He was just using her. Bonny kept away from Gloria's when Eric was around, he could not stomach the giggling fool of a man. He had warned Gloria about getting involved with a married man, but Gloria was convinced Eric was going to leave his wife and kids and settle down with her and did not want to hear anything different.

Bonny always kept a change of clothes at his mother's home and had a key so he came and went as he pleased, often bringing her takeaway food and sometimes bringing Mark and Melody to see her. At least he had options, so life was not that bad. Bonny Roberts was a glass half-full type of man.

He crossed the street and turned right into Hope Street when a police van suddenly slid up besides him. A police van cruising on a hot summer's evening should not in itself trouble a man in his thirties without a criminal record and with a reasonably clear conscience, but this was Liverpool 8 and things were different around here. Bonny knew without looking that the vehicle would be full of bored, sweaty, foul-mouthed uniformed men who did not look like him and who lived in faraway parts of the city he had never seen or wanted to see.

Bonny had never left Liverpool for more than two days except when he went to Colomendy, a youth camp in North Wales, for a week to give his Mam a break after the fire. He made a point not to look at the van directly but its menacing shape filled the corner of his eye and he could hear its engine and feel hostile stares burning into his body like piercing lasers. It made him tense his shoulders and think of a dozen things he did not like to think about. There was no one else around, no witnesses, so they could do what they liked.

Could this be the day the law caught up with him, he wondered. He did not consider himself a villain or dishonest, he was one of the few of the boys without a criminal record.

Bonny liked to dream fantasy situations where he makes a big hit on the pools, buys a nice house in Green Heys Road near the park, and takes the family on nice holidays.

As far as official records were concerned, Ronald Robeson Roberts was born on the 19th September 1943, the birth registered at Mount Pleasant Registry Office, Liverpool, his mother's named as recorded as Esmee Clarissa Roberts and in the space where his father's name should have been it was marked "Not known".

Ronald Robeson Roberts went to St James School, he lived in St James Street, right opposite the Anglican Cathedral, until he was 14 and then he disappeared from official records. It was as if he no longer existed; he had simply dropped off officialdom's radars. He was not registered with a GP, had never had a pay slip and had never been in receipt of state benefits. He saw no reason for dealing with the state or its agents and always kept well away from the police. They were trouble.

The occupants of the police van, he would bet a wager and Bonny Roberts was a gambling man, were going to arrest him and worse. Beat him up for sure, maybe plant some weed on him and send him to jail. Bonny was nervous, afraid almost, and Bonny Roberts didn't scare easy.

"HEY YOU, where ya goin'?" a gravelly voice devoid of charm and compassion bellowed from the police van.

Bonny ignored the salvo and walked on. He had thought of making a dash for it, had thought of nothing else in fact, but there were few escape options. No

Pure Pressure

little streets to run down, just the Cathedral park and cemetery on his side of the road and the large, the posh Edwardian town houses of Gambier Terrace across the street that spanned three hundred yards without a break or crannies or gaps in between to hide behind. If the police stopped and called him over or got out of the van, he would climb over the Cathedral railings and lose them in the park. He had escaped their attention many times over the years. He thought only naïve people or those who were foolhardy or slow-footed got caught in this game and Bonny Roberts was none of these.

He heard the gravelly voice shouting from the police van again, but more insistent.

"Where're ya goin', jungle bunny?"

Bonny glanced at them without turning his head and then looked straight ahead again.

'*Jungle bunny*', that was a new one on him. They must have learnt that in the police college.

"What did you juss fuckin call me, pig?" Bonny said to himself. "Come on, I'll take you all on."

Instead, he wished he had a hand grenade so he could throw it across the street into the open window and blow them all to smithereens. He could see the newspaper headlines:

MYSTERY BOMBER KILLS POLICE PATROL IN LIVERPOOL 8

BLACK POWER REBELLION IN LIVERPOOL 8

IRA GRENADE KILLS SEVEN (or was it 8?) POLICEMEN IN LIVERPOOL

He knew to remain calm and ignore them. If they got out of the van, he would jump over the railings and they would not catch him. He heard the engine suddenly roar and was deeply relieved to see the police vehicle accelerate away. He watched it turn right onto Upper Parliament Street and disappear from view down the hill towards the docks. Bonny stopped walking, took a deep breath and looked up to the cobalt sky then he stared at the brown stone Cathedral, that breath-taking edifice, that lavish building whose presence had dominated his childhood and thanked it for helping him get out of this mess. The Anglican Cathedral had never stopped gob smacking him. Every time he looked at it he got a slight tightening of the chest like the building itself was reaching out to him, overwhelming him, frightening him, protecting him.

As a child growing up a few hundred yards away from its huge presence, he thought the Cathedral was God, or at least God's base on earth because it was the most imposing building he had ever seen then and since. If God was going to live anywhere, he would live in Liverpool's Anglican Cathedral, the biggest of its kind in the world. The Cathedral was the God of Liverpool, the God of Over-the-Water; the God of Wales even, because you could see Wales sometimes far in the distance on some days. He wondered for many years almost into adolescence whether every area had a huge God overlooking them like the one that overlooked him. He knew Brazil had their own God because his mother had a colour picture on the back kitchen wall of this giant statue of Jesus Christ on a hill, arms extended, overlooking the sea and all the Brazilians.

When Bonny did wrong as a child he would kneel in front of his bedroom window, stare at the Cathedral and pray to the house where God lived. He would plead for the evil spirits to be chased away, evil spirits that were sure to infect his mother's mind when she discovered his wrong and screamed at him or even beat him with whatever came to her hand. One day she threw the old heavy iron at him. Had he not been blessed with nimble limbs and quick reactions the iron would have shattered his left foot and he would never have been able to run middle distance for St James School or be one of the star men in the celebrated Jaycee Football Club, the best Liverpool 8 team ever according to some of the old-timers.

He will marry Valerie in this very cathedral one day he said to himself. What a wedding that will be, everybody would be there. First, he had to get his hand on some real money. He sometimes wished he had the bottle to rob a bank, but gambling was his thing and he hoped tonight would be a very lucky night at Robbo's.

Bonny usually went to Robbo's gambling house most nights except Wednesdays, because that was football-training night and he liked to relax afterwards. He had not been to Robbo's for a while. Not since Zacky left town six weeks ago. He always went to Robbo's with Zacky, his best mate from time.

Zacky and Bonny were like a physically contrasting double act. Zacky Pong, tiny, one of the smallest men around, barely five foot tall, slightly built, sharp features, slim moustache, light skinned, loose dark European hair and full of chat and spiteful wit.

Zacky once challenged Bonny to a 'who's-got-the-biggest-cock' competition, when Zacky was drunk, and Bonny lost by several clear inches. In his defence, Bonny said better a small one that works than a large one that doesn't. Zacky scoffed at his response and said that he had had no complaints.

"Anyway," Zacky added, "that was a stock response of all men with small cocks."

Bonny Roberts, six foot, athletic, a round face from which his nickname was derived, dark skinned, and no intellectual except in a Cathedral-is-God kind of

Pure Pressure

way. Bonny was awkward most times in women's company. He was more a man's man, a listening man's man.

There was nothing else to do at night except go to either one or more of the three gambling houses and the 14 clubs that all operated within ten minutes walk of each other, and he and Zacky were night people. They also went to the Blues party on Selbourne Street or Mulgrave Street or wherever as venues frequently changed. The music was good, there were always people there and you could buy a drink right through until daylight, and Zacky liked his drink. They had stopped going to Robbo's altogether because Zacky was barred when he was caught cheating, a capital sin at Robbo's, and instead they went to Turkey's gambling house on Sandon Street. Since Zacky left for Scotland Bonny had to do the rounds on his own. No wonder Valerie left, she could not adapt to the life of a hustler, a full time job with long hours and irregular income.

Bonny was not going to Turkeys' gambling house tonight because Gloria—game generous glorious Gloria—gave him a little dropsy this evening; she had touched lucky herself at the casino in town last night whilst he was babysitting for her. He intended to invest this bonus at Robbo's place and come out with lots more. Win enough perhaps to find Valerie and the kids in London and bring them back home and take them on that summer holiday he always promised but never quite delivered. Because that is where they had gone, Valerie's Mother had told him so when he went to her house looking for them.

"And she's na com'n back so don't you ever come knock'n on dis effin' door again," her Mother had told him with characteristic bluntness.

Nevertheless, he would get her back, and the kids, and the furniture and his sound system and his priceless record collection   everything. He would get them all back. He would rent a nice flat by Princes Park—on Green Heys Road maybe or off Lark Lane and get himself a job as a Youth Worker or even a Social Worker. That would please her. That would keep her with him, having a real job, a proper job. Bonny Roberts had wanted to be a Social Worker because of Penny who was his Social Worker when he was a kid. He would listen in on the conversations Penny and his mother shared, Penny talking about her job, his mother talking about the olden days and even singing Negro Spirituals to her. He could still be a Social Worker. He would go back to school and work in clubs for the money. Then he would become a Social Worker and carry a briefcase. He would show Valerie. He would show everybody.

Bonny had reached the corner of Huskisson Street when he saw the same police van heading towards him. He knew it was the same vehicle because he had clocked the registration number when it sped away.

"Shit," he cursed.

He should have guessed they would come around again if he had not let himself be caught up in his childish fantasies and reminisces. He was never going to be a youth worker or social worker; Valerie and the kids will never come back and he will probably lose all his money at Robbo's tonight, as he did most times. He felt at that moment more than at any other time in his life, deep down to his very bones, that he was a loser and that is the fate of losers, they always lose.

Bonny's potential escape routes had narrowed further, with only the now forty-foot drop into the cemetery on his right, but that was a risky strategy, he could seriously injure or even kill himself. He felt damp under his armpits and his heart was pumping blood more vigorously than he felt was healthy for him. He decided to wait until they made the first move out of the van. Head fixed ahead, glancing from the corner of his eye at the pale faced uniforms, the anticipation of a kill bursting out of the open van windows. He knew what was coming next. They would try to get him in the van so that they could beat him up and then charge *him* for assaulting *them.* They had never caught him before but he knew what would happen, it had happened to so many before him.

He imagined the policemen singing in the van as they approached him, just like the 'Jet' chorus in West Side Story, one of his favourite films of all time.

> We're gonna catch us one of them—t'niiiite
> We're gonna get us one of them—t'niiiite
> If he decides to run, fair flight
> But if we catch up wid 'im we'll bust him with miiiight
> Tonight!

As the van slowed to a halt a few feet ahead of him, twenty yards away to Bonny's left a group of half a dozen people came out of one of the Georgian houses on Huskisson Street. The men wore rigorously parted hairstyles; two of them wore graduate clothes—black capes with light blue lapels and a black cap with tassels at the back. One was a cleric with his dog collar and the last man carried himself like a leader in his full traditional dress. Their two female companions, draped in brightly coloured robes, were laughing and joking as they sashayed down the stone steps as if they were on a fashion shoot.

Sensing a way out of his predicament Bonny Roberts grinned at his good fortune. He quickly crossed the road walking past the front of the now stationary police van in the group's direction.

"Mister Ogunboro," he shouted to the man in traditional dress waving his hand to attract his attention. "Mister Ogunboro," he repeated.

The group stopped laughing among themselves and looked uneasily at Bonny heading straight for them as if he knew one of them.

Bonny thought of telling them "I'm being harassed by the police, can you help me," but knew he would not get far with that approach as they would all probably get in their cars in double fast time and drive off. '*Ha, no troobal please, tank yu*'.

Bonny Roberts put his hand out in a handshake and the man, who seemed the senior person in the group, instinctively shook Bonny's it after extravagantly tossing the wide sleeves of his top over his shoulders as big shots do.

"Mr. Ogunboro? I'm sorry I made a mistake. You look juss like our priest at the black church, Mr. Ogunboro," Bonny said almost in a whisper but his face beaming still in recognition.

"Yes," replied the bemused Nigerian man in a soft educated accent, "I do think you have mistaken me for someone else, young man."

Bonny kept on smiling and shaking the man's hand, until he saw the police van driving away, whilst the man as politely as possible was trying to disengage his hand which Bonny was squeezing like his life, or at the very least his liberty depended on it.

As soon as the van turned right into Falkner Street, Bonny released the man's hand and ran as fast as he could, oblivious to the group's startled looks. They had served their purpose.

Bonny ran past Holy Mary who was plying her trade on the corner of Parly: high heeled white shoes, transparently white skin, dark red hair, micro skirt, ruby red lips and a white blouse revealing the ever-present large silver crucifix from which her nickname derived. Bonny waved at her as he dodged the fast moving traffic across Upper Parliament Street towards Windsor Street.

Bonny leapt up the Toxteth library steps by the corner in one stride, pressed his back into the large wooden door and waited, a vein on his forehead pulsating steadily. A few breathless seconds later he saw the police van drive down Upper Parliament Street indicating to turn into Hope Street. The seven policemen, or was it eight, were not giving up the chase.

Suddenly Bonny's legs gave way as the Library door opened and made him stumble and knock books out of a young lad's hands. He recovered quickly said "scuse-me" and helped him pick his books up from the floor.

"You're one of the Lewis's aren't ya," he asked the youth. "Wha' 'appen young Lewis,"

"Hi Bonny," said young Lewis through tight lips.

"Wha' ya readin', bra? Woy yoy yoy! *English Law!* Youze gonna be a lawyer, young Lewis!"

Young Lewis grinned uncomfortably. He did not quite look down to his shoes but it was close.

"Let me look at dem odder books."

Bonny read their titles aloud as if he was announcing annual school prizewinners.

"*Introducing Sociology*; yeah man, Youze gonna be a so-cio-lo-GIST! *Geography Today*, not tomorrow but today; youze gonna travel the world as a jog-ra-feean!"

Young Lewis smiled despite himself, exposing a full set of steelworks, as he stepped outside through the doors clutching the books that were going to give him so many job choices and waved at Bonny with one arm as he clutched the books with the other.

Bonny looked up at the redbrick and stone library. The last time he had been inside was during his schooldays but he remembered the rows of shelves heavy with colourful books, the strips of light making the long, high-ceilinged room as bright as daylight.

He turned away from the building, looked up and down the street then resumed his purposeful stride.

By the time he had reached Selbourne Street, five minutes later, Bonny had passed another packed police vehicle cruising along Park Way and two policemen, walking together down Princes Avenue like they owned the place. They stared at him, daring him to say something, anything or make a run for it but he simply ignored them. He could deal with two of them on foot; he only got nervous was when they were team-handed. Bonny was concerned about the amount of police on the street. It was unusual, it was as if they were preparing for war or looking to start one.

Robbo's gambling house was situated in a double fronted, three storey terraced house in Jermyn Street at the bottom end of Granby Street, nearest Princess Park. Jermyn Street was a quiet street, lined with tall, pollarded plane trees, containing two dozen large Mid-Victorian terraced houses on each side. Overgrown dark-green privets on both sides of the gateless gateway to the house covered the front room windows from view and spilled towards the sidewalk over the waist high brick wall. Two stone steps led to a solid wooden door with peeling green paint. Exterior maintenance was clearly not a priority in this household.

Pure Pressure

Jermyn Street was somewhat more reminiscent of its past grandeur than the other nearby Ducie Street and Cairns Street were. For a start there were fewer boarded up houses with their tiny front gardens that attracted a variety of detritus. Jermyn Street looked genteel at night, partly because some of the streetlights did not work but mainly because of the trees forming a dense green canopy and gave it suburban feel. Even in day time hours the leafy shadows went a long way in hiding the creeping decay, the broken pavement and the pitted road, accentuating instead the venerable homes that had seen so much over the hundred odd years of their existence.

Directly outside the gambling house, half parked on the pavement, was Robbo's dark blue Audi. He was doing all right that Robbo, thought Bonny as he brushed his hand against the shiny-clean car. Billygoat's hand painted black truck was parked up behind the Audi and then Maureen Ajayi's veteran red Austin with the SOS number plate, SOS647C. There was a battered old Simca parked directly behind Maureen's car he had not seen before.

JD opened the door to Bonny's rings, three short rings and one long, the accepted signal. JD was short for Jimmy Duncan. Jimmy forced the nickname on others since he was 14 years of age, when developed a passion for America and JD sure sounded more American than Jimmy Duncan did. JD was Robbo's go-fer, a tall heavy-shouldered man in his late forties who liked gold jewellery and colourful sportswear. Today was grey tracksuit bottoms with orange trims, matching trainers, an oversized Chicago Bulls basketball shirt and a backward-facing Dodgers baseball cap.

"Many in?" Bonny asked walking past JD into the dimly lit corridor.

"Just a few, the usual," JD replied curtly closing and locking the door.

"Go in," he said to Bonny as he went up the stairs. "I'm having a break."

Bonny walked past the staircase to a half open door on his left and pushed it. The room was 20 foot by 14 foot, brightly lit by two bare 150-watt bulbs hanging from the ceiling at each end of the room. The small air-extracting machine in the corner hummed monotonously and with the whirr of the large ceiling fan together they made a sound not unlike a constant stuttering melody, like avant-garde background music. A strong smell of scented chemicals pervaded the room—fly spray mixed with air freshener. That was if you could get past the ever present cigarette and ganja smoke that hung heavy in the room. Gamblers had access to a clean bathroom with soft toilet paper on the other side of the hallway, but the rest of the house was strictly off limits. People said Robbo kept mounds of money up there. The house was well protected and there was always somebody there.

Robbo did not live there and few knew where he actually lived; secretive man was Robbo.

No alcohol permitted, unlike other gambling houses, but food and soft drinks were free. There were no flies buzzing around as you would usually get in this hot weather; Robbo was on a crusade to exterminate all house flies forever.

People still talk of the time when, in the middle of a big poker game, with an audience of one hundred and thirty-six people if you believed everybody who said they were there that night, head to head for big money with Georgiou (a Greek-Cypriot who owned a thriving restaurant in Widnes), Robbo's body suddenly stiffened. Robbo stared up towards the ceiling. Everybody turned round to see what put the shock all over his face. What nobody but Robbo had seen was a fly enter the room. He told JD to hold his cards and started chasing the fly down with a rolled up newspaper. Everybody laughed at him except JD. It took several minutes of frantic swats before Robbo squashed the creature and after delightedly scrapping the fly's remains off the wall, he then resumed the game as if nothing had happened.

There was a large rectangular shaped table in the middle of the room around which were seated a group of people. There were two smaller square tables tucked in the corner under the back room window surrounded with empty chairs. Under the front window, draped by heavy dark blue curtains that shut out any hint of light or sound from the outside world, was an old tan coloured leather settee. Blue-tacked on the wall next to the larger table and against the wall by the kitchen door, dominating the whole room, was a near life-size black and white action picture of Muhammad Ali. Ali was staring down defiantly and triumphantly at a distraught Sonny Liston, stretched out on the canvas with a faraway look in his eyes; the date (*25th May 1965*) was written in black letters at the bottom of the picture and a hand written note glued under the picture read: '*I am America. I am the part you won't recognize. But get used to me. Black, confident, cocky; my name, not yours; my religion, not yours; my goals, my own; get used to me.*'

There were seven people sitting around the larger table: Robbo (who was keeping scores), Maureen Ajayi, Billygoat, Chico, Trinidadian Trevor, Jimmy Howard (who was spectating as he had lost all his money) and a sweating American, introduced by Robbo as Shep-from-Ohio with a face that was vaguely familiar to Bonny.

Trinidadian Trevor, a round-shouldered dark-skinned man in his fifties with a small Afro wearing an Hawaiian shirt and a pork pie hat, was the only one who did not acknowledge Bonny's "wha' 'appen" greeting because that's the way he

Pure Pressure

was. Billygoat merely sucked his teeth loudly in what passed as a welcome, his face glistening with sweat, a sure sign he was losing.

Trinidadian Trevor called to win the game.

"Me gan 'ome," he announced as he rose from his chair.

"Where the friggin' hell you think you're goin' with all the winnings?" asked Maureen brusquely.

Trevor ignored her and walked out of the room without looking back. Robbo pressed an intercom button on the wall next to him to summon JD to let Trinidadian Trevor out of the house. Bonny sat in Trinidadian Trevor's still warm chair.

"Yu so quick in 'im grave," Billygoat said to Bonny. "Anyway, how is your spa Zacky, still in Scot-lan'?" he added giggling strangely.

"Wha' you on about," Bonny replied, "of course he's still in Scotland, out in the North Sea somewhere."

"Don't mind him," said Maureen who knew what Billygoat was hinting at. "If you got money join in."

"Me gan too," said Jimmy Howard.

He tried to cadge some change for a newspaper, cigarettes and a tin of soup for his dinner, but nobody was listening; gamblers have no pity except for themselves.

"Watch yerselves, there's loads of pigs around tonight," Bonny shouted after Trinidadian Trevor and Jimmy Howard as they left.

"You eez pure paranoid about de police," Billygoat said to Bonny.

"I'm tellin' yer, the streets are crawlin' wid 'em," Bonny persisted.

"Yeah, yeah, me know," said Billygoat humouring him.

"You won't be laughing if they get yer. I'm tellin' yer I've never seen so many on the street in years. They're lookin' to bust some black heads tonight, mark my words."

"Yeah," concurred Maureen, "they've been around all day. There must be sometin' goin' on. Me kids don't hang around the streets, so they're okay, but anybody else had best look out."

"You don't have to hang around the streets t'get picked up by the pigs; you juss have to go to the shops, or on your way home, they'll stop and harass you anytime," said Robbo.

"It's that 'sus' charge isn't it," Maureen said firmly. "The law says the police can stop, search and arrest anyone they feel like; juss on suspicion that they have committed a crime and most people they are suspicious about or they feel like stoppin', searchin' and arrestin' are black people."

"Dem didn't need no "sus' to do wha' dem doin'. Dem stoppin' n' searchin' black people since we 'ere, I tell yu," said Chico nodding in agreement.

"Dem kids dem wild," said Billygoat. "Ef dem nah cause so much choble the Police nah come; ya nah see it?"

Billygoat sucked his teeth and tilted back his trilby.

"What's the stake?" asked Bonny.

"Twenty five," Robbo replied. "Are you in?" he added, his raised eyebrows indicating he was pleasantly surprised that Bonny Roberts would be able to play high stakes.

Bonny felt the insult and retorted recklessly: "Why don't we make it fifty quid, make it more interesting."

"You won the Pools or som'n, Bonny," said Maureen patting her hair, an explosion of black corkscrew curls.

Robbo looked at the other players for agreement.

Chico shook his head. "Me's leaving dis one, man, dis is getting' too 'ot for me. Man muss know when to wi'draw," he said, pulling his chair a few inches away from the table.

"Like when a man don' wanna get a beef pregnant?" said Robbo. "I'm coming in to this game, to bring it back up to five players, any objections?" said Robbo.

"The more the merrier," replied Bonny.

"Must be new packs then," said Maureen suspiciously.

"New packs it is," said Robbo unwrapping two new packs of cards from a bag by his feet.

Shep-from-Ohio, his face covered in sweat, placed his money carefully on the table and the rest followed. Robbo gathered the money into a neat pile.

"Faites vos jeux, rien ne vas plus," Robbo announced in a mock French accent as he shuffled the cards this way and that like a magician with his long thin fingers. "New cards, new player, new game; cut for deal."

"Who's been winning?" Bonny asked no one in particular.

"That jammy bastard Trinidadian Trevor," replied Maureen with a leer. "He wins our money and pisses off without givin' us a chance to win it back; the friggin' ponce. Oh, and Mister ten-friggin'-per-cent here, who's been rakin' it in good style all day," she added pointing her head in Robbo's direction.

Maureen was one of few women who frequented gambling houses, women gamblers went to the bingo, the casino, or the bookies. You had to have a thick skin to put up with the gambling house banter and be able to toss it back. Maureen passed on both counts. As well as a thick skin, Maureen had bad skin. The pockmarks made her face look like an orange peel, but these blemishes had stopped being a source of embarrassment for a long time now and she never wore make-up. Small and well built with a permanent air of defiance, she had light brown skin, her aforementioned frizzy shiny black hair and a full mouth shiny with Vaseline. Her vibrantly hued caftan matched her colourful personality; she called herself an alpha female. She had been at the table since just after three that afternoon. Starting off well and then, just when she had been thinking of going home and treating the family to a Chinese takeaway from Lau's in Prescott Road, she began losing. Now she was in Shit Street, as she would have put it, unless she won this game with her last £50. Make or bust, notwithstanding the £200 worth of cheques that Robbo had cashed for her with 10% commission on top. Those cheques will bounce to the other side of the water and the bank will then take their piece of flesh as well.

Seventy-nine was the house game. Seventy-nine is a variation of Rummy, played with two packs of cards with jokers removed. There is a maximum of five players. Each player is dealt seven cards face down from the double pack then the following card, the kick card, is placed face up on the table next to the remainder of the pack, called the deck which is placed face down. The basic game strategy is to improve one's hand by forming sets and eliminating dead, or non-matching cards. There are two types of sets: three or more cards sharing the same rank, and runs of 3 or more cards in sequence of the same suit. A player's dead cards are those not in any set. The dead card count is the sum of the point values of the dead cards—aces are scored at 1 point, face cards at 10, and others according to their numerical values. When a player wins a hand he calls by putting his cards on the table. A player can call with one set so long as his dead cards total no more than seven points. The losing players must then total up the points of their dead cards. A game is lost when a player has accumulated more than 79 points. Players alternate in clock-wise sequence to deal the cards after each hand. On each turn, a player must draw either the face up kick card or the facedown top card from the deck. The player has the option of keeping that card and exchanging it for one of his seven cards or throwing it face up on the dead pile. The second player has the choice of picking up the discarded card from the dead pile or the top face down card from the deck. The following player can only pick up the top card from the dead pile or from the deck. The strategy is to try not to hold too many high value cards as dead cards when another player calls.

Robbo ran his gambling house personally. He never seemed to sleep, keeping scores or gambling or both, and when he was not there JD invariably was but more often than not, it was both of them.

A Smithdown Road Hospital baby Robbo was as local as it is possible to be. Tall, skinny, pale skinned, closely cropped light brown hair, small prying green eyes, a prominent chin that cried in vain for a beard, crooked teeth and gaunt cheeks dotted with large freckles made more conspicuous by the summer sun.

"The kind of face only a blind mother could love," Maureen had said about him.

Robbo was dressed in cream coloured shapeless trousers and a crisp, short sleeved, open neck white shirt with a thin gold chain around his neck. Known also to be a big weed man, Robbo had been running the gambling house for nearly two years. His was the only gambling house never raided by the vice-squad. This meant either he was giving more bribes to the police than the other gambling house owners were or that he was a police informer; many suspected it was both.

Sometimes games went on for 48 hours non-stop, but mostly they started late afternoon until there was nobody left, usually the early hours of the following morning. A steady stream of people came, got bust or won and went and others took their place. Onlookers were discouraged; you came to Robbo's to gamble, nothing else.

Bonny had gone right through St James School with Maureen although she had been in the A stream and he mainly in the B until he stopped going altogether a year earlier than the legal school-leaving age. He only ever liked the English and History classes and he soon got bored both.

Maureen had been a gambling house habituée since her late twenties. She usually went to Robbo's on Thursday evenings rather than the higher stakes Fridays. However, today had been treat night having backed a 25-to-1 winner in the first race of the day. She hired two videos for the family to watch and then headed straight to Robbo's with the aim of playing big and winning big. Next to Maureen was Billygoat, a small, wiry man in his late fifties, with wide nostrils that looked like the business end of a twelve-bore double barrel shotgun. Born in Barbados, he came to live in Liverpool on his 24th birthday to join his elder brother Ken. Ken and Billygoat had a building trades business and rented out a dozen small houses they owned in and around the area. Billygoat always wore a brown trilby which, with his open necked shirt, his baggy trousers bellowing over dark socks ensconced in brown open sandals and his sallow almost yellow complexion, made him look like a 1930s sepia photograph come to life. His real name was William Goolsby, but everybody called him Billygoat. He was a Friday night regular. You always knew when Billygoat was winning because he became chatty, cracking jokes, usually at other people's expense and laughing loudly.

"Me is de king o' seventy-nine," he would proclaim on these occasions.

Right now Billygoat was silent and feeling down having been gambling for over five hours and only just about breaking even.

Seated between Billygoat and Bonny was Chico from Jamaica via Wolverhampton. A medium sized, medium-built, wispy bearded, dark brown-faced man in his late fifties with a long face, high cheek bones, thinning hair dyed the blackest of black and thick lens glasses His accent was as liltingly Jamaican as it was over 40 years earlier when he first came to England through the Royal Air Force during the war. He was another Friday night regular. Tonight, though, was not Chico's night as, unusually for him, he was losing heavily.

Shep-from-Ohio was built like a bull terrier. Short bandy legs, a small nose, a neck like a tree trunk and a square jaw; he sported an unfashionably large roughly combed Afro and had a toothpick in his mouth that he chewed constantly. Dressed in creased navy blue trousers and a half zipped up black leather jacket, which did not seem the most appropriate attire on this hot summer's night and was probably the reason he was sweating so profusely. JD had brought him along because he had money to lose and Robbo, who normally was suspicious of newcomers, was charmed by his accent, which reminded him of Muhammad Ali. This was Shep-from-Ohio's fifth game and he had lost all of them.

"How long you in Liverpool for?" Bonny asked Shep-from-Ohio.

Bonny had not heard him speak yet as he had just grunted when introduced. Shep-from-Ohio took the toothpick out of his mouth, wiped his drenched forehead with the back of his hand and frowned quizzically as if he had been asked a trick question. The silence lasted a long time. Robbo repeated the question on Bonny's behalf, more slowly and with an American accent in case he had not understood.

Shep-from-Ohio stuck the toothpick back in his mouth, blew a bead of sweat off his nose and said without opening his mouth; "eh . . . few . . . few days, man, y'know, passin' through."

"Me Dad's from Chicago; you ever been there?" Robbo asked him.

Shep-from-Ohio hesitated again, but this time Maureen intervened: "We'll all have time to go for a piss and come back before he answers," she said.

Maureen snatched the cards off Billygoat, gathered the cards together by tapping them on the table and urged everyone to cut for "who's gonna friggin deal the friggin cards." By the time Shep-from-Ohio replied "no" everyone had forgotten what the question was.

Shep-from-Ohio drew the lowest card and thus had to deal the cards, which he did so slowly that Maureen took out her knitting and Bonny started building a spliff. Not that Bonny was a slouch at building a joint. Legend had it that he could build a five skinner walking in a gale without spilling a speck.

Louis Julienne

"Is a slow boat ya all on den?" said Chico from the sidelines as he skinned up too.

Shep-from-Ohio ignored the remark and seemed not to sense the strange looks he was attracting from around the table. His eyes fixed on the shiny cards, he carefully and slowly distributed the cards as if it was his own money he was sharing out.

Bonny Roberts silently mouthed to Chico out of Shep-from-Ohio's view: "The man's blocked up," meaning he thought Shep-from-Ohio must be stoned out of his mind on some funky substance. Robbo caught the comment and asked Shep-from-Ohio if he was all right.

"Juss tired, y'know man," he replied cagily. "And I keep on losing, man; dunno what's happenin' to me, man."

"Why ya nah take a ya jacket off, star, is no wonder ya ah sweat like a pig," said Chico.

Shep-from-Ohio ignored him, finished distributing the cards and flipped the kick card over.

"Did you hear about your Paul mashing up Shirley Bassey bad in the blues last Saturday for no reason," said Robbo to Bonny as he gathered his cards.

Shirley Bassey was the nickname given to Vinny Kitson because when dressed up and out on the pull he donned a huge black bouffant wig, sweeping false eyelashes, displayed exaggerated hand movements and wore expensive cocktail dresses looking more like Shirley Bassey than Shirley Bassey herself does.

"De man's crazy sometimes," Bonny conceded. "But dat Shirley Bassey can be an aggressive bastard."

Bonny felt duty bound to defend Paul Leung being first cousins and all. Robbo acknowledged the concession without hiding his displeasure.

"Shirley had to go to hozzy; busted nose, split lip, the works, lah; for wha', for noffin'," added Robbo, pressing the point.

"I'll talk to him," said Bonny with a tone intimating that that was the last he wanted to hear of this particular topic.

The ten of spade was the kick card. Billygoat snatched it off the table and buried it in his hand, which he had fanned out close to his face.

"Pass de 'erb, nah man," Billygoat said nudging Chico.

"Got your friggin' set, then?" said Maureen to Billygoat. "Crash callin'? Ready like friggin' Freddie are we?"

Maureen Ajayi (she never used her married name) had been married to Colin Smith for over 20 years. Colin worked as a milkman at the large dairy on Upper

Parliament Street, having worked for them from when he left school, when they were based in Selbourne Street and had live cows on the premises. Maureen and Colin had two children, Maxine and Dion aged 18 and 13 respectively. Maureen's elderly Dad, Nat, also lived with them or rather they lived with him since it was Nat's house. She named her son after Dion Di Mucci, the US sixties singer on whom she had a crush for a long time. Alan Leung, probably her best male friend, said it was a good job she did not have a thing about Fats Domino or Screaming Jay Hawkins.

Maureen worked part-time as a supply teacher with the local authority the wages from which funded both her gambling and her bank overdraft. The housekeeping money kept in a joint account with Colin. Maureen had hoped Maxine would have gone to University but she got pregnant in the middle of her 'A' Levels and dropped out. She still hoped that Maxine would go to College as a mature student as she had done after Maxine was born. Gambling was the only vice Maureen had as far as she was concerned. She had given up smoking on health and cost grounds and seldom drank alcohol. She had a passion and talent for politics and was a self confessed barrack-room lawyer. As for sex, that became a chore for her after Dion was born, so gambling was her only thrill and she thought she was good at it, gambling that is. When she hit a winning streak, it seemed to go on for weeks. Lucky streaks were Maureen's orgasms. However, Maureen was known as a fish (a reckless gambler who relied more on intuition than the run of the cards and from whom pickings were relatively easy). For example if you have one set of cards, say the three kings and the other four cards are say 2 tens and 2 threes, a prudent player would discard the tens before discarding the threes because he would hold less high scoring dead cards. Maureen on the other hand would throw away the threes, on the basis that someone is more likely to throw her a ten than a three because low point cards are usually at a premium.

There had been no gambling orgasms for Maureen today. She did nurse sexual fantasies, however, and only for one man and it was not Colin but Bonny Roberts; beautiful, beguiling, blazing Bonny. She always fancied Bonny, from when they were at school. She often reminded herself of the School's Annual Sports Day in 1960, out in the playing fields of Allerton when she was in pole position for the girl athlete of the year being by far the best player of the Netball team and a swimmer for the school. She was not overweight then, sturdy yes, but curvy as well. She knew if she won the title she would make a lap of honour with Bonny Roberts because he was bound to win the boys' title, he always did. He would have to notice her then, maybe hold her hand as they ran around the track with everybody clapping and saying what a lovely couple they were. Bonny Roberts won of course, but Philomena Brown won the girls' title because she was the best track athlete Miss Tomkins, the Deputy Head, told her when Maureen went to complain, but Maureen was convinced it was because Philomena was better looking and lighter skinned than her. Therefore, it was Bonny and Philomena together who got all the applause, the attention, and any chance of a romance between her and Bonny disappeared that afternoon.

She had never been with another man apart from Colin, but if she ever did, she hoped it would be with Bonny Roberts or someone like him.

Maureen was quite content in her life. Probably not the happiest she had ever been; she knew she could do better, and she believed she was only one big win away from total happiness. Right now, however, she was in serious trouble and with the baby's christening tomorrow, she did not have enough money left to pay the balance for the lunch. She had to win this game, and then she would definitely go home.

"What was that kick card?" she asked Billygoat

"Ten of spades; you're supposed to show the kick card so everybody can see," said Robbo to Billygoat.

Billygoat sneered.

"The man's ready to friggin' call," said Maureen psyching herself down as if she was fated to lose.

Billygoat threw out a king of clubs; Maureen ignored it and went to the pack to pick a card. She held the card close to her face, stared at it with disgust and threw it on the table as if it was on fire; a king of diamonds and she needed tens to go with her existing pair to make a set and Billygoat had just picked one up. Robbo ignored the card, took one from the pack, looked at it for half a second and threw the card, the jack of clubs, on top of the king of diamonds.

Bonny Roberts opened his hand carefully so that no one else could peep at them; three kings and the two, three and four of clubs. He had two sets, a double set! This was a brilliant start.

His seventh card was a nine and he needed seven or under to call. He picked a card up from the pack, the ten of hearts and put it on top of the dead pack. Shep picked up the ten of hearts from the deck, slotted it amongst the cards he held in his hand and studied it as if it was a hieroglyphic tablet, then slowly placed it on the dead pack. Billygoat ignored the card and went to the deck, plucking out the seven of diamonds and so it went on until it was Robbo's turn and he chucked out a seven of clubs for Bonny who jumped out of his seat whooping with delight. Bonny sat back down and carefully positioned his upturned cards on the table next to the seven. A wide grin covered his face.

"Call for seven," he declared triumphantly.

"You friggin' jammy bastard! The man was double friggin' set," shouted Maureen her face contorted with awe.

Billygoat showed his own hand. He had a set of three tens, two Jacks and two fives-thirty points. Maureen had two tens, one eight, two sixes, one three and two aces; forty-five points. Robbo spread his cards on the table revealing two kings, two queens, two nines and one ace; fifty nine points. Shep-from-Ohio had thirty-seven points.

"That's a brilliant call, man, ab-so-lute-ly bril-li-ant," said Bonny Roberts emphasising every syllable.

Robbo wrote the scores on a sheet of lined paper in neat columns.

JD came in during the game from upstairs.

JD used to be a semi-professional boxer who had trained with national champions. He ended a never promising career into unlicensed fights and brain damage. JD could still throw a mean punch but it took a long time to get there and his mind left unpolluted by ideas.

"Where ya bin man, we 'ungry," Chico asked him.

"Kippin' upstairs but couldn't get a proper kip wid all dat noise," JD said. "I may as well come and see wha' all de fuss's about. We didn't finish until after eleven this morning and started up again at free," he replied and went straight into the kitchen.

"Bonny holds 7, Billy holds 49, Mo 34, Shep-from-Ohio 42 and I hold 20; Maureen to deal," announced Robbo reading solemnly from the score sheet.

"Gi' dem a good shuffle, Billygoat," said Maureen tiredly.

"Billy Goolsby's de name," he replied impatiently.

"Is not wha' dem call yu, is wha' yu h'answer to," said Chico.

Billygoat shuffled the pack vigorously and distributed the cards swiftly. He picked his own cards up and squeezed them open slowly just in front of his face. He prayed for a good hand to a god he did not believe in and, as he slowly unfolded the cards, he cursed to himself but kept his features neutral. He had seven disparate cards as divorced from one another as cards could be; at least they were relatively low cards totalling only 35 points, but if someone called now he would be out, five points over the limit. He thought he had shuffled these cards too well.

Maureen dipped into her bag and took out a colour photograph, showing it to Bonny.

"That's me first grand child," she said gloatingly. "He's getting christened tomorrow at St Bernard's; you can come if you want; quarter-to-one. His name's

Martin. Maxine had to name him within seven days of his birth, because according to Yoruba beliefs (me Dad's a Yoruba you know) a baby who is not named within seven days after its birth will die before its parent of the same sex. When I told our Maxine that she soon stopped dithering about and named him sharpish, I can tell you."

Bonny Roberts picked up the photo. "Dat's a white baby," he said teasingly.

"Don't be friggin' cheeky," she riposted, "that's our Maxine's baby, Martin. Our baby's black on both sides, let me friggin tell you; the father's one of Derek Freeman's lads."

"It's got red hair," Bonny persisted.

"So friggin' what? You're so friggin' blocked up with that shit you're smokin' you can't friggin' see. You've never seen a red headed nigger before?" she said pointing to Robbo.

"Hey, my hair's brown not red," Robbo protested with the air of someone who has had to protest on this issue many times before.

"What time's the food Robbo? I'm starvin' like Marvin," asked Maureen impatiently.

"Soon come," answered Robbo. "JD's taking care of it."

"Shit! What kind of friggin' hand is that you've dealt me?" Maureen said staring at Billygoat threateningly. She pushed the kick card aside and plucked one from the pack.

"Dis all bluff," Billygoat said bitterly. "I betcha she double set."

"Billygoat's gorra good hand, he's talkin' again," said Robbo with a grin waiting for Maureen to throw a card. "What you waiting for, scared to play in case you give me a set? Play the game, gal, throw me a ni-cee key-ard," he teased in his best Jamaican accent.

"Don't '*girl*' me, mister Frederic friggin' Robinson, don't let me start on you, shitty arse," warned Maureen wagging her finger and shaking her head side to side. "Here's your friggin' card."

"Me gone 'ome now, man," said Chico rising to his feet. "Who gon gi' me liff?"

"Get a friggin' taxi, you've won enough money to hire a friggin' limousine," riposted Maureen.

"A taxi, he'll be lucky," said Bonny. "Taxis don't stop for no black people in the day time let alone at night time."

"Eez true," said Chico. "Eez true, so who gon gi' me liff?."

"Never mind taxis won't stop for us," said Bonny. Then to Robbo, "remember when even the bus wouldn't stop for us?"

Pure Pressure

"Goway," said Maureen urging him on, despite having heard the story before.

"Yeah, man. Me and Robbo got to the bus stop by the ol' people's place on Parly just as a bus was comin'. We puts our hand out and the bus juss drove past us widout stoppin'. We were cursin' the driver we couldn't believe it, true t'God. Not like it was late at night or the bus was full or anything. It was teatime on a Sunday and the bus was near empty. Anyway, as luck would have it the lights by the Rio turned red and the bus had to stop. So me and Robbo dashed to the next stop on Catharine Street and get there well before the bus and again put our arm out. The little slimy bastard looks at us, doesn't even slow down, and drives straight past us again. True t'God man, we couldn't believe it. But lissen to dis, de nex' fing is a taxi comes right after and stops for us; ironic innit? Anyway, we gets in the taxi and tell him to follow the bus. We followed the bus all the way to the terminus at the Pier Head. We weren't gonna lash him or anyfin', is it Robbo?"

Robbo took up the story.

"No, we just wanted to pull him and put a complaint against him. By the time we got there, the pigs were there; he must have called dem on his radio. I wanted to put a complaint against dem but Bonny said to leave it before they arrested us. You know what they're like."

"Besides," added Bonny, "we had a film to go and watch. Remember dat?"

"*Zulu*, how could I forget? We go to see this film Zulu, right. We thought it'd be good to see the brother warriors in a movie. It was terrible. A handful of John Bulls killing hundreds and hundreds of Zulu warriors; when dem lights come on I've never felt so embarrassed in me whole life. Me and Bonny were de only white men in de whole picture house. We felt shame, lah, pure shame."

"You call John Bulls what we call Jim Crow?" asked Shep-from-Ohio.

"Friggin' 'ell!" exclaimed Maureen, "he can talk."

"Yeah, John Bulls, or JBs or Jays for short," answered Robbo.

Bonny Roberts' heart began racing, he could not believe the cards he had just been dealt—three fours and the ten, jack, queen and king of hearts. A double set. One crash call straight after the other; this had never happened to him before.

Valerie, Mark and Melody here I come.

Robbo threw his spare card down and spread his cards wide on the table like an open fan, triumph shining vibrantly in his eyes.

"Call-for-noffin'," Bonny said as evenly as he could with a grin that was dying to burst out into the loudest laugh in the world.

"You're a friggin' cheat, Ronald friggin' Roberts; I don't care what you friggin' say, you're a friggin' cheat. There's somefin' goin' on 'ere. You come in 'ere and as soon as you sit down; two straight friggin' crash calls," said Maureen, incredulity spilling out of her every pore.

She rose to her feet and deliberately knocked her chair to the floor.

She had lost three hundred pounds tonight so far and she was not going to give it up without a fight. She had the bank to answer to and that party to finance.

"Hey, easy on the furniture," said Robbo sharply as he picked the chair from the floor. Then more firmly: "There's no cheating goes on in here, I make sure of that. So don't come with this cheating shit here."

Maureen sneered at him but she knew she was out of order. She knew also that her outburst had deprived her of any chance of getting further credit off Robbo. However, Maureen was like that sometimes, reckless. She could burn her bridges without any matches in an instant.

"I take it you're out, Mo," said Bonny turning her cards around. "Anybody else?" he asked hopefully.

"I'm bust," said Robbo.

"Same here, you win the game. Come on let's double it, man. A ton a game" said Billygoat.

Robbo threw his cards on the table resignedly as did Shep-from-Ohio, still showing no emotion.

"I'm never coming back to this friggin' shit hole, ever again; d'yer 'ear me, never am I gonna set foot in this place again for as long as I live, as God is my witness," she declared, swinging her heavy bag over her shoulder without looking back as she walked towards the door. Losing graciously was not a Maureen forte. She was a born poor loser.

"Make sure dem cheques don't bounce, Maureen or I'll send JD to go lookin' for you," Robbo shouted after her and then to JD "come an' see Maureen out."

JD came out of the kitchen with a tea cloth on his hand and a chef's hat on his head. JD took his job seriously.

Robbo took his cut and pushed a roll of notes towards a happy and smiling Bonny.

"Everybaaady don't fuckin' move!"

Billygoat jumped out of his seat and held both arms up rigidly in the air in a gesture of total surrender. Everybody else stood stock-still.

It was Shep-from-Ohio with a cocked revolver in his hand and a wild look in his eyes.

"If y'all take it easy, everythin's gonna be awrigh'. I want money and jewellery."

Pure Pressure

With his free hand, he took out a small holdall from under his jacket and slowly, keeping everyone in his sight with darting nervous eyes, placed the holdall on the table.

"All I wancha t'do is handover ya cash and jewellery; do like I tell ya or I'll kill ya. You, big mouth," he gestured to Maureen. "Put all the money in the bag. Everybody empty ya pockets in the baaag."

"What's goin' on?" Bonny asked Robbo without speaking by knotting his brow and jerking his head towards Shep-from-Ohio.

Robbo's shrug meant he did not know the man, and looked to JD with a critical stare for answers. JD glanced at the gun in Shep-from-Ohio's hand, looked at Bonny and Robbo's accusing eyes and shook his head, imperceptibly lifting his eyebrows at the same time, in a plea of innocence. JD gestured for him to attack Shep-from-Ohio but Robbo shook his head slightly but unmistakeably. No heroics.

"Empty yer pockets!" ordered Shep-from-Ohio, interrupting the clandestine conversation, his voice low but impatient.

Billygoat, standing stiff still with his arms still stuck straight up in the air, emitted a big noisy wet fart but nobody cared. Robbo took out bundles of cash from his pockets and placed them in the bag, not too quickly or too slowly, he was not going to antagonise this crazy guy. The others followed suit.

"The watches, the rings, everythin' in the baaag; EVERYTHIN', c'mon let's go."

Robbo slid his gold watch off his wrist and a thick gold signet from his middle finger. JD took off his jewellery but more reluctantly. He had a lot more to give up; his jewellery did not come cheap.

Robbo was quietly incensed; he prided himself on providing a nice place for people to gamble, safe from police raids and gangster stuff; that's why some of the top card players from all over Liverpool came to gamble with him, Chinese, Greeks, even some of the heavy white guys from the North End. Now this little twat from Ohio is about to ruin his reputation. He will find him and punish him as he has never been punished before, Robbo promised himself.

Nobody who knew Robbo ever crossed him. The man was crazy, he was not known as a hatchet man for nothing, he would chop you down if you crossed him.

Maureen was disappointed in Shep-from-Ohio; she had imagined him a quiet, lonely and romantic American who had probably had his heart broken. She had felt quite maternal towards him. So long as people just gave him what he wanted nobody would get hurt and this Shep guy from Ohio would just go away. All this could turn out quite excitingly, she thought. She had no money to lose so it was no skin off her nose. She might even come out better off, if Shep takes her cheques as well. What a story to tell Colin and the kids, or maybe not, Colin hated her gambling and would use this episode as a battering ram against her bloody obsession as he called it.

"Empty your baaag," Shep-from-Ohio said to Maureen. He had spat out his toothpick and little balls of spittle and chewed wood lodged into the corners of his mouth.

Maureen hesitated; he surely did not want what was in *her* bag.

"Empty your baaag, you Motherfucker; ain't got all night!"

With a look of 'you asked for it', she turned her shoulder bag inside out tipping its contents into the holdall.

You could tell a lot about Maureen Ajayi interests, hobbies, concerns and habits by what she carried in her bag. Two balls of light blue wool and two knitting needles told you that she was a new grandmother who could knit; a blood donor card informed you of her regard for others; heaps of crumpled William Hill betting slips indicated an unlucky serial gambler. The folded Red Star newspaper pointed to a woman on the left of the political spectrum, confirmed by a hand-written list of towns she had visited last year along with other activists, including Alan Leung, on the bike ride from Liverpool to Port Talbot in South Wales to help raise money for the Steelworkers' strike. Sweet toothed (a half-full packet of wine gums and a few loose dust-speckled liquorice allsorts), literary (two well-thumbed paperbacks—James Baldwin's *Giovanni's Room* and Salman Rushdie's *Midnight's Children*), busy (a dog-eared A4 diary), a community activist (old Minutes of a John Archer Youth Centre management committee meeting) and strong wristed (a one kilogramme rubber hand weight). In addition, the bag also found room for half a dozen ball point pens, hand-written shopping lists, a cheque book, an address book, dry cleaning tickets, old letters, new letters, three sets of keys, a packet of chewing gum, curled up photographs and a purse jam-packed with receipts.

"Take all this shit out," he said to her, impervious to any humour in the situation.

"Make up your mind," she replied defiantly, convinced he was not going to shoot anyone.

When Shep-from-Ohio was satisfied that everyone had diverted themselves of their valuables he turned to Robbo and with the gun barrel a few inches from his face asked him.

"Where do you keep the money?"

"What money?" Robbo replied intimating there was no further money.

"Don't fuck with me! Where do you keep the rest of the money?"

"Tell him, for godsake, it's only money," pleaded Maureen.

It took a few anxious seconds before Robbo answered "Upstairs."

Shep-from-Ohio ordered everyone up the stairs.

The 'money' was kept in a bare room save for a divan bed, inside a wall safe hidden behind a black and white poster of Muhammad Ali, legs wide apart hands held low, swerving away from a Sonny Liston right hook.

Robbo opened the safe and invited Shep-from-Ohio to open it.

"You empty it out and put it all in the baaag," Shep ordered.

Robbo took out a large wad of used notes tied with an elastic band and handed them to Bonny who was carrying the hold all.

The safe emptied, Shep-from-Ohio marched everyone down the stairs back into the gambling room. Both Billygoat and Maureen wondered how much of *their* money was in that bundle, the biggest bundle of cash she had ever seen. Billygoat being a building man accustomed to handling cash estimated the bundle to be worth between £2,000 and £3,000, plus the £2,000 or so already in the bag and the jewellery. He considered Shep-from-Ohio to be a very lucky man.

"Where's the phone?" Shep-from-Ohio asked Robbo.

"Haven't got one," he replied.

"You sure," Shep-from-Ohio insisted.

"I'm sure."

"Good," he said. "Give me your caaar keys."

JD handed him a set of keys.

"I wan' everybody to stay in this room. The big girl is coming with me. If anybaaady comes out, she gets it. Pick up the baaag," he gestured to Maureen.

Maureen had not bargained on being a hostage so froze with fright. Shep-from-Ohio grabbed her by the hair and pulled hard. Her hair came away from her head in his hand sending him slightly off balance.

JD immediately pounced on the hand holding the gun. He had been waiting patiently for his moment. They struggled locked together for a few seconds, then the sound of the gun firing surprised everyone it was so loud.

Billygoat fell heavily, spread-eagled and apparently dead before his body hit the ground.

A second shot rang out and JD clutched the side of his neck as blood trickled through his fingers. Chico was sitting down as still as a statue.

Bonny had Shep-from-Ohio in a headlock on the floor and the gun slipped from Shep's fingers onto the floor. JD kicked the gun away from Shep's hand and

Robbo stood on his wrist. Maureen bent down and picked up the gun, cradling it in her hands, mesmerised.

Another shot rang out.

Maureen had fired into Shep's chest and watched in horror as the force of the bullet slammed his body to the floor. Maureen dropped the gun in horror as if it was contaminated with some unspeakable disease.

"I didn't mean to shoot, oh my God! I didn't mean to shoot, it just went off."

The stench of gunpowder overwhelmed the room.

"Wha' we gonna do?" said Bonny kneeling next to Shep-from-Ohio who was lying very still on his back staring at the ceiling.

"How's Billygoat?" asked Robbo looking at his body lying prostrate on the floor.

Billygoat rose slowly blinking unscathed; one of life's dramatists.

"What about you JD?"

"I'm okay," JD replied. "Just a flesh wound; I've had much worse than that in the ring, believe me."

"Wha' we gon do?" asked Billygoat anxiously.

"Who we?" said Chico. "Not me; I'se too old for all a dis, me gan' 'ome."

"Call the police," replied Maureen. "It was an accident."

Despite the shock, Maureen still had the presence of mind to pick up her wig and hastily fit it back on to regain some propriety.

"Nobody's calling the police. Everybody stay calm. Stay Chico and lissen," Robbo said firmly. Robbo was adamant he was not calling the police; he did not want them crawling all over his business.

Bonny Roberts did not want to get involved with the police. He could walk away, nobody could stop him, but then in his absence they might shift the blame on to him. He needed some answers.

"Who is dis guy? Who's his woman? Who does he knock around wid?" asked Bonny impatiently.

JD, holding the now bloodstained towel pressed against his neck, answered in a croak: "I'd juss been buyin' some premium bonds and comin' out de Post Office on Myrtle Parade when I bumped into him. I vaguely remember him a good few years ago, in the One-O-One Club. I bought some cases of Thunderbird and King Edward cigars off his mate from the PX at Croughton base. Anyway, we got chattin' and he said he had some bread and wanted to gamble so I brought him here. He said he was here on 'olidee, stayin' in a hotel on Mount Pleasant for a couple of weeks. He was drivin' an old banger, said he won it playin' poker with

Pure Pressure

the manager of the hotel. I swear on me Mam's grave I had no idea de guy was going to hold up de place, I swear on me Mam's life."

Robbo patted JD on the shoulder to calm him down as JD looked like he was about to cry and kept repeating what he had said.

"Like I says, I was juss comin' out de Post Office on Myrtle Parade, after buyin' me premium bonds when I bumped into him . . ."

"It's okay, lah," said Bonny, cutting him short. "I don't see how we have a choice but to get rid of de body."

Maureen, on quick reflection, did not want the police involved as she had visions of cross-examinations by some sharp suited, grey wigged QC in the Crown Court, the case splashed out all over the front page of the Liverpool Echo.

Maureen became tearful.

"I swear it was an accident; youze all seen it, didn't yers? It was an accident, I didn't mean to shoot the poor man," she said wringing her hands.

"Maybe you did it coz Shep shame you. All dee years me know you, Maureen, me didn't know you wear a wig. You know she wear a wig Chico?" said Billygoat earnestly.

"Leave she alone, man, tcha," Chico rebuked.

Bonny suggested dumping the body in the street, near Scotland Road. "De police'll fink he 'ad no business bein' dere and dat's why he got shot."

Bonny got no support for his proposition.

Chico was washing his hands off the whole business: "dun wan nutin t'do wid dis ting, man. Me's too ol' fe dem tings dem."

Bonny suggested taking the body to a waste ground somewhere to burn or bury it.

Robbo, who was now clearly in charge of the situation, agreed with Bonny and set out a plan.

Maureen, Chico and JD would stay behind and roll up the carpet with the bloodstains. Bonny, Billygoat and he would take Shep-from-Ohio's body into his car and drive out somewhere quiet and burn the car with Shep-from-Ohio in it. They would throw the gun in a river on the way.

"Why not use Chico's car rather than yours, that way we kill two pigeons with one stone and you get to keep your car?" asked JD feeling good about himself for making a contribution.

"Not my car, silly arse," Robbo said to JD. "His car," he said pointing to Shep on the floor lying like a broken marionette, staring open-mouthed at the ceiling.

"'E brought 'is car with him didnee, and 'is keys must be in 'is pocket, right? Come on; let's get the show on the road. Open the window JD to let the smoke and that smell out. And don't open the door to nobody."

"Can't you shut his mouth and eyes, it's giving me the friggin' creeps," said Maureen. "It seems like he's staring at me and wants to tell me somefin'."

"Yeah, like I'm gonna haunt you," said Bonny lowering his voice sinisterly.

"Lissen," said Billygoat to Robbo. "Me and Chico dun wanna get involved in all a dis, yer na hunnerstan'? We too ol' for all a dis, man," he implored.

Robbo put a lanky arm around Billygoat's shoulders in a hug. "It's alright, B. If we call the law, we could all end up in jail for a long time anyway. Yer know how de police operate. A gang of niggers with a body; they'll charge us all with conspiracy. I'm tellin' yer, this is the best way, believe me."

Robbo offered to give everyone back the money they had lost. The gesture melted reservations like a hot sun melts ice, except Chico who insisted he wanted to leave.

Robbo's eyes narrowed.

"You're not goin' anywhere," he said threateningly. "JD, you make sure this man don't go nowhere."

"Done," said JD. "It's stopped bleedin'," he added with a smile pointing to his neck wound.

"Nice one," said Robbo.

Chico sat down on the chair resignedly.

Bonny found Shep-from-Ohio's keys in his pocket and Maureen went to open the car and check there were no onlookers. The room was silent now except for the creaky ceiling fan and air extractor. Mohammed Ali looked imperiously displeased at the killing of a brother.

Bonny Roberts, Billygoat, Robbo and JD surrounded Shep's body and in unison lifted him off the floor, as they did so Shep-from-Ohio's head rolled and blood poured out of his open mouth.

"Shit," swore Bonny, "all over me clobber!"

Maureen came back in to the house to say the way was clear.

They carried the body upright as if he was drunk in case any neighbours were watching and laid him out on the back seat. The streetlight by the house was broke so they felt relatively safe in the shadows.

A car drove past down Granby Street but the driver did not look in their direction.

Billygoat was not happy when Robbo told him he had to drive Shep's car with the body in it with Bonny, because Bonny did not know how to drive and JD

Pure Pressure

had to stay behind with Maureen and Chico. He opened his mouth as if to protest and gathered by the expression on Robbo's face that it would be futile. You just don't argue with a man like Robbo, the man was too mean.

Robbo led the way in his own car. As he turned left into yellow-lit Princess Avenue from Granby Street, he saw the flashing blue lights of two police vans parked outside Princes Park gates less than 200 yards away. Instinctively he braked and Billygoat drove right into the back of him with the sound of breaking glass that seemed to reverberate throughout the street.

The police must have heard it, Robbo thought his heart pumping fast.

With his eyes fixed on the police vehicles, Robbo waved for Billygoat to reverse. If the police came over they would be in real lumber, he thought. However, the police, who he could not see in the darkness, did not move, the vans remaining stationary the lights still flashing.

Billygoat slowly reversed Shep's car back into Jermyn Street and Robbo followed, all the time his eyes fixed in the direction of the flashing blue lights.

They struggled again to get the body back into the house with more blood being smeared on Bonny's clothes as if it was personal.

"There's somefin goin' on," Robbo told Maureen, Chico and JD's startled expressions. "The place is buzzing with pigs. We had to bring him back."

They laid out the body in the middle of the floor and wrapped the bloodied carpet around it. Robbo's Plan B entailed dumping the body immediately in one of the derelict houses in the street that he used to hide weed. Some of the properties had been derelict for years, the owner-occupiers long gone to whiter pastures in suburbia and beyond.

"Then we'll bury him there in the morning. Nobody'll take any notice, believe me," he added trying to convince the sceptical looks reflected back to him.

"Billy G, you can get some digging tools and builders' clothes can't you?"

"Me don't like dis one little bit, y'know," he answered Robbo fretfully.

Suddenly the front door bell rang.

The police, it must be, they all thought and, as one, they all instinctively fixed their eyes on Maureen with a 'nothing-to-do-with-us-you're-on-your-own-on-this-one' look.

Maureen put her hands over her face as if the gesture would make the police go away. The air extractor and the ceiling fan were the only sounds left in the whole world it seemed.

The bell rang again; three short and one long ring.

It was a regular, it had to be or it could be the police who had found out about the code.

Robbo raised a finger to his lips with one hand and made a calming downward movement with the other.

The bell sounded again.

"It's the law," mouthed Maureen panic illuminating her eyes like a neon sign.

Everybody was rehearsing their own defence to the situation in their heads, ready for the worse. No one budged or made a sound. Whoever was at the door, they lifted the letterbox whistled through it. It was the two-tone whistle; it had to be one of the boys.

"I'll handle it," Robbo whispered tensely.

He left the room, closed the door behind him and walked into the hallway towards the front door, wiping sweaty palms on his pale trousers. He looked through the keyhole and recognised Paul Leung. He opened the door a fraction, the tension easing out of his body as if he was shedding a set of worn skin.

"Wha' 'appen' Paul; can't let you in, gorra private game on."

Paul felt like this was a déjà vu. Mad Danny Odegunji had said the same thing to him yesterday in the Gladray Club.

"Wha' 'appen'; is JD or Greg there?" Paul Leung asked Robbo.

"There's no Greg here," Robbo replied shaking his head.

"JD was driving with him earlier on; he's a Yank and that's his fingy there isn't it, his car?"

"Oh him; yeah, he was here earlier, lah. Couldn't get his car started so he gorra a taxi; but that was ages ago. What's up anyway?"

"How long's he been comin' to your place?"

"First time; I've never seen him before. Who is he?"

"Ar' Beryl's ex; he's been a bit fingy, y'know, naughty and I'm lookin' to sort him out. Does JD know where Greg'll be?"

"JD doesn't even know the guy, just met him in the Carousel I think, and brought him here to lose some money. Okay Paul, catch yer later, lah."

"Yeah, later; take it easy," said Paul walking back down the steps. Then he added, "if you see him don't tell him I'm looking for him . . ."

Robbo had already closed the door.

"Who was it?" Bonny asked Robbo when he came back into the room.

"Your kid, your Paul; I told him it was a private game," he replied deciding not to share what he had just heard. There was no point complicating things at this crucial stage when the corpse was still relatively anonymous.

"Anyway, let's get him out, get it over with," said Bonny resignedly.

"He's beginning to stink," said Maureen curling her top lip.

JD unlocked the back door and Robbo warned him not to put the outside lights on.

JD carried the legs, Robbo was propping up the middle section and Bonny and Billygoat carried an arm each as they struggled into the small yard. The night was clear and warm, the moonlit sky blue-black velvet dotted with myriad white shiny dots. In the small yard surrounded by ten-foot high walls, Billygoat slipped and fell on the uneven concrete floor and Shep-from-Ohio's body dropped on the floor.

"Shit!"

"Quiet!"

"'Don't panic."

They picked Shep's body up and JD gingerly opened the back door leading to the back alley.

As JD looked up and down the alleyway, he saw Peach fifteen feet away staring at him. Peach was leaning against the wall, her skirt hitched up high above her waist, with some white man he had never seen before thrusting himself frantically between her bare legs.

"JD," she said without breaking the rhythm, "What are you doing?"

JD dropped Shep-from-Ohio's legs as the others dragged him sharply back into the yard and JD, not sure what Peach had seen, said hesitantly at first: "Noffin'," then more boldly: "Go on, piss off; go and do your business somewhere else."

Peach and the white man stopped what they were doing, rearranged their clothing and JD watched them as they hobbled down the alley until they turned right into the street. He could still hear Peach's educated voice (she had six GCEs at O level) echoing in the distance for quite a while.

"He was carrying a body; he's a murderer that Jimmy Duncan," she complained as she stumbled along the street in her high heels with her companion. Peach was to repeat what she saw to a few people over the weeks that followed, but nobody paid her any mind it was the booze and the dope talking they would surmise.

They picked Shep-from-Ohio's body up again and struggled to carry him five doors down the alley to a derelict house. They had to prise open the corrugated sheet that covered the back door before they dumped the body in what used to be a kitchen and then had to replace the corrugated sheet on the way out. They got back to the house sweaty and exhausted. Robbo used nearly a full can of air freshener all over the room in an attempt to get rid of the stench. JD opened the windows wide (the first time they had been opened in two years) to let the fresh air circulate.

Everybody got a bath or a wash eventually and everybody except Maureen and Chico was wearing clothes provided by Robbo and JD, putting their own clothes in a bundle on the floor for a planned bonfire. JD started cooking some food.

Robbo generously distributed the house money amongst everybody, including giving Maureen her cheques back, as a way of buying their cooperation. It was not an easy gesture for Robbo to make but he was a businessman and sometimes businessmen had to make sacrifices to keep their interests safe. Robbo wanted everybody to stay and then in the morning Billygoat would go fetch building work clothes, his van and tools so they could all join in digging a hole in the yard of the derelict house. The house of death Bonny called it.

"It'll all be done in a coupla hours," Robbo reassured them. "Then everyone can go home and forget about the whole fing, just as if it never happened."

By the time Chico and Maureen had managed to convince Robbo that it would be okay for them to leave the food was ready, so everybody ate the fried fish and rice.

JD's fried fish was renowned in the neighbourhood for its succulence. His fried fish was on a par in reputation with Lee from the Gladray Club's fried chicken. The magic was in the marinade with its closely guarded secret concoction of herbs, spices, sugar and vinegar and marinating time.

It was after four o'clock in the morning with daylight well broken into when Chico and Maureen left promising to return later on to help out. Robbo realised that he should have paid them after the burial not before. He knew they were not coming back later.

Chapter 4

Crazy Baldheads

3:30pm Saturday 4th July 1981

Walking around the path for the fifth time hands in pockets, slow-paced, Googie felt his mind relax. He had declined three opportunities to go out to the exercise yard. However, getting some fresh air and maybe talking to some people, seemed a good means of thinking less emotionally about his situation.

Looking around the fifty or so people walking around with him, well, not exactly with him but at the same time as him, he had clocked already there were a few black people in the file, maybe one in five, but none he could recognise by name and most he had never seen before. He did nod briefly in Freddie Nash's direction, an old acquaintance of his brother Alan, but only out of politeness. Freddie was infamous for having spent more time in prison than he had at liberty. Freddie did not acknowledge the nod. Googie had no desire to walk with Freddie and by the grimace on his face and the wild look in his eyes and the gap that had built up in front and behind him; Freddie was in no mind to have anybody walk with him.

All prisoners in the exercise yard (not one Rasta among them—all baldheads) either walked in pairs or singly, dressed mainly in the navy blue and grey house colours, snaking around the thin strip of concrete that formed a misshapened circle in the middle of four prison blocks. Only the sky above was visible in the exercise yard. He guessed a yellow sun was shining bright outside in the real world.

Googie nearly tripped over when someone trod on the back of his shoe.

"Sorry mate," a fair-haired man with a smiling face said to him. "I was miles away."

Googie replied it was okay and smiling face asked him how long he had been on remand. Googie muttered a vague answer and smiling face said he was up next Tuesday when he was sure of getting bail. He had beaten up his wife's lover he boasted. Would Googie believe it, he told him, his own brother, his own flesh and blood was shafting his missus., He introduced himself as Harry.

For a few minutes, Googie listened to his voice without hearing the words and just nodded periodically. He was really getting into the business of being a listener who did not listen.

Googie asked Harry whether he had a recent copy of the Echo. Googie wanted to see whether his case featured. He told Harry about his daughter Michelle and his concern about her safety and the whole business with the police and the charges. Harry did not have a paper but gave the impression he would move heaven and earth to get one for him. Googie gave him his mother's phone number and Harry said he would get one of his visitors to ring her and tell her where he was, and not to worry about him not writing the number down as he had a good memory for phone numbers. Harry advised him to ask to see the Governor so he can phone his mother to let her know where he is. Googie thanked Harry for the information as they trooped off exercise back to their cells.

As the cell door was slammed and double-locked behind him, Googie looked at Fazakerley, stretched out on his bunk, both hands buried inside the top of his trousers fiddling with his willy, and wished he was somewhere else.

The next morning was Sunday and Googie was going to Church. Not out of any religious convictions, and he had many, but because he would get away from Page Moss's constant chatter. Despite himself, Googie knew more about Page Moss's cousins than he knew about his own. Cousin Charlotte was a transvestite musician who played alto-saxophone in Styal women prison's brass band. Cousin Hector's son-in-law was the welterweight kickboxing British Champion. Cousin Bernie, doing nine years at Gartree prison, was a safecracker respected throughout the criminal fraternity. Cousin Gerry's "Judy" was one of the dancers in the *South Pacific* at the Empire. Page Mosstalked about other relatives but Googie could only remember those mentioned at least three times. He was going to pray to Jah to spare the world from the Page Mosss and their kin.

On the way back from exercise, Googie had seen church services written on a notice in the television room.

9am-10.am Catholic Services

10.30am-11.30am Church of England Services

He then had an interesting but frustrating conversation with one of the screws

No, there were no services for, what did you call them, Rastafarians.

"That's not a religion. Well at least none that I've heard about," the officer said.

Pure Pressure

When Googie told him that Rastas believed deeply and were guided by the Ten Commandments he was not impressed.

"What if he was a Muslim or a Jew, or Hindu or Buddhist; are there services for all of these religions," Googie persisted.

There was a service for all "main" religions at different times, but nothing for Rastafarians.

Googie told him that Rastas worship Haile Selassie, Emperor of Ethiopia, ordained by God to be his living presence on earth the prison officer thought Googie was making it all up and told him to get back to his cell.

The Chapel, which was next to the visiting room, was packed. Every seat taken and there were more people standing herded together at the back of the room. At the front, a large table draped in white cotton and blue and purple insignia looked to be an extension of the priest dressed in similar garb. The priest wore thick glasses and thin hair and welcomed everyone to God's house. The captive congregation, eager to spend time out of their cell, chanted the tunes heartily not knowing the words, and when the priest began to preach, a low drone of hushed conversations could be heard from different parts of the room; it was the singing they had come for not the preaching.

"You're a fuckin' nonce, you, aren't yer?"

Any doubts Googie had that the question was directed at him soon dissipated as he received a hefty shove in the back that propelled him to the row in front of him and off his chair. Googie turned around, angry and ready to protest.

The first thing you noticed about the man who had pushed him was his size. His face was twice that of a normal person and the rest of him was in equal proportion to that face.

"You're a nonce aren't yer?" The Face repeated.

"No, of course I'm not," Googie stammered his mouth suddenly dry.

"Wha' yer in for?" The Face demanded.

"Assault, I'm being framed by the police," Googie said quickly

"So what you doin' walkin' round the exercise with that nonce?"

This voice belonged to another prisoner, sitting next to The Face, with popping eyes and a burly frame.

"He's not a nonce, he's in for GBH," Googie protested on Harry's behalf and now wishing he had not.

"He's a fuckin' nonce and so are you, and I'm gonna 'ave both a' yers," The Face promised.

The Face was not long in carrying out his promise. It happened on the landing coming back from collecting the evening meal. Googie had seen Harry but deliberately avoided eye contact. When Harry approached him, Googie said "cha" dismissively and turned away from him.

There were about thirty people separating Googie from Harry, as they all shuffled back to their cell balancing their meal on metal trays; he made sure to keep as far away from Harry as he could.

Had Harry been there outside the Rialto when the police abandoned his daughter to fend for herself, Harry would have kidnapped her and done all sorts of nasty things to her because that was the way these people were. He might even have killed her, bastard.

Harry had reached his cell door when a metal tray came down on him like a guillotine. The Face's mate, the one with the popping eyes did it, dropped the tray and walked away as if nothing had happened. Harry's face was slashed from ear to mouth producing copious blood and unmerciful screams.

The Face was right behind popping eyes and glared at everyone in case any of them wished to remember the incident and talk about it. A grass is as bad as a nonce; Googie had soon picked up prison lingo.

"What wuz de service like? Ours was brill'," said Page Moss as soon as Googie walked into the cell.

"Crap," Googie shot back adopting a Jamaican patois. "Me in no mood t'talk, yer get me,"

Page Moss had never heard Googie express himself that way before, maybe it was tribal fight talk, and maybe he had better shut up.

Googie did not sleep well that night, tossing, turning and sweating profusely. The next morning, he did not leave his cell to collect his breakfast and closed the door shut behind Page Moss so he would need a Screw to open the door when he returned. Googie was only leaving his cell at ten o'clock that morning to see the Governor. He was not taking any chances and did not want to end up like Harry. He sat on the chair, elbows on the table, fingers clasped together as in prayer, eyes tightly shut. Googie knew he was about to cry so he pursed his lips together firmly to stop the tears.

The loud bang on the door startled Googie and made him jump out of his chair, his locks swaying.

In the spy-hole, was a glaring eye that could only belong to The Face.

"I'll have you, you fuckin' black nonce," The Face growled.

"I'm not a nonce, you got it wrong."

"Can't 'ear yer, wha' yer sayin',"

"I'm up for Assault and possessing cannabis, I've been set up by the police," said Googie approaching the door.

The wooden pole that broke through the glass missed Googie's eye by a whisker, bouncing off his temple and drawing blood.

This is turning into a nightmare, thought Googie as he dabbed the wound with the pyjama top he never used because it was too coarse for his skin.

He had to get out of this cell; he had to get out of this prison. He lay on his bed drawn up into the foetal position and relived that fateful Friday.

Roll out of bed, into the bathroom, long piss, brush his teeth wash his hands and face, back to his room, finish the roach from last night, cup of tea made dem with mint from de yard prepared by him Mother. I and I can do dem tea too, but Mam she like to fuss she pickney, and then off to work. Walk fast him usually get there in get there in six minutes, but today him would take it easy, enjoy the sun on his skin and breathe in the air. Apart from Joe, the caretaker, him would be the first in the office as usual. Him would pick up any letters dem from the hallway and open the important looking ones at his desk next to the two phones. The first call on Fridays always seemed to be Marianne, ringing in sick. Marianne loved to get paid on Fridays but did not like working on Fridays. She always rang early to catch Googie rather than Treasa. It was easier to lie to Googie, such a sweet lad. Everybody liked Googie.

Treasa would come in, complaining about the heat, and ask if everythin' wus gran' without waiting for an answer. She would be carrying a rucksack on her back as she always did, though nobody wore a rucksack unless they were mountaineers.

Googie would say where are you going with that rucksack on your back and Treasa would reply: "I'm gonna a conference on youth work in Leicester, it's part av me course, it's for de whole weekend."

She would then disappear in her tiny office for most of the morning, gabbing away on the telephone. Googie would work through his lunch to finish off his work and as soon as Treasa left to go for that weekend conference, he would tell Bobo Jones, he had things to do, would be back later wishing him a good weekend.

Off he would go in the Jaycee bus, windows down, and drive straight to Englefield Green.

He would bounce up the concrete staircase two steps at a time like a man in a hurry, go in, say hello to drunken Elsie and tattooed Hank, and take Michelle in the van,.

He would stop at the shop, get back in the van, spot Slim with his head in the bonnet of his car and drive straight past as if he had not seen him. He would take Michelle home and not move out for the whole weekend.

The bleeding had stopped by the time two Screws escorted Googie into the presence of the Governor. The Governor was very old and dressed in grey tweed. Flesh was hanging from his face like grapes on a vine; his eyes, when he glanced up at Googie above his half-moon glasses, looked more verticular than horizontal, as if the sagging cheeks below them were dragging his eyes out of shape. The Governor's voice was laboured and of the officer class.

"You wish to make a phewn call, what is stopping you, you only have to aask, we have proceedures here, don't you know."

"I also want protection from a dangerous inmate," said Googie firmly.

"Sir!" the two screws shouted at Googie in unison and with equal vehemence.

"Sir," repeated Googie. "Sir, I have been threatened by a nasty looking character with serious harm because he says I have been locked up for interfering with kids. I have told him that is not what I'm here for but he won't listen."

"Who is this man that is threatening you," the Governor enquired.

"I can't say, sir, reprisals and all that."

"Has this got something to do with what happened yesterday, violence on one of the inmates?"

"I don't know sir, but I don't want it happening to me."

The Governor pondered a little before giving his judgement.

"You will be moved to a single cell and be excused exercise. You will collect your food before the other inmates and eat it in your cell. We will allow this regime to continue until you go to court and then review the situashorn."

The Governor turned his attention to one of the screws and instructed him "to ensure Roberts gets to make his phone call and has the means of writing to his Mother, presumably with a Visiting Order Request. Case dismissed. Also arrange for the Probation Officer to visit Roberts to discuss his concerns."

Relieved and thankful, Googie marched to the telephone with his escort. For ten minutes, he tried his Mother's telephone and for ten minutes, it remained resolutely busy. Then it came to him. Doreen was home for his Mother's birthday and she would spend all her spare time ringing London, getting her money's worth; the selfish cow. He loved Doreen of course, she was his favourite sistren and all, she had always looked out for him from small.

Googie put all his belongings in his bed sheet and followed the screw to his new cell. As he walked along the landing inmates were banging on their cell door as he passed and cursed him.

"Fuckin' nonce."

"Yer dirty bastard."

"Castrate the black cunt."

Googie tried to hide his face behind the bundle but succeeded only in tripping over and sending his belongings scattering along the polished floor.

"You beast, hope you die in pain; you're a shame to yer race."

Googie recognised the voice from the last comment as that of Freddie Nash.

All that evening until teatime a constant barrage of noise and curses directed at Googie kept him on the edge of his bed, head in his hands rocking himself gently. He chanted old reggae tunes to distract himself until he was hoarse. It seemed the whole prison was ready to kill him.

Chapter 5

Screw Face

5:55am Saturday 4th July 1981

Lizzie woke up before six every morning. She had drunk more than a quarter of a bottle of expensive vodka last night and two pints of milk, but she did not have a hangover, she never did, or rather, she never drank enough to have one. She lay in bed wide-awake thinking of the day ahead.

Sixty-five years of age today and if this were to be her last day on earth what would she do with it? Strange that she had not thought that way before although she could remember her best friend Gwen always saying 'live your day as if it's going to be your last'. Gwen died in childbirth before her 22nd birthday, God rest her soul.

Well, for a last day it should be better than most. The big party tonight, her new black dress from Lewis's store that Martine Goolsby altered to perfection, the family, the friends, the food and the music to dance to, she hadn't had a dance in years, but you never forgot, the rhythm stays with you forever although it's more in your head than your limbs as the years creep up. That Googie had better show up, typical of him not to ring to say he wasn't coming in for the dinner, so thoughtless and disorganised sometimes.

Lizzie had dozed off in front of the television and fallen into a deep sleep in the armchair when Paul woke her. Then she went to bed and had barely slept a couple of hours but still woke up at her usual time. Between 5.50 and 5.55; that's what it said on the digital clock that Googie had bought for her out of his first proper wages, bless his cotton socks, not that he wore any, summer or winter; it wasn't the style no doubt.

Not one to linger in bed, Lizzie eased her legs from the squashy bed. She put her bare feet on the little brown rug Beryl had bought for her in Atlanta with the picture of Dr. Martin Luther King in Heaven surrounded by angels. She stretched

Pure Pressure

out for a cigarette from the closed pack, next to the alarm clock she never had any use for, lit her first cigarette of the day, and drew the smoke deep into her lungs. This provoked a reaction that began with a number of slight, almost polite coughs that slowly turned to throaty barks. The rasping wheezes that followed seemed to come from the sole of her feet, up her legs and through her lungs where the sound turned a nasty navy-blue in its furore and erupted like a volcano through her open mouth as her head nestled between her knees.

"Clearing the cobwebs," Lizzie called her first cough of the day.

She put her slippers on and wrapped a diaphanous scarf several times around her sagging neck so that the sags were no longer visible.

Lizzie cursed the passing years, flying past her at the speed of light, dragging her to territories she dreaded. The sagging flesh, particularly her neck which was starting to hang in ugly knots; no symmetry there, it was like the Himalayas upside down, she once moaned to her sister and used the joke ever since. She despaired about the creeping shapelessness of her figure. Lizzie was not blessed, like her sister Esmee, with the insect thin frame amplified by a prominent bust that hardly lost its bearings over the years, like Jane Russell or Dorothy Dandridge. She had not seen big-breasted Esmee since the fire. No, she tells a lie, there was the brief interlude when their mother died. Esmee had moved into that flat in 1975 and Lizzie had had only been there the once, when her Paul drove her there to drop off some curtains. Everybody needs new curtains when they move to a new place. Some are grateful for moving-in gifts, not Esmee.

"Do you think I need yer charity, Mrs Stuck-Up-Your-Arse? Well I don't! So buzz off and take yer manky curtains wid yer!" Esmee had screeched as she stood in the dark hallway.

Lizzie had never heard Esmee behave like that before and she promised herself never to speak to her again.

Lizzie had brought the curtains because her son Paul had told Lizzie that his Aunty Esmee had newspapers stuck on the windows instead of curtains.

Goddammit, Lizzie cursed with quiet rage. Esmee would get a gold medal in the Olympics for burning bridges if it was in the competition and if they had a relay team, she would win that and all. Nobody did it quite like Esmee Roberts. She had no friends and lived like a recluse in that tiny Corporation upstairs flat in a horrible Corporation estate just off Warwick Street by the Army barracks, a leisurely eight minutes walk from Lizzie's Imperial House, as Esmee sneeringly dubbed it.

Esmee's mind had never been the same since the fire, Lizzie conceded, nevertheless, Esmee had gone too far and her tolerance could only stretch so far.

At least Lizzie had all her marbles; better have your marbles than big titties, she thought.

The multiple birdsongs drew Lizzie's attention as she let out the grey smoke through her mouth and nostrils in turn. Food and sex hunting musicians, that is what she called the birds; a winged orchestra including screeching seagulls, cooing pigeons, machine gun sounding late thrushes, chirping sparrows and male blackbirds sounding like deranged adolescents. She could identify birds by their sound. The birds were sharing their songs of summer and Lizzie loved it, imbibing the chorus deep inside her, as pleasurable as Vodka and milk in the evening and the second cigarette in the morning. It was at these moments when she seemed all alone in the world, as if only she and the birds existed, that she missed Kai. The man who had promised a lifetime of happiness and security but, ultimately he could not deliver because he died too early. They had not reached their peak as a couple; he was mostly at sea and she was mostly busy having babies most years. However, when he came back ashore he was home every day all day. Although the house was full of clinging children, the time spent together, talking about every day things, doing every day things; that was when they re-bonded and it became as it was before the children. Laughing and giggling, talking, arguing about nothing and realising it straight away. They had their issues Kai and Lizzie Leung, of course. Her narrow view of the world, caused by her Liverpool 8 prisms, was always on the agenda and him being away, but these things were never going to be fundamental to what they had. A relationship she hoped all her children would find in their own lives. That relationship was so right that she often blamed God for ending it so early. God only took the good early, because he wanted them for himself sooner rather than later.

She decided to go back to bed, a first time, an indulgence, but a permitted indulgence when you are 65 years old. She looked at the two framed photographs that dominated the polished bedside table for probably the 10,000th time. The smallest photograph was Lizzie and Kai with Paul as a baby. They were dressed in their Sunday best, her fake pearl earrings and necklace and his starched white shirt and real silk tie, told you that. These three pairs of eyes were looking straight back at her with barely discernable self-conscious grins.

Kai Leung was a seaman for 35 years in the merchant navy since he was 17; he died aged 55, nineteen years this Christmas, in an accident at work on the docks. Kai's father was a seaman also, who settled in Liverpool from Kowloon and his mother, Aida Birch, came from a long line of North End barrow girls, selling fruit and vegetables near the city centre.

Pure Pressure

Lizzie had deep roots in Liverpool's black community; five generations of black women preceded her, starting with Elizabeth Evans who came to Liverpool as a fifteen-year-old freed slave on a steamer ship from the Bahamas to work as a domestic for the family of the man who had owned her and her parents and grandparents before her. Lizzie's father, Dennis Duncker, was a Cape Coloured stowaway who had ended up inadvertently in Liverpool when he expected to dock in New York. He stayed for ten years without legal papers until he died of a massive heart attack, long enough to father five children with Marjorie Roberts—Margaret, Elizabeth, Esmee, Leonard and Elrica—without being able to give them his name. The second, larger photograph had 22 people crowded around Lizzie and Kai on their wedding day outside Mount Pleasant Registry Office. Monday the 30th of March 1931, there was no Great Depression that day. Kai was working with Uncle Kwan in the laundry and he was doing all right; Lizzie was getting by helping out in the Chandler's shop on Park Lane and doing some cleaning here and there.

Everything went haywire less than a year later of course. The Depression got to everybody in the end. Lizzie's Dad's attempts to keep running the corner grocery shop he had acquired a few months before fell through. The bank had no money to lend, they said.

"No money to a coloured man, you mean," her Dad protested.

He never got another job after that and was never the same. He stopped singing and laughing after a while and grew old quickly and the heart attack finished him off.

Uncle Kwan had to close the laundry, as business was so bad. He could not get a buyer and lost a lot of money, and then his young wife ran away with Mr. Bernstein, the ticket man, who left his wife and children. She's forgotten the girl's name now, but the last Lizzie heard she had left Mr. Bernstein after spending all his money and got herself another mug and was living large in Chester. What was her name again, Gertie Richardson's girl, Phyllis, Veronica, or some such name.

Dressed in a pristine cream dress bellowing daringly just below her knees with a small bouquet of white lilies held in white gloved hands, a dainty white hat perched at a gravity-defying angle on top of her bouffant hairstyle and a wide smile underlining that this was the happiest day in her life. Kai wore an awkward grin but looked so smart with his double-breasted striped suit, dickey-bow and white carnation in his lapel. Most of the craning faces in the large black and white photograph were now dead. Her mother and father, Agnes and Dennis, Uncle Kwan was there of course dressed in black tails with his new young wife holding on to his arm. Her mother's sisters Aunties Johanna, Mary and Eileen and her brothers Uncles John and Philip; her cousins Jenny, Peter, Barbara and Oliver took up half the photograph; they were always pushy those Harrisons. Mr E. A. Williams, a Sierra Leone man and the only black coal merchant in Liverpool (nobody knew what the 'E. A.' stood for, many suspected it was invented for some spurious effect). Mr Olowale, from the African Church, with his hair widely parted in the middle making it a double Afro, one above each ear and a Charlie Chaplin moustache. The only white faces in the photograph apart from Mr Bernstein, the ticket man who made a living selling expensive small loans, and who had made his luxurious car available free of charge to the newly-weds, were Mr. and Mrs. Fitzpatrick, who lived next door to the Roberts family in Beaufort Street before they moved to Nelson Street. All of them dead and buried, long gone, their stories ephemeral, untold and quickly forgotten, as if they never existed, society's invisible people.

All the men wore broad lapelled loose-fitting dark suits, except her brother Lenny whose suit was single breasted, light brown when everybody else's suit was grey or navy, and cut much tighter than the other's. Lenny also wore his sultry, posy Byron pout whereas everybody else just looked happy. Lizzie's other siblings were also there, of course. Esmee and Rica, and Lizzie's best friends Gwen Davies and Victoria Benjamin, as bridesmaids, co-ordinately dressed in white and burgundy. Maggie, a bridesmaid also, was not having any of it and dressed in pink and white so she could stand out from the rest, but you could not see the colours in the photograph so it did not matter.

It was a glorious day, it did not rain, and although the sun shone shyly, it was not cold; there were no winds, God-ordained weather for that time of year. The reception was at the Berkeley Arms pub on Berkeley Street. It was the first time black people were allowed to drink in the front parlour. The rule was not lifted until after the war when black G.I. money opened the doors again.

After the reception, everybody came back to the family home and everybody drank until daylight. The food was a veritable feast. The souse, the spunky pigtails and rice, the glutinous Fufu and Palm Nut soup, and Uncle Kwan had had delivered half the menu from the Golden Dragon restaurant.

The Jim Gray Combo provided the music with Charm-Boy's high-pitched voice bouncing off the basement walls. Jim Gray and Cayenne were ostentatiously plucking killer rhythms from their guitars. The drunk percussionist, Biggy Avaricious, half drunk and thumping the shit out of his bongos, totally oblivious to the beat he was meant to follow and it was his last gig with them anyway as they were sacking him, so what the hell!

The dance of the moment was the Turkey Trot, straight from the States; everybody Turkey Trotted that spring, nothing else came close.

Pure Pressure

Lizzie and Kai did not stay very late. Lizzie was exhausted, being five months pregnant with Paul at the time. Kai's friend, Woof-Woof (real name Jimmy Wolf), drove them to their semi-furnished top floor flat on Falkner Street just after midnight singing all the way.

If there was a heaven Kai would be there, but she feared that there was no heaven. Heaven, she had long realised, was when Kai was alive and the kids were growing up. She thought those days would last forever. Hell was loss, pain, unfulfilled dreams and broken promises here on earth. Not that she was scared of dying; she was more scared of how she was going to die, praying not for some heaven against hell but for a quick and painless death. Not that she was in any hurry to die, far from it.

Lizzie opened the bedside table's top drawer and reached out for her cocktail of pills, taken religiously every morning and night, and she gulped them down as one with a quick sip from the glass of water she always kept by the bedside table. Next came the final ritual, the second cigarette taken immediately after finishing the first; the only time of the day she smoked two cigarettes one after the other. She lit it with her Statue of Liberty shaped silver lighter and pulled at the cigarette deeply with tight lips. Lizzie immediately began the rasping cough that finally brought up the phlegm that the first cigarette couldn't bring up and carefully placed the slimy liquid with her tongue on a tissue and examined it for worrying hues; there were none, all was fine. Now her day could start.

Lizzie reached for the latest book she was reading, a birthday present from her sister Maggie. She had found *In the Ditch* by Buchi Emecheta a really good read. Lizzie liked nitty-gritty books that depicted life as it really was or had been for people like her. Not for Lizzie escapist, fantasist, glamorous novels describing middle and upper classes on their middlers and uppers. She had saved herself the last few chapters as a treat for her birthday. She slipped her reading glasses on and turned to the first page inside of the book to read again her sister's message, written fluently in blue biro, each word written without lifting the pen from the page, like a teacher in a hurry.

To Lizzie mfs Welcome to the PENSIONERS Club, love always Maggie xxx.

MFS was their code for My Favourite Sister. Esmee and Maggie were as opposite as chalk and cheese; Esmee was beaten Maggie was brash, Maggie travelled the world chasing the sun and fleshy pleasures, Esmee was a hermit who barely saw daylight and had probably stopped masturbating years ago, if she ever did, Maggie said about her.

The events in the book reminded Lizzie of her own childhood, so far away in years but so very present in the way she did things and thought about things. Her goals of big house, big family and financial security were all achieved. She had built a strong barrier against ever going back to the embarrassing poverty, the attic rooms with the overcrowded basement rooms where the sun never shone, bellies stuffed with white bread and potatoes and having to wear constantly mocked antwacky clothes that had scarred her childhood. The financial security she enjoyed now had come at a terrible price—Kai's death—so she had well paid for that.

"*Christmas went, but the cold began,*" Lizzie read adjusting her glasses.

After finishing reading the remainder of the book, in less than one hour, Lizzie stretched her arms, yawned and rose from her bed. She coughed up the rest of the phlegm that had still been lying determinedly on her chest. It took a couple of wet, whooping, barking minutes before she brought it all up, rolled it to the tip of her pale pink tongue and carefully placed it on the damp tissue like she had dug up a nugget of pure gold that she could take to Mister Greenberg's pawn shop and get cash for no questions asked. She examined the phlegm for traces of illness.

> Pearly white means all right
> Pale green means clean (ish)
> Dark green means not too keen (ish)
> Red means blight.

The phlegm was pearly white with a trace of pale green. She folded the tissue carefully over the phlegm and put it in the ashtray, feeling as if she had just undergone a thorough medical check and passed with flying colours. She would live to ninety-three, no problem.

Shopping in the morning and the hairdresser's in the afternoon.

She checked Googie's room hoping he would be there, fast sleep and snoring, but the room was empty. She shrugged her disappointment then went downstairs full of anticipation for a soon to be satisfyingly full house with Beryl and the twins on their way as soon as this nonsense with that little American shithouse had been sorted out. She went straight into the kitchen and made herself a mug of milky tea with the last of the milk. Bashir's shop down the road was open but she would not venture out for at least another hour, even in broad sunny daylight, until she was sure the night people had disappeared off the streets.

She took the pack of cards out from the cupboard door, opened the back door into the yard to let some breeze in and sat down in her nightclothes at the small

Pure Pressure

table, and laid the cards out carefully in front of her for a game of Patience. She lit a cigarette and immediately began to cough, a darker, wetter cough. She spat that out on her tissue.

Thick but pearly white that was alright

The queen of clubs, her favourite, was the first card she turned over. An omen that meant she was bound to win after days of unsuccessful tries, and she did.

The phone rang. It was Beryl wishing her a happy birthday and to say she would be back soon with the twins and confirming they would have breakfast with her and then shopping in town.

Upstairs, Doreen was running a bath, preparing herself for worship.

Doreen came down the stairs at 7.40 fully dressed and looking glum. She rang home while Lizzie poached some eggs and burnt some toast trying to listen in on the conversation.

"How's everyfin at home?" she asked Doreen as soon as she came off the phone, eager to start a conversation.

"Fine, why, shouldn't it be?" Doreen answered with a tone that made Lizzie uncomfortable.

"I was juss asking, luv, that's all. What time you going to church, luv?" Lizzie asked sweetly trying to cheer Doreen up.

"Half nine, and stop calling me luv all the time, it's embarrassing." she replied sharply.

Doreen ate her breakfast in silence while Lizzie glumly returned to her cards.

"I'm going to the Arab shop," said Lizzie after a while discomforted by Doreen's silence. "I've run out of milk. Do you want anyfin, a newspaper, a bar of chocolate or somefin," said Lizzie just stopping herself adding '*luv*' to her sentence.

"I don't read newspapers, Mam," Doreen replied dryly, "and no thanks for the chocolate, but thanks for asking."

"Yes, of course you don't read newspapers, they're full of lies aren't they," Lizzie said with a hint of sarcasm.

Lizzie disapproved of her daughter's devotion to the Seventh Day Adventist Church. Why could she not adopt a mainstream religion, Lizzie asked her once. Doreen replied with such a withering look that she never asked Doreen again about her religion.

"Beryl's coming over shortly," Lizzie added as she slipped on her coat, "we're going to town, are you sure you won't come with us? You could miss church for one week, I'm sure. It's not often I see you, Doreen; it'd be really nice if we could all go out together, on my birthday and all . . . Doreen," she was begging now.

"I never miss church, Mam, so no thanks," Doreen replied gathering the empty plates.

"Thanks for the breakfast, Mam, and happy birthday."

Doreen took out a small neatly wrapped parcel from her handbag. Lizzie opened the parcel and took out a gold chain and cross. They kissed and hugged and Lizzie's eyes and nose began to water.

As she walked down Kingsley Road, hurriedly, almost illicitly away from Doreen's censorious glances, Lizzie lit a cigarette and pondered on Doreen's behaviour. Jekyll and Hyde that girl, she must be having problems at home, were initial conclusions. There were, of course, undercurrents that had never been discussed between Lizzie and Doreen that went back to that dark freezing January morning, twenty-two years ago.

After taking a few deep pulls of the cigarette and coughing in the process, Lizzie expertly extinguished the cough maker with two fingers and put the stump in her pocket before walking into the shop.

"Hello Bashir," she greeted the Yemeni shopkeeper, grey smoke coming out of her cranial orifices like a steam train engine

"Hello Madame," replied Bashir behind the counter. "Are you fine today? Still smoking?"

"It's my birthday today," she said quickly changing the subject.

"Your birthday, today? Can I ask how old you are?"

"Guess," she said flirtatiously.

"No, it is not right to ask lady for his age," Bashir decided.

"Go on, Bashir, guess," she teased.

"Maybe you forty five, maybe you fifty five, maybe you in between. I doono."

"Sixty-five," she said proudly.

"No, not sixty five," he replied. "You lie to me."

Lizzie left the shop uplifted and smiling, carrying a lot more than she had planned to buy, including three pints of milk, a dozen eggs, two packs of bacon, two cloves of garlic, a pound of onions, two newspapers and cigarettes.

She heard a car horn and looked round to see Billy Goolsby waving at her from his passing truck; she did not wave back but merely nodded at him because she was a civil woman. She never liked the man after he had tried to overcharge her for a plumbing job he and his brother botched up.

She walked back home taking deep pulls from her strained, bent stump of a cigarette. Doreen was sufficiently upset without having to put up with her smoke, she reasoned. One day, she promised herself and anybody who would listen, as she had done many times before, she would stop smoking altogether. She took two quick final pulls and threw the spent cigarette straight into the gutter with a practiced flick.

Lizzie had just finished emptying the carrier bags in the kitchen when the phone rang. She was quick to answer it to get away from the awkwardness between Doreen and herself who had simply sat there on the stool, on the telephone, watching as Lizzie came in struggling with the bags, without offering to help.

As soon as Doreen put the phone down it rang again.

Doreen picked it up and passed the phone to her Mother, her face tight and resentful.

It might be Googie, wishing her a happy birthday and spilling with excuses, Lizzie hoped.

"Hello," Lizzie answered.

"It's me, happy birthdee," said her sister Maggie.

"Hi, thanks; how are you girl, you okay?"

"I'm fine,"

"And everybody?"

"Yeah, they're fine too. You okay?"

"I'm fine,"

"Is everybody alright?"

"Yeah, everybody's fine."

"I need a favour. If Jim asks; tell him I'm in Liverpool with you and that I've just gone out and I'll be back later. I'm supposed to be with you from this afternoon and I'll be there until a week on Wenzdee."

Although Maggie had lived in Cardiff for over forty years, her Liverpool accent was as strong as when she left, but her kids were pure Welsh, they had red dragons printed on their hearts. Her three kids, Barry, Helen and Herbert, had been to Liverpool a few times over the years but it was not really their scene, it was not Welsh enough for them.

"Wait," Lizzie said. "I'll take this in me bedroom."

She placed the phone on the table and went upstairs, lifted the phone on her bedside table and shouted down to Doreen to replace the phone.

"What are you up to, Maggie Roberts?" said Lizzie after shutting the bedroom door behind her. "Thanks for the book, by the way, I finished it this morning and really enjoyed it. The bit about the rat not being afraid of her made me sick; It reminded me of the old days in Beaufort Street. Remember, we used to be overrun with them."

"Don't remind me. I thought you'd enjoy the book, Miss Martyr, who likes to wallow in it."

"So, what's going on?"

"I've got this friend," Maggie giggled. "He's taking me on a cruise for a week."

"You're kidding, a cruise, for a whole week? You're never going to get away with that. Who is this fancy-man, I know it's a fancy-man, come on, who is it?"

Maggie did not answer.

Oh no, thought Lizzie, Basil the glazier. Basil the glazier had left Maggie stranded at Orly Airport in Paris when his wife appeared out of nowhere and marched him out of the terminal before Maggie could get her return ticket off him. She had to go begging to the British Consul for her fare back. She had sworn on her kids' lives she would never talk to that man again.

"Basil the glazier," Lizzie said resignedly.

"What, you must be joking! That spineless, lying half a prick! No, you don't know this one. He's brand new and single. His name's Winston and he's a widower."

"With a name like Winston he's bound to be black."

"Winston Churchill wasn't black."

"No, but he's the last white man to be called Winston. How old is he?"

"He's 68."

"A bit old for you, I thought you liked them younger."

"He looks good for his age, at least ten years younger on a good day and I've only ever seen him on good days."

"Is your Jim likely to ring?"

"No, of course not, unless there's an emergency. You'll just have to remember it when you see him if he brings it up. You know Jim, he never says a word unless he has to. Winston wants me to leave Jim and go and live with him in Barbados."

"Don't be daft, you'll never leave Jim, he's the only man who could put up with you."

"Winston could, he'd do anyfin for me; Winston really loves me."

"Does Winston now? You couldn't leave Jim. It would break his heart. It would kill him."

"I know, I'm really thinking about leaving very hard. It's cael a chael, touch and go. The kids taught me it. They can speak Welsh fluently you know. He's

Pure Pressure

a lovely man this Winston, really kind and knowledgeable. He's got a house in Barbados, well it's his mother's house but she's 90 odd; it's near Oisin, a beautiful place on the South West Coast . . ."

"Maggie, I've never been to Barbados and I never will. So why don't you stop dropping these names about places I've never heard and care even less about."

"Anyway, I'm sure Jim'd manage in the end. And I'd always come and see him; and the kids will always look after him."

"Mind you, you said you were gonna leave Jim for Pig Face, what was his name, and that didn't last very long."

"Melvin? That was different, Melvin had no money and kids all over the place, and he'd been telling me lies."

"You're an 'oower, Maggie Roberts, noffin but a dirty 'oower, I swear to God. You're only going with this man because he's got money."

"Hey, you know as well as me that you can't live on fresh air alone. When you get to my age, you're looking for a little more than fresh air I can tell you. Oldish people, you, me—all older people, need comfort and comfort cost money. Am I right or am I wrong?"

"Yes, Maggie, you're always right. Anyway have a good time."

"How's Esmee?"

"The same as far as I know; I don't see her from one year to the next. She's cut her phone off so nobody can ring her. Her Bonny goes there quite often so I'm sure she's alright, so I suppo . . ."

"I'll bring you back somefin nice, Madeira cake, we're stopping at Madeira; it's part of Portugal apparently, and Agadir in Morocco. I could get you some nice leather slippers from there. They've done it all up, Agadir, since the earthquake; remember that earthquake in Agadir?"

"I'd prefer duty free cigarettes and a bottle of good Russian Vodka. Talk to you when you get back."

"Don't forget, from today until a week Wenzdee I'm staying at yours. Me kids know where I'm going, so don't worry about them. Seeya sis, happy birthdee."

Lizzie slowly shook her head at the antics of her elder sister. Sixty-seven next birthday and she acted like she was 27 and had the energy to prove it. As the elder sister, Maggie was supposed to guide Lizzie through the straight and narrow by virtue of her seniority, but she was more like Lizzie's younger sister, always had been self centred and needy.

As she walked back down the stairs, the front door bell rang out. Beryl arrived with the twins.

Beryl carried a box under her arm and was so pleased to discover it was a wide-brimmed straw hat, which was just what she wanted against the sun. Happy birthdays were wished and kiss and hugs shared around. Alice sang a little poem she had made up about the wonder of Granma.

She told Beryl to go wake Paul while she cooked breakfast and dashed around the kitchen with her hat on, and the twins took the table and chairs into the sunshine dappled yard.

Beryl said Paul did not want any and Googie's bedroom was empty.

The girls ate the breakfast and Lizzie took out her knitting because there was a worry lump where her empty stomach should have been.

"Mam, what's up, why aren't you eating?" asked Beryl.

"Noffin, girl, everyfin's fine; I'm not hungry."

"Look, Granma, what's those big white birds?" Alma shouted from outside.

"I wonder what's happened to Googie," said Lizzie to no one in particular.

"They're seagulls," said Doreen. "You only see them by the sea."

"We live miles from the sea," said Alice.

"He could have rung at least. He was supposed to be bringing little Michelle for the weekend," Lizzie continued.

"We don't have a sea in Atlanta," said Alice, "but we have shopping malls and microwave ovens."

If Lizzie could persuade Doreen to come to town with them maybe they would find time to talk things over, just the two of them. Maybe not on reflection, Lizzie was sure Doreen would start a scene if she brought it up, crying, cursing and accusing, the charity of her faith cast aside while she vented twenty-two years of pent up feelings. Perhaps tomorrow she would find time for them to be alone; go for a walk in the Park before everyone got up from the party. Doreen had to get it out of her system; you could see it bubbling up inside her.

Lizzie wondered if Doreen had told her husband. Probably not, Evelyn would be horrified and judgemental; he was training to be a saint.

Lizzie, Beryl and the twins mingled with or rather stood out from the bustling all-white Saturday crowds of shoppers and strollers along Church Street. Lizzie felt coquettish in her straw hat and asked Beryl several times if she looked all right with it on before venturing outside with it on. They had walked all the way from home to make the best of the warm weather. On Princes Road Alice wanted to know whom William Huskisson was to have such a big statue like that.

"Some slave trader from the 18th Century," said Beryl confidently. "They were all slave traders in them days, getting fat on our blood," she added with touch of venom.

"You know Mam, I'm absolutely amazed that we must have passed hundreds of people in town and I didn't see one black face, not one" remarked Beryl.

"Really, I didn't even notice," Lizzie replied. "Hang on," she remembered, "There was that man at the bus stop."

"What bus stop, I didn't see no black man."

"Facing Lewis's," Lizzie said. "He looked like an African man."

"Well, just one, the exception that proves the rule. Where are they, where are all the black people in this town?"

"They're probably still in bed, luv," Lizzie replied with a smirk.

"That's not funny, Mam, that's playing to stereotypes. I mean, there must be thousands of black people in Liverpool and most of them live within fifteen minutes' walk from town yet you'd think you were in Utah . . ."

"In where?"

"Forget it, Mam. Let's go in there and look for my outfit for tonight," Beryl said indicating a large departmental store, the most expensive in town. "I'm gonna celebrate your birthday in style."

Beryl had already selected her outfit in her minds eye; either a plain black or brightly coloured dress, no in-between. It had to have long sleeves to hide her fleshy arms, a low cleavage for showing her pushed-up breasts, baggy enough to smother her generous hips and *de rigueur*. power-crazed shoulders.

"See that woman with the screw face and the green scarf," said Lizzie to her daughter. "Don't look now, but she's been following us ever since we walked into this shop."

Beryl turned slowly round as they rode up the escalator and spotted the woman a few feet below them.

"She's a floor walker, a store detective," Lizzie explained, "and imagines that all black people must be followed because we are all thieves."

"Are you sure, Mam; she looks just like any shopper to me."

"I'm sure, watch her," she said with a frown.

They took the escalator to the next floor up. Screw Face with the green scarf trailed them. When they stopped, she stopped, pretending to look at some merchandise. When they moved on, she moved on, keeping them in her sights throughout.

Beryl was astonished. Why did this woman want to follow us, she mused. It was not because she was a famous ballerina, or her Mother was Winnie Mandela. This woman was following us because we looked like potential thieves.

Beryl walked straight up to Screw Face, invading her space, face to face.

"Are you security or are you in love with me because your eyes have locked on to me for the past half hour?" Beryl said her voice soft and composed their noses almost touching.

Without waiting for an answer, Beryl pointed her finger at Screw Face's nose and said in a loud voice.

"Instead of hounding honest black shoppers with money in their pockets like us all over the store, you'd be better doing your job properly by keeping an eye on the little white Norfenders who are busy robbing stuff while you pursue your obsession that all black people are shop lifters."

She then turned to Lizzie adding, "come on, mother, let's go and spend our money in a store that respects black people and doesn't treat them like thieves."

Both embarrassed by people staring and impressed by her daughter's feistiness, Lizzie followed Beryl and the twins down the escalator without looking back.

When they got outside the store, Lizzie said to Beryl, "you'd have to go back to Atlanta to find a store that respects black people, cos you won't find one in this town."

"Now I know why you don't see black people in town. It's scandalous," Beryl protested.

"This is Liverpool," Lizzie said wearily. "And you're gonna have to get used to it if you're gonna settle back here again."

Lizzie bought ice creams all round as recompense.

They went to three other stores before Beryl found a dress she wanted. In each store they played spot the store detective and won each time, although there were a few false alarms, as one suited man was eyeing Beryl up, not because he thought she was a potential thief but because he thought she was the most beautiful girl in town, and he told her so. Beryl did even blush rather she was disappointed by the corny chat up line.

Next, they went to St. John's market to buy meats and vegetables and then made their laden way back.

It was too hot to climb up the hill that Hardman Street represented so they got the 86 bus.

"Way yuze goin' girls, Parly?" Keith Jones, the bus driver asked.

"How's your Mum, Keef?"

"Yeah, she's fine, Aunt," replied Keith. "How are Aunty Lizzie, you're looking well."

"I'm okay. Tell her I was asking about her."

Lizzie put a note on the tray to cover the fares.

Keith pushed the note back and smiled.

"You look after yourself, now," he smiled.

"Beryl Leung!" he shouted on recognising her. "Ain't seen you in years, I hear you're a Stateside girl now; you on holiday?"

"Yeah, somefin like that," Beryl replied with a grin.

They got off the bus on Upper Parliament Street, walking along Mulgrave Street, they passed three old timers and Lizzie stopped to exchange words with all of them.

Lizzie knew everyone.

Further on, by Cawdor Street, Lizzie pointed out an elderly, bald, bloated, red-faced white man.

"He used to be dead handsome in his time, like a film star, all the girls used to talk about him, although it was obvious he didn't like chinesses. And sixty years later I still don't know his name although he's been around all me life. You wouldn't guess by looking at him but he's years younger than me."

Lizzie loved to give running commentaries on locals.

A teenager sauntered on the other side of the road.

"Do you know him too?" Beryl challenged her.

"That's one of Etta Mitchell's grandkids or great-grandkids, for sure; the same tiny eyes and big chin you can't mistake the Mitchells," Lizzie replied proudly, adjusting her glasses.

"Okay Mam," Beryl conceded, "you know your community."

"I should do, I haven't lived anywhere else."

"That's your problem, mother, you should get out more. The number of times I've invited you over . . ."

"You know I couldn't bear the thought of flying. I'd die of a heart attack."

Beryl shook her head. She remembered her mother reading The Echo and whenever a name she recognised had been charged or convicted of some crime or other she had a set of stock answers.

"Well, it runs in the family, his uncle went to jail for the same thing back in 1948," she would say peering above her glasses.

"Her grandmother, who worked hard for every penny she possessed and never stole anything from anybody in her life, will be spinning in her grave with embarrassment."

Or the time Jake Mensah was mugged.

"What goes around comes around. His grandfather was the most violent person in Liverpool—a bully—and he would beat up anybody anytime for nothing and anything."

As they reached the corner of Beaconsfield Street and Granby Street, a female voice shouted Beryl's name. They looked around to see a woman waving at them 100 yards away in a wheelchair by Hatherley Street near the Mosque.

"Who's that?" asked Beryl.

"That's Cilla, Cilla Jenkins," she replied. "Keep your purse in your pocket," she warned.

Lizzie walked ahead with the twins as Beryl ambled towards Cilla Jenkins.

Beryl was shocked when she got closer. She had not seen Cilla since she left Liverpool to live in the States fifteen years ago. She remembered Cilla as a plump and well-groomed woman, but the Cilla in front of her was unhealthily thin, her face gaunt and her eyes sunk deep in their socket, her uncombed frizzy hair roughly tied back in an untidy bun. However, she had lost none of her gregariousness, lost none of her front.

A waif-like brown haired young white-looking teenaged girl pushed Cilla's wheelchair. Both Cilla's legs were missing from the knees down.

"How are yer, girl?" Cilla said in her familiar spunky voice.

"How are YOU?" Beryl replied. "What happened to yer legs?"

"Oh dem, I 'ad to get dem cut off cos of infection, the needles, you know. Dis is me daughter Chantelle, you remember her Dad, Little Johnny from de Bull Ring."

Beryl remembered Cilla was going out with a white guy before she left, a shifty-eyed, ferret-faced man who looked like he had never done a day's honest work in his life and planned to keep it that way.

"He's dead now," Cilla said. "He died from an overdose when Chantelle was a toddler. Are you on 'olideez or 'ome fer good?"

"Home for good; I got homesick, you know. How's your Sandra?"

"She's alright. Yeah, yer always better off wid yer family. Can yer lend me a coupla pound for the chippie?"

Beryl remembered her mother's warning but found herself taking out a £5 note from her purse. Cilla's hand sprang from her lap and took the note with the unexpected speed of a chameleon's sticky tongue lapping up an unsuspecting insect, shoving the note down her bra. "God bless yer, girl, tell yer Mam I was asking about her," she said with a smile as Chantelle spun the wheelchair around and went off in the opposite direction.

"I should not have given her that money," Beryl thought. "She'll probably spend it on crack or heroin."

Beryl watched them cross the road towards the Avenue, making a car swerve and beep the horn impatiently.

Walking up Granby Street on her way home, a van drew up alongside Beryl. It was Bonny Roberts, her cousin, with Billygoat driving.

She had not seen Bonny since she left the first time for the States. He looked pleased to see her. They used to get on well as kids growing up and it was good to see him again.

Bonny insisted Billygoat dropped her off at the house although she insisted it would have been quicker for her to walk. That is the way she remembered Bonny, not the brightest child in the family but always helpful.

They passed her mother who was chatting away with a contempory.

"Drop me here Billy, thanks," Beryl said and waved as she stepped out of the car.

"Guess who's just helped me with the bags?" she said to her mother.

"Bonny and Billy-Goat," Lizzie replied.

"How do you know?"

"Do you think I'm blind as well as daft?"

"This is Charm-Boy," Lizzie introduced the fat old man.

"That's what they used to call me back in the day," explained Charm-Boy, who may have been charming but clearly had not been a boy for many decades. "Me name's Johnny Davies, I've known yer Granma all me life."

"She's me Mum not me Nan," replied Beryl.

"You don't look old enough to be her daughter," said Charm-Boy.

"Take no notice of him," Lizzie interjected as she walked away. "I'll see you again Johnny, and take care of yourself."

"He knows quite well you're me daughter," she said to Beryl when Charm Boy was out of earshot, "he sang at your Christening, lovely high-pitched voice, like a girl's. He's trying to flatter yer. Why do you think he's called Charm-Boy? Did you give that Cilla Jenkins any money?" Lizzie asked as she inserted her key in the front door.

Beryl did not have to answer it was written all over her face.

"She'll only spend it on drugs," Lizzie rebuked her. "She's got her daughter on the gear as well and she's only seventeen, poor sod."

"Have we got everyfin ready for tonight?" said Beryl not wishing to dwell on the matter.

"Well, did you?"

"I had to, Mam. I felt so sorry for her and felt guilty for being able-bodied and healthy. She looks likes she's gonna die very soon and she's not yet 40."

"It is a shame, but money won't help her," said Lizzie as she opened the door. "I only need some liquor; I've had the beers for weeks in the cellar. I'm waiting for Paul, that lazy brother of yours, to get out of bed to go and get it; he's getting it at discount price from one of his cronies."

They had not finished emptying the shopping when the front door bell rang. It was Doreen.

"Have you only just got back from church?" Beryl asked her. "It must be good to keep you there all day."

Doreen walked past Beryl acknowledging her with the briefest of nods and went upstairs.

"She's been in a strange mood all day. I think she's having problems at home," Lizzie said to Beryl by way of explanation. "Don't say noffin to her, though, she'll be okay later, I'm sure."

Chapter 6

Burial

7:45am Saturday 4th July 1981

Billygoat stifled a yawn as he drove up Jermyn Street in his truck wondering how he got himself in this mess. All he did was go to play some cards and now he was about to commit a crime that could send him to jail until the day he died, a man who had never had any problem with the police nor the taxman. He paid all his taxes, as little as possible of course, but he paid them and on time. Martine did the books. She did the books for all the family businesses, Felicia's restaurant and her own sewing work; although Martine charged so little money there was not much to count. Billygoat was not a regular churchgoer but he feared God as much as the next man did. He had long convinced himself gambling was not a mortal sin in God's eyes. If there is such a thing as Heaven, his ticket to blissful eternal life was booked, for sure. until now.

Doubts were creeping in, despite him having accepted that the death of the American was an accident, pure and simple, and it was not as if it were he who had pulled the trigger. Denying a man a proper burial was overstepping the mark, he feared. Yet, what else could he do, it was too far to go back now. He should have walked out, wiped his hands from it all, and called the police. However, the thought of desperadoes like Robbo and JD after his tail was not a comforting one. Coercion, Lord, I swear. God understands but would the Police? He could go to jail for a very serious crime; murder at worst, manslaughter probably, or at best concealing and unlawfully carrying a body. Billygoat knew his law; he had not watched so many crime dramas on television and read about court cases in the newspaper not to know about these things.

He had driven the long way round from his home in Percy Street through Kingsley Road (waving to Mrs Leung, Bonny's Aunt, as she carried her groceries home) avoiding Granby Street in case his daughter Felicia caught sight of him. He had promised to help her prepare for her busiest day of the week at the restaurant but he could not face her, not before he had finished what he had started and put the whole business behind him. Billygoat did not want to face his wife Martine either but had had no option.

Martine gave him her well-rehearsed me-don't-care-where-you-been-all-night-you-whoring-master look when he walked in as she sat knitting something or other for her sister's grandchild in Canada.

Billygoat tried to tell her he had been gambling all night. He took out a bundle of notes as his alibi but she stopped him in mid-sentence with her withering "me don't care where you been all night Wi-lli-ham, you whoring master, dat eez wha' una eez; yu tink me nah no yu," Martine said without looking up or missing a stitch.

"Me's gone out again to do a job," he said, pretending to ignore her comments. "Me'll be gone all day; you wanna lif' to de church?"

"Me 'af a lif' awready," she replied curtly pursing her lips and then sucking her teeth long and slow.

Martine Goolsby sucking teeth was more eloquent than words in displaying her displeasure and Billygoat had come to terms a long time ago that protestations were hopelessly futile when Martine thought he was in the wrong, even when he was in the right.

Only once had Billygoat erred during his forty-one years' marriage, just the once and, whenever he was late or appeared deep in thought, the treatment started. The treatment usually involved the words *whoremaster* in the first two sentences (Martine didn't curse she was a religious woman, a pious woman) followed by days, sometimes weeks of long silences regularly interspersed with the notorious sucking of teeth whenever Billygoat made an attempt to coax her out of her mood. However, he loved the bones of that woman, sometimes in spite of himself. She had a good heart and they had been through so much together.

Billygoat parked his truck behind Robbo's car. He loved the sun beaming down on him; he felt the sunrays were burning up the toxins accumulated in this wretched country with its polluted atmosphere. Billygoat cursed England most days of his life and rhapsodised about Barbados, but deep down he loved England above all other countries. Billygoat was an Englishman now. Not your proper Englishman, he still supported the West Indies cricket team even though the selectors purposely excluded Bajans from the team, they even blocked Gary Sobers in his early days. Sure Billygoat missed Barbados, that is why they went back there every two years for a whole month. All the family had gone now, dead. There were only the nephews and nieces and their children, and most of these had emigrated to Canada or the US and were no more Bajan than he was. Martine, however, had all her family to visit—her mother was still alive, and aunties, sisters, brothers, or rather brother, as the other three were long dead, cousins, even school friends—still alive, still kicking. The women always live the longest and it is always the women who complain the most about how sick dem is.

Martine made little money with she dressmaking but she save that little money for Barbados, sending money through the wire like she a millionaire when she so thrifty at home.

Martine could lie, boy, she could lie; and she made him lie too. Not nasty lies, Martine does not have a nasty bone in she body. Lies like she met the Queen in a garden party at DE PALACE and drank Earl tea with no milk with DE QUEEN sheself, and wore a flowery hat, a blue dress and white gloves and matching shoes. The Queen thank she for she work in the church. She also said that she shop in the same store as the Duke of Marlborough and know him by name, but she call him Your Grace and he call she Miss G. She would call on him as a witness.

"Isn't that so Willi-yam?"

"Yes Martine."

Billygoat was sure that when they returned next year she would swear and make him swear that she went to London to see Lady Diana and Prince Charles' wedding in the flesh.

Billygoat walked up the steps full of trepidation as he knocked on the door. JD answered the door and looked very tired with dark brown bags under his blood-shot eyes.

"You took your time gettin' 'ere," he said as he closed the door firmly behind Billygoat, "what kept yer?"

"Youze ungratefool man, wha' 'appenin' wid you?"

Billygoat walked straight past JD sucking his teeth, not quite in the Martine class, which was a gift of nature, but enough to emphasise his annoyance.

Bonny and Robbo were playing cards. All traces of the night before had disappeared. The bare floorboard where once there had been the blood soaked flowery carpet had been swept and mopped. The Muhammad Ali photo still dominated the room, an illustrious if silent witness to its secrets. The air extractor and the ceiling fan were on full power screeching and whirring in unison of sorts, like two muffled helicopters, attempting to suck out of the room the remnants of death and cordite. Shep-from-Ohio's body scent still lingered on guiltily in all of their nostrils and would remain there until their dying day. Except Robbo who did not have a sentimental bone in his body.

"Y'all ready?" Billygoat asked impatiently.

"You got all the tools?" asked Robbo looking up from his cards.

Billygoat sucked his teeth again translated as 'do you need to ask' stance.

"Go get 'em, then," said Bonny.

"Eez wha' missus Goolsby bring me into dis life, fi be slave for una. Cum 'elp me get de tools nuh; end de game an' cum we go, cha man."

Bonny helped bring the tools and equipment and a set of dark blue dirty overalls, heavy gloves and painter's masks.

The four of them, Robbo, JD, Bonny and Billygoat trundled through the back door, one behind the other, down the entrée, retracing their steps from the night before.

They could smell the corpse before they had fully opened the kitchen door. Five pot-bellied rats scuttled away into the shadows as JD entered the room, followed by the other three.

The dust masks they all now wore did little to counter the stench from Shep-from-Ohio's body. His face covered with buzzing flies gave the illusion that it was moving, like a heaving black mask. It seemed every fly in the area had decided to feed on the smelly corpse and invited their friends and families from further afield to the unexpected feast.

Robbo recoiled.

"I'm allergic to flies," he said and turned to walk away.

Bonny Roberts stood in front of him blocking his path out of the yard.

"You ain't goin' anywhere," Bonny told him firmly. "It was your idea and you've got to see it through."

"Well get rid of the flies then," he retorted his face damp with apprehension.

JD lifted his spade high over his head and smashed it on Shep-from-Ohio's buzzing mask. The dull thud of the blow made Billygoat cringe; the flies dispersed for a few seconds revealing Shep-from-Ohio's now eerily familiar open-mouthed face. His eyes balls where missing, as was the fleshy part of his broad nostrils, chewed away by the rodents.

"Bloody hell," cursed JD. "A few days or so and all we lef' t'bury'll be clean bones," he said trying again to disperse the persistent swarm with his spade.

Bonny Roberts said he was not into rats and waited outside scouting around the crevices in the back yard wall with furtive eyes for any scuffling apparitions.

They had to lift eight flagstones with the crow bars before starting to dig the earth that soon baked dry hard in the summer heat, all the time fighting off swarms of flies and other insects, and having to put up with Billygoat's full complement of Bajan curses, some of which they had never heard before. Robbo had brought one can each of fly killer and air freshener and was spending as much time spraying the flies away and trying to deodorise what could not be deodorised as he was actually digging. The spraying served only to increase Billygoat's annoyance.

"Spray, spray, spray; is all you can do?"

Robbo threatened to spray Billygoat's mouth and stuff the spraying cans down his fucking throat if he didn't shut it.

Bonny had to calm Robbo down and warned Billygoat to stop moaning.

It would take seven solid backbreaking, hand-blistering hours before they had finally laid Shep-from-Ohio to rest in a four-foot deep grave covered with earth and rubble and packed tight with the cracked flagstones on top. JD jammed a yellow-headed dandelion in one of the cracks to pretty it up a bit.

Now that it was all done, they all hoped without saying so that they would never again hear about this man from Ohio. They hoped he had no family, or friends to come looking for him and it would be as if he had never existed.

Robbo knew that Shep-from-Ohio had a family all right, and what a family, they were everywhere. Shep-from-Ohio, or Greg as Paul Leung called him, might only have been an in-law but Robbo feared that it would all come to back to haunt him.

Billygoat asked "Gad" solemnly (his head bowed, his eyes downcast, one boot resting on his spade's head) to bless Shep-from-Ohio's soul, adding, "none o' we want de man fe dead, none o' we. De man bring it on he self; we juss protec' we self."

Billygoat made the sign of the cross and whispered Amen first and the others followed, heads down not daring to look at each other in case their eyes betrayed guilt. After a few uncomfortable seconds of silence and standing rigidly still, apart from who was, they all trudged silently back through the alley, head bowed, except Robbo who was busy swatting insects.

Bonny, Robbo and JD normally had the hands of bureaucrats, smooth and not used to physical work, but today they were raw with burst blisters. Only Billygoat, the professional builder, the foreman of the work detail, trained to work all day in all weathers, was physically unscathed and proudly so, skitting the "aunty men" for their soft hands and weak backs. As the only one present and alive not to be locally born, Billygoat could not help throwing in a last dig, metaphorically speaking, adding, "you all been in de country too long, man, you too English man, you forget what hard work is."

The burial complete, the deed done, they all sat in the gambling room mulling over their ordeal.

"I wonder wha' Shep's short for?" said JD.

"The only Shep I know is Shep from the Limelights," said Bonny.

"Daddy's home, Daddy's home to stay, oooo, ooooo ooo,." croaked JD.

"And his name was Sheppard," said Bonny who knew a thing or two about Doo-Wop. Shep's name was probably named Sherman, dem Yanks dem love fangancy nagames."

"Sh-itonyerdoorst-ep," said Robbo with a smirk.

"The man was a teef, that's all, a teef. De man dun deserve fe die, but eez 'im gun dat kill 'im; is not we fe blame," said Billygoat by way of conclusion as he rose to leave, followed by Bonny.

Bonny, like many of his generation, was mesmerised by American culture—the films, the music, even the language. The love affair with America ended when he caught Valerie kissing and hugging with Montgomery, a slick-arsed gold-toothed GI stationed at Lakenheath base. Though they still had the best tunes, he conceded.

Bonny asked Billygoat to drop him at his sister Gloria's flat in Chinatown. He could get a long bath, some sleep, and a change of clothes. He would chill out there until Monday and then go to town and buy himself a new outfit, he told himself patting the wad of notes inside his pocket.

They drove down Granby Street; the sunny weather had brought out many people, dressed in their best summer fineries, which made Bonny feel acutely self-conscious in Billygoat's dirty overalls. No one had ever seen Bonny Roberts in dirty work clothes before; nobody had ever seen Bonny in work clothes period. He hoped not to meet anybody on the way. He had a reputation to keep.

They both got in the truck and drove off towards Granby Street. Bonny saw a young woman struggling along Jermyn Street carrying shopping bags who seemed familiar. They caught each other's eye.

"Hello cuz," he shouted through the open window, gesturing for Billygoat to stop the vehicle.

"Hello Bonny," Beryl Leung replied.

Bonny jumped out of the truck almost before it stopped. Beryl put down the bags and they embraced.

"I didn't know you were in England," he said to her.

"I've only been here a few days."

"Hey, you've got a Yankee accent."

"You're bound to pick it up after fifteen years."

"It's been that long has it? How long you here for?" he asked.

"I'm moving back to England."

"Really, with the family?"

Pure Pressure

"The twins only, I've split up from me husband. What are you up to these days?" she asked looking at his work clothes.

Bonny blushed.

"I've been helping Billygoat out," he said quickly, lowering his eyes.

"Do you work for him then?"

"Yeah, no . . . sort of . . . are you going home? Let me help you with your bags."

"Don't be soft it's only round the corner."

Billygoat sounded the horn impatiently.

"Hurry man, me 'ave tings t'do."

"No problem," he said to her, ignoring Billygoat. "Jump in."

Bonny grabbed her bags and put them in the back of the truck.

"Come on," he urged her. Then to Billygoat, "you remember Beryl, me Aunty Lizzie's daughter. We're just dropping her off with her shopping; she only lives up the road."

"Me know where she live, man," Billygoat muttered through gritted teeth that turned instinctively into a welcoming smile as he greeted Beryl.

"Hello daarlin'," he said to her in the patronising voice he usually reserved for women, "I juss see yer mudah dis marnin' doin' she shoppin'."

Beryl climbed in and Bonny squeezed in next to her. They drove down Jermyn Street into Granby Street, then Princes Avenue and round the corner into Kingsley Road. During the couple of minutes it took to get Beryl to her destination, the electricity generated just by having his thigh pressed against hers strangely exciting; Bonny wished they were driving to London and back. Bonny detected a faint whiff of perfume mixed with sweat coming from her, so he took a deep breath through his nose to try to bottle it inside his brain.

"You've grown lovely," he heard himself saying to her.

"How's Aunty Esmee?" Beryl asked.

"Up and down, but she's alright. Go round and see her when you've got time, she'd be really pleased to see you," he lied. "She lives in Thackeray Street, 26b."

"Sure, I'll bring the twins as well. Tell her I was asking about her."

Billygoat parked the truck outside Lizzie's house, behind Paul Leung's grey Jaguar. Bonny reached for Beryl's bags and skipped out, holding the door open for her.

"Why don't you come in for a bit; me Mam's in, and our Doreen's just come down from London for a few days?"

"I'd love to but I've got to get changed," he said looking down at what he now perceived as the ugliest, most disgusting clothes he had ever worn in his life. "Say hello for me."

"Why don't you come round this evening, we're having a little family do for me Mam and our Paul's birthday."

"That's right they share the same birthday. Yeah, I'd luv to; what time?"

"Anytime after 8," she smiled. "You don't have to get all dressed up, it's all quite informal."

"After 8 it is, then," he replied placing her bags on the top step as if they were made of the finest crystal.

He got back in the truck and barely had time to slam the door behind him before Billygoat accelerated away in a screech of tyres.

Bonny turned on the radio to listen to listen to the horse racing results.

"Ya want some food from me daughta's place, ya know, *Spices*," said Billygoat.

Bonny nodded.

"Ya comin' in?" asked Billygoat.

"Are you mad," Bonny replied, "in these clothes?"

Bonny shook his head. "I'll wait here; take me ticket to the bookies I got two winners in me Canadian bet. I'll get me money back at least. Oh, and I'll have some fish, any fish would be nice with rice and peas and salad but no tomatoes, I hate tomatoes."

As Billygoat stepped down from his van he turned to say to Bonny with a grin, "dere your in-law."

Bonny looked in the direction Billygoat nodded towards and saw Eric Wilson coming out of *Spices* with a takeaway in his hand. Bonny watched Eric saunter over to him dressed in pristine white clothes and trainers. Bonny hated that man with a passion and Eric knew Bonny hated him with a passion. Of course, it was mainly due to Eric's relationship with his sister. Something else about Eric angered Bonny; Eric was a heroin dealer and, in Bonny's estimation, heroin dealers were only one notch up from paedophiles. Although smack was mainly a white kids' poison, he knew people who were on the gear, he had seen the effects on them and it was ugly. Rumour had it, and Liverpool 8 was always awash with rumours, that Eric supplied half the smack heads in Birkenhead. Everybody knew what Eric did, which meant the police knew what Eric did, which meant to Bonny that Eric was paying the police and probably informing on people as well in order to keep sweet with them.

"Hey, Bonny, my main man," said Eric and he laughed nervously extending his hand in greeting. "Ha-ha-ha-ha-haa."

Eric always laughed when he was nervous.

Eric tried to do a soul handshake but Bonny slapped his hand in a high five before Eric could grab it and Eric's face registered a low five as the corners of his mouth dipped at the snub.

"I've juss got some food to take back to your Gloria's," he said, ignoring the slights. "You been workin'?" he asked noticing Bonny's clothes.

"Yeah, been helping Billygoat out as a favour."

"Boy, you look rough," Eric said and laughed.

"Boy, you look like a school girl with all that white gear and cheap jewellery," retorted Bonny without smiling.

"Cheap! Is joke yua a joke; dis jewellery's worth thousands, man, thou-sands."

Ha-ha-ha-ha-haa, he laughed as he walked away waving.

"Catch yer later, Bonny."

No quiet bath in Gloria's tonight then, Bonny thought.

Billygoat came back, gave him his winnings and his food, and dropped him at his mothers' home on the Thackeray estate instead.

"Change yer plans, huh," he said looking at the back of Eric's Mercedes as it drove off.

"I hate that bastard," Bonny said twisting his mouth as if he had inadvertently eaten a live fly straight off Shep-from-Ohio's face.

"Me knew him mudda and fadda, nice people, me did dem kitchen, me do it cheap for dem too; dem both die in car accident when young Eric still pickney; 'im 'ad a hard life y'know, a damn hard life, lef' t'fen' for heself from young young."

Bonny sniggered. "That's not like you, Billy, goin' all sentimental on the man."

The Thackeray Estate's reputation for neglect was not as bad as the enjoining Englefield Green Estate, but the litter on the street and in the gardens seemed to indicate that it would soon catch up. It would have been easy to assume that community spirit had all but collapsed under the weight of burglaries, vandalism and other street crimes. Lenny, Esmee's brother, dismissively dubbed the estate a Corporation dumping ground for the wretched.

Louis Julienne

As far as Esmee Roberts was concerned, living on the estate suited her fine. Esmee never ventured outside her door, so it mattered not to her what happened out there

Outside Esmee's flat Bonny was trying to find his front door key. His belly was starting to make a noise because he badly needed to shit. The hall and stairway were painted in the ubiquitous Corporation scatter colours: tiny speckles of green, reds, yellows, blues and whites on a pale mauve background.

Bonny was getting exasperated after searching every pocket of the overall (they had eight pockets) at least twice and the clothes in the bag (a further four pockets) before it finally came to him he had lost his key. The shit, he felt, had reached up to his throat, bursting to shoot out from whatever end. He wanted to fart but did not fearing a wet smelly deluge would follow; he cursed, took a breath and gingerly knocked on the door; no answer.

He counted to ten in his head, tightened his arse muscles as they had never been tightened before and knocked again. No answer.

He counted to ten again and knocked once more. Still no answer.

The aroma of the takeaway meal made his mouth water and his stomach rumble even more furiously. Urgent and conflicting needs of ingestion and elimination battled simultaneously, and elimination looked like winning.

He put his ear to the door and shut his eyes trying hard to detect any sound, then lifted the letterbox flap again and shouted almost authoritatively:

"Esmee, it's me."

Silence; had something happened to her he wondered?

He shouted again through the letterbox with desperation in his voice propelled by concerns about his mother's well-being as well as by the demands from his rear end.

"Esmee, are you there!"

Bonny began to dance not in the smoothly rhythmic way he did so well but in an undignified, uncoordinated way, clutching his belly and twisting his body in different directions.

There was a few seconds silence then he heard Amin bark followed by his mother's voice:

"What do you want?" she said.

"It's me, Bonny; I wanna come in."

"I know who it is. D'you think I'm gaga or somefin?"

"No, Mam, no, of course not; can you let me in?"

"Where's your key?"

Amin barked.

Pure Pressure

"I've lost it, Mam,"

"What did you say, I can't hear you for that dog barking. Shut yer gills, dog."

"I've lost it, Mam,"

"You've lost it!" she thundered.

That was the wrong thing to say.

"Well you're not getting another one I can tell you that for noffin."

"Can you let me in, Mam, please?"

"Go back to where you've been sleeping for the past two weeks. Go back to your 'oowers. You think I know noffin don't you."

"Whores, Mam, wha' you talkin' about?"

"Never you mind," she hurled back, "you muss think this is a hotel, a doss out for your convenience."

Esmee's voice was getting louder with each sentence.

"Mam," Bonny pleaded, "Shshshsh, don't need to shout."

""Don't shush me."

"Don't shout Mam."

"I can do what I want in me own house. Do you pay the rent here?"

"Don't shout Mam. No Mam, you . . ."

"Do you pay the rent? No, I pay the bloody rent here, nobody else but me. Don't forget that."

"Yes, Mam."

"You think I'm soft, don't you, but not anymore, oh no, I'm not having you treat my home like bloody Lime Street Station, no siree,"

Esmee began to sing in a measured, almost middle-of-the-road manner.

"Yes sireee, no sirrree, pleeeeze siree, not today siree, I don't want your grief no sireee, I want my own company, yes sireee, . . ."

"Mam, please, can you let me in PLEASE, please."

Esmee abandoned MOD in an instant to an angry scatting mode, "tededlititideleti-no siree-youyouoo, tutututu, saaa-eee-reee.

In normal circumstances Bonny would have appreciated his Mother's ability to improvise musically and invent catchy tunes on the spur of the moment, but right now all Bonny wanted to do was have a shit; a monster shit, a hippopotamus of a shit, a stream of hippopotamuses, the biggest shit he has ever had in his life.

"I know you pay the rent, Mam, and I dunno wha' I'd do if it wasn't for you, Mam. Please, Mam, lemme in so we can talk about it, and I'm dying to go to the lav."

"Oh, so you think my home is a bloody shit house," Esmee shot back in mid song. "Anytime you wanna shit just come to Esmee Roberts's house."

Esmee broke into an agonising falsetto, "bloooooody shit house, bloooooody shithouse, my home is a shit house, read the toilet sign outside my door, doooo bring your friends and your enemies to Esmee Roberts houoooooose . . ."

Bonny started to panic, what if she would not let him in. If he attempted to go downstairs and shit outside, he knew he would not make it.

Bonny leaned his back against the lobby wall his eyes shut tight trying very hard not to shit his pants.

It sounded to him that thunder and lightning was raging in his belly.

"Mam, look I'm sorry, true to God, I'm sorry," Bonny begged, "I lost me key."

Bonny by now was standing first on one leg and then the other, desperately trying to stop nature taking its downward course.

"Don't you come here blaspheming, calling the name of the Lord in vain, go on, on your way Riley, you bloody heathen."

"Mam, please let me in, I'm begging you."

"Don't beg when you're old enough to steal, when you're old enough to steal don't beg . . ." Esmee sang returning to MOD mode.

"Mam, please," Bonny winced, holding his stomach.

"I've got noffin to say to you Mister Ronald, your time is up and a new chapter unfolds . . ."

Bonny heard the sound of a door opening behind him.

"Is everythin' alrecht, loove?"

It was the neighbour from across the landing, a red headed middle-aged woman in a blue pinafore with a Scottish accent. He had never seen the woman before; he guessed she was a new tenant.

Bonny explained to her, as quickly and politely as he could who he was, that his Mother was not well, indicating with his forefinger to his temple that the illness was mental not physical and could he use her toilet please.

At that precise moment, the advance cavalry had pierced through noisily.

The stench instantly invaded the corridor and blue pinafore visibly flinched.

The Scottish lady slowly closed her door with one hand and held her nose with the other, all the time staring at him in case he did something criminal on the floor.

Bonny put his hand on the hard lump to stop it sliding down his trouser leg.

"Mam, will you let me in, please?" Bonny said, close to exasperation, close to tears.

Silence.

Bonny considered whether attack might be the best method of entry as he struggled to keep his shit in place and prevent the whole regiment coming down.

"Mam lemme in!" he shouted boldly.

"Who d'you think you're shouting at. I'm still your mother, don't you forget that."

"I know Mam; I just want to come in to have a chat, you know . . ."

"You lyin' bastard, you only come here because you want to use my home, the only home I've got in the world, as a bloody convenience. Coming here trying to bully me, who the bloody hell do you think you are?"

Bonny sensed he was losing the battle and tried a new tack.

"I've got a job, Mam. I'm in me overalls and I need to get changed."

The Scottish woman came out again.

"Will yer keep yer voice doon, I've got a wee one I'm tryin' tae gie sleepin'," she said and closed her door again.

Bonny heard his mother's shuffling footsteps. She was looking through the spy hole, probably inspecting his overalls.

He heard the lock turn and saw the door open and left ajar.

The hallway was in total darkness.

He felt Amin sniffing his trouser leg.

Bonny turned the light on and followed his mother into the unlit living room.

"You've got loads of mail, here Mam," he said looking at a dozen letters on the floor just inside the door.

"Pay them no mind," Esmee said without turning around. "They're letters from the encyclopaedia people wanting their money. They'll have to take it out of me face cos I ain't got a dime. Buddy can you spare a dime," she sang, "we're in the money, come on, my honey, let's **lend** it, spend it . . ."

His mother was dressed in a thick beige dressing gown and brown furry slippers.

Amin followed Bonny into the living room.

"Out! On your way Riley!" Esmee ordered, indicating the lobby to the dog with a stern finger.

Amin looked up at Bonny and pleaded with his eyes "please don't let her send me in that dingy dark corridor."

"He knows he's not allowed into the living room but he'll never stop tryin'," she said.

Amin looked at Bonny with doleful eyes but saw quickly that he was getting no support for gaining entry into the living room, so he slow marched back out into the hall without looking back.

Bonny headed straight towards the toilets.

"And don't be shitting down the sides like you did the last time. I had to clean it all up after you, you dirty bastard."

Bonny was oblivious to his mother's ranting and just had time to lower his trousers and sit down on the bowl before a noisy avalanche came spurting out.

Much relieved, Bonny walked back into the living room, drew back the curtains and opened the windows. Daylight could not reach every dark corner in the room but it was enough to take in the usual disorderliness.

"Did you leave the bathroom window open and shut the door behind you? Your shit stinks."

The living room was where Esmee lived and slept, hardly making use of her bedroom. Two old sofas fought for dominance of the room with a large elaborate Welsh dresser lined with crockery, figurines, and unframed photographs and other mementoes of a life too quickly gone by. Pride of place was a black and white photograph of a young, bright-eyed Esmee smiling widely at the camera whilst shaking the hand of Paul Robeson. It was the largest of the photographs and the only one in a frame.

Esmee had the same round brown eyes as her sister Lizzie but the sparkle had gone. She had incongruously large breasts for so thin a frame. Unlike Lizzie's elegance, Esmee's thinness looked more like a sign of neglect.

Esmee Roberts lived alone and spent most of her time alone, with only spasmodic visits from her two children. Twice a week including Sundays, Harry, a neighbour, would send one of his kids over with a hot cooked meal. The lad downstairs got all her messages from Windsor Street and Berkeley Street corner shops, although the lad was expensive as he always kept as much of the change as he thought he could get away with without her noticing.

Esmee did not eat much and most of it came from cans. She had left her flat only once since February 1975 when she moved in, and that was to attend her grandson's christening in November 1979. She religiously watched all the documentaries and the news on the little colour television her daughter Gloria had brought her for one of her birthdays, but mostly she sang some tunes, some of which she made up herself. It was not just mindless singing; this was serious singing with a full orchestra. She would point to the guitarist or the vibraphonist, depending on the song, to come in for a solo and she would play the instrument with puckered lips. She would take up the song again after the solo with a wave of

Pure Pressure

thanks to the trumpeter or the vibraphonist; the brass section would always come in with the chorus and she would conduct them by waving both arms as if she was flapping wings, but in time with the music.

When she was not watching TV or singing, she would study one of her innumerable dictionaries or encyclopaedias.

Her only constant companion was Amin, a large dog she named after Idi Amin, because white people feared Idi Amin and she liked that.

Amin's father was the notorious Sloopy, the most rampant mongrel that Liverpool 8 had ever seen. Sloopy would shag anything walking—cats, dogs, human legs, tree trunks—you name it and he'd shagged it or tried to and usually got it pregnant. Someone once calculated that Sloopy had sired over 150 puppies, but Sloopy denied all knowledge, he was selfish like that.

"Do you know what '**palingenesis' means, Ronald?" Esmee asked à propos of nothing in particular.**

Bonny sighed.

"Sumfin to do with the Bible?" he ventured.

"Wrong," she said triumphantly.

Esmee picked up a large dictionary and read aloud: "It's got four meanings. It's either a rebirth or regeneration. In biology, it's the embryonic development—that's a nice word embryonic isn't it—the embryonic development that produces the ancestral features of the species."

Esmee looked up from the book. "Are you listening, you numbskull, don't you want to learn anyfin?" "Yes, Mam." "It also means a Christian Baptism . . ."

"I knew it had sumfin to do with the Bible, so I'm not altogether a numbskull am I?"

"It also means the doctrine of transmigration of souls. So you've got a job, at last," she continued, looking at his overalls. "I'd never thought I'd see the day. How long you been doing it?"

"Eh . . . not long . . . eh . . . it's only temporary. I'm doing a job for Billygoat."

"Doing what, you can't do anyfin. What would a skilled man like Billygoat want with someone like you with two left hands; you're lyin'," she said. "You can't fool me. What are you up to?"

"You hungry, I've bought some food," Bonny said quickly lowering his eyes.

"Wha' you up to Ronald?"

"Noffin, Mam, noffin."

"Don't believe you."

This exchange went on for some minutes with Bonny fighting against his mother's persistence. Esmee knowing there was a bone to chew if she dug deep enough, kept on digging.

"There muss be som'n up," she said, "I can tell when you're tellin' lies."

"No, you're right, I haven't got a job," Bonny admitted. "I just said it so you'd open the door. I've been helping Billygoat out that's all," he said looking down at the overalls.

"What's the food?" she asked.

"Oxtails from Felicia's on Granby," he replied taking the container out of the bag.

Esmee did not know who Felicia was and had not been to Granby Street for years.

"Get a plate and cutlery out of the kitchen," she said.

"Are you going to have some with me?"

Just bring me a spoon, I'll pick some off your plate; it smells nice but it's probably too spicy for me. The hot pepper sauce you bought is still there in the top cupboard by the window."

Bonny opened the kitchen door and jumped with fright when he saw two long tailed dark rats gnawing away at a bone on a plate on the small kitchen table. They looked up at him and went back to their meal not the least bit put out by the interruption. Bonny made a whooshing noise with his mouth and waved an arm to frighten them away but they carried on as if he was not there. He rushed out of the kitchen closing the door firmly behind him.

"What's the matter with you?" Esmee asked him.

"Rats," he shouted. "there's rats in your kitchen eating your food!"

"Oh them; pay them no mind they live under the cupboards but they only come out in the kitchen. I leave them little tit bits . . ."

"Esmee, rats are dangerous, you could get nasty diseases from them; they could attack you. I'll call the 'Corpy' first fing in the morning; they'll soon get rid of them."

"Call the Corporation? I'm not having them crawling all over the house, rooting through me fings. Stop fussing; when I've had enough of the rats, when they get too many, I'll put some poison down."

Esmee rose unsteadily from her chair.

"A big man like you and you're scared of rats. I dunno," she said shaking her head as she walked out of the room. She came back a few seconds later with a plate, cutlery and the bottle of hot pepper sauce. After the meal, ate in complete

Pure Pressure

silence, Esmee suggested he made some coffee for himself or a can of beer that he had left in the fridge on a previous visit.

No inducement was big enough to make Bonny enter that kitchen again, overrun as it was by sharp toothed evil little devils whose instincts he knew was to jump up and sink their spiky teeth into your jugular vein, particularly if they could sense your fear, so he politely but resolutely refused.

Bonny could feel his mother staring at him.

"Why you staring?" he said uncomfortably.

"You look just like McCarthy, your father, sat there," she replied not taking her eyes off him. "Everybody called him McCarthy, even me. But when we were alone I'd call him Ronald or Ronnie if I wanted som'n."

"I thought I looked like you; Aunty Lizzie thinks so."

"Yer Aunty Lizzie's talking through her bloody arse, she always does."

Esmee closed her eyes and started softly humming tunelessly.

"I've just finished burying this guy," Bonny said suddenly.

"What do you mean? Who died? Who's funeral?"

Perhaps it was the need to get the burden lifted that led Bonny to tell his mother the events in the past 24 hours. There was a good chance she would not repeat it to anyone, as she never left the house.

Bonny told his mother about the events that were troubling him. He began with the hold up the attempted hold up, the shots, the death and finally the burial. He did not mention any names. He talked in a slow, deliberate and monotonous voice as if he was describing scenes he was not directly involved in, as if he was describing a boring sequence of an action movie, detached and unreal.

Esmee listened intently, asking questions without offering an opinion until he had finished.

"The poor man didn't even get a proper Christian burial," she said shaking her head.

The tension of the previous hours had been building up inside Bonny without him realising. Now that he had told her everything, he felt some relief. Esmee put a comforting hand on his shoulder. She would have liked to cuddle him but she had forgotten how to, it had been so long.

Bonny also wanted to tell her about Valerie leaving with the kids but Esmee never liked Valerie and would just lecture him, "told you she was no good."

"I need a bath," Bonny said as he walked out of the room.

"Don't forget to give me some money for the hot water. It don't come free you know," said Esmee as she sucked the marrow out of a piece of oxtail, put it down on the plate, sat back on her chair, closed her eyes and began singing her song.

> Lemonade and Sherry burned my Joan and Harry
> Lemonade and Sherry took my Joan and Harry
> I didn't hear them scream
> I was only having a dream
> Lemonade and Sherry Equal Fire and Death
> I'll sing this till my dying breath
> They'll come back one day
> And show me the way
> So don't worry
> My little Joan and Harry

"Stop torturing yourself, Esmee," Bonny shouted from the bathroom. "It's doing you no good."

Bonny bathed quickly, washing the tub after climbing out as his mother shouted for him to wash the bathtub when he finished. He went to his bedroom, opened the small wardrobe and took out a pair of black trousers and a white tee shirt from wire hangers. He threw the overalls in a corner, sat on the single bed, covered his face with his hands, and silently cursed himself for telling Esmee about Shep-from-Ohio. She might tell somebody, the Scottish neighbour perhaps, and next thing is he will be in court on a capital charge. He went back into the living room. Esmee was still singing her song repeatedly looking blankly in the distance.

"Esmee," he said to her, "don't tell anybody or I'll end up going to jail for a very long time."

"God will be your judge, son, not me," she said simply.

Bonny's taxi reached Lizzie's house at 10.30 that night. He had stopped off at Brahim's late night grocery store on Northhill Street to buy the largest box of chocolates in the shop.

Cars lined both sides of Kingsley Road from the Boulevard right past Cawdor Street. If a passer by wondered why there were so many cars parked the street, the booming sound of the music would have removed any doubt there was a party going on.

Doreen was on door duty responding to the doorbell with a strained smile. She would rather be somewhere else, like two hundred miles down the motorway with her brood. At least Doreen was trying; she was wearing a dark blue dress cut just below her ankles. Beryl had suggested she put some make up on, but Doreen would rather eat a kilo of horse manure than smear anything on her face.

"Hello Bonny," Doreen said, "long time no see."

"Hiya cuz," said Bonny giving her a chaste hug.

Bonny entered the front parlour, the 'best' room of the house, where Lizzie was sitting in pride of place, like a birthday queen, sipping a glass of a Vodka cocktail, surrounded by her contemporaries from Upper Stanhope Street circa 1950s.

There were twenty odd people in the room and none younger than 60. Bonny recognised most people and timidly wormed his way to where Lizzie Roberts was sitting in between Aunt Peggy and Mrs. Williams. Aunt was a courtesy title as Peggy Evans was not a blood or marriage relative. April Williams was the doyenne of Liverpool 8 who was supposed to be 92 but many said she was really only 86, but there was nobody left who could testify authoritatively one way or the other.

Bonny kissed Lizzie on both cheeks, wished her happy birthday and handed her an envelope that contained a card and a £10 note and a large box of chocolates.

"Hello Bonny," said Lizzie. "I'm so pleased you made it. How's your Mam?"

"Fine, Aunty Lizzie, these are for you," he said.

"Thank you. I hope you're hungry, there's plenty of food," she said to Bonny.

"I hear your Sweetness has been misbehaving hisself again?" said Mrs. April Williams to Mavis McKenzie who was sitting on the couch opposite.

"Whadyamean?" said Mavis feigning not to know what was coming.

"He got our Barbara's granddaughter pregnant and she's only 17, still at College. I'm sorry to have to say this, Mavis," croaked Mrs. Williams gravely. She took a deep breath as she had to when she got a bit emotional, "but that man's a beast. He should have been castrated the day he was born; a bloody menace to women that man is."

"It takes two," replied Mavis feebly.

"Don't talk nonsense, Mavis," reposted Lizzie. "A bloody menace to women, juss as April says. Barbara's granddaughter is just a kid and Your Sweetness's a hairy-arsed, seen-it-and-dun-it-all man."

"I'm not defending him. But I'm saying a lot of them girls want to get pregnant."

"It's not your fault, he's only your son, but I juss thought I'd bring it up so that you know we're not happy," April Williams concluded her voice now fainter.

"Anyway," April added, "we haven't come here to argue about men but to celebrate Lizzie Roberts' 70th birthday," she said teasingly.

"Sixty-fifth, if you don't mind," Lizzie riposted, "dat's old enough for me for gettin' on with. Ronald, will you bring some drinks from the kitchen, just us three the rest can get their own, there's a good lad," Lizzie asked Bonny who took the orders.

Mrs Williams shook her head.

"Not for me lad, it goes right through me and me nappy's damp already," chuckled April.

"You should get him to change it for you," whooped Mavis lasciviously.

"What's happened to our music, Billy?" someone asked. "All we can hear is that jungle music from the back."

Billy who was in deep conversation with his wife Miranda in a corner, turned to the record player and within seconds had some of the old timers on their feet.

Peggy Evans grabbed hold of Bonny's hands, whipped them around her waist and started to tango. She twirled Bonny slowly around the room her mouth open in an expansive smile, gums gleaming.

"Oh Mister don't touch me tomatoes," she sang loudly almost drowning out Josephine Baker's voice "Touch me dis, touch me dat, touch me everytin' I've got. All you have to do is feel up, feel up," she crooned caressing Bonny's bum.

Bonny was trying as politely as he could to pull away from Peggy but she was having none of it. The dance went on for an age and Bonny was sweating with embarrassment but trying hard to look like he was enjoying it all. Alfred Morris, well into his seventies, pushed a grateful Bonny out of way and grabbed Peggy, swaying his hips suggestively to the rhythm.

"Mmmmm, shake it baby," he roared.

"Always a lady's man Alfred, that's why they used to called him Moby Dick," shouted April in Lizzie's ear.

"Mobile Dick you mean, he's been with everyone," retorted Lizzie.

Bonny made a quick retreat out of the room and saw Beryl in the crowded hallway. Bonny thought best to play it cool at first, not to seem too eager. Beryl put her arms around his neck and kissed his cheek.

Beryl wore a dark red jacket with power-crazed shoulder pads (which would not have looked out of place on a Miami Dolphin quarterback) over a sleek black dress; her curly shiny dark hair dangled around jewelled ears.

"You look stunning," he said to her, meaning every word.

She thanked him, took his hand and led him into the kitchen.

"What you gonna have? Champagne, brandy, what's your poison?" she asked him.

"I'll have lemonade if you don't mind," he replied timidly.

"Are you driving?" she asked, surprised at his choice.

"Huh . . . yeah . . ." he muttered.

"What kind of car you driving, did you buy it off our Paul?"

"Yeah . . . er . . . no . . . I'm not driving, I don't drive . . . er, I'm not a heavy drinker really, I prefer to start off with lemonade."

"Saving the hard stuff for later, hey?"

"Yeah sumfin like that."

She plopped two cubes of ice in a tall glass and filled it up with lemonade.

"Help yourself when you need a refill, you're family," she said as she walked back into the hall.

"Beryl," he called after her, but the heavy beat of *going back to my roots . . . yeah* got in the way and she did not hear him. He was too self-conscious to go after her, after all, they were first cousins and they grew up together, almost brother and sister. They had had their little thing in Granny's house, Bonny and Beryl. They were barely into their teens. They were playing hide and seek and she asked him did he want to kiss when they were hiding in the pantry. He had never kissed a girl before, it had never occurred to him to kiss a girl before. He kissed her but he did not like it, moreover, neither did she.

"Eeeeee, you can't kiss, you're a slobberer," Beryl whispered so the others would not hear, scrubbing his germs determinedly off her mouth with the sleeve of her cardigan.

He grinned at the memory. He always liked Beryl's style—loud, funny, and tomboyish then. Now she was this gorgeous self-assured woman with a Yankee accent and she was single now, just as he was.

Bonny pondered whether to go after her but instead decided to have a spliff to calm his nerves and ponder his next move. He had to think this through carefully, like a military campaign, the forbidden love fighting the army of family traditions, like Romeo and Juliette.

Bonny went into the yard. There were a handful of people there including Doreen drinking coffee whilst talking earnestly to an older white man who was also drinking coffee who Bonny recognised as Father Dominic. Bonny knew, from old gossip, that his coffee was adulterated. He liked a bit of whiskey did old Father Dominic.

Bonny was not keen on joining that conversation; he could not trust himself to confess all to the preacher man in front of everyone. He wanted to build a spliff but there was no question of that with watchful Doreen there. He took in the warm air for a while, thinking of Beryl and then decided to go back inside and talk to her, or at least look at her. He had to be careful, he did not want to get carried away and make a fool of himself.

Beryl was standing by the kitchen door with a drink in her hand talking to her brother Alan.

Bonny stood there for a few seconds, looking at her, admiring her, loving her. She looked beautiful. He was going to say something to her, ask her about America. Maybe not such a good idea talking about America she might mention her missing husband.

He will ask her to dance; there is nothing unusual about asking someone to dance with you at a party, it is expected.

He walked towards her smiling to himself.

"Hello, Porky-Boy."

It was Hilda Deforo, Bonny's Godmother. She always made a fuss of him whenever she saw him.

"Hello Aunty Hilda, you're looking well."

"I don't feel well you know," she replied with a grimace. "Haven't been for ages; it's me arthritis and me kidney. You know I've only one kidney left; dey took the udder one out two years ago last April. I'm bearing up though, well, you have to don't yer? I'm not ready to lie down and die, let me tell yer. You know the last time I saw you was at May Marshall's funeral and that was at least five years ago. How you keepin' me lad, how's your mudder, haven't seen her in yonks either. In fact, the last time I saw her was at her Mother's funeral and that was back in the Sixties. Is she alright?"

"She's fine, Aunty Hilda," Bonny replied. "She doesn't get out as much as she used to but she's fine."

Bonny looked over at Beryl.

She was laughing now with Alan and the others in the kitchen.

"Tell yer Mam yer Aunty Hilda was askin' about her. Don't yer forget now? D'yer look after her, Porky-boy?" Aunt Hilda added raising her forefinger at Bonny's right eye.

"Of course," said Bonny quickly.

"I shouldn't call yer Porky-Boy, should I? Yerra grown man now, but yer know I don't mean any harm, doncha lad?"

"Of course, Aunty Hilda; you can call me what you like, you've well earned the right."

"That's right lad," she acknowledged. "Changed yer nappies, used to spoil yer with sweets, and yer've never ever given me a word of cheek, ever. Always polite, always helpful; yer a credit to yer mudder you are, you and Gloria, you both are, and so would Harry and Joan if they were still alive, God bless their little souls."

Aunt Hilda took out her handkerchief from the sleeve of her cardigan and blew her nose loudly into it, looked at its contents as if she expected something moving to emerge, satisfied that there were no moving parts, and shoved the handkerchief back up her sleeve.

"I'm juss gonna get meself a drink, Aunty Hilda . . ." Bonny said anxious to get away and closer to Beryl.

"You know my Stan's not well," Hilda continued as if Bonny had not spoken, "emphysema, it's all the smoking. He's stopped now, bless him, but it's like shutting the stable door after the horse has bolted. He's on oxygen, bless him."

"Do give Uncle Stan my regards and I hope he gets better," Bonny said, thinking it was a good way to end the conversation.

"He's never gonna get better," Hilda said quickly, "but he's a fighter my Stan, a real fighter."

Beryl was still standing in the kitchen doorway. Bonny finally caught her eye.

"Are you alright?" she mimed looking at Aunt Hilda as if he needed rescuing.

Bonny raised his eyebrows slightly indicating that it was not all right and that Aunt Hilda was going to keep him there chatting all night.

Bonny inched his way towards Beryl.

"I hear you've settled down now with a nice girl from the Nortend? Aye, Porky-boy, yer can't go far wrong with a Nortend girl, dat's where I'm from originally. I've been living in the Soutend since I was a young girl. Two kids you got now or is it three?" Aunt Hilda said inching along with him.

"What are you having, Aunty Hilda?" Beryl intervened.

"You know wha'," Hilda replied, "I was sent on a message to get the drinks ages ago and talkin' to Porky-boy here, I forgot; muss be gettin' old."

Hilda paused, closed her eyes reeled off her order.

"A large Rum for yer Aunt Hilda, with a bit of blackcurrant on top, a Pernod and lemonade for Peggy, a gin and orange for Mavis, a Vodka and milk for yer mudder and Champagne for old Leon if dere's any left, if not any wine will do but only white."

"I'll get you a tray Aunt Hilda," said Alan as he lined up the glasses.

Louis Julienne

"Shall I give dese a rinse?" asked Aunty Hilda haughtily, scrutinising the glasses for marks as she held them aloft.

"Sorry, luv, I'll give them a quick rinse," said Alan apologetically.

"*Luv? Luv*? Who yer callin' *luv*? Don't you '*luv*' me, Aunty Hilda to you if you don't mind. Bloody hard-faced you are," Hilda said clearly offended.

"*Luv*," she repeated, "like me n' 'im went t'school togedder, luv, Hey," she said to Alan as he polished some glasses. "I don't remember you bein' at school wid' you. Do you remember being at school wid me, Alan?"

"Sorry, Aunt Hilda, juss a slip of the tongue," Alan said as he lined up the gleaming glasses, "what was your order again, Aunt Hilda, rum and black for you and what else?"

Beryl and Bonny teased Alan the rest of the night about being disrespectful to AUNTY Hilda. Still, Bonny could not find the right moment to ask Beryl to dance. Twice he went to ask her and each time someone distracted her.

It came as a thunderbolt when Beryl asked him to dance.

"Do you fancy a dance?" she asked him sweetly.

After the third dance, Bonny was silently begging the deejay to play a slow tune. It had been frenetic dance music one after the other. He was enjoying dancing with her, captivated by Beryl's shapely body gyrating stylishly to the music. Above all, Bonny wanted to hold her in his arms and dance to a romantic record, press his cheek against hers and feel the warmth of her body against his. He wanted to inhale her perfume and whisper in her ear that he loved her.

The fourth song was *Rock Me Baby*, a compulsive dance tune that did not lend itself to close contact.

". . . *woooman, take me in your arms and rock me baby* . . ."

How appropriate the words if not the tempo, thought Bonny.

When the singer had finished rocking his baby, Beryl paused, her face shiny with perspiration, and said to Bonny that she was feeling her age. She grabbed his hand and led him towards the kitchen. The next record stopped Beryl in her tracks. She whooped as *Everybody Was Kung-Fu Fighting* filled the room

"My favourite dance song" she sang lifting both arms in the air.

". . . *those cats were as fast as lightning* . . ."

Bonny swayed his shoulders to the rhythm and smiled at Beryl's joy. The next tune however was a godsend for Bonny. If ever there was a song to dance to with someone you wanted to get close to it was The Dells' *Stay in my Corner*. The record was slow, passionate and lasted for over six minutes, giving ample time to make a move. They danced coyly for the first minute or so, keeping their bodies at a first cousin distance. By the middle of the song, their cheeks were touching and near the end their lips brushed

"You've come a long way since that kiss in Granny's kitchen," she whispered in his ear.

Chapter 7

Ten O'clock Road Block

Saturday 10pm 4th July 1981

On leaving Cliffie's down town snooker hall, Paul and Alan Leung, Jazz and African Henry, darkness was quickly wrapping its stifling cloak on the city. Jazz was leading the way, dancing a joyous jig. Jasminder Manmohan Singh, to give him his full name, had suckered a long list of punters at snooker, playing with his left hand as a handicap, and was celebrating the windfall. Jazz was a snooker and pools prodigy with the talent but not the dedication to be a professional. Tall, hairy and handsome, in his mid-twenties, born in Liverpool of Indian parents, Jazz was a friend of Alan Leung from College in Ormskirk who was now working as an Administrative Officer for a shipping firm in town.

"Did you see that guy's face when he handed me his money, pure venom in his face," he laughed.

"He only gave you the bread cos I was there to make sure he did. We should go halves,"

Paul Leung insisted.

"Don't worry Paul, I'll give yer a dropsy," said Jazz generously.

As they strolled up Fleet Street, African Henry, Paul Leung's right hand man, tried in his usual unorthodox way of entertaining his companions by throwing an empty beer bottle in the only tree in the street. The effect was instantaneous as a cacophony of birds' alarmed screeches rang out in the still hot night. A small man in his thirties, African Henry, whose full name was Henry Owusu, worked in Paul's garage. The three horizontal marks on each cheek identified him as an Oyo man from Ghana.

"What d'yer do dat for, dick-head?" growled Paul.

"To provide some free wonderfool music for my friends," Henry replied brightly.

Pure Pressure

"Yeah, you know all about freebees," said Paul, "you're the only one who didn't buy a drink tonight, youze shameless, man, pure shameless."

These sorts of comments were water off a duck's back to African Henry.

Alan was furious when he saw what he thought was a parking fine notice stuck on the front windscreen of his car. Funny place to put a parking ticket, he initially thought until he saw it was a *Free Nelson Mandela* sticker.

"Who's Nelson Mandela?" asked Paul.

Alan looked at his brother in the eye.

"For a moment there, I thought you were serious," Alan said to Paul

On the way back "up the '*Souf-end'*, Alan was driving along Grove Street coming up to the junction with Upper Parliament Street, making great play that his new company car was power-driven by ostentatiously guiding the wheel with one index finger, when he noticed an obstruction right across the street. Alan thought it was an 'official' roadblock because in the middle of the street were familiar signs of white arrows on a light-blue background and a vehicle parked in the middle of the street. An accident maybe, some Saturday night cowboy had overtaken at the wrong place and at the wrong time and ended up wrapped round the traffic lights. What other possible reason would there be for a roadblock at ten o'clock in the evening in the middle of Liverpool 8.

Alan was not concerned about a roadblock, drinking and driving was not on his agenda, he had too much to lose, all his papers were in order and he never gave lip to the police. As he got closer, he noticed an unusual darkness and it took him a few seconds to realise all the streetlights were off. Once his eyes accustomed themselves to the shadows, the obstruction revealed itself as an overturned car.

Alan stopped his car and a slim man wearing a ski mask walked slowly towards him carrying a large piece of wood with both hands. The scene seemed eerily like a war zone in Belfast. Alan pressed a button and the driver's windows slid down.

"You can't come through," said the man who wore a grey jogging suit with the bottoms tucked inside white socks giving him the look of a military man.

"What's happenin'?" Alan asked the masked man.

"We're stoppin' all cars from going fru. We're waitin' for the pigs to come," the masked man replied.

Despite the camouflage, Alan recognised the voice as Kenny Brown, a habitué of the Jaycee

"Join us if you want," Kenny Brown said as he walked back towards the barricade.

Louis Julienne

"These guys are crazy," said Paul. "Come on, it's still aygerly, let's go over to the Gladray and get a few jaygars in before we go to the paygarty."

Alan parked the car on Mulgrave Street on the other side of the barricade. A dozen or so youths were hanging around the overturned car puffed up with anticipation. Paul led the way as they walked down Parliament Street passed the Caribbean Club and up the wide stone steps of the Gladray Club.

"Som'n's gonna happen tonight, for sure," said Alan looking back at the barricade now some 200 yards away.

Paul took off his rimless glasses and stuck them in the case he carried in his back pocket with one hand and pressed impatiently on the doorbell with the palm of the other.

Mad Danny Odegunji, the hefty jovial doorman opened the door.

"Wha' 'appen'; sorry but yers can't come in," he said in his deep chocolate brown voice that belonged to a bass singer in a soul band. "The O'Connors' 'r 'avin a private do."

"Wha' 'appen'; the O'Connors, hey? I'm alright wid dem; tell dem it's me. Go on tell dem, it's sound," said Paul firmly.

Mad Danny Odegunji shut the door quickly, but not that quickly to risk Paul being offended. He came back a few moments later, opened the door wide and let them in. Indicating Jazz he said, "Who's the cha-cha man?"

"He's alright," Paul replied. "He's a mate of our kid."

"What's with the cha-cha business?" said Alan as they walked in.

"It's alright," Jazz assured him recognising the insult although he had never heard it before. "I've been called a lot worse, NIGGER," he said purposely to Mad Danny.

There was a moment of stunned silence, everything seemed to stand still, poignant suspense hanging heavy in the air. Danny made to grab Jazz. Paul quickly stepped between them.

"I'll kill that fuckin' . . ."

"You're not gonna kill anybody Danny, you're gonna apologise to Jazz. Then Jazz is gonna apologise to you," Paul said calmly.

"Don't mean nuttin' by it, lah," Danny said to Jazz by way of apology. "But you're bang out of order for calling me nigga. Nobody calls me nigga and gets away with it. Are you gonna lerrim gerraway wid it Paul?"

"I can't fight you but I'm not having anybody oppress me with their insults without retaliating," said Jazz by way of apology.

Alan was impressed with Jazz's reply; he would have liked to have said the same thing in similar circumstances. He printed the sentence to his memory.

"Don't ever let me hear you use that word again, get it, and apologise properly to me cuz Danny here right now!" Paul ordered.

"I'm sorry Danny," said Jazz quickly, "but one insult deserves another."

Danny muttered something that sounded like its-okay-lah-but-don't-do-it-again and then changed the conversation.

"See dem crazy kids out dere, lah?" he said in his cavernous voice pointing towards Grove Street. "D'ave been frowin' bricks at the cars and taxies."

Then slipping into backslang, Danny gave Paul his verdict: "It's bayghad for bayghizness, lah, know warra maygheen? You kaygant taguell dem, dey dagont layghissen. 'Ere sign the book."

"Hey, you were just as bad if not worse at their age," said Paul as he picked up the pen. "Remember Park Road, remember Earl Road, remember Sussex Gardens," he recited, recalling the street gang fights of their youth when 'the boys' fought neighbouring white gangs in the streets.

"Imitation is the greatest form of flattery," Alan laughed recalling his earlier ditty about the historical battles in Liverpool.

The Gladray Club was a Liverpool 8 institution run by two black Liverpooleighters middle-aged women, Gladys and Rachel. It was supposed to be a members-only club to circumvent the English licensing laws that decreed no serving alcoholic drink on licensed premises between 3pm and 5.30pm and after 11pm except for members-only clubs. In reality, anybody could and would come in and sign themselves in as members or guests of members who were not really members.

The guest list could be quite startling. Elvis Presley, Vera Lynn, Rudolph Valentino, Batman and Ronald Reagan, had all had their name signed in the past few months, and all four of The Beatles, several times each. Ringo Starr was the most frequent, probably because he was the only Beatle who was a Southender, a Dingle lad. However, the John Smiths, Paddy and Mary Murphys and Dean Vincents predominated. No, not Gene Vincent the singer of *Bebop alula* fame, Dean Vincent was a genuine name, a bricky from Widnes who came to the Gladray six days a week. He loved the place or rather the strippers, and one stripper in particular, Gloria, a star turn.

The Gladray Club was one of the first drinking clubs to put on strip shows in Liverpool back in the early seventies. In the afternoons, always its busiest, particularly Sundays when there was no breathing space. The afternoon clientele were mainly white men ranging from those working locally in the building trade to office types, but also working girls and clients known as mushes in the argot of the time and other locals looking for an illicit drink on the day of the Lord. At night, it would be less of the same but a different atmosphere, not raucous except for the edgy gangsters. The local lads came for a gamble, a drink and a chat; this was not pulling pussy territory for them. Most single women only came to get their drinks bought for them, promising their whole body and more, but made a runner when they had been sufficiently tanked up.

The club walls were colourfully decorated with larger than life hand painted murals by Pauline Wiggins, a local artist and songstress, depicting Muhammad Ali, Queen Nefertiti and Angela Davis in regal poses. The bar, behind which the proud busty owners reigned, was festooned with neckties cut from past customers' necks and hung up like bounty trophies.

There were about thirty people in the smoke filled room. Dean Vincent was not one of them; he only came in the afternoons for the strip shows. Donna Summers was wailing about needing '*some hot stuff . . . and bringing a wild man back home tonite*' on the jukebox. Kathy Kirkby was dancing blissfully alone in the middle of the floor next to another working girl in a tiny skirt clutched by a mush dancing un-rhythmically with his eyes shut. Kathy Kirby was not her real name, of course, that was the name of some fifties singing star, but the fact that Kathy McDermott came from Kirkby and had back-combed platinum blonde hair when she first appeared on the scene was enough to get stuck with the name fifteen years later.

Bull O'Connor was holding court by the bar surrounded by his crew; three of his brothers, Terry, Leo and Lecky and four other men, all dressed in short sleeved shirts hanging over sharp-creased slacks and wearing enough gold (on fingers, wrists and necks) between them to open a jewellery store. The O'Connors were a white gang from the North End of the city who specialised in armed robberies but had now moved into the drugs market, mainly heroin and amphetamines.

Bull was accurately nicknamed with his thick neck, snub nose, muscled torso and skinny legs. You expected jets of steaming anger to shoot out of his nostrils at any moment.

"Awright blue," bellowed Bull in Paul's direction.

He always called black people he knew 'blue', not as an insult—Bull O'Connor had no shortage of really offensive words with which to call black people and he used them often—but as a put down, like he could not remember his name. It could not have been any worse if he had called him 'watcha-name-again'.

"Awright al' arse," said Paul extending his hand, which Bull shook with just a little too much vigour. The contest had begun.

"We were in Borstal together," Bull said to his entourage by way of explanation as to why he should be letting black people into their company. "We kept all the Geordies and Mancunians in check in dere; right blue?"

"Bloody right we fingeed, blue." said Paul bouncing back the insult.

"Wha' yers 'avin'," Bull offered.

Paul wanted to answer 'I don't want or need your fucking drinks you little piece of shit.' However, sensibility prevailed as they were outnumbered.

"Brandies all round, right lads?" Paul asked his companions.

"Four large brandies for the boys, Raich, there's a good girl," and Rachel behind the bar smiled; she always smiled when she took orders.

Alan was nervous; he knew of the O'Connor reputation as a vicious family. If a fight broke out they were outnumbered against eight of them with just Paul, Mad Danny Odegunji (and he would have divided loyalties) and Shadow (who was selling trinkets and maybe would not want to get involved) being the only black men in the club who could handle themselves. Alan had ruled out African Henry and himself from any physical confrontation because they were not fighters, although Jazz talked a good fight. Paul could see the tension written all over Alan's face.

"Don't worry, ar' kid," Paul said reassuringly. "Nuffin's gonna 'appen; yer fingy, yer wid me."

The four of them sat down at a table with their drinks as far away as possible from Bull's party.

"I think we should get out before there's a fight; I can see it coming they look all tanked up already," said Alan.

"Don't worry," Paul said in a reassuring voice, "we'll finish the drink, nice and easy and gerroff, and pop into The Clock to see what's shakin' there."

"Hello Alan, how are you?"

Alan recognised the modulated voice instantly although he had not heard it for over a decade. It was Peach, an old bitter flame, his oldest flame.

"Peach, it must be over ten years since I last seen you," he said.

They kissed on the cheek.

It was eleven years and three weeks almost to the day since he last saw her, the 16th of June 1970, when she came to the cell below the Crown Court minutes after he had received a five-year prison sentence.

"What you been up to?" he asked turning towards her.

"This and that, you know," she replied grimly, turning her eyes away.

Peach's name was Doris Anderson, but got her nickname because her skin was incredibly smooth and glowing with a touch of red on her cheeks, like the fruit.

Peach was sitting at the table next to them with a leering white man, one arm around her waist, drinking Special Brew straight from the bottle. She was wearing a mini skirt exposing acres of brown flesh and a tight blouse fighting a losing battle in containing large breasts. Her face was as pretty as he ever remembered it, although it had a sadness to it as if she had been crying ever since. The sadness in her face and the two extra stones of bad fat she now carried made her look 15 years older.

"He was the love of my life," she told leering-white-man.

"And you're still the best looking girl in Liverpool 8. Where you living these days?" Alan asked her.

"With a mate of mine in Halewood, a fifteen minutes' drive to hopelessness."

Paul catching the conversation whispered in his brother's ear. "What you doin' talkin' to dat slag, do you want to go back to jail or wha'?"

"We're only talking, she's an old friend," Alan whispered back. "That's all."

"Got any kids?" Alan asked her.

Her face darkened and he knew it was the wrong question to have asked.

"Frigging Social Services, more like the frigging Gestapo," she cursed. "They took them off me, the three of them; lovely kids and all."

"Yeah, I'm sure," he replied.

"The eldest, Derek, was to a mush, a regular, a nice mush, or at least I thought he was nice. Said he wanted to marry me but he frigged off before Derek was born. James is to Sweetness McKenzie, but I'm not with him anymore. We were together for nearly two years then he buggered off and all before Robert, my baby, was born. I tried the best I could to be a good mother but it is hard when you have not had a proper mother to show you how. I just could not cope on my own. They are gone now, but I'll get them back eventually. I'm getting myself together again; I'm waiting on this flat from the Council, well away from the South End; this is a bad place for someone like me."

"It'll come good don't worry," Alan said without conviction.

"I heard you've got a good job up in Yorkshire, senior management," she said, ignoring leering-man tugging at her arm.

"In Middlesbrough, yeah it's not a bad job."

Peach smiled her broadest smile, leaned over to him and planted a loud kiss on his cheek.

Pure Pressure

"Take care of yourself, Peach," he said as he saw her eyes fill up.

Johnny Nash began to sing *I Can See Clearly Now* from the jukebox presiding on the small stage in the window bay. Cue for Shadow, a large bearded Trinidadian, to put down his tray full of little trinkets and attempt to grab everyone's attention by singing along to the tune or rather trying to overwhelm with his booming baritone voice both the song and the busy conversations swirling round the room. Shadow sang, wide mouth, wide arms and word for word to a tune he had sung dozens of time before in the same location.

"NOOOTHIIIING BUUUUUT BLOOHOOHOOO SKIIIIEEEZZZ," Shadow hollered adding more notes and cadences than the songwriter ever intended.

At the end of the song, having by then silenced all conversation, he milked the applause like a true showman, bowing and waving, declining offers of drinks from around the room with the well rehearsed rejoinder "juss give me di money, man" in his lilting accent.

Bull sent another round over to them. Alan poured his drink into African Henry's glass.

"I'm driving," he explained, not that African Henry was complaining.

Half an hour later, the jukebox turned off and the lights dimmed, a smaller stage between the bar and the women's toilets was suddenly lit up and a pert little blonde woman came on, big smile, big tits, in a skimpy cowboy outfit.

Cheers came from those crowded around the stage as she began to wriggle to an instrumental version of a tune everyone knew but no one could remember.

Intrigued by the show as he had never seen a live strip show before, Jazz stood up but he could not see past the craning necks and he was mindful of his companions' studied nonchalance to it all.

"It's awright," said Paul, detecting Jazz's interest. "Go and 'ave a look; it's yer first time."

Jazz looked embarrassed.

"Go on, it's okay. We've seen it all before," Alan confirmed with a wink.

Bull O'Connor sent another round of drinks over to their table and everything was going fine with no thought of leaving in a hurry. The stripper had no clothes left to discard and was hiding her dignity behind her huge Stetson hat.

"Gizza look at yer minge, Mary," a punter shouted.

Then with a theatrical flourish she tossed the hat behind her and, legs asunder, showed her audience what it had been impatiently been waiting for. Mad Danny Odegunji had to use his considerable bulk as a shield in front of the stripper to stop groping sweaty hands from touching the untouchable.

Then a commotion broke out. Jazz had inadvertently knocked Bull O'Connor's drink on the floor. If you were going to accidentally knock over someone's drink in the Gladray Club that night, Bull O'Connor's drink was the last one you would want to knock on the floor. The Bull snarled and threw a punch at Jazz's head. Jazz, who was nimbler than he looked, evaded the punch by moving his head two inches to his left. The punch would have shattered his jaw had it landed. Jazz rushed over to the others, blind panic etched in his eyes, pursued by Lecky O'Connor and The Bull sporting a large wet stain on the front of his white shirt. Paul rose quickly from his chair and grabbed Lecky in a headlock. In normal circumstances, Paul would have punched him unconscious but these were not normal circumstances, the O'Connor posse was out in force. The Bull swaggered over.

"Lerrim go, blue," he threatened, looking at his brother's head immobile in Paul's vice-like grip.

"Tell him to behave himself," replied Paul easing his grip.

"Leave it," The Bull barked to his brother. Then looking at Paul he continued, "I think it's best if you an' yer fuckin' mates just fuck off, otherwise dere'll be fuckin' murder t'night, d'yer get me?"

Paul was convinced he could knock out Bull O'Connor no problem, but he also knew that Jazz, Tony and Alan, as pacifist non-combatants to a man, could offer little or no physical support against the rest of Bull O'Connor's gang. On the other hand, Paul felt his reputation as a hard man, probably the hardest man of his generation (well, perhaps after Big Les and maybe Kenny and Chippy) was on the line. Paul was not sure whether his ego would let him walk away, despite the odds. As he pondered what to do next, Mad Danny Odegunji came over, putting himself in front of The Bull, and whispered to Paul in back slang: "Lef' it, Paul; gago agome magan. It is de faguinger's pagarty. He's pagut a lagot o' bragued behind the bagar; lef' it man."

The gist of his message was 'go home, leave now'.

Alan rose from his seat and gently pulled Paul's arm.

"See yer around, Bull," Paul said, staring directly into Bull O'Connor's face, a last act of defiance.

"Yeah, see yer around, blue," said Bull hands clenched and with a disturbing smile on his lips.

"Yer did de right fing, dere cuz, I'm tellin' yer" said Mad Danny as he followed them to the front door.

"It takes a man to walk away in dis kinda situation, believe me. Live and fight another day," Mad Danny added as he opened the front door.

Alan was the first to come out of the club. He was surprised to find the street wrapped in darkness. All the lights on Upper Parliament Street were out of action. It was one thing knocking the lights out on corner of Grove Street but to take out all the lights in Upper Parliament Street from Lodge Lane to the Rio that took some doing. Who were those guys?

A few yards to his right a dozen or so youths were throwing missiles at shining objects fifty yards to his left. It took a few seconds for Alan's eyes to separate the forms from the shadows and the shining objects turned out to be rows of about sixty uniformed policemen spread right across the street crouching and slowly moving away from the youths.

The youths were shouting and throwing missiles, some of which burst into flames on impact. The police retreated and the youths were picking the missiles they had thrown off the floor and hurling them again and police cordon retreated a few more feet.

Every so often, a policeman would get hit and then stumble or fall and some of his colleagues would drag him behind their lines. The ground between the youths and the police was littered with pieces of masonry, bricks and broken glass. The missiles made thudding noises accompanied by shouts of encouragement, triumph and pain.

The four of them stood there staring in absolute amazement at this incredible scene. Paul was the first to react. He jumped down the steps in two leaps, picked up a piece of concrete off the sidewalk, ran a few yards and threw it in an arc towards the dark blue line.

The brick landed a few feet short, splintering as it fell.

"You wouldn't get into the javelin Olympic team on that showing," Jazz shouted.

Paul found another piece of concrete, edged a few feet closer and threw it way off target.

With the third projectile, a half brick which he weighed with his hand like he was weighing a small melon in a grocery store, then, arching his whole body this time and shouting to give himself more leverage and strength, he threw the half brick with venom.

He followed the missile in flight and watched with considerable satisfaction as it landed on a policeman's upper body and made the man fall down.

Paul yelped with satisfaction and acknowledged his companions' cheers with an exaggerated bow. Emboldened, African Henry and Jazz, who had never consciously committed a criminal offence in their lives, picked up pieces of brick and concrete and threw them at the police line, gingerly at first then with passion, whooping with delight at direct hits.

Alan spotted a few lads from the community centre in the crowd and immediately went into pillar of the community mode and shouted at his brother: "Have you gone crazy. Do you want to go to jail or what?"

They patently ignored him so he shouted that he was going to the party and walked away, his hands deep in his pockets.

"Lef' 'im," shouted Paul as he went looking for another missile to throw.

As the police line retreated the throwers, whose numbers seemed to be growing by the minute, were able to pick up the same bricks and pieces of masonry they had thrown earlier and throw them again. This went on for twenty minutes, with the police stumbling backwards a further 200 yards just beyond Park Way. The crowd had grown to over 50, mostly youths in ghetto livery (low-cut baggy trousers and loose tee shirts) versus little helmets and shiny buttons.

Paul was now at the head of the crowd, and had perfected his aim. He no longer flung missiles directly at the line, where more often than not whatever he threw hit the shields or the black dustbin lids the police had picked up as impromptu protection. Instead, Paul lobbed his missiles over the shields and with almost every throw, he was hitting flesh and bone. Then, without prompting, he charged towards the police lines screaming at the top of his voice. Others quickly joined in the rush, caught up in the exhilaration. The police line held for a few of seconds and they roared as one when the line broke off in disarray as every policeman turned away in utter panic back down Upper Parliament Street; from tactical retreat to frantic flight.

The navy-blue uniforms of domination no longer held the same mystique—these were just frightened men retreating in disarray, like leaderless sheep chased by hungry wolves.

Paul picked up a police truncheon lying on the ground and chased after the police, baton raised, bulging veins and clamouring mouth. Paul caught up with a stumbling policeman and whacked him hard on the back of his head. The blow was deflected by the man's helmet, which rolled off his head to the floor. The encounter galvanised the policeman's legs as they suddenly spurted and avoided Paul's second baton swing. Paul watched the policeman run towards the shadows, picked up the policeman's helmet off the floor and stuck it on his head, like a trophy. As he walked back up the street he was overtaken by the kids from the road block with their balaclavas and track suit hoods pulled tight over their heads and scarves over their mouths.

The youths pushed the police back a further two hundred yards from Park Way to the Florence Nightingale building effortlessly until more police reinforcements arrived. There was a momentary standoff, then a barrage of missiles crashed into the reformed blue lines, and the masked ones charged again, taking running jumps into the shields and pushing the line back to the Rialto buildings.

Paul was convinced that if they carried on like this, they could batter the police all the way into the town centre and what a prize that would be, the town centre's shops filled with all manner of goodies.

A vehicle with flashing lights appeared from behind and startled Paul who instinctively took off the helmet perched on top of his head and threw it to the ground, thinking it was a police vehicle.

"Hey mate," shouted the ambulance driver through the opened door window. "We've got a patient who's just had a heart attack; do you think you could get us through please, we're desperate?"

"Yeah, lah, no problem," Paul replied sensing an opportunity. "Follow me."

"We've already had stones thrown at us down by Verulam Street," the ambulance driver said.

"Don't worry, I'll take care of it," Paul replied authoritatively.

Paul ran ahead of the ambulance waving his arms and shouting, "Let them through, let them through!"

African Henry and Jazz followed him. The sea of combatants split to let them pass and Paul indicated for the ambulance to drive through.

"Thanks Moses, you might have saved a life here," said the ambulance driver sticking up an approving thumb before driving away.

Paul felt a hand on his arm and turned quickly around, his arms up in defence. It was African Henry.

"Dat's enough now, you gettin' carried away, man. Dis a young man's game," African Henry said pulling him gently by the shoulder.

"Yer right, you know," Paul answered, suddenly feeling very weary.

They walked back up Upper Parliament Street. The road was like the aftermath of a battlefield, littered with debris. Paul was out of breath and could barely get the words out.

"You know what, that was payback time for the cops. They will never forget that. And you know what they deserved it, lah, every single one of them."

They found Jazz at the back of the crowd carrying a brick in his hand.

"Man, that was fun," he said smiling and letting the brick drop to the floor.

They passed a few people, mainly young and mainly black, eagerly running towards the fray.

"You surprised me Jazz, you did well," Paul said to Jazz. "Throwing bricks at the pigs; where's your father to see you now?"

Jazz was embarrassed but pleased by the compliment. His father would not have been happy, no doubt about that. He wanted his son to be a surveyor, like him, or an architect. He did not want him wasting his time as a snooker hustler and would be mortified at the thought that his beloved Jasminder was a rioter. Maybe his father would understand the feelings of relief Jazz felt right now, as if he had redeemed a debt owed to him. He had struck blows against the police tonight, a situation that could have seen him spend the best part of his life in jail. The thought terrified him but could not overcome the feelings of power and satisfaction that was welling inside him until he felt like bursting.

Jazz was not a violent man, in fact, he had avoided violence all his life, but this was different. It was a once in a lifetime chance that he could not have ignored. Not that Jazz had anything personally against the police. It was more an institutional thing for him. Getting away with getting back at the police for what they had done in the past against demonstrators, like Blair Peach and Grunswicks. Jasminder Singh, brave of the missile, mighty of the half brick, participant in urban battle against no longer powerful oppressors, in the spirit of Tegh Bahadur; how good it all felt.

They walked slowly, Paul was still breathing hard.

"Boy, I tell ya . . . I'll have to start . . . going to the fingy again," he gasped.

"The gym," Jazz and African Henry said in unison.

African Henry began chuckling, whether it was about Paul always saying fingy or the whole craziness of the evening, no one was sure. It caught on; the three of them started giggling like schoolboys after a successful daring prank and ended up laughing uncontrollably, like Richard Pryor himself had just cracked the funniest joke in the world.

"This was the police's worst fingy come to life," he said after regaining his breath. "Black people daring the police to come and when they finally do to whup them the way they did. Man, this was Muhammad Ali whuppin' Brian London."

"Yesss man, yesss, man," said African Henry.

"Let's get to the party," said Paul, "me Mam'll be fingyin' where the fuck we've been."

Paul opened the front door with his key. They walked in the house and into the brightly lit front parlour. Lizzie was in her element at centre stage, dancing a sedate version of the jitterbug with Uncle Leon to a lively 1954 tune with the venerable black and white Upper Stanhope Street posse clapping in tune.

'I'm like a one-eyed cat peepin' in a seafood store. I'm like a one-eyed cat peepin' in a seafood store . . .' sang Big Joe Turner.

"My lad Roger said to me," Betty shouted in Peggy Evans' ear trying to overcome the thumping sound of the music, "he was going to the clinic to get checked out because his wife wasn't getting pregnant and they've been married three years. I told him not to bother; it was her that needed checking out, not him. There's never been a McKenzie male who can't make kids, I told him. If the McKenzie males can do one fing and one fing only, I told him, then that's making babies. Thirty eight grandkids me mother had from her five lads when she died. And the new generation is just as prolific. Sweetness alone has twenty-three kids. Can you imagine twenty-three-children? And the poor cow is wondering how come they're not producing babies. It's obvious isn't it? They can't produce babies cos she's bloody infertile, that's why!"

Further down the hallway, the back parlour was in semi darkness, with a dozen or so couples dancing cheek-to-cheek, belly-to-belly, to a smoochy 1968 Chicken Shack tune. The average age in the room had dropped at least three decades.

'I was juuust, I was juuust, and I was juuust sittin' 'ere thinkin' . . . I would rather, I would rather go blind, boy, than to see you walkin' away from me . . .' sang Christine perfectly.

The three of them went into the kitchen where Alan and a tipsy-eyed Our Wayne were serving the food and drinks. At this moment Our Wayne was sucking the tonsils off a pretty, young black girl in a staggeringly tight skirt, both his hands clasped firmly to her backside.

Our Wayne was Paul's estranged son, a 22-year-old-going-on-16 lippy hedonist. The *Our* was because that's what all the family called him, never Wayne always Our Wayne. It was the family's way of making him feel a part of them and to let the outside world that he was part of their family. Everybody called Wayne *Our Wayne* now, even those who were not related.

Paul saw very little of Wayne when he was growing up and Wayne still is resentful against his father. To be fair to the lad, as Lizzie often said, he did make an effort with the rest of the family once he had found them. He always brought presents for Lizzie's birthday and at Christmas and attended most family get-togethers. Lizzie did not care much for him at first; he had lived too long in Bootle, miles away from his roots, in a district that Lizzie had long ago put on the list of godless places. However, blood was thicker than water and he was always polite and respectful and had such a lovely voice.

Wayne looked white but he sang like a black man. Wayne had become quite famous locally with his band MISCHIEF, Paul told Lizzie proudly. Wayne did not get his voice from Paul as he could not whistle in tune let alone sing.

Our Wayne was tall like his father with the same square head and raised shoulders and their smile was identical, yet to all intents and purposes, Our Wayne was European. Africa and China had been wiped off completely from his features with his thin lips, bony nose and tight nostrils, straight light brown hair and round dark blue eyes.

"Hey barman," said Paul jovially to his son. "Get back on duty and serve the bloody drinks."

"What did your last slave die of?" Our Wayne asked releasing tight skirt for a moment.

"I fingeed him for insubordination. How are you son?"

African Henry walked into the kitchen and grabbed a bottle of Cognac from the kitchen table and some plastic cups.

"Don't come the father with me, Paul. You should have tried it when I needed it."

"You missed out," Jazz said to Alan. "It was eerie man, you should have stayed. We caned those pigs proper, and we were that close to a fight in the Gladray with Bull O'Connor. Lucky your Paul was with us or we would have got battered."

"I was in the Gladray with youze, remember," said Alan patiently. "How much have you drank, Jazz?"

"Where're your Aunty Beryl and Aunty Doreen?" Paul asked Our Wayne, keen to keep the atmosphere light.

"Beryl's in the back room necking with Bonny and Doreen's gone to bed," Our Wayne replied defiantly excluding the prefix 'Aunty'.

"Bonny, you lie," said Paul. "Whadya mean neckin'. Kissin'?"

"And rubbin' up," Our Wayne said smiling sweetly.

"That's fingy, that's blasphemy."

"Incense, you mean," said African Henry as he poured brandy into the cups and distributed them.

"Dat too," Paul replied.

Alan grabbed Paul's arm as he went towards the back parlour.

"Leave them, let them enjoy themselves; they're big people," he advised his brother. "They know what they're doing."

Paul was not going to let it go, he was the family's enforcer, it was his duty to safeguard the family's honour. His first cousin trying to take advantage of his sister's vulnerability, he could not let that go, not in a million years.

Paul pushed Alan's arm aside and strode into the back parlour, fire in his eyes, chest puffed up with indignation. It took a few seconds for him to locate Beryl and Bonny in the darkness, not kissing perhaps but their bodies indecently close to each other in a real slow dance.

Paul pressed the light switch on but nothing happened, the room remained obstinately dark.

"Who took the bulb out?" he growled as he marched over to them demanding to know what was going on.

"Piss off," Beryl replied bluntly.

Paul was taken aback, shocked. It was not that he expected contrition from her, Beryl does not do contrition very well, but her rudeness broke all the rules, you do not talk to your ELDER brother that way in public, you just don't. Their Mother would be mortified.

"Show respect to your elder brother, particularly in public," Lizzie would have said.

"Wha' did . . . wha' did you say?" Paul stammered disbelievingly.

Bonny kept his head diplomatically turned away from Paul. He was not going to get involved, but he admired Beryl for standing up to Paul and maybe telling the world that she wanted a relationship with Bonny, taboos or no taboos.

"You heard," Beryl repeated pressing herself closer to Bonny, "piss off!"

Paul was at a loss what to do. He could not spank her like the spoilt brat he thought she was, as much as he would like to, because she is a mother herself. He could hit Bonny but that would cause a commotion and it would not do to spoil the party.

Paul stood there in front of them feeling like a sour lemon for a few seconds, not sure what to do next. Finally, he turned around in silent fury and walked out of the room.

Had Paul been a cartoon, smoke would be pouring out of his ears and nose and his eyes would be bright red with a dark cloud above his head.

"Well?" asked African Henry who had expected fireworks.

"Mind yer own fuckin' business, okay!" Paul snarled at him.

African Henry was naturally thick skinned, particularly when it was his turn to buy a round of drinks, but on this occasion, he knew when not to press a point

As the song ended, Bonny reluctantly released his arms from Beryl's hips, as she gently pushed him away.

"That was nice, I enjoyed it; you really dance well," she said and left the room.

What about that kiss, he wanted to ask her, you can't walk away after kissing me and holding me the way you did.

She had walked away, with nice words and a nice smile, and Bonny was left listening to some soul-funk folly.

He followed her to the kitchen.

"Can I get you a drink," Bonny asked her.

Then, to show that everything was all right as far he was concerned, he asked Paul where Alan had gone. African Henry said he was around somewhere and Paul echoed that by shrugging his shoulders.

"White wine and lemonade for me," Beryl said, "I'll be outside for some fresh air. Can I talk to you," she added looking in Paul's direction.

Paul followed her into the yard.

"Don't you ever do that to me again," she warned Paul, finger pointing in his face.

Bonny followed them out keeping a respectful distance.

"You two on with each other," Paul said looking at Beryl and Bonny in turn. "I hear youz two've been rubbin' up in there."

Bonny thought he would willingly give a year of his life were that true.

"He's bloody family," Paul said to Beryl. "It's not right."

"Rubbing up?" said Beryl, "what are you on about?"

Our Wayne had come out with the pretty, young black girl in the outrageously tight-fitting mini skirt.

Paul turned to look accusingly at Our Wayne, who quickly led the girl back towards the kitchen.

"That little toe-rag," cursed Paul. "He told me you two were up to no good."

"You owe me an apology, mister, trying to make a show of me in there." Beryl said to Paul.

"I owe you fuck all," Paul replied. "You were so close to each other you may as well have been makin' babies. If anyfin' you owe ME an apology for the way you fingeed back dere"

That was an additional two years sacrificed out of Bonny's life if only they had been making babies. If this went on much longer, Bonny thought, he will have wished himself into his fifties before he left the house.

"You're sick," said Beryl contemptuously. "Come on, Bonny let's go back in there, my kissing cousin and the father of my future babies and leave this poor fool stewing in his fetid juices, they're playing my tune."

Despite her defiant words, Beryl was playing it cool. That was the last dance he had with her that night. He did not get to speak to her much as she was in the front room with the oldies listening to exaggerated stories from yesteryear and joining in singing endlessly the Real Thing's *Liverpool 8 Medley*. Bonny was deeply disappointed, building himself up all evening that Beryl felt the same way as he felt about her. He would always blame Paul if they did not make it as an item; Beryl must have been affected by Paul's intervention.

"What if we are related, we're not brother and sister," that is what he should have said to him.

Maybe he could have declared his intentions that moment.

"No Paul," he should have answered, "we are not an item but I would love it if we were because she's everything a man would want," and he would have found the words to describe her beauty, charisma and intelligence.

That is what he should have said and cursed himself for not having said it. Maybe she would have been overjoyed to have a love declared so boldly, so publicly or maybe she would have slapped him down with her words and put him in his place. Bonny closed his eyes, imagined the toe-curling scene and shuddered.

Bonny went back out into the yard alone and surreptitiously built a spliff, resigned to mourning Valerie and the kids rather than celebrating a new and exciting chapter in his life.

The party continued until well after daybreak, with a dozen or so stay-behinders until Doreen came down with a disapproving look in her eyes, muttering on that she did not get any sleep with all the noise. Everyone left except love struck Bonny who was following Beryl around like a faithful puppy and African Henry who Paul had to prise literally finger by finger away from the kitchen table still loaded with free alcohol.

"I'll help you clean up if you want?" Bonny asked Beryl and she agreed wearily.

It was past eight o'clock when they finished cleaning up and the place looked like it usually looked—spick and span.

Doreen, Lizzie, Beryl and Bonny ate breakfast together in the kitchen. Was this the start of something big between them, Bonny wondered.

Chapter 8

Waiting In Vain

11:30am Saturday 4th July 1981

Felicia Goolsby-Power-Wright was getting ready for the lunchtime crowd. Saturday was her busiest day of the week, and Gary was late again. Some of these Youth Opportunity Programme kids were so unreliable, this was definitely the last she was taking on. Gary had only been with her for a couple of weeks and had been late most days. She should have known after getting the so-so reference from the Jaycee. Gary had probably been to the Babalou Club or wherever it was young black kids hung out these days until the early hours, not caring about the responsibilities they had the following day. She only took him on as a favour to his Nan, Mrs. Small, because she was a friend of Felicia's mother from back home since before Felicia was born. Felicia will need to find somebody who can do the job even if the wages she can offer are not exactly top dollar because she cannot do everything—cooking, serving and washing dishes. Felicia's father had promised he would be in the restaurant before nine to help her prepare.

"Is promise me promise," he promised her. "Me'll be dere sarduh mornin' furss ting, rahti gal, stop fussin'."

"Dad, you know how quixotic you can be with your promises," she had told him, raising her eyebrows.

"You too Eengleesh," he replied as was his wont whenever Felicia said a word he did not understand. He used to say the same thing when she started to straighten her hair, or started wearing shorter skirts.

Felicia had spoken to her mother on the phone at nine-thirty enquiring about her father's whereabouts but her mother had told her with thunder in her voice.

"'Ee not been 'ome all night. Is eider him out gamblin' or him out tom-cattin' or is bot', me dunno. Aks ee when yu a see 'im."

Pure Pressure

Felicia had been in her restaurant, since 8 o'clock that morning getting all the prep done, peeling and washing ground food, preparing salads, wiping tabletops and scrubbing the floor and frying 18 pieces of chicken. She had already seasoned the various meats, prepared the sauces, cut up the vegetables the night before after closing time, and put the red beans on to soak, now she was ready to open shop.

The first thing you noticed about Felicia was her hair. Bright orange and sticking out of her head like a burning bush, 'an incandescent spiky globe', Peewee, her husband of ten years, called it (Peewee found a new description for her hairstyles most days). Her crimson painted lips seem to burst out of her face, as did her teeth. She was thirty-one years old, medium built with generous hips; dark-skinned like her mother, and had her father's wide slightly upturned nostrils, which gave her a slightly porcine look. Her enemies at school used to call her '*oink-oink*'.

A large colour Jamaican Tourist Board poster dominated one wall depicting two white people lying on a sun kissed beach, frothy waves lapping at their feet as they laughed.

Visit JAMAICA—the Paradise Island

She had asked the Jamaican High Commission for a different poster, one with black people in it, but they said that was all they had in stock. It would have to be a make-do poster until she found another to hide the large patch of dampness on the wall from the flood upstairs.

Two small speakers were perched high on the wall above the poster; the sound coming from them was vintage Calypso.

> Coconut wooman is callin' aout
> and an' aout in de street yu can 'ear she shout . . .
> get your coconut watta
> Coconut
> man it's good for you dauta
> Coconut
> coconut got a lot o' iron
> Coconut
> make you strang like a lion
> Coconut
> Cococo, cococo, coconuuuut

Her first customers were regulars, Tiny and Elliot, the local basketball team coaches.

"Got the chicken, without the skin, the fried dumplings and the carrot juice ready, Felicia me love?" asked Elliot, at six foot four the smaller of the two. "We've got a big tournament in Nottingham this evening."

"Eighteen pieces, been marinating all night, without the skin and fried fresh this morning, all by meself, and thirty six baked dumplings," she replied proudly.

"What happened to Gary, no show yet?" asked Elliot.

Felicia's lazy shrug answered the question.

"Probably boogieing all night," said Tiny. "We have that problem with some of our youngsters but I just drag them out of bed; it's the only way. I know, cos I was exactly the same meself at that age."

Felicia disappeared into the kitchen, emerging a few minutes later with four bulging plastic carrier bags.

"I was always motivated me, from time," said Elliot "Me Mam's heavy hand helped as well like."

"See ya, Felicia," they both said on leaving.

"Yeah, have a good game."

Three lads in their mid teens strolled in doing the infamous Granby Walk, a slight dragging of the right leg as if it was heavier than the left and dipping the left shoulder with every other stride. All the teenage boys who thought they were bad and cool walked like that. The trio had similar build—elastic limbs, narrow shoulders and long necks. Felicia did not know their name. They not only looked alike (brown-skinned, big teeth, freshly razored skiffle haircuts) but dressed almost identically in track suit bottoms carried low over the hip and tee shirts and box-fresh trainers. As usual and infuriatingly for Felicia, they occupied three different tables across which they bantered loudly to each other. Felicia thought them rude and silly but they were regular customers (they always came on a Saturday) and meant money in her electronic till so she treated them politely and patiently.

"Yer can't tell me that Jacky gal loves ya, man, when I catch her kissin' Little Pete in the doorway. Her tongue was so far down the man's throat she was eatin' his tonsils," said the one with green-rimmed sunglasses to the one with pimples all over his face.

"Yer lie," laughed the third youth with a magazine stuffed down his back pocket

Sunglasses and Magazine slapped each other's hand and then clicked their fingers with choreographed shakes of the wrist.

"Hey, at least I can get a gal," said Pimples looking at Magazine.

"Wha' ya mean? Me can get gals anytime meself," was the defensive retort.

"Have you ever seen Rodin with a gal, ever?" said Pimples.

At least Felicia knows the name of one of them now.

"I've juss remembered," Rodin said. "I've lef' me magazine at the Barber's."

"No, you haven't," said Pimples pulling the said object out of his back pocket.

"Are you three people together?" Felicia asked politely.

They nodded.

"So why don't you all sit at the same table? It would save me having to clear and clean three different tables instead of one."

"We like our space, knowarramean?" said Rodin.

"We'll leave you an extra tip," said Sunglasses with a smirk implying that the tip would be of a sexual nature rather than a monetary one.

"Don't be so damn cheeky I'm old enough to be your Mother," Felicia said sharply.

They rigorously inspected the menus as if they were unsure what to order.

"Three yam and sweet potato soups, one without dumplings, as usual?" Felicia suggested with a hint of impatience.

"Yeah, man, wicked," was the eventual answer like it was a new dish they had never thought about before.

"You know my name is Felicia and I like to know my customers. What's your names, I know you're Rodin," she said pointing with her pad towards him.

Rodin swaggered with a look that said, "Everybody knows me".

"What about you two?"

"I'm Kay, short for Kwaku, but some call me by my middle name Kojo," said Sunglasses smiling. "And he's Alex," pointing to Pimples. "I'm the leader so any problems from dese two come direc' to me."

"I'm de leader," protested Alex. "Dis man is a born follower. I and I is the leader of me brethren," Alex continued, spreading his arms as if he was a messiah.

"I'm me own leader," Rodin chipped in as an afterthought.

Felicia tittered at them and returned to the kitchen.

As she was warming up the soup on the stove, she heard Alex shout:

"Can we have some real sounds?"

"If you don't like me music bring your own," she shouted back.

"You're on; I've got the best tunes in Liverpool."

She gently dropped the pre-cooked yam and sweet potato with a spoon into the soup and nudged up the temperature. She heard someone coming in and hoped it was Gary.

It was Solomon Howard.

Forty-two years old, small and skinny, wearing a thick, dark grey army overcoat that reached down to his ankles on what promised to be the hottest day of the year. To say that the bright yellow rubber washing up gloves that covered his hands and arms right up to his elbows were bizarre would be grossly underestimating their visual impact.

Soloman Howard was shy but friendly, well read but could be monosyllabic for long periods; he never combed his bulky hair but was always scrupulously clean.

"Hello Solly," Felicia sang out to him.

"Hello Felicia," he answered back in his high-pitched voice.

"Why are you wearing those gloves and the overcoat?" Felicia asked him.

"It was a bit chilly this morning when I got up and they're the only gloves I own," he replied lowering his eyes.

"Well it's not cold now, is it? What can I do for you today Solly?"

"A bowl of rice to eat in please, if you don't mind Felicia," he replied his eyes fixed on the floor.

"Do you want some chicken with it, I won't charge you extra?"

Solly grinned and shook his head.

"I just like coming here," he said raising his eyes slowly. "Coming here talking to you and that; I think you're lovely, the best girl in Liverpool."

"You know I'm a married woman," she said.

He nodded. "I don't mean it that way," he added quickly.

Felicia called him into the kitchen.

He hesitated at first, still standing in the doorway.

"Come on," she insisted, "I want to speak to you."

Solly had never been in the kitchen before and felt privileged by the invitation. Only staff were allowed in the kitchen. There was a notice above the kitchen doorway stating as such. '*Staff Only*' it warned.

"Do you want a job here, Solly? Only a few hours a day and I pay crap wages."

"Me?" he said incredulously. "Me?" he repeated. "Yeah," he said. "I'd work here for free. But I can't cook," he cautioned.

"Not cooking," she replied, aghast at the thought.

Felicia Goolsby Power-Wright was the self-styled best cook in Liverpool 8. She classified herself better than Jimmy Duncan, better than Lee from the Gladray Club, and better even than Junior, and he was good.

"Not cooking," she reassured him. "You know, washing dishes, clearing tables, cleaning up, that sort of thing."

"Can I play my tapes as well?"

Spices was notorious for playing the same three 90 minute tapes of soca and calypso over and over again from the time it opened at eleven thirty in the morning to when it closed at nine in the evening, ten thirty on Fridays and Saturdays, closed Sundays except for pre-booked private parties.

Felicia ignored the insult. "Of course, but can you start right now? I'm rushed off me feet."

"Yes, but do you mind if I go home first to get my tapes?" he asked. "And to get changed," he added.

"You won't be long, will you?" she pleaded as she returned to the stove.

Solly came back thirty minutes later cradling a carrier bag full of tapes, dressed in a white boiler suit that must have previously belonged to a giant and still wearing his bright yellow rubber washing up gloves. The man was ready for action.

Spices' eleven tables were all occupied; 29 people's noise swamping John Holt's fruity voice.

Felicia was looking visibly distressed with the volume of work. She had to send Solly to get some rice and vegetables from the grocery store because she was running out of supplies. Inwardly Felicia was elated by the turn of business. Today was turning out to be one of her best trading days, if not the best, since she started. Gary Clarke had finally showed up and was taking orders with a morbid face. Customer care was not something that came naturally to Gary.

Solly ambled into the kitchen and Felicia pointed him to a pile of dishes angling on the sink's drainers. He smiled broadly and ran the hot water; he had been washing dishes since he was a kid, being the eldest of a large family, and he knew exactly what to do. Two hours later and Solly's assiduousness was rewarded as Felicia asked him to take orders as well as wash dishes. He peeled off his gloves and stuck them down his boiler suit trousers, relishing at the prospect of his new duties.

"We've got everyfin on the menu except fried chicken and dumplings," Felicia barked breathlessly at him. "We're not doing takeaways until four thirty and take these to the white woman with the two kids."

Solly had been a professional singer in his time, in fact the only jobs he ever had were singing jobs. Starting out in 1956 after school when a group of them, sometimes as many as ten, would rehearse singing American songs in harmony, always accappella because no one could play an instrument; then after leaving school five of them became a local doo-wop group, The Specials. They did mainly local clubs and pubs and birthday parties and benefit nights for someone who was ill, dying or dead, but it provided them with more income than the majority of their peers who were shuffling and scuffling to supplement their Dole money. The Specials thought they were part of the people the Prime Minister had said at the time had never had it so good. You never saw them hanging around, they were always rehearsing, every day; when they were not performing they were rehearsing in one another's house sometimes but mainly in Stanley House because the community centre had a piano. This went on for three years but Solly, concluding he was carrying the group, wanted more.

Then answering an advert for a new lead singer from a white rock and roll band, The Echoes, against the odds, Solly got the job. He called himself Lucky and stayed two years with them, touring up and down the country until he had what was described to him as a nervous breakdown. Solly returned to Liverpool, hung about for a bit and then rejoined as lead singer with The Specials who had reformed as The Special Ones with two singers, a drummer, two guitarists and a sax player. They played mainly Tamla and Stax. That lasted a further four years and things were going well, they even got a record at number 49 in the local charts, but Solly, who had renamed himself Lucky Solly, had another breakdown. He recovered after a few months but by then The Special Ones had discovered a young kid who sang exactly like Levi Stubbs so they did not want him back, although he was the only reason the group had lasted so long, Solly told them.

Lucky Solly became Solly Howard again and he dropped out of singing for a living altogether. Now, he was washing dishes at Spices restaurant and had found a new vocation.

"Can I play my tapes, now?" he pleaded.

"Later, later, Solly, we're busy, can't you see," said Felicia hurriedly as the tested the firmness of the steaming rice.

It was another half hour before Solly got to put his first tape on the machine The tape began with a distinctly posh speaking voice backed up by an eerie, out-in-space melody.

"*When the white eagle of the North is flying overhead and the browns, reds and golds of autumn lie in the gutter, dead . . . remember then . . .*

Several of the animated conversations stopped in mid sentence, some were mystified, some looked amused by the strange beatless sound and Gary looked close to horrified.

"Heh-heh, what eez deece dat eez playing, a politeecal speech? Eez not Kwame Nkrumah."

"Put the calypso back on, man!"

"Maybe they're not quite ready for the Moody Blues," Solly said ejecting the tape. "I'll play something more commercial, shall I?"

The Beatles caused a few amused looks and Gary's disapprobation. Felicia was too busy cooking to care.

Forty-three sit-downs and seventeen takeaways she had served by six o'clock when the last customer left. She was exhausted but counting the takings perked her up. She felt, at last, that maybe this was the turning point, the beginning of a successful business to prove all her detractors wrong.

"**Mi cyan 'elp yuh wit dat problem,**" her father asserted firmly, when she asked him for a loan to help start the business. "People dem go out tuh eat food dem cyan cook at 'ome an' everybody dem can cook Caribbean food. Yu nah see how many properties dem empty on Granby shtree', where your bizness ago come from eef nobody nah live dere."

The three banks she approached for a loan would not entertain her. Felicia was convinced it was because they would not lend to a black woman. Peewee, her dear husband, her loyal and supportive better half, who was supposed to stick by her through thick and thin, would not back her, saying it was a waste of money. He said the location was what put the banks off not her colour.

"Everybody around here is on benefits and can't afford eat in no restaurant," Peewee cautioned. "Eyetalian, Chinee, Greek, fast food, is where the money is. White people won't buy food from black people. Granby Street is the last place you should invest money in, the place is a dump full of dealers, junkies, prostitutes, poor people."

Her mother appealed to her father's sense of duty, so he eventually agreed to provide the finance necessary to kick off her business.

"Yu only chile'," her mother chided him, "'ow yu cyan 'elp she, yu flesh n' blood."

The business started reasonably well but that did not last long. However, despite the steady downturn, Felicia persevered. She lowered her prices, laid off staff, and, she cut some sharp corners (not on the cooking, as Felicia was almost religious with her food) as she regularly swapped the labels to a lower price at the Cash and Carry and prayed she would not get caught.

As many white people came as did black people but not enough of either to keep the place going. More days like this and she would be all right for sure. Solly had been a revelation as a versatile and hardworking worker; Gary was just Gary—sullen and grudgingly cooperative—but the cash till was full and customers left looking reasonably happy, except for Trinidadian Trevor. He had asked for Souse although it was not on the menu and stormed out vowing never to "set foot in de place again" when Felicia told him that his national dish was not available because Felicia did not serve slave food and least of all pork.

The irony was that although Felicia did not serve 'slave' food she paid slave wages to her staff. The bulk of the staff pay came from tips and the food. She would say to staff: "I don't pay much but you can eat all you want so long it's not sea food or ackee, these cost real money."

The customers were gone, the door shut, all the dishes washed and the place sparkling clean again. Felicia sat down and sipped some lemon tea. Solly's tape had Bob Dylan rhyming *child's balloon* with *sun and moon*.

"What do you think about Prince Charles and Lady Di's wedding, Felicia?" Solly asked her.

"Thanks for the tea, Sol. Are you a royalist then?" said Felicia half mockingly.

"I love all that glamour," Solly said and twirled on the spot on the tip of his toes, closing his eyes for images of pomp, pageantry, luxury and indulgence.

"I thought you were an intelligent man, Solly," Felicia said affecting exasperation.

"They're having a huge fireworks party in London tomorrow night. I heard it on the news. I would love to go and see that. I love fireworks, the noise the colour. I never miss the Chinese New Year celebrations in Chinatown."

"You know what," Felicia said getting up from the chair. "I wish that old vampire the Queen Mother dies on the day they get married so we get everything, the wedding and the funereal in one week and get it all over with. Then I hope some big star gets murdered or commits suicide and everybody will forget about the bloody royal family for a while. This country's obsessed with them, I tell you."

"She's not a vampire, she's an old dear, pampered yes, but sweet," Solly protested following Felicia into the kitchen as she took off her apron.

"She sucks people's blood, been doing it all her life, living off the fat of the land," persisted Felicia.

"She drinks gin not blood," said Solly grinning.

"But she's been so well fed that she'll probably live for ever like all vampires."

"Can I go home now?" asked Gary suddenly, the conversation having blissfully passed him by.

"Yes, you did well," said Felicia. "And don't be late tomorrow, we've got a Christening at twelve, 18 people," she continued reverting to her don't-mess-me-about voice.

A silver grey Mercedes convertible stopped outside the restaurant, the driver jumped out of the car without opening the door. Eric Wilson knocked on the locked door until he was let in. He swaggered in, a brown-skinned man dressed like a baseball player advertising gaudy jewellery; medium height, muscle-bound, dark sunglasses and dressed in white Bermuda shorts, white ankle socks, white trainers, and a Phillies tee shirt pulled tight against a flat stomach. Gold sparkled in the sunlight from his fingers and neck.

"That's a vampire if ever I saw one," said Solly to Felicia nodding towards Eric Wilson.

"Keep your voice down, that's Eric Wilson; he's a bad man," whispered Felicia gulping down her tea.

"Whasappenin sis," Eric sang towards Felicia in what he thought passed for a New York accent.

"Everyfin's just fine," she replied, "juss come back from the gym?"

"Yeah man, gorra keep fit y'know," then looking directly at Solly he said: "You're one of the Howards aren't ya, the crazy one?"

"I am Solomon, the eldest Howard," Solly corrected him looking up directly in the eye.

"Youz've all got biblical names in your family, how many of you, a dozen?"

"Nine actually," Solly insisted, still staring at him. "Ruth, the youngest, then David, Naomi, James, Joseph, Simon, Mary, Peter and me, Solomon."

"Hey," Felicia intervened. "Leave him alone, he's not crazy and he works here."

"Keep yer hair on Felicia, I was only jestin'."

Eric rubbed Solly's head as a peace offering but it may just as well have been the table he was rubbing for all the empathy he seemed to put into the gesture. Solly responded like a pet, almost rolling his eyes with gratitude. It was not that Solly was intimidated by the man or by what he had said to him (as slight and small as he was Solly had a back as broad as the Boulevard, insults bounced off him like rubber balls), Solly was just glad of the attention.

"'Av' ya got red bean soup and plenty o' napkins, I don't wanna stain me outfit, seen?" he asked Felicia and burst into laughter.

"Large or small?" asked Solly.

"Large," Felicia and Eric said simultaneously.

"A large portion for a large man," Eric laughed. "And dun firget de fried dumplings on de side and a large mango juice. What you recommend today for main meal chef?" he shouted.

"The oxtail and butter beans are all we got left; had a busy day today," Felicia shouted back from the kitchen.

"Yeah man, dat sound nice," he approved and sat down at the table nearest to the window so that the world could see Eric the Man.

"Got anyfin' to read while I'm waitin'," he asked Solly.

"We've got the Caribbean Times, the Mirror or the Daily Post and fashion magazines." "Gimme all of dem, me's a fast reader," he said laughing.

"Y'know," he shouted to Felicia, "y'should have tables and chairs outside on de pavements when it's nice like this; whadyaasay?"

"Yeah, good idea, Eric, I'll give it a fink." answered Felicia from the kitchen.

"How's yer daddy?"

"He's fine, and me Mam as well; he was supposed to help me at the restaurant today, I'm waiting in vain."

Eric's laugh boomed across the room as if he had heard the funniest joke in the world.

Solly brought the soup in a large bowl and Eric spread the paper napkins all over his clothes tucking them in neatly.

Mally Gibson came in cradling a pile of printed papers, dressed in patched up denim and open sandals.

Lenny Roberts called him the revolutionary without a cause. Mally Gibson had not long been freed on parole on a six year prison sentence for trying to rob the post office on Upper Hill Street armed with threats and a scowl, and came out of prison militantly politicised.

"I'm no teef," he declared to the jury, having sacked his legal team. "I'm only takin' from de man what he took off me."

"Wha' appenin, star; there man, straight off the press," he said handing a small pamphlet to Eric.

"What's this?" Eric asked holding the pamphlet by the tip of his fingers and well away from his clothes in case the ink came off.

"This is the third edition. *L8 Lynx* tells it like it is and makes the links between perception and reality in the Liverpool 8 situation on an economic, political and cultural level. Read it bra, you'll learn somefin' for sure," Mally replied earnestly. "It's well written, simple but fearless."

"How much?" Eric asked suspiciously.

"I accept donations, whatever you can afford, if you can't afford noffin' give me noffin'. I don't get no grants for this you know, it's all done by me for free and whatever shilling I can raise coz all donations goes straight to the *L8 Lynx*."

'*STOP KILLING GRANBY STREET*' read the headline with two photos of Granby Street underneath, one taken in 1955 and the other last month.

"Hey," said Felicia, "I remember those days. There's the school and Mr. Smith's sweet shop. We used to buy glasses of Sarsaparilla and bright green Cream Soda by the glass there. Oh, there's the Greek chippy on the corner of Hatherley Street, and on the opposite corner there's Waterworths the fruit and veg shop. Remember Mr. Price's chandlers shop on the corner of Parly, I used to deliver paraffin to his customers for some pocket money; those were the days. How things have changed," she lamented.

"Okay, let me read it and I tell ya wha' it's worth, seen," said Eric.

"Yeah man, whatever you say, take yer time; hey sis, wha' 'appenin' wid you, everyfin' tight."

Felicia smiled at Mally and gave him fifty pence—big money for two A4 sheets.

"Everyfin's fine Mally, you having a chicken patty?"

"Yeah, sis, the usual for me; the best chicken patty outside Jamaica, I swear."

"When were you ever in Jamaica, Mally," she asked him playfully.

"Soon man, soon," he grinned.

"So what's all this about, who's killing Granby Street?" she said taking one of the sheets.

"The Corpy dey're killing Granby Street; when people leave they don't relet the house to some new tenants and keep the place alive, but board it up so that now half the houses in the area are standing empty. It is so they can knock all the houses down because nobody will want to live in a ghost town, and employ their friends to build new ones. They are destroying a long-standing community. You must be feeling it if there's less people about. Read it nuh, sis, and nex' time I pass you and me gonna discuss it, right?"

"Right," Felicia echoed placing the pamphlet on the counter and reaching for a patty from the cold display with thongs and placing it into the microwave for a

Louis Julienne

few seconds. Felicia placed the patty into a small paper bag, took Malley's money, carefully gave him his change and warned him as she always did not to eat it for a few minutes until it cooled down a little as it was still cooking. As usual, Mally ignored her and bit deeply and noisily into the pastry like he had not eaten in an age.

"Yeah sis," he cooed between mouthfuls, "you'll have to give me the recipe."

"Next time," she assured him, "next time."

"Hey man that's good," said Eric to Mally as he handed him a £5 note, adding, "Keep the change, buddy. Me always likes ter support de community, seen?"

Mally's startled look lasted a second and he almost snatched the money and left the restaurant with a happy look on his face.

"It's been a brilliant day today," Felicia said to Solly as she sat down at the 'staff' table counting the day's takings. "I've hardly got any food left. I'll have to raid me Dad's freezer for the Christening tomorrow and get some stuff from Danny's."

Eric had just finished wolfing down his dessert and was stretching his arms.

"Me's belly's full and my man is glad," he exclaimed. "Muss rush me darlin'" he said to Felicia has he handed her money for the bill. "Keep the change sweetheart," he added and walked out adjusting his tee shirt which appeared to have shrunk around his midriff. A few seconds later Billygoat walked in.

"'Ello me love, 'ow eez bizeeness?" he announced.

"Where've you been," she said reproachfully, "I've been waiting for you since morning?"

"Work, me darlin', me's been workin' all day," he replied showing off his stained overalls as testimony.

"You could've ringed me, Dad; we've been rushed off our feet all day."

"Good, good," he replied. "Me want some fish, two big-big portions, wid rice n' peas and salad; 'urry nuh, I'se starvin'."

"Sorry, Dad, not much left. The fish is long gone, there's some oxtails left, and white rice, no rice and peas; that's all I've got left."

"Can you make that two oxtails and rice, fe me spar outside as well, but quick gal?"

"Five minutes then," she promised, "it's still warm."

"Is wha' 'appen to the bwoy Gary, you sack 'im," Billygoat said looking suspiciously at Solly, taking in his clothes and the wide-eyed innocence and marking him down as a crazy man.

Pure Pressure

"He's been and gone; Solly saved me life today, he's been a Godsend. If he hadn't turned up I dunno what I'd have done, seriously."

"Solly, dis is me Dad," she said.

"So bizness eez good today den, yes?" said Billygoat shaking Solly's hand without looking at him.

"Pretty good; if it carries on like this I'll be minted."

"And pay ye Daddy's money back, huh?"

She handed him the dinners in a cardboard container and wrapped in a plastic bag and warned her father: "I'll be round t'night to raid your freezer; I've got a function on early tomorrow."

"Wass wrong wid de shop?" he said as he brought the packaged food to his nose, took a deep breath and nodded appreciatively.

"All the good meat shops are closed on Sundees and I know you always stock good meat."

"Cha man, you never bring food back, never," said Billygoat kissing his lips churlishly.

"I've got an arrangement with Mum," she replied with a wink,

"Is she who put de food on de table or is me? Nobody tell me anytin'; in me own haouse, I tell ya," he muttered, "eez 'ow much me owe yu?"

"The food is on me," she replied with a smile.

Felicia finally locked up the shop at nine thirty. She bought some groceries from Bashir's store on Kingsley Road just before he closed then dropped Solly off on the Boulevard near where he lived and drove home as the day was turning into night.

Home for Felicia Power-Wright was a two bed flat on the Bedford Street South estate. Recently built and run by a housing association, the estate was comprised mainly of flats in three storey blocks. Well-kept and sought after in the area, the small estate of sixty mixed households, mixed in that there were as many working people as '*economically inactive*' people, there were quiet retired people and noisy young couples. Most residents were white with sprinklings of other ethnic groups.

Felicia lived there with her 42-year-old husband, Beresford Power-Wright (everyone called him Peewee). Peewee had serious form as a skirt chaser who liked to keep his love options as wide open as possible so it took some heavy pressure to get Peewee to finally consent to settle down and then to marriage. It was a quiet affair, no big ceremony; a wet weekend in London for their honeymoon, a play, a film and two meals out, that sort of thing. But it felt good to be Mrs. Power-Wright. Everybody still called her Felicia Goolsby so she readopted her maiden name and added it to her new double-barrelled name to make it a treble. Not many people outside of aristocracy had three surnames.

Peewee could have helped out in *Spices* but he had no interest whatsoever in cooking, serving or cleaning, as he was fond of stating.

He was dead set against the restaurant idea from the beginning. Why she could not be satisfied with her job as a Staff Nurse with good promotion prospects Peewee would never know. He could never understand her, always pushing the boundaries, always wanting new challenges.

"You say it yourself and other people say that I'm a brilliant cook, and well organised."

"Yes darling but cooking for five or six people is not the same as cooking for fifty or sixty people a day, every day."

"How many people do I cook for whenever I've had a function? I'll tell you, as much as 150 people and every single one of them is starving and every one of them is pleased by the food I cooked for them. Don't tell me about the difference between domestic cooking and COM-MER-CIAL cooking, because I know all about it, from time. I'm a chef as well as a cook"

Felicia parked her car, an old mini estate, and walked up to her block. She opened the door into the flat and immediately the smell of rum hit her nostrils. Every single night Peewee drank that stuff, and every single night he said he could handle it and he does not have a problem.

"Hello, luv," she shouted to him as she opened the door, "I'm home."

Peewee, stretched out on the sofa in his underwear in the dark, looked weary. The curtains were drawn with the flickering images from the television filling the room.

He was eating strawberries and cream liberally laced with Bajan rum from a saucer with a spoon.

"You okay?" she asked him.

"Not bad," he replied. "I've had one of me attacks but I'm over the worst of it. I've been feeling cold and my hip's been playing me up all day. I haven't moved outside the door only to put a bet one. I had to ring in sick. How was your day?"

Felicia knelt beside him and caressed his face.

"Brilliant, really busy," she replied without enthusiasm, and then, perking up, she added."You've got a hard on,". "My, are you pleased to see me," she smiled.

She kissed him full on the mouth. Peewee felt cool to Felicia's touch despite the heat.

"You okay?" she said.

"Of course I'm okay," he replied turning his eyes wearily back to the flickering images.

"I'll soon cheer you up. I'm all sweaty and smelly and need a bath to wash it all away. I'll be back to deal with your pro-tu-be-rance" she said suggestively.

Felicia came out of the bathroom twenty minutes later, naked save for a short robe that barely covered the top of her legs; her body was shiny with perfumed oil. She stared at her reflection softened in the mirror by the darkness; she was proud of her firm breasts that hung from her like ripe avocados. Tonight may finally be the night she gets pregnant, she mused, stranger things have happened.

Felicia lay alongside Peewee on the sofa and caressed his hip. She was pleasantly surprised at Peewee's erection. Wow, she thought, one look at her and zoom he reaches the sky. Had it been like this more often she would have had a houseful of kids by now.

She reached towards the rigid flesh but Peewee flinched away.

Felicia exploded.

"What's the matter with you? For weeks you tell me you can't get it together because you feel ill, or you're too tired or something. And now," she shouted and jumped up to switch the lights on, "now that you've a whopping hard on, if you'll excuse my French, you still don't want me near you. What's going on Peewee? Would you rather toss yourself off than have sex with me?"

"I've had this . . . hard on since this morning," he grimaced. "It won't go down. It's not sore but it is very sensitive."

"What's the matter with you, what's the matter with it, have you got a venereal disease?"

Felicia's voice had risen several octaves.

"I've got a hard on and it's very painful and it won't go down," he said.

"I don't understand."

"Neither do I but it's not comfortable."

"Douse it with water," she suggested. "It works for dogs."

Felicia went into the kitchen and returned with a salad bowl full of water.

Peewee dipped his sore member into the cold water and waited and waited but nothing happened, his cock was still standing up to attention.

"If anything its gone worse," he said wincing.

"You'll have to go to hospital, to Casualty," Felicia suggested.

"I don't think so," he said. "What will I say to them: 'Excuse me but I've got an erection I can't get rid off, can you help? No but I wouldn't mind my feller having your condition,'" he continued mimicking an imaginary conversation with the hospital receptionist.

"You can't ignore it; you don't know what lasting harm it could cause."

Felicia persuaded him to let her drive him to the hospital, despite his pleas that 'it might have gone by then.'

He slipped a pair of knee length shorts leaving the fly open with his inflexible penis jutting out like a bald solitary sentinel and threw a coat over his shoulders carefully fastening the buttons to hide the painful protrusion.

The walk to the car was slow and uncomfortable. They drove out of Bedford Street into Myrtle Street and the car stalled. Felicia tried to start the car several times before she realised she had run out of petrol.

They had to trek back to the flat with Peewee walking as if barefoot on broken glass.

"We'll have to call an ambulance," said Felicia in a tone that tolerated no argument as she dialled 999.

Engaged, she had to try eight times before getting through.

"Emergency, which service please," said the answering voice.

"Ambulance please," Felicia said.

"Hold the line please," said the impersonal voice.

Felicia held on for many minutes and wondered what was going on.

"Ambulance Service, how can I help," another impersonal voice offered.

"My husband is in terrible pain," said Felicia anxiously.

"What is the problem," rejoined impersonal voice number two.

Felicia thought for a moment and decided that impersonal voice number 2 would not be too impressed with 'he has a very painful erection which will not go down,'

"It may be acute appendicitis," said Felicia choosing her words carefully. "He's taken pain killers but they don't seem to work."

"Where are you located?"

"Bedford Walk, Liverpool 8."

"I'm sorry," she said quickly, "but emergency services are inundated with calls right now and I don't think we can come out to you for at least half an hour, possibly longer. The police have advised us that several main roads are barricaded and they have no idea when these will be cleared Can you drive down to A & E or get a taxi?"

"I'll try a taxi," Felicia answered. "Thanks for noffin."

Felicia picked up a taxi card by the phone and dialled the number but received an engaged signal. She grabbed the large telephone book, located and dialled five taxi numbers and all of them were engaged. She dialled the first number again and it rang for five minutes before a voice answered.

"ABC Cars, can I have your address please?"

"Bedford Walk, Liverpool 8," she answered.

"I'm sorry but we are unable to send any cars in the Liverpool 8 area presently because of the riots."

"The riots," Felicia replied perplexed, "what riots?"

"Yes, riots. Two of our drivers have had their cars damaged by rioters; I'm sorry."

"Not as sorry as me," Felicia said before slamming the phone back on its cradle.

"What's the matter?" asked Peewee.

"There are riots in Liverpool 8 apparently; roads have been blocked off and they're not sending out any ambulances and taxies are either engaged or they won't come out here because of these riots. The way they're talking you'd think there was a revolution going on. I don't know what we're gonna do."

They sat down. Felicia looked pensive whilst Peewee had a pained expression etched on his face.

"I'll call me Dad, he'll drive us," said Felicia stretching for the phone.

"Not your Dad," Peewee pleaded. "You know what he's like, taking the piss all the time and he'll tell the whole world."

Felicia accepted Peewee had a valid point; she could picture her father giggling and lewdly entertaining his cronies for years to come.

For several minutes, they went through all their family, friends and acquaintances that lived nearby, drove a car, would not take the piss and could keep a secret.

Neither could think of anyone who had all the required attributes. There was a winner, with three of the four requirements, so Felicia rang her.

By the time Gloria Roberts arrived, it was one o'clock in the morning.

"Can I have a look?" Gloria asked Peewee as if she was the doctor who was going to put it all right.

"No, you can't have a bloody look!" barked Peewee, hiding the swelling with his overcoat, "you make me feel like a circus act."

"Oh go on, Peewee, just let her see the shape," urged Felicia.

Peewee reluctantly took his arms away to reveal his overcoat with a little mountain in the middle.

"And it won't go down, that's amazing," Gloria said incredulously. "Hey, I know some people who would be glad of one of them more often," she continued smiling broadly.

The requirement Gloria failed was taking the piss. Gloria Roberts was a known piss-taker. Peewee threw a despairing told-you-so look at Felicia about her mocking bitch of a friend while Felicia busied herself packing overnight stuff in a little holdall.

"Are you ready then, I've got my baby in the car fast asleep," she said turning towards the front door.

All the way to the Royal Hospital, less than a mile away, Felicia wanted to talk about the riots, Trisha wanted to talk and laugh about Peewee's erection and Peewee did not want to talk about anything to anybody.

"What caused it," asked Gloria looking down at Peewee lying on the back seat, struggling for space with the sleeping infant. "Were you like . . . eh, y'know . . . like . . . eh, having it?"

"No we were not," Felicia said pointedly. "Did you see any trouble on your way?"

"Chinatown's quiet. I only saw loads of police buses parked up on Catherine Street. Has this happened before Peewee?" Gloria said turning towards him on the back seat next to little Eric as they stopped at a red light.

"First time," Felicia snapped, "there wasn't much on the local news on the radio and Peewee was watching some detective thingy on the telly. The taxi people said there were barricades across the road, just like in the Russian Revolution."

"More like Northern Ireland," countered Gloria. "It wouldn't surprise me if they brought the Army in. Have you got any idea what caused it?"

"The riots?" asked Felicia.

"No," replied Gloria nodding in Peewee's direction, "his erection."

"We don't know," said Felicia, "but we hope to find out."

"Have you tried cold water, it works with dogs," said Gloria.

Gloria dropped them off at the hospital and Peewee and Felicia made their way inside. The hospital was like a supermarket on a busy day. There were people everywhere, but the people did not look like shoppers they looked like they had been in a war. Nurses, doctors, and porters wheeled people with bloodied makeshift bandages on trolleys. Everybody, wounded and staff, was in uniform and everybody was on overtime and everybody was white, except Felicia and Peewee.

"What's been happening here?" said Peewee as he shuffled along propped up on Felicia's shoulder.

Pure Pressure

"Looks like the police have taken a right caning, look at them," said Felicia.

The reception area seemed like a police station with perhaps seventy uniformed men, most of them seated or lying on the fixed benches. As Felicia and Peewee walked slowly towards the reception desk, the room went quiet. Some were staring at them as if they did not smell nice.

"I think me elbow's broken," grimaced the policeman in front of them to the receptionist.

"If you take a seat someone will call you as soon as possible," she said after taking his details.

"Your name," the receptionist said to Peewee.

"My name's Power-Wright, I'll spell it for you shall I?"

Peewee explained his problem to an unimpressed receptionist and sat down.

At regular intervals, a nurse came into the reception area shouting numbers like a bingo caller.

"P.C. Hawkins, 2547." [Fractured shoulder]

"P.C. Williams J. 3987." [Head wound]

"P.C. Marsden, 3409." [Shirking]

"P.C. Vaughn, 4431." [Head wound]

"Clifford Barrymate." [Civilian—appendicitis]

"P.C. Williams D.1907." [Fractured arm]

"P.C. Moore, 2155." [Fractured foot]

"P.C Woods, 9874." [Fractures finger]

It took nearly two hour before Peewee was called, twisting in his seat trying to assuage the pain, his erection having lost none of its inflexibility. Felicia waited while Peewee followed the nurse, hobbling timidly.

"Your condition is known as priapism, after the Greek god of fertility, Priapus," Dr. Thavendra, the chatty Sri Lankan doctor, told him. "Statues and pictures of Priapus show him with an abnormally large and erect penis," he added with a smile. "More seriously, if the erection is maintained for six hours or more it could lead to impotence or worse. As the blood becomes stagnant it starts to acidify and starves the penis of oxygen, which means the penis could become gangrenous and have to be amputated."

Gangrene, amputation, Peewee cringed and wriggled and squeezed the sides of the bed on which he was lying, trying hard to convey that he was not panicking.

Why me," Peewee protested meekly.

"It could be leukaemia or, more probably, Sickle Cell disease," Doctor Thavendra opined, "Sickle Cell anaemia is one of the most common genetic disorders in the world and particularly affects people of African, Middle Eastern and Indian origins. It is caused by a mutation producing abnormal haemoglobin, the molecule inside red blood cells that carries oxygen. While healthy red blood cells can bend quite easily, the abnormal haemoglobin makes cells stiff and sickle shaped and consequently they can't squeeze through small blood vessels. This stops oxygen from getting through to where it should and causes severe pain and damage to vital organs such as the heart, lungs and liver, as well as to joints and, as perhaps in your case, prolonged and painful erections. My uncle had the disease, so I made a point of looking it up."

"If I have got Sickle Cell how did I catch it," said Peewee clearly rattled.

"It's not a disease you contract like flu or venereal disease, it's genetic, probably from one or both parents," said the doctor.

"I got my nose and nature from my father and my lips and love of books from my mother and sickle cells from both," thought Peewee as he began to contemplate his body going into convulsions starved of oxygen.

Blood samples were taken from Peewee to be analysed, the doctor promised he should get the results imminently.

The results when they came confirmed Sickle Cell anaemia.

The treatment was not for the squeamish and Peewee was among the most squeamish people who ever lived. The local anaesthetic was bad enough, then they cut a small hole at the side of his penis with a fearsome looking needle and drained the blood off and, like a miracle, his penis regained its wonderfully flaccid state again.

It was past five in the morning when Felicia left the hospital, still packed with injured and defeated policemen and hurried medics. She saw a taxi with its hire lights on but the only response she got for her frantic waves was a sneer; she sneered back and had to walk all the way home.

She got a jerry can from her kitchen cupboard, walked the two miles to the Smithdown Road petrol station, filled it up and walked all the way back. She waved at two more taxis but they just drove straight past; the third taxi stopped (a kindly soul, rare among the breed that calls itself Liverpool taxi drivers and she was going to tell him so but the taxi-driver would not let her in his cab when he saw she was carrying petrol.

Felicia cursed all the taxi drivers in Liverpool and promised herself to write to the licensing authorities to make a formal complaint.

Felicia had form in writing letters of complaints. The gas and electricity boards, the newspapers, the health authorities over the IVF treatment that does not work; she had queried every one of her parking fines and had at least half of them cancelled it. She would organise a petition and get as many black people as she could to sign it. That would add weight to her letter; letting the authorities know it was not a one-off but that it happened all the time.

Dear Sir/Madam, she would begin, *this is a formal complaint against drivers of black taxis in Liverpool. Today, Sunday 5th July between 5.45 am and 6.35am I flagged five black taxis with their hire lights on. None of them were carrying passengers and all of them saw me, yet they drove past me, one of them even glared at me. He had a red tee shirt, a bald head and a dark moustache, his car number was either WRO, WRA, WRD, or even WRL 639 or 839; It was near the corner of Edge Lane and Tunnel Road.*

These are not the only such outrages I have been subjected to; it has happened to me on at least twenty separate occasions and more, particularly at night.

Nor am I the only black person to whom this has happened. For your information, I have enclosed a list of other black people who have also been victims of this discriminatory behaviour from drivers of black taxis, not black drivers as I have yet to see a black man driving a black taxi in Liverpool. Is there a bar on black taxi drivers the way there used to be on black bus drivers?

To help solve this problem I demand firstly that where these taxi drivers can be identified that they should have their license revoked forthwith and secondly, that all taxi drivers should undergo Equal Opportunities and Race Awareness Training and pass the test to ensure they are able to provide a service to all regardless of race, colour or creed.

Please respond by 31st July 1981. If I have no response by then I will barge into your office, grab you by the goolies and twist them until your eyes water; if your eyes remain dry I'll spit in them to make them wet. This is not threat it is a promise.

That is a bit strong, thought Felicia, the good manners instilled into her by her parents prevailing, so she would close the letter with, *if I have no response by then I will contact my MP to take the matter up with you directly.*

In anticipation, I thank you for your assistance and cooperation in this matter.

Yours truly

Ms. Felicia Goolsby-Power-Wright

Felicia had reached the top of Upper Parliament Street by the time she had finished mentally reviewing her complaint letter. She stopped to take a breather, put the jerry can on the floor and leaned against the pavement railing.

She heard the screeching of tyres in the distance and popped her head around the corner. She looked down Upper Parliament Street and in the middle of the road, a few hundred yards from her rested the burnt remnants of a car around which a crowd of what looked like teenagers were milling around. The screeching car was being driven erratically across the road and pavement by skinny youths.

Stolen cars, she reflected, those kids should be sent in the Army to straighten them out and get some discipline in their lives. Like Peewee did when he was 18, stayed for twelve years and came out a skilled man.

"You lot wanna get out of that car and get home before the police catches up with yers," she warned them.

The car drove away past her, the youths waving at her.

Further down the road, she recognised Gary, her Youth Opportunity employee, standing on his own with his back to her, his hands deep in his pockets staring at the burnt out car in front of him.

"Gary," she shouted with just a hint of doubt in her voice in case it was not him. They all looked alike from a distance.

"Gary," she repeated, as she got closer, "what are you doing?"

Gary turned around slowly.

"I'm watching the car burn," he replied in a matter-of-fact voice.

"Did you set it on fire?" she asked him.

He laughed.

"Me, no," he replied shaking his head.

"So what you doing standing there, you could get yourself locked up. What would your Mum and your Nan say if they saw you now?"

"They'd cry," he answered with a broad grin.

"So why don't you go home and come into work in the morning," she suggested.

"I'm goin' now," he said defensively reasserting his familiar rebarbative persona.

"You could come home with me and go straight to the restaurant from there. We'll get an early start with that Christening," Felicia said reaching a hand towards him.

"Hey missus," Felicia heard a young voice say. "Is dat petrol you're carryin' in dat can?"

"Mind your own business," she snapped back walking away with her hand firmly on Gary's shoulder.

"Hey you, don't fuckin' walk away from ME when I'm aksin' yer som'n. Is dat petrol in de can I says?" said a heavily built teenager she did not recognise, bunching his shoulders and rolling his head like a hard case.

Pure Pressure

"Who the bloody hell do you think you're talking to, mister big stuff?" replied Felicia sharply.

"Yeah well, what you doin' walkin' round with a can full o' petrol like youze gonna buil' some petrol bombs or som'n'?" he asked defiantly hitching his low cut baggy trousers up.

"You're one of the Gallaghers," she said staring at him. "You're Prinny's lad, aren't you?"

"So wha', wharrif I am?" he replied the aggression seeping out of him.

"I've run out of petrol and I'm taking this to get my car going. Is that okay Master Gallagher?"

"Tom!" someone shouted after him. "Tom. Come 'ead, man, leave 'er alone."

"Wha' you mean, she's family, man, she's safe, man, pure safe," said Tom indignantly, saluting her politely as he Granby-Street-walked away.

Felicia and Gary walked together through the Faulkner estate. She made him carry the jerry can and he was carrying it as if it was the heaviest article in the whole universe, puffing and panting, frequently changing hands.

Coming out on to Grove Street, they stumbled upon a convoy of Police buses parked up head to tail alongside the sidewalk.

"Don't panic," Felicia whispered to Gary as a few policemen stared as they walked in their direction.

Gary suddenly dropped the jerry can to the floor and began running back into the Faulkner estate at speed. However, he ran straight into another group of policemen lounging on the grass verge in the early morning sunshine. They grabbed Gary and frogmarched him to a police van as he shouted "I ain't done nuttin, leave me alone."

A burly sergeant picked up the jerry can lying on the floor and carefully unscrewed the top.

"Hey, hey, it's petrol!" the Sergeant exclaimed triumphantly.

"That's mine," protested Felicia trying to grab the can off him.

The Sergeant pushed her away.

"So you're both in it," he said to her, "makin' petrol bombs."

"My car's run out of petrol and the lad was helpin' me carry it," she protested.

"Carryin' the can for you is he," laughed the Sergeant at his own joke. "You're under arrest lady."

A young Inspector marched up to them oozing importance with every deliberate step.

"What's going on?" he asked authoritatively.

"I've run out of petrol and had to buy some petrol from the garage in Smithdown Road," Felicia explained breathlessly shaking the sergeant's hand off her shoulder.

"The young lad you've just bungled into the van was helping me to carry it to my car," she added. "It's parked on Myrtle Street around the corner, a mini estate; go an' check if you don't believe me."

They did check and they let her go, the Inspector ordering the Sergeant to pour the petrol into her tank.

"Thank you, officer," she said relieved. "What about Gary, the young lad, are you going to let him go."

"Of course," replied the Inspector smiling.

"I'll come with yers and take him home myself, make sure he doesn't get into mischief."

Peewee felt very uncomfortable lying flat on his back in bed with his penis swathed in white bandages like a Mummy. The pain from the hole they had drilled, or at least it felt like it had been drilled, although dulled by the painkillers, the pain was still there like a little devil digging its little fork into his flesh ploughing away at Peewee's resolve.

He was in a small ward with eight beds, all of them occupied with wounded men; Peewee was the only civilian and the only black person in the ward.

"What happened to you?" a Northern voice said to Peewee.

Peewee opened his eyes and swivelled them slowly towards the voice, careful not to move his body unnecessarily in case it provoked more pain.

The Northern voice belonged to a young man in the bed next to him with a bandage draped around his head. Peewee knew he was a policeman because the man's helmet was propped up on the chair next to him. The voice was not friendly or unfriendly, just Northern.

"You won't believe it," Peewee said shaking his head.

"Try me," replied bandaged policeman.

"I had a very painful hard on that lasted for nearly five hours so they had to drill a hole in the side to get the blood out from my penis."

Before bandaged policeman had started to say "You joking or what" Peewee swung the sheets aside to reveal his bandages as if he was showing off valour medals.

"They drilled a hole in your . . . cock!" said bandaged policeman squirming in his bed both hands cupped over his nether region for protection against an electric drill.

"They don't know what's caused it but it could be either Leukaemia or Sickle Cell disease."

Bandaged man tried to shake his head gravely but he winced with pain instead.

"What happened to you?" Peewee asked him.

"I've never heard of that before, it sounds scary," bandaged policeman added. "Will it work again?"

"It wasn't working too good before so I don't know if it'll work again," Peewee answered.

Peewee shivered at the thought of impotence. Felicia was a hot-blooded girl she was bound to find someone else.

"So what happened to you?" Peewee repeated.

"My name's Pete, by the way," bandaged policeman said.

"My name's Beresford but everybody calls me Peewee."

"Anyways, Peewee, I can hardly believe it meself what's happened to me," Pete said drawing a deep breath.

"I'm a copper," Pete began, not as a boast but matter-of-factly, like saying he was a plumber or a bus driver. "There I am in me garden playing with me little nephews and nieces on me week-end off, the first in six weeks, minding me own business. Then we gets this call, me brother and meself, to report to the station to go to Liverpool because of riots. I live in Bolton. Bloody riots, I thought they only happened in bloody Northern Ireland and on training courses, rather than in Liverpool. Liverpool, for God's sake, home of the Beatles, Penny Lane and Strawberry Fields Forever. Dockers' strikes yes but not bloody riots."

"So you're a poet as well," Peewee interrupted sardonically.

"Not really, but I read a lot," Pete replied taking it as a compliment, "you don't get much time for poetry in this job, let me tell you. Anyways, the call came at five o'clock just before dinner, that we ended up not having and at six o'clock we waz on the police buzz haring down the motorway and by ten we're getting brick and stones and petrol bombs thrown at uz from hundreds of kids. I couldn't believe it, man. They give uz these tiny shields but they waz bloody useless man. Tony, me brother, he's a sergeant, so he didn't get injured. They stay behind with the officers. This piece of concrete or some bloody something hit me on the head and the next thing I know I'm in the ambulance. In and out of the bloody operating room in five minutes with eighteen stitches in me head, scrapes and bruises all over me legs where they must have dragged me fifteen bloody miles man. All this for what, I don't even bloody know. Do you know what it's all about? The Super said something about outside troublemakers and local hooligans."

"It's not really like that," said Peewee shifting himself into a more comfortable position. "There's a lot of angry young people in the area and they're angry because they're harassed by the police and because they can't get a job, just because they're black."

"I'm not sure," said Pete trying to shake his head and wincing. "I couldn't tell if they were coloured or white kids but I'm told it's the other way round, it's kids who harass the Bobby on the beat. In Bolton we don't get any problems with the Paki kids or the adults; they keep themselves to themselves and get on fine."

"If me and you are going to get on," Peewee said, his tone suddenly turning cool and measured, "then you have to stop using words that I really find offensive. Calling people coloured or Paki or Chink is the same as calling them nigger."

Peewee lifted his hand to discourage Pete from replying.

"Don't tell me you don't mean anything by it," he continued, "because it means a lot to me and people like me."

"I'm not a racialist," Pete protested, lifting his bed cover defensively.

"Oh yes you are," Peewee insisted. "Only you might not realise it. Every white person in Britain is racist; they can't help it because it comes with their milk, it's part of your culture."

"You sound like a birrer man," Pete said sadly.

"I'm not bitter, I'm just in pain right now," Peewee groaned and closed his eyes, trying to shut out the slow throbbing pain that was surviving the effects of the pain killers Peewee had been administered.

Within minutes, he was asleep.

Chapter 9

Burnin' N Lootin

8:15 pm Sunday 5th July 1981

Cars had always been Paul Leung's passion, from when he was young. He stole his first car when he was 13 and did not stop robbing them until he got out of Borstal when he was 17.

On his release, he bought his first car whilst still banned but never robbed a car again. It was not just that he stole them he rode them at ferocious speeds, risking serious injury or death like only the young or the foolish do.

Paul had watched and sometimes helped Jimmy Deforo, who ran a car repair business, when he should have been in school. His mother was too busy looking after his siblings to control him, his father was always away at sea and the truant man was scared of him.

When Jimmy Deforo was suffering with prostrate cancer, he relied mainly on Paul to keep the business alive and when Jimmy died Paul's father gave him the cash to buy the business off the Deforo family.

The garage provided Paul with reasonable income. He drove big expensive cars and funded his hobby of car racing, it was only hot-rodding but to Paul it may well have been Formula 1.

Paul became known as Juan Fangio on the hot rod circuit, after the Argentinean driver who won Formula 1 Championships for fun in those days. More precisely, Paul told everyone on the circuit that he was its Juan Fangio after winning the only race he ever won in Plymouth back in the sixties. He still kept an expensive interest in car racing but his driving days were long gone, the thrill now was building the cars and watching them race. He had done all right in that respect, won quite a few races, not big ones, but big enough for him.

He owned the yard and workshop where he ran his business from and paid Billygoat to put in a shower and toilet in the rooms above. Paul would sleep there whenever he worked late which was often. He seldom worked on Sundays and the rest of the staff never did, except African Henry who was always around the place.

Paul had just finished fixing a reconditioned engine in a Honda. African Henry was polishing a five-year-old Ford ready for putting out for sale on the forecourt. That was another line of Paul's business, buying and selling cars. He usually went to the car auction on Friday mornings in North Wales but he had to give it a miss with his sister home from America and preparations for the party.

Paul employed two other people, Paul had known Lloydy, a genius with bodywork, since they were kids, and Donald, a Guyanese ex-RAF man, who was the only qualified car mechanic at PL Motors but he liked to chat too much. Paul had taken on Lolly as a Trainee because. Lolly's grandmother, Mrs. Beckles, had pleaded to give him a chance. He was a good worker was Lolly, the keenest in the shop. Maybe Paul would leave the garage to him when he died. African Henry should have been his heir as he was Paul's main man, but African Henry loved his liquor too much and the business would fold if he were left in charge. Paul had been thinking about his mortality since his 45th birthday. He had been diagnosed diabetic last year, his smoking was excessive and he was carrying too much weight.

Nobby the plasterer was passing by and dropped in for a moan about times being hard and his missus was still spending money like water. He also told Paul and African Henry there were burning buildings, looted shops and barricades everywhere.

"The people have taken over the streets," Nobby said with trepidation.

When Nobby added that the Racquet Club was also on fire, immediately Paul jumped into his car and drove off with no explanation. Paul felt it was too good a chance to miss, thinking that he might be able to salvage something from the fire, something nice to put into his above-the-shop abode. Within minutes of leaving his garage, he had parked his car outside the large grey stone building.

Paul had been inside the Racquet Club once before, albeit very briefly. The only person he knew that had ever gone inside its august portals. Paul was astonished by the lavishness or gob-smacked, as he put it when recounting his discovery to others, the otherworldliness of it all with its sweeping staircase, large paintings of the upper classes at play from bygone days, leather chairs and chandeliers and acres of polished wood. Paul was putting a leaflet advertising his business through the letterbox when he noticed the front door was open. He went inside and had time to look briefly at most of the ground floor rooms until someone came and quickly ushered him out.

Pure Pressure

The Racquet Club opened in 1877 as a 'Gentlemen's' Club with a sporting twist (Racquets Courts and American Bowling) on Upper Parliament Street, right in the middle of the ghetto, yet close to the grand town houses of the Georgian quarter a few of hundred yards away. With a membership drawn from all over the North West and beyond, there had never been a black member, not even the great John Archer in his prime could have got in.

Upper Parliament Street was full of people, like a carnival but quieter and more sinister. The Racquet Club was indeed on fire, flames fanning out of the shattered downstairs windows. Down the road, the copper cupola roof of the Rialto building was glowing with the flames that surrounded it.

Paul walked gingerly towards the Club trying to avoid the debris strewn all over the street. He saw Bobby Harrison creep up behind Lewis Green and crash a piece of limestone on the back of his head. That was probably for Lewis sleeping with Bobby's wife while he was in jail. Lewis staggered to the floor blood streaming from the wound. In normal circumstances, Paul would have intervened or at least come to Lewis's rescue but he had bigger fish to fry and time was short.

Paul looked down at his feet to see he was walking across one of those large canvas paintings he had spotted s few years ago on that first brief visit, but shorn of its frame and ripped across the middle. What a waste, probably worth thousands, he thought, as he climbed the small railings fronting the building and peeped through the broken window into the large dining room. He knocked the rest of the glass from a window pane and scrambled through the window, reckoning he probably had a couple of minutes to get in and out safely before the flames overwhelmed the room.

Only one of the three chandeliers was still hanging from the ornate ceiling, the rest were lying shattered across the floor. The long table with the white cloth and been turned over and chairs thrown on top of it to look like a Bonfire Night pyre, hissing and spitting threateningly and discharging clouds of black smoke. The heat was so fierce and the smoke so dense that Paul had to retreat. However, determined not to leave empty-handed, he grabbed two mahogany chairs with dark green leather seats and backrests and placed them carefully, one at a time, outside the window. He ordered one of the young lads standing around to help him load the chairs into the back seat of his car.

Paul heard a familiar two-tone whistle and turned to see Alan outside the next door building, the old people's hospital (known locally as the home of the incurables because apparently nobody came out of there alive) as it was being evacuated by ambulance and police personnel with Alan and others escorting them through.

"That's ar' kid, the community leader," thought Paul proudly, as he waved to him.

A groggy and bloodied Lewis Green was among the procession of older people escorted to the two ambulances as he staggered onto one of the ambulances before they sped off with blue lights flashing.

African Henry was in the process of locking up the garage when Paul returned, as proud of his booty as a Genghis Khan marauder. African Henry told him there were two phone calls but he did not get to the phone in time to answer them as he was still working, adding pointedly "working on a Sunday night, ha."

African Henry rebuked him about not going to *Quicksave* supermarket to bring back some booze. After dropping off his precious chairs, Paul drove to Smithdown Road looking for liquor. On the way there, they were surprised to notice half of the shops on Lodge Lane were ransacked and some were on fire.

"Hey dis is fingy, man," Paul said to African Henry as he slowed down to avoid various obstacles littering the road. "Any minute now and you expec' some guy to come out fingyin' a Tommy gun; it's like in de movies."

When they reached the supermarket, there were dozens of people spewing out of the shop carrying all manner of goods. One of the younger Bootmans ("they all look alike in that family," said Paul), dressed in shorts and tee shirt made no attempt to hide his face as he wheeled away two large trolleys full of bottles of spirits and liqueurs. There really was no need to hide your face, as there was nobody there except the looters. The neighbourhood had been hi-jacked by its residents; for the first time in their lives, they had taken control of their neighbourhood.

"What an opportunity," Paul thought, a unique opportunity and everyone was taking a piece of it.

"Dis is a revolution," said African Henry, "so let we enjoy it while 'im last."

An empty-handed elderly white woman asked young Bootman if he had any Drambuie as she had not had any since her husband died ten years ago. Young Bootman searched briefly in one of the trolleys and fished out the requested article. She thanked young Bootman profusely and calmly walked away clutching the bottle like it was a newborn baby; Paul would swear blind when he retold the tale that the old lady was kissing the bottle and talking to it. "My little Drambuie," he quoted her as saying, "I'm going to take you to a good home."

Paul pulled rank on young Bootman and commandeered one of the trolleys. African Henry quickly filled the boot of the car and they drove off.

Paul carried the chairs up to the flat, so pleased that the chairs were in mint condition, whilst African Henry was carefully transferring the bottles from the boot into carrier bags so that none broke.

Paul placed each chair against the wall next to each other and stood back to admire them. The chairs did not particularly match the rest of the sparsely furnished room, but then few of the rest matched each other: The burgundy leather chesterfield sofa he bought last year belonged to a much larger room. The highly polished red wood coffee table from Angola was bare apart from a 6 inch thick Concise Oxford Dictionary and a well-worn English/Cantonese dictionary. The dictionaries and *Hot Rod* magazines were the only literature in the flat. Paul was not an avid reader, he never bought newspapers as he got all his news from television and radio, and from African Henry of course, who knew everything about current issues. The final piece of furniture was Paul's centrepiece, an exquisitely carved and lacquered Chinese cabinet from Shanxi he had shipped over from China when he went in search of his roots three years ago. It had cost him a lot of money, so much so that he was too embarrassed to tell people the true price. Not even African Henry knew. The coffee table had a tale to tell. Paul bought it when he was in Angola where he and two friends had gone to volunteer to fight for the Angolan government and the Cubans during the war against the South Africans. Jolla Walker, Dave Ankrah and Paul drove all the way from Liverpool. Dave did not quite make it as he fell in love with a young woman with generous lips and plump hips in Senegal when the car packed up whilst they were waiting to get a lift from a cargo ship to Angola. Dave stayed in Senegal and then the Gambia for two years with that young woman but had to get repatriated back home because by then he was destitute.

Jolla and Paul spent nine months in the Angolan Army. Paul learnt to speak Portuguese rather well, Jolla less so. They were mainly driving trucks and did not kill anybody but they saw enough danger, misery and death in those few months to last a lifetime. Paul would have stayed longer, but Jolla caught malaria and was very sick so they came home to a hero's welcome. A special welcoming party held at the *Carousel* pub on Myrtle Street raised £75 for an Angolan charity. The family were all there, all the boys also, some he had not seen for years. Uncle Lenny brought some white lefties. That was the first night Paul met African Henry.

If only he could write a book what a lot he would have to say, Paul often said. Maybe Uncle Lenny or Alan could put it in proper English, he contemplated, and it would sell in its thousands.

The walls of the flat were bare except for a burgundy coloured framed (to match the settee) print of William Windus' *The Black Boy*; Paul had seen the original picture at the Walkers Art Gallery in town and was mesmerised by it. He did not care much for the clothes the boy wore, but the boy's honest face, button nose and wide forehead looked a bit like him when he was younger.

Next to the *Black Boy* was a Chinese calendar from the Peking Duck restaurant and next to that an unframed black and white photo tacked to the wall next to the calendar. The photo was of African Henry and Paul, both smiling broadly, with Arnold Dyson in the middle taken outside the gym Arnold ran on Princes Road. Arnold was once Mr. Universe; he was the strongest man in the world in 1953 and a good friend, Paul told everyone, although it was a fair bet that Arnold Dyson did not know Paul Leung from Adam.

There was a strong smell of lemon air-refresher about the place and everything was neat and orderly, the Leung way. The adjacent room was just about large enough for a double bed and a small rosewood wardrobe he inherited from his Uncle Kwok.

"I hope you're taking those bottles home," Paul said impatiently to Henry as he struggled with three carrier bags full of bottles. "I don't want them around littering the place."

Paul grabbed Henry by the shoulders and kissed him hard on the lips, with angry passion.

African Henry pulled away.

"You forget how to kiss," Henry said wryly.

"Leave it," Paul replied edgily. "Juss fuck off home and leave me, okay? And leave any brandy and vodka bottles behind."

As soon as African Henry left with his stash, Paul switched on the television and watched Liverpool 8 burning and being looted on the 10 o'clock news.

"*CS gas, commonly known as tear gas, was deployed for the first time on the British mainland to help quell the rioting in the Liverpool district of Toxteth. Dozens of buildings including businesses were on fire, some of them completely destroyed It is reported that the fire and ambulance services have been prevented from entering the areas by missile-throwing youths . . .*"

"Yer lie, fuckin' liars," Paul shouted at the television.

"*Our special correspondent Richard Clerkwell-Smith reports directly from Toxteth . . . Residents were forced to use fire hoses abandoned by fire-fighters fleeing rioting youths . . .*"

A film of civilians with fire hoses dousing a building was showing on the screen. Paul put on his glasses and immediately recognised his brother Alan, then Maureen Ajayi's son and Bobo Jones from the Jaycee. Paul quickly switched on the VHS tape recorder to record the image but just as quickly, the picture had gone and replaced with that of a very senior police officer with so many stars on his shoulders he looked like the night sky had descended on his shoulders. With a wry grin, the very senior police officer promised to restore law and order.

"There are no no-go areas in Liverpool," he said forcefully

Paul rang his mother's house but there was no answer.

He looked up in the yellow pages for the BBC.

" . . . Hundreds of police officers are reported to be injured and hundreds of arrests have been made since the rioting began on Friday night . . ."

Paul gave up trying to find out how to get a copy of the news film after ringing three different numbers; he would try again tomorrow.

He switched channels until he found other news programmes.

"Toxteth is aflame . . ."

"What's wid all this 'Toxteth' business," he asked the newscaster, "it's the Souffend, not Toxteth, it's Liverpool 8; fuck Toxteth!"

Chapter 10

Keep On Moving

1:30am Sunday 5th July 1981

Dion had fallen asleep fully dressed on the armchair watching a video on the TV set in the living room as he often did at week-ends after everyone had gone to bed. Woken by the sounds of a commotion—shouts, a crash and more shouts—he opened his eyes and looked around the room. The flashing, snowy crackling television screen lighted the room. The noise was out in the street and sounded like it was some distance away. In the shadows, he could make out the sleeping silhouette of his grandfather stretched out on the sofa. Dion switched off the television and slightly parted the curtains. He peered out at the dark familiar street opposite lined with maisonettes and flats. Dion thought the noise might have come from St Saviours School across the street but there was no one there. The street was deserted. He closed back the curtains and went to the front door, opened it and gingerly stepped outside. About two hundred yards to his left, past the estate, he could see an overturned car burning in the middle of Upper Parliament Street and could barely make out silhouettes throwing objects at the flaming car. He looked at his digital watch (a fourteenth birthday present from Mum and Dad), and was surprised how late it was: one hour, thirty two minutes and seventeen seconds past midnight precisely. He peered over at his Granddad, assured himself that he was still asleep, slipped his trainers on over bare feet and eased the front door shut behind him, putting the lock on the latch so he could get back in without a key. There would be hell if they found out, but both Granddad and Dad were heavy sleepers and early risers so would not know he was gone.

Dion ran at breakneck speed towards the road junction keeping his focus on the burning car, anticipation welling up in his chest. The car had crashed into the traffic light and thick black smoke rose in plumes from the wreck. The flames were fizzing and dancing, lighting up the dark street and the people standing around it. There were more than two dozen people looking at the fire with practiced disdain.

Dion recognised a few of the lads standing around the vehicle; there were mostly older than him and they barely noticed him and did not acknowledge his greeting. He stood in the middle of the road, feeling the heat of the flames licking his face with a giant dry tongue. Hands in pockets, eyes bright and wide, he waited for the fire engines to come and do their heroic duty as they surely would.

Anytime now, the firemen would announce themselves with screaming sirens and flashing lights, with their smart uniforms and brusque manners, like in a film on TV.

The authorities would have to take this car off the street straight away because it was in the middle of the busiest road in the area and he would want to watch that as well when it happened.

The sound of shrieking tyres startled Dion and he turned around to see a car careering at speed directly towards him. At the wheel was a boy from the estate, Big Johnny, bare-breasted, a waving arm out of the window. Big Johnny was always a bit of a show off.

Dion had no time to react except to close his eyes tight shut and brace himself and wait for the impact but none came. The car had swerved away, spun back to front and stopped, like in the films, its back wheel a couple of inches away from Dion's feet. The car roared off back up the road, its tyres singing in the night.

Big Johnny had now acquired an audience including a few middle-aged drinkers straggling from the Dressler Club. Gathering speed the car veered on to two wheels, clipping the sidewalk, and zigzagged in Dion's direction. Dion ran to the other side of the burning car for protection and watched the car crash into the burning wreck. Big Johnny emerged from the crushed car smiling and waving his arms like a racing driver after winning an important race, but it was hard to tell whether he was limping because he injured himself or because he was just doing the Granby Walk. Dion was impressed.

One tall boy threw a bottle half-full of liquid at the car and like a grenade exploded in a ball of yellow flames. Dion recognised the missile as a Molotov cocktail, having read about them in modern history. He stood there just watching the fire slowly and loudly overwhelm the cars until the fire had almost burned out. Warped brown and grey metal was all that remained from the cars and still the Fire Brigade did not arrive. As there was no fire to put out now so Dion decided to go home. As he turned to walk away, he saw them. Dozens of policemen, three lines of them, advancing slowly up the street behind large see-through shields. They were banging their shields as they advanced hoping the noise would intimidate the youths.

"Pigs!" someone shouted.

"Fuckin' pigs!" shouted another.

"Come on den," dared another.

Out of nowhere, it seemed to Dion, a barrage of bricks, pieces of concrete and iron railings took to the air and landed on the shields with echoing thuds. The shield banging ceased but still the police lines marched forward.

Crowds of young men came out of side streets, most of the faces Dion had never seen before. Some of the youths had broken into the milk depot where Dion's Dad worked and taken out milk floats which they then drove at the police. The leading float was on fire and, as it crashed against the shields, a ball of flame sprang up and scorched the police lines. There were flashes of light coming from cameras. Dion was sure these men were journalists, they wanted a show, and they were getting it, thought Dion; the photographs would be in all the papers.

One after the other the floats were set alight and driven straight at the police lines with the drivers jumping out at the last minute. The flames ignited a few shields put they were soon extinguished. The police lines continued advancing.

A large earth digger chugged along from the top of the street. The police line stood firm until the machine came within feet and then the line broke up in disarray as more missiles came raining down.

Dion watched as the youths ran after the police and melted in the darkness until he could just make out some animated silhouettes. He was disappointed the police did not stand their ground and fight back, after all these were only kids. He was about to make his way home when another fire caught his eye. The tyre shop was ablaze. This was the largest fire Dion had ever seen. The whole building was aflame and tyres were exploding sending multi-coloured flares up in the sky. Dion ran towards the building marvelling at the explosion of colours brightening the ink dark night but could not get any closer than fifty feet because of the choking black smoke. He stood still and stared at this gigantic bonfire. He had heard on the news about a huge fireworks display in central London to celebrate the engagement of Prince Charles and Lady Diana. Dion was certain that the exploding tyres on Upper Parliament Street rivalled the royal show.

The black smoke engulfed him and he became afraid. The time was four o'clock, seventeen minutes and twenty-four seconds and daylight was breaking out. Dion had never been outside the house at such time, ever. His father would be up for work any moment now. He reluctantly left the scene and ran all the way home as fast as he could.

As he lay in his bed in total darkness, Dion could feel his heart was still racing wildly. This had been the most exciting night in his life. He was sure all the debris would be cleared up by the time he got up and it would be as if it had never happened except perhaps for the car carcasses, the wrecked milk floats and the burned down buildings.

Dion sighed, still caught up in the excitement of the events he had witnessed. He relived it again, remembering and storing in his mind every detail—the flames yellow, white, green and red and the smoke thick and all encompassing, the fizzling sound of the paint in flames like fireworks, and Big Johnny and his pals' road show. It was a huge disappointment to Dion that no fireman turned up for the blaze. Maybe one day when he grew up he would become a fireman in the city of Liverpool. That would be something. That would make everybody at school envious of him. Duncan Forrester, his worstest of worstest enemy, would wish he was him, Dion Ajayi-Smith, the fearless fireman with his helmet and his uniform with shiny buttons and big leather boots, and the fire hose, 'fighting fires and saving lives'. That's what it said on the recruitment poster for firemen on the wall above Dion's bed and under Howie Gayle's photograph ('*Liverpool Football Club's first black footballer*' and Dion's current hero).

"Howie Gayle, the quickest player in the Liverpool, squad, the quickest man in the whole of the football league," he would tell his Evertonian friends with relish.

He looked at his luminous watch under the blankets. Four thirty-nine and twenty eight seconds, Dad's alarm clock would go off soon.

The alarm clock went off at 5 o'clock precisely, this being Sunday, one hour later than other days. Within two minutes, Colin was bouncing round the walls. He was at his best early in the morning that's why he was a milkman. Although he had gone to bed late watching videos with Dion, when the alarm went off he sprang out of bed like a jack in the box. He was a different man from that first waking moment, full of energy and in control until he clocked off six hours later.

Today was a special day for the Smith family, the Christening of their very first grand child. Maxine and the baby had gone away on a Gingerbread trip to the Lake District but there was some problem with the minibus and instead of coming back yesterday, they were now due in at 10 this morning, less than three hours before the event.

Maureen had been in bed all day yesterday, recovering from her gambling binge. They would all go to St Bernard's church at quarter to one and then to the restaurant in Granby Street for the dinner.

Colin was thirty-nine, born and bred in Liverpool 8, four years older than Maureen, thin, five foot five with balding wispy fair hair. He had never been to a *'rest-o-rant'* before and he was looking forward to showing off his new black Chelsea boots and the blue silk tie Maureen had bought especially to wear for the ceremony. He was relieved that Maureen was there lying next to him fast asleep when he woke up. He thought she might have sneaked off to go gambling again, she had done it before. He had known her to stay in them places 24 hours non-stop and come back home stone broke and deeply depressed. However, she was a gambler when he first met her just after leaving school when she used to put her mother's bets on for her and have one herself, and he reckoned she would die a gambler. That is just the way she was. Colin had never gambled in his life, he was not a man to take risks.

He boiled himself two eggs, five minutes exactly, soft but not runny, with two rounds of buttered toast and a full pint of creamy sweet tea in his grubby but much-loved plastic mug that he had bought for himself with his first pay packet all those years ago. The mug had a dent where the plastic had melted because Maureen has left it too close to the cooker's flame and it had lost much of its colour. He had to rescue the mug a few times from the bin where Maureen had consigned it. Colin loved that mug; sweet tea did not taste as good in any other receptacle.

"It's like a friggin' idol that mug," Maureen told him once. "If you were a Nigerian man I'd swear it was juju; I dunno why you juss don't throw the friggin' manky fing away."

Colin would not swop his mug for a full Meissen tea set; some things you just have to hold on to.

After breakfast, he had a quick shave and rinsed his face with cold water, always cold water to close the pores and save getting spots. That is what he had been used to and that is what he advised Maureen to do to get rid of her awful skin but he guessed her skin was too far gone for that. He slipped on his uniform; a short-sleeved light blue shirt and navy blue trousers. You had to wear your own shoes and they had to be black and proper shoes, no trainers; management were strict on that.

Colin dressed quietly mindful of not disturbing Her Royal Highness, Queen Maureen. He glanced in the wardrobe mirror, pleased that everything was as it should be and tip toed down the stairs. He made two cups of tea. His cup was weak and milky with two sugars and Dad's black with no sugar because of his diabetes. Dad liked waking up with the sun in the summer with a nice cup of tea. It was one of the perks of having to give up his bedroom to Maxine and the baby;

Pure Pressure

he got his first cup of the day prepared for him. Colin felt deeply embarrassed about Dad having to sleep on the couch. In making Dad give up his bedroom, Maureen had shown a dark side that he did not suspect she possessed. Colin had seen it coming when she took down the photograph of Dad shaking hands with Bessie Braddock, the local MP, from the sideboard in the living-room wall. It was taken in the town hall and Dad looked a real gentleman with his dark suit, white shirt and neat tie. A big row ensued. Maureen said she was fed up looking at that woman on the wall. Bessie Braddock was a misplaced hero for black people, she affirmed, because she voted for an immigration act that stopped black people from settling in UK and she had voted for the rearmament of Germany. Dad defended the MP saying she had always supported black people in Liverpool.

Colin suspected that Dad regretted now having passed the ownership of the house over to Maureen to save having to pay the taxman when he died. Out of guilt Maureen had suggested to Dad that he could sleep in Maxine's room (Maxine's room!) while she was away for the weekend but out of pride Dad had refused. Colin had called Nathaniel Ajayi Dad from when he first met him; Nat was that kind of man and because he looked like a Dad. To be honest he looked like a Granddad but calling him Granddad would have been disrespectful.

Nat lay on the couch by the kitchen door covered with a blanket. He reached out for his glasses on the chair next to the sofa.

"Tank you, Colin; you make best tea in Liverpool," Nat said wanting to smile but avoiding to until he had put his teeth in.

"I bet you say that to everybody, Dad," Colin said smiling openly.

The telephone rang. Instantly Colin thought something terrible had happened to Maxine and the baby; maybe the minibus had crashed. Maybe they were badly injured or even dead. He rushed for the phone dreading the worse.

"Hello Colin," the voice said.

"Who's that," Colin said tentatively.

"It's Graham from the depot. There's been some trouble in Parliament Street. Nigger kids have been riotin' like bloody savages. The police have advised us not to open the depot, it's too dangerous."

Colin was trying to filter the information in his mind and make sense of it.

"What do you mean '*nigger kids acting like bloody savages*'? My kids are black, don't you forget that."

This was not the first time he had to object to racist language at work. No black people had ever worked there and racist banter was normal practice. Eighteen men and two women worked at the dairy all of them white and in the middle of Liverpool 8. It took him years to summon up the courage to start directly challenging their racism; he had to get the union involved because the managers were just as bad as the workers were. Because of his stance, Colin took his breaks on his own or with Denise in the office who was married to a Malaysian man and sympathised.

"Look Col," Graham replied apologetically, jerked out of the monotony of repeating the same message eleven times so far with three to go, "I'm just repeatin' what Jim said to me, don't shoot the bloody messenger, mate. Anyway, the management are keepin' the depot closed until further notice; you don't have to turn in today. The management are reviewin' the situation and'll probably call a meetin' on Monday. We'll let you know. You'll still get paid but not Sunday rates. Okay?"

The phone went dead before Colin had time to reply.

"The bloody cheek," Colin cursed with pursed lips.

Nathaniel Garba Ajayi limped into the hall dressed in his pyjamas. A 68 years old man, medium height, thin, dark skinned, white balding hair with a small greying Hitler-type moustache and thick-rimmed glasses perched on the end of a broad nose.

"Whassa matta, twuble," Nat asked Colin.

"It's the depot, Dad. There's been riotin' on Parly and they're keepin' the depot closed."

"I dun 'ear nuttin'," Nat replied, "dem pay am?"

"Yeah, but normal rates; I'll talk to me union about dat on Mundee."

"Who was that on the phone, was it our Maxine?" Maureen shouted from upstairs.

"No, it's the depot," Colin shouted back. "There's been trouble on Parly and they've told me not to go in."

"Are they paying you?"

"Yeah, but at normal rates," Colin shouted back. "I'll see the union about that first thing Mundee morning. I dunno how long I'm gonna be off for, I'm due in right fru to Fursdee."

"Yeah, I know. Didn't they tell you what happened," Maureen shouted back.

"Keep yua noise, gal; yua de wake Deeo!" said Nat in a loud whisper.

Maxine and Martin arrived at the house at 10.30. Maxine had a quick bath, complaining the water was cold because Maureen had used up all the water, and changed into her best dress, a cute pink number with a low cleavage, and dressed Martin in a white fluffy woollen suit with false pearls sewed all over it made especially by Martine Goolsby, the best clothes maker in the neighbourhood.

Nat wore the worn black baggy suit he had worn on special occasions for the past thirty years, a white shirt that was now two sizes too big for him around the neck, his black brogues and a tie that dazzled in its multi-colourings.

Maureen wore a long blue dress with black patterns on the collar and cuffs bought when the family had holidayed in Lagos eight years previously and only worn twice since. Colin wore his grey suit with the electric iron scorch mark on the sleeve, and a white shirt with a blue silk tie. Dion wore his Liverpool Football Club tracksuit and strutted around as if he was Howie Gayle himself.

They all crammed into Maureen's tired car and chugged off reaching the church with seconds to spare. A crowd of relatives and friends were loitering outside. The Murphys (Maureen's family on her mother's side) were out in force and dolled up to the nines; dolled up in their parlance involved a lot of gold; no shiny yellow metal passing off for gold for them, not when the family numbered some of the most prolific shoplifters and pickpockets on Merseyside. Whenever there was a family religious event—wedding, funeral, christening or communion—it was guaranteed the Murphys would turn up gang-handed.

It was not just the free food and free booze the Murphys came for as they always contributed generously to the food and alcohol kitty. It was a chance for them to pray, and sing and dance, '*en famille*'.

The doyen of the Murphy family was Uncle Albert. Aged 65, but his bent body, heavily lined vividly florid face and his sad eyes suggested he was 15 years older. Uncle Albert was wearing what many took to be his demob suit (light grey stripes on a dark grey background, straight out of the pawnshop and going right back in on Monday morning until the next family gathering). Double-breasted tight-fitting jacket and baggy trousers with a turn up that had collected all manner of debris over the years. Uncle Albert's suit was oddly set off with a flash pair of cracked black and white patent leather shoes that looked older than the suit. The suit might have been sober but Uncle Albert certainly was not. Glassy-eyed and three alcohol units away from bursting into song and dance, four units from turning nasty and abusive and five units from slipping into a coma. Luckily, since he developed emphysema, Uncle Albert had given up his 60 roll-ups-a-day smoking habit, because a match lit within close vicinity of his breath would have caused an explosion that surely would have blown half of Liverpool 8 away.

The Murphys called themselves the Radcliffe Estate mob (evacuated from the Four Squares in the seventies, the toughest estate in the North End), to emphasise their geographical credentials. They consisted of Uncle Albert, Aunty Franna, Aunty Maria, Aunty Bernadette, Aunty Aida and Aunty Teresa and a dozen of their assorted children most of whom were carrying colourfully wrapped presents and greeting cards in envelopes.

It was quite a crowd with five of Nat's old African friends, some with their young partners or wives; Colin's mother and father looking positively sedate. Denise, Colin's work colleague, and her husband Anwar were there also. Cilla Jenkins, in her wheelchair with Chantelle her waif-like daughter, was outside the church gates. They just happened to be passing when Cilla saw the crowd of people waiting in the warm sunshine outside the church. Never one to spurn an opportunity when it presented itself, Cilla Jenkins made a killing, successfully begging almost as much money from the congregation as the church received in its collection boxes that day.

Baby Martin's godparents and Jimmy Freeman, baby Martin's boy-father, were already inside the church, waiting agitatedly for the ceremony to begin. Outside the church, the crowd murmured appreciatively as Maxine emerged from the car clutching her baby, some of the Murphys applauded.

The Priest, Father Eustace, looked a robust and convivial man who enjoyed his food and drink. He was dressed in long shiny garments and was making eye contact with everyone, nodding at regulars and frowning slightly at those who only to came to church for special occasions like these. He led a small procession of choristers and ushers up the aisle, climbed four stone steps and turned to face the congregation.

"Dearly beloved," he began solemnly, "we are honoured with the privilege of being present here today to witness and support in faith the baptism of . . ."

Father Eustace consulted a list.

"Martin James Colin Nathaniel, Pascal Daniel, Marie, Maria, Suzanne, and Mary Mabel Eve. Quite a mouthful of names here on this blessed day," he said with a grin. "You have been invited here as family and friends as your prayers and spiritual support in the life of . . . [he consulted the list again] . . . Martin James Colin Nathaniel, Pascal Daniel, Marie, Suzanne, and Mary Mabel Eve. It has been said that in a Baptism . . .

"You've left out Maria, Father," shouted a female voice at the back.

"And Maria," Father Eustace continued with a nod, "It has been said that in a Baptism Heaven comes down and surrounds . . ."

This time Father Eustace read out the names very slowly.

" . . . Martin James Colin Nathaniel, Pascal Daniel, Marie, Maria, Suzanne and Mary Mabel Eve with God's love for which the effect is lifelong, we join our thoughts and sincere goodwill, asking that Christ's peace might embrace these families and an arc of God's light surround these children for all of their days."

"Martin. Where did they get the name from?" Uncle Albert asked Aunty Franna from the corner of his mouth.

He got a frown for an answer.

"They shoulda called it Albert after meself, a good Cat'lic name."

Uncle Albert had a peculiar way of talking, like a ventriloquist; he spoke from the side of his mouth, his lips barely moving. It was a legacy from being in prison when it was forbidden for inmates to speak to each other, so, like ventriloquists, they learnt to speak without appearing to speak and Uncle Albert had it down to a pat.

"Shshshsh," shushed Aunty Bernadette.

"The baby's named after a saint. Saint Martin was black you know," whispered Aunty Franna. "The only black Saint there ever was I tink."

"Dat's awrigh' den is it, named after a nigger Saint," said Uncle Albert.

Aunty Franna was going to tell him to wash his mouth out with carbolic soap and holy water but Aunty Bernadette's impatient "Shshshsh" put an end to that sentence before it came out.

Aunty Aida shushed Aunty Bernadette and pretty soon everyone was shshshshing everyone else.

The choir started hymning:

> *"Come down, O Love divine,*
> *Seek thou this soul of mine,*
> *And visit it with thine own ardour glowing;*
> *O comforter, draw near,*
> *Within my heart appear,*
> *And kindle it, thy holy flame bestowing."*

The Murphy Aunts sang the hymn word perfect without looking at their hymnbook.

"Sounds very sexual to me dis hymn," said Uncle Albert to everyone on his row, emphasising his point with a wink and a giggle. "Ardour glowing. Ardour? Bloody cock glowing, dat's wharrit means. Holy flame bestowing, me arse, dat means shooting yer bloody load, dat's wharrit means."

Aunty Franna, standing next to Uncle Albert, raised the level of her singing voice to drown his out.

"O let it freely burn," she sang

Uncle Albert started giggling which brought on a cough.

"Crooua, crooua," coughed Uncle Albert.

Uncle Albert's coughing fit, suspiciously keeping a steady rhythm and sounding like a bullfrog with laryngitis, counterpointed the female Murphys' high voices.

Till earthly . . . crooua, crraaa, . . . passions turn

To dust and ashes, in its . . . crooua, crraaa, craaa . . . heat consuming;

And let . . . crooua, crraaa, craaa . . . thy glorious light . . . ."

Maureen's eyes had become moist as soon as she entered the church. The ceremony brought back memories of Maxine's christening. Eighteen years did not seem that long ago. Eighteen years had just flashed by, half of her life, a quarter of the rest of her life, gone forever. Then she saw Shep-from-Ohio's face, blankly staring at her, open-mouthed.

"I could go to jail for 10 or 15 years," she thought and her eyes dried up. Maureen was convinced she would die in jail. The stress would kill her for sure.

The feeling of doom that rose within her tasted bitter. She turned and looked at Colin seated next to her, pretending to sing.

Maureen thought Colin's body was not suited to a suit; denims and any old jumper were his constants. He had loosened his tie and the top button of his shirt.

She nudged him and whispered, "fasten yer tie it looks terrible. Loosen it when we get out, after the photographs."

"It's bloody hot in here," Colin pleaded. "The collar's too tight to fasten the button," he explained to her.

Maureen decided at that moment that she could no longer live with Colin. She respected him for being a good father to the children and for being a hard worker, in and out of the house, but alas, there was no future for them as a couple, she had suddenly come to realise. She wanted more than devotion from him; she wanted to devote her self to him but could not, not anymore. She needed someone to be devoted to, someone she could be in love with, someone like Bonny Roberts. She also knew then that she had to fall in love before another eighteen years passed or her life would be wasted and unfulfilled. Colin was not in love with her either, she knew that much. Obedient, certainly, full marks for obedience; three bags full of obedience and devotion was Colin Smith. They may as well split up, Maureen reasoned. This sudden realisation seemed to lift her spirits, and she began to sing with the others, her voice getting stronger with each verse.

"In the name of the Father, and of the Son, and of the Holy Spirit," said Father Eustace.

"Amen," responded Maureen louder than anybody else did.

"Let us pray," invited Father Eustace. "Heavenly Father, by the power of your Holy Spirit you give to your faithful people new life in the water of baptism. Guide and strengthen us by the same Spirit, that we who are born . . ."

Several people began to giggle at Uncle Albert as he fell asleep slumped on his chair a low rumbling noise oozing out of his mouth. Aunty Franna gave him a shove that made him fall to his knees.

Father Eustace carried on valiantly with just a slight raising of an eyebrow in Uncle Albert's direction to communicate his displeasure.

These distractions displeased Maureen, spoiling this most important of days. Uncle Albert falling asleep was not totally unexpected, in fact Maureen would be quite happy if that was the worst thing he did today given his track record for creating havoc at family gatherings. Aunty Franna, the eldest of her aunts and the one she least got on with, did not have to push old Uncle Albert off his chair that hard, that was just bullying; but it was the giggling that annoyed Maureen most, it just threatened to turn the whole thing, the key family event of the year, into a farce. Maureen sought out and silenced the gigglers with withering stares.

"Jesus gave unto us two great commandments, which we should strive in heart and mind to obey. Both are of Love. Love God with all our hearts. Love others, as we would have others love us. These two things our Lord and Saviour Jesus Christ commands of us . . ." intoned Father Eustace.

One of the babies at the altar began to cry. Maureen was not sure if it was Pascal Daniel, Marie, Maria, Suzanne or Mary Mabel Eve, but it sure as hell was not her little Martin. He knew how to behave in public; he was an Ajayi.

"As Godparents to Martin James Colin Nathaniel," Father Eustace said to Michael Freeman, Jimmy's cousin who looked barely 16, and Becky Thorpe, Maxine's best friend, tiny and dressed all in white, including white shoes with vertiginous high heels that still did not get her past the five foot high mark.

"God will give you the wisdom and ability to hold within your heart forever the spiritual welfare of this child. You are charged with the responsibility of seeing to the spiritual welfare of this child should the need arise and it is you who stands as spiritual counsellors. Do you accept this duty and charge?"

"We do," they said in perfect unison, like a well-rehearsed accappella duo.

"Do you promise to love, honour, support and encourage Martin James Colin Nathaniel throughout his life?"

"We do," Michael and Becky repeated as if they had been saying it all their lives.

"As Godparents to Pascal Daniel, God will give you the wisdom and ability to hold within your heart forever the spiritual welfare of this child . . ."

Felicia Goolsby-Power-Wright had stuck bunches of white balloons on the walls with tape and given firm instructions to Solly to play only her tapes, none of your avant-garde stuff she told him, it wasn't appropriate for a christening party. Gary had yet to turn up as usual although he was on his final warning. She thought Gary was probably part of the mobs that rioted until the early hours on Upper Parliament Street.

Solly had turned up at eight o'clock on the dot, as instructed, but she had to send him home. It was his dress. Very short and very tight beige shorts and what was meant to be a white, or rather off-white, or, to be blunt, a dirty cream poncho that was really a bed sheet with a crude hole in the middle for his head and two cruder holes for his arms. The Army and Navy industrial black boots he wore—the toe caps of which he had whitened—looked as if they weighed more than he did.

"You can't work in me restaurant dressed like that, Solly," she told him exasperatedly, "and you can't wear the white boiler suit you wore yesterday because it is full of stains. Go back home and find the cleanest, most respectable clothes you possess and wear them. They don't have to be white; it's not you getting christened and you're not Eric."

The cleanest most respectable clothes Solly possessed turned out to be 11 year old silver grey bell-bottomed trousers and a five year old sleeveless, garishly coloured fair-isle sweater and a pair of light brown canvas shoes; very 70s but respectable for working in a restaurant Solly assured her.

"What you need," she said to him, "is a good woman to teach you how to dress."

"Are you offering?" he asked boldly.

"Solly! I'm a married woman."

"Not as a wife," he laughed. "I wouldn't know what to do with a wife, but as a friend who could guide me like."

"Yeah, sure, when you've got some money saved I'll come to town with you and help you choose some clothes that'll suit you; deal?"

"Deal," he agreed with a grin. "I've £38.76 saved in me Post Office account."

"That'll do it," she assured him. "Your shoes are nice, even though they don't go with the rest."

They shook hands by way of conclusion.

The Christening party came in at 2.30 as planned, a few minutes before Gary came in with not one word of apology for his lateness. There were 25 of them including the baby when Maureen had only booked for 18. Felicia did not complain, the more the merrier said her electric cash register.

The *Spices* restaurant was unlicensed, therefore Maureen brought alcohol from the off-license a few doors up. A couple of crates of beer for the white men, fortified wine for the white women, sweet white wine for the black women, Cola, Sarsaparilla and Lemonade for the kids, whisky for the African men, *Spices*' own carrot, mango and pineapple juices for the teetotallers and strong black coffee for Uncle Albert.

Later on after everyone had finished eating, the entertainment began. Urged on by his nieces, with fake reluctance Uncle Albert revealed his well-rehearsed party trick.

He grabbed two tablespoons and showed them to everybody like a magician who was about to make them disappear. He put one spoon with the bowl down between his thumb and index finger, the other bowl up between his index and middle finger and began tapping his foot rhythmically as his mouth hummed de-dum-de-dum-de-dum-dum-dum, and his head nodded like a conductor preparing for his orchestra to start playing.

He had not drank a single drop of alcohol whilst in the restaurant, Aunty Franna made sure of that, so he was quite steady on his feet. He began moving the spoons with his wrist and his thumb and made a clinking noise that was in step with the toe tapping, the de-dum-de-dum-de-dum-dum-dum and the head nodding, the noises blending together to form an unmistakeable polka beat. This went on for a little while, to get the audience warmed up then, with a flourish, he made a drum roll by opening wide the fingers of his free hand and dragging the spoons up and down them a couple of times and then smashing the spoons against his leg like an enthusiastic cymbalist. All the time a toothless mouth made short bubbling sounds in time with the spoons. He repeated the move a few times and then hit his shoulder with the spoons. Two solemn drum rolls on one of the tables was the prelude to the main part of the show. Uncle Albert hit his knee with the spoons in a grand gesture, but the sound of crashing cymbals came not from the spoons but his mouth; appreciative but muted applause rippled around the room. The cutlery went up and down the inside of both arms, another drum roll and he paused. He winked at Aunty Aida and played a series of clinking notes on her back followed by two more drum-like rolls. Uncle Albert bounced his spoons off his knee, Aunty Aida's open palm, Aunty Bernadette's puffed up cheek to make a hollow sound, then he did the horse gallop across Aunty Franna's bosom.

Emboldened by a little ripple of applause, Uncle Albert repeated the performance. This was a mistake as the audience's attention had rapidly faded.

Nat and some of his friends were discussing politics by the open front door and appeared to have little interest in the Murphys' party pieces. The subject of discussion was corruption in Nigerian politics. Nat was arguing that Gowon's regime was more corrupt than the present one. Kojo Ankrah and Samson strongly disagreed, with the latter stating, as a good Yoruba, that Obafemi Awolowo should have got into power and corruption would have ended. Nat mocked Samson's naivety and laughed at him for being a 'fool fool' and Josiah dismissed Kojo's opinions on Nigerian politics, as he was Ghanaian and therefore genetically negatively biased in Nigerian matters. Samson maintained that military government was best for Nigeria because for every corrupt Army officer there are ten corrupt politicians.

Kojo agreed enthusiastically because he was a Midshipman before independence, one of the first Nigerian officers in the Nigerian Navy when most of the officers were British, a boast Kojo brought up at every opportunity.

"Yes, we know," said Nat raising his eyebrows. "You tell we once you tell we a million time."

"What language are you speaking now, Grand?" Dion asked.

Nat put his hand on Dion's head.

"We de speakin' Yoruba and pidgin," Nat replied, "one day I de teach you."

Uncle Albert finished playing his spoons with a flourish, and only then, Aunty Franna allowed him a can a beer that he gulped down sloppily but swiftly with great relief.

"Come on Dad," shouted Maureen, "give us one of your songs."

"Yes, Nat, one of your native songs," said Aunty Aida.

"Go on Grand," urged Dion.

"I will sing one for yua," he said to Dion smiling. "I will sing a song about Nigerian language."

"Yes," Maureen encouraged, "I like that song."

"But first I have something to say," Nat insisted.

Nat wiped a tear from his face. That was unusual, Nat Ajayi did not cry easily.

"Big boys no cry," he said, a smile forcing itself through the wet creases on his cheeks. "But ol' men dem do."

Everyone smiled and aahed.

"Enough of this ole man nonsense," Nat said a broad grin taking over his face, "me feelin' like me feelin' when a young boy, no different, excep' me face all screw up, me hair gone and what left white like snow. Me can't run no more bicos me leg nah let me. Me have me pickney and me gran' pickney and today me great-grandpickney get christen', today is special day,"

Nat stood in the doorway, shuffled his feet and tapped a rhythm on his thigh.

"I de sing de language melange een Nigeria.

Which of dem we go speak?
One metre,
We travel to Umunede, we go speak Isoko,
One metre,
We travel to Borno, say na Fulfulde,
We travel to Ughelli, dem go speak Urhobo,
We travel to Buguma, say na Kalabari,
One metre,
We travel to Kaduna, dem go speak Hausa,
We travel to Okene, dem go speak Ebira,
We travel to Abbi, dem go speak Kwale,
Ogomola, dem go speak Okrika,
One kilometre means another language,
half a kilometre means another language,
One metre

Kojo and Samson had lost some of their initial reserve and joined in Nat's rhythm by clapping their hands and encouraging others to join in.

Maureen rose from her chair dragging Solly by the hand and began to dance.

One metre,
We travel to Sokoto, dem go speak Fulani,
We go to Benin City, dem go speak Edo,
One metre,
We travel to Onitsha, dem go speak Ibo,
We travel to Asaba-Asa, den Bendel we go,
We travel to Gboko, dem say na Tiv,
One metre,
We travel to Otukpa, dem go speak Idoma,
We travel to Akure, dem go speak Yoruba,
We travel to Ase, dem go speak Aboh,
We travel to Uyo, na Ibibio,
One metre . . .

We travel, we travel, we travel, travel, travel
Me saying, we travel
One metre . . .
We travel to Patani, dem go speak Izon,
We travel to Vom, dem go speak Berom,
We travel to Ekpoma, dem go speak Esan,
We travel to Auchi, dem go speak Etsako,
We travel to idah, dem go speak Igala,
We travel to Bida, dem go speak Nupe,
We travel to Ogbakiri, dem go speak Ikwere
One metre

After the food and drink had been consumed and Uncle Albert been carried to a taxi comatose, and the rest were about to leave, Felicia asked Nat whether he would be attending the meeting on Monday. For sure, he will be attending, he replied, reminding her he had only ever missed three meetings in five years. Felicia then asked him whether he had heard about the trouble last night.

Nat had seen the two burned cars on Upper Parliament Street on the way to the church, and that they had closed the dairy because of it.

"Dozens of police got injured, according to the news on the radio," Felicia told him. "This is serious, we must do somefin'. I want to bring it up at the meeting," she insisted.

"Eez wha' you de propose, dat we nurse de police, make am better, mejore su salud?" Nat laughed at his own joke.

Nat could speak many languages. Yoruba, Igbo, English, French, Spanish and both French and English pidgin; he could also speak some Swahili, some Cantonese and could understand some Urdu languages. He picked up these languages on his travels. First as a stowaway, then as a galley boy, then as a fireman and finally as a cook, in all forty eight years in the merchant navy, retiring at 60. That is how he first met Liverpool, as a stowaway before the war.

He lived down in Pitt Street in those early days in Mrs. Clarke's boarding house in an area that became known as Chinatown but was really *Everybodytown* with every shade, ethnicity and nationality and religion represented. Africans from the West, Africans from the North, from the South and from the East. There were Muslims, Christians, Jews, Buddhists and many with no religion at all; Asians, Chinese and Poles but mainly Black and White and in between Liverpudlians.

It took Nat twenty years to stop using the term 'Half-caste' substituting it with 'Mulatto' or 'Métis'. He always distrusted the term coloured and rejected the term Negro; it might sound okay in America and Britain but in French, it meant Nigger.

Elsie used the word half-caste right up to the day she died and she meant nothing derogatory by it, Elsie was not like that.

Nat brought up Maureen not to mix with "half-caste boys" because he believed for a long time that they were all no good up to no good. When Maureen started going out with white boys Nat was not too alarmed, thinking she would grow out of it and marry a nice Yoruba man or even an Ibo. But God no butta 'im bread on dat one and she ended up marrying Colin, nice enough fellow, but a milkman when he expected her to marry a Big Man in the Merchant Navy.

"I go see you tomorrow, Felicia. An' de food de nice," he said.

Thanks," she said. "I didn't know you could sing and dance like that."

Nat loved compliments. His cheeks dimpled when he answered: "If you can walk you can dance. If you can talk you can sing."

Most of the christening party went back to Aunty Bernadette's house off Netherfield Road in the North End of the city to carry on the merrymaking. Nat went home with Dion because Dion complained of having tummy ache, the trade off for his gluttony with the cake and chocolate, said Maureen.

Felicia, Solly and Gary spent two hours cleaning up the restaurant back to spick and span. When it was all done Felicia took out money from the till, paid Solly what he was due and Gary double what he was due.

"I don't think it's worked out for you here, Gary," Felicia told him as she handed him the money.

"Wha' ya mean?" he replied looking even more glum than usual.

"I can't cope not knowing when you're gonna turn up; your time-keeping is not good enough, I'm afraid."

He grabbed the money from her hand.

"You're afraid? You should be furrin' terrified for messin' wid me yer furrin' bitch," he muttered as he turned away from her.

"Hey, you mind your bloody language, I'll tell your Nan off you," she warned him.

"It's noffin t'do wid me Nan, it's t'do wid me an' you," he said defensively, moving away from Felicia's face.

"Get out of my shop," Felicia retorted pressing her advantage. "You ungrateful swine, after all I've done for you."

Gary slammed the door noisily behind him as he stepped out into Granby Street. The job was no big loss to Gary he had only ever worked there under duress from his mother. He would ask Treasa at the Jaycee if he could work there full time instead of part time. He liked it there it was a better job than *Spices'* lousy café. He thought that he would learn to cook there, and then maybe open a café of his own. When he did own his café, he would employ Felicia and not because she was a particularly good cook (Gary was not keen on all that black food, he was a fish fingers and chips guy with loads of tomato sauce on the side). Gary would employ Felicia so he could persecute her, dock her wages when she was even one minute late; make her clean the mirrors right into the corners and make her scrub the floors on her hands and knees, like they did in the olden days. Right now though, Gary was a million miles away from being a cook, let alone a restaurant owner; he was a million miles away from being anything.

Gary had left school with four CSEs not quite ready to conquer the world, or even wanting to begin to make a mark in the adult world. Gary Brown was totally devoid of realistic ambitions. Sure, he had fantasies, more than most probably. His ambition to own and run a restaurant was a passing fantasy rather than an ambition. Gary's future was populated with passing fantasies. Professional footballer: he was totally uncoordinated and hated sport except as a spectator and had more chance of being crowned King of England than ever becoming a professional athlete of any kind. Consultant Surgeon not a Doctor, let alone a Nurse but a Surgeon like the one he had seen on a favourite medical programme. However, he had a deep revulsion of blood.

On the corner of Granby Street and Cawdor Street Gary passed two guys, Lolly and Kenny, loitering with intent. He knew them from school. His Nan called people like them 'no-marks'.

"Ya want sum'n?" mumbled Lolly.

Gary shook his head and looked straight ahead, as he had been coached to do if approached to buy or try drugs.

"Me 'af nice weed 'ere," Ernie said with a grin in an accent suggesting he had spent the whole of his life in Kingston Jamaica when he had never been further than New Brighton.

"Furroff," Gary snarled and hurried his step.

As he crossed Granby Street, impervious to passing traffic, Gary nearly got run over by a car that had to break quickly and swerve to avoid him. The driver beeped his horn furiously.

"Why you no look, you idiyat you" the driver cursed through his open window.

"Furroff," Gary shouted back.

Today would be the day when Gary told everybody who bugged him to 'furroff' and feel good about it; yeah, furroff everybody cos I'm not in the mood.

The driver, Warsame Hussein, a tall thin Somali man with staring eyes, stopped his car, stepped out leaving the driver's door wide open and the engine running and walked purposely towards Gary who stood in the middle of the road. Perhaps if Gary had known that people from his clan nicknamed Warsame *Wiil Waal* (crazy boy), and Liverpool people called him 'Warrior', although that was more because they could not pronounce Warsame. Had Gary known about these things perhaps he would not have stood there so brazenly, in a defiant hands-on-hip pose.

Warsame was in the foulest of moods. His father had been roughed up and abused two weeks previously by "half caste boys". The culprits were still running free and as far as he was concerned, Gary was probably one of them.

"Wha' d'yer want, go on furroff," Gary repeated.

Warsame Hussein punched Gary hard in the face and watched him collapse onto the warm tarmac road. He swiftly got back in his car and drive away without so much as a glance back at a now prostrate Gary.

Gary wanted to cry, he could feel the tears welling up in his eyes and his nose was throbbingly sore and leaking blood. He sat up, still in the middle of the road, leaning on his hand and tilting his head back so the blood would run down the back of his throat instead of on his clothes. Three cars one after another beeped their horns at him as they had to slow right down to try to get past him, but Gary was determined not to move until the bleeding had stopped and the buzzing cleared his head.

How was he going to explain to his Nan when he finally got home about his broken face and his bloody clothes, and sacked from the job she had pulled strings for him to get.

A police patrol car stopped right in front of him.

"What the hell are you doin' dere lyin' in de road, sunshine?" asked one of the policemen getting out of the car.

"Furroff," said Gary.

"What did you say?" said the policeman taken aback.

"Furroff," Gary repeated bracing himself against a blow he was sure was coming.

"You're nicked," he heard the voice say.

The policeman lifted to his feet, cuffed his hands behind his back and bundled into the back of the police car. Gary did not struggle, he did not even protest, he was too frightened to react; this whole thing was turning into the worst of nightmares.

Gary's body was contorted across the back seat with his head jammed one way and his manacled arms jutting the other. There were banging noises and Gary was not sure whether they were the sound of blows on his body or whether the banging noises were coming from outside the car. He opened his eyes and Ernie and Kenny were banging angrily on the police car window.

"Why yer takin' 'im', he's dun noffin', lerrim go; he's special needs," Ernie was shouting.

The driver, a ruddy-skinned man with sleepy eyes, looked startled by the intervention.

"What d'you mean special needs?" he asked looking back at his prisoner searching for physical evidence.

"I've got Asperger's," croaked Gary.

"Asperg-what? What's that?" said his sleepy eyed colleague.

"Some sort of mental illness," replied the colleague not too sure of his ground, "but I think we'd better let him go."

"And stay off the roads in future," said sleepy eyes feeling a bit embarrassed as he sped away.

"Did the pigs do dat t'yer face?" Ernie asked.

"No, it was some madman, for no reason," Gary replied the tears now mixing with the blood to form pink rivulets dripping from his chin. "He juss punched me on de nose for no reason."

"Yer lie," Kenny said shaking his shaven head. "Was he Somali?"

Gary shook his head sticking out his tongue to catch the pink tears.

"That'd be Warrior. You can't mess wid him, he's one cra-zee bastard. He tried to run over me spa de udder day, for noffin' as well. I tell ya de man's a complete loon, 'e should be locked up, fer true."

"Is bess if yer get yerself home sharpish, lah, or de pigs'll be back for yer," Lolly advised.

Gary needed no further prompting and ran all the way home with the presence of mind to stop running whenever he saw a police car, which was twice in the quarter mile to the middle end of Upper Warwick Street where he lived. He had learned that a black man running in the street meant only one thing to the police: he was running away from a crime and had to be stopped and searched, stands to reason.

Nat Ajayi was pleased to get the chance to spend a few hours with Dion; it was not very often these chances came. He was not expecting the rest of the household until late. When the Murphys partied, the parties went on all night with full breakfast the following morning. They were not the type of parties in which Nat felt comfortable. Race would always come up and sometimes turn nasty like when

Maureen poured the contents of a flower vase on the head of one of her cousin's boyfriend for telling anybody who would listen that Africans came from Apes and Europeans from Homo sapiens. The boy was drunk and he thought he was bright because he had a couple of GCEs. That was the major drawback to the Murphy parties; they were always lively, too lively. His time would be better spent with his grandson than with the Murphy tribe, besides his friends left early, it was not their kind of party either.

With relatives like the Murphys, Nat felt he needed to protect Dion from them, he felt it was his duty to inculcate into his progeny that they should never be the enemy of Africans, the enemy of black people; particularly the lighter skinned ones like Dion who could pass for white and be more prone to anti-black indoctrination.

Nat was in the kitchen spicing and warming up a fish soup he had cooked yesterday and preparing the Gari. He looked at his watch, nine thirty; he had told Dion, who was playing out on the estate somewhere, to be in before it got dark, which should be any minute now. Right on cue Dion walked through the door sweating profusely.

"You don land Deeo?" Nat greeted him.

"Hi Grand; I've been playing football and I'm dead thirsty. Can I have some cola, please, Grand?"

"You should always drink water when you are thirsty and if you muss drink cola drink for taste not to bury you own thirst."

"Yes Grand."

"You ready fe nyam?"

Dion shook his head.

Nat mixed the boiling water into the Gari to produce high consistency fufu. He put the mixture on the flat plate and filled two bowls with the soup.

Nat and Dion sat round the table tearing cobs of fufu to scoop up the soup. Nat was pleased to watch Dion eating like an African.

Dion grabbed the salt ready to douse his soup with it.

Nat stopped him as if he was about to commit a mischief.

"Salt no catch dis soup at all," he said gravely. "Salt no good for you, give you high blood pressure and weaken yua heart," he warned before hooking a piece of flesh from the soup.

"You know such a lot Grand; why didn't you become a doctor; you could have made a lot of money," remarked Dion without irony.

The remark was pointedly felt by Nat. Dion was commenting on the fact that his grandfather had no money.

"It take a lot edjucashun to be doctor and me prefer to play rather dan study when me was pickney. And now me is old and poor, *sans-sous* as de French say, *indigente* say de Spanish, living on 'small small' penshun. Don make same mistake as yua Granfadda, Deeo. Edjucashun de only ting dat bring you good pay, remember dat, Deeo, dis is very important for nah future, o."

Dion dug his fufu into the bowl and shovelled out a mouthful.

Dion would ask some of his school friends what their Grandad was like to see if they compared with his. But most of them didn't have a father let alone a grandfather. So Dion knew he was privileged compared to other kids.

"You're not poor, Grand, you own this whole house."

"Let me tell you a likkle story from back home den you tell me how old me is."

Nat told the story of an old man who lived with his son and his wife and their son in a nice house. Everything was fine but as the old man was getting older, he became frailer and clumsy, spilling things on the clean floor, breaking things. This disturbed his son's wife, a very proud housewife and she told his son how terrible it is living with the old man. Then one cold and wet night while they were eating dinner, the old man was dribbling his soup down his chin, on his clothes and on the floor. His son's wife was outraged and said that the old man must leave, so the son ordered his father to leave the house.

"Before you leave," the son said to his father. "Take this blanket to protect you from the cold and wet."

The son, his wife and their child watched as the old man walked slowly away from the house towards the woods. Then the little boy ran after his grandfather and took the blanket off his shoulders and tore the blanket in two, gave his grandfather one half of the blanket and returned to the house with the other half.

"What did you do that for," his father asked the little boy.

The little boy replied, "I'm keeping this half for when you grow old, Daddy."

They ate in silence while Dion thought about the story. "You're not going to die soon, are you Grand?" he asked.

The question took Nat by surprise and he had to chew his food longer than he would normally while he prepared his answer.

"Me English paper say me is 75, but really me is 70, cos I lie and say to custom man, me is 17 when me is 12, cos dat what the cook tell us to say," he said. "But if God spare me, me will die when me is 107, so me 'ave plenty years lef'. You nah granfadda yuaself well before I die, ha-ah," he replied raising his eyebrows.

Pure Pressure

Nat's '*ha-ahs*' meant nothing in themselves, it was all in the intonation and loosely translated into 'I really mean that, this is not a joke'. Dion watched out for these little expressions like 'o' at the end of a sentence and again the intonation of his voice clearly indicated that 'o' meant to emphasise the sentence that went before. "I go beat you if you bad, o," he often used to say to Dion but never once carried it out.

They sat in the small kitchen on opposite sides of the table eating noisily. Nat was studying his grandson with a predicting-the-future eye.

Dion had his round dark eyes, not knowing and rheumy like his but innocent and inquiring. Nat often thought as he did now about the contrast in skin colour between him and his Grandson. Dion's Africaness did not lie in his skin colour or his features. Dion's cheek bones had a hint of West Africa certainly, but the European genes had elongated and thinned out the wide bulbous Ajayi nose, and made it pert and cute, Scandinavian almost. In addition, to Nat's great chagrin, Nat's fleshy lips had metaphorsed through two generations into two thin slices of ham. Nat laughed aloud at the comparison and when Dion asked him why he was laughing Nat got out of his seat and round the table and hugged him

"Me is laughing bicos you have your Granmudda mouth."

Dion instinctively covered his mouth with his hand.

"Everybody says that," he said and returned to the soup.

"I is laughing bicos you is my precious boy and yua make me happy bicos you will see and do big things by the time you ol' like me," he said planting a peck on top of Dion's head.

Dion promised his Grandfather that he will teach his children to cook the African way and tell them of Nat's stories. That was more important than looking like him, Nat always concluded when he despaired at his grandson's features. However, he had told Dion many times that if God made man in his own image and the first man was African then God must be black as well.

"I tell you how I die even after I die," Nat said, in between mouthfuls. "If yua 'ave yawa pickney wid a white gal, den me will die cos Africa will gone from yua pickney forever and ol' Nat Ajayi and him ancestors going back long long time, since de beginning of time, since de sons of Oduduwa turned bad lands into fertile lands, all dem will disappear from yua pickney."

"I won't let them forgot you, Grand, and I'm going to marry somebody rich and beautiful. Are there any rich and beautiful Yoruba women?"

"Many beautiful but not so rich," Nat said

"Dere's plenty black women in Liverpool, pretty pretty as well as from good good family," urged Nat.

Yes, Dion had met them all these prospective wives when visiting his Granddad's friends. Snarling Idowu, gabber mouth Taiwo and skinny Jennifer. In any case, Dion didn't like girls; they were mostly a waste of time.

"Marry someone darker than yua or we don disappear forever as if we never exist."

The meal finished, Nat told Dion to do his homework while he washed the dishes and cleared the kitchen.

Dion came back with his homework as Nat was plumping the cushions on the settee. "Here Grand, do you want to read it," he said handing him his homework.

"No yua read am, me no know were me own eye-glass is," Nat replied.

Chapter 11

Pass It On

4:45pm Sunday 5th July 1981

The John Archer Youth Centre's Management Committee had never met on a Sunday before. This was unprecedented; Sunday was a 'me' day. A varied bunch that committee, with varied Sunday preoccupations. The repeats of '*The Untouchables*' and game shows on TV, worshipping and preaching, sleeping or simply catching up, so it was difficult for many members to attend. Nevertheless, Alan Leung had been most insistent, imperative even, although he only provided a few hours' notice, that after the events last night, the meeting had to be brought forward from Thursday. Today it had to be. Alan Roberts's edicts on timing of meetings had to be obeyed.

Prior to main meetings Alan always held a one-to-one meeting with Treasa Doherty, the centre's manager. Sometimes their meeting lasted two minutes and sometimes one hour. Today they met in Treasa's tiny office fifteen minutes before the rescheduled meeting was due to start. Treasa was not pleased either at having to come in on a Sunday evening. That was the time she reserved for the Irish centre on Mount Pleasant, particularly at this time in the middle of the hunger strikes and all. She was already clocking up at least 15 hours a week more than her contractual hours. On top of which Alan had asked her to come to the Centre at 4.30 for their pre-meeting and he turns up late, again. Undervalued, taken for granted, underpaid, she could go on, this could turn out the worst job she had ever had.

Treasa's appointment as the Centre's Manager had been controversial because she was white; some even resented her for being Irish, although they were far fewer. The selection panel led by Alan overall were impressed with Treasa Doherty's passion and the experience she had gained working with deprived youths in Belfast and Dublin. The pickets that followed her appointment petered out after a few days and the users of the Centre liked her from the off, won over by her no-nonsense enthusiasm.

An attractive but unfussy woman in her late twenties, Treasa was dressed as always as if she were on a demonstration. Khaki dungarees, comfortable shoes, hair tied back by a bandana and an extra large black tee-shirt, the shoulders reaching past her elbows, with a picture of Bobby Sands on the front and the inscription *Bobby Sands will live for ever* written underneath. Treasa liked to dress down to dress up. She also sometimes wore *MI5 kills* and *Cuba Libre* tee shirts with eye-catching graphics.

Treasa face was startlingly oval-shaped face, like a pear. Her childhood had been plagued with the grating nickname Pear Drop. People still called her Pear Drop behind her back, even some of her comrades.

Treasa pointedly stared at the watch on her wrist holding up her arm prominently to indicate to Alan her annoyance at his lateness. Alan ignored Treasa's signal and sat down in her chair (the old posh brown leather number donated to the centre by a relative of Lord Derby).

"I'm already clocking more than fifteen 'ours a week in time aff in lieu whaich I'll never be able ter take," she said evenly.

"Okay, okay, I'll talk to the Treasurer about paying you some of that time," Alan replied, clearly irritated by the diversion.

"That's waat yer said last time whaen oi wanted ter take sum time aff in lieu."

"Yes, yes, I know," said Alan his impatience growing. "I'll talk to him. Now, this meeting has to finish by seven at the very latest; I've got things to do. I need decisions so I'm gonna have to cut short those on the committee who love long discourses," Alan said in a tone suggesting hope rather than certainty despite his smacking his hand on the top of Treasa's desk for emphasis. "Also, I want this to be the shortest Service Report you've ever presented to committee. We'll go into details at the next meeting or I'll take Chair's action."

Sunday evening in Liverpool was choir practice night for Alan and he did not want to arrive too late, they had started at six. Whenever he was in Liverpool on a Sunday, Alan would always fit choir practice in; it was the best buzz in town.

Treasa sighed shaking her head.

"There's a lorge agenda, an' there's other issues as well, line manager's issues whaich yer promised we wud discuss the day."

"I told you to ring me and we can discuss these issues on the phone."

"I've tried Alan but you're alwus oyt an' yer never return de call."

"You're always engaged," Alan lied. "Back to this agenda," he continued indicating that that particular issue had ended and there were other and more important issues to deal with.

"Let's cut the agenda right down or better still, postpone it and have a single item on the agenda: how we gonna respond to this war that's raging out there."

"Oi don't tink they'll agree ter dat," said Treasa with half a grin.

"Have you got a copy of the agenda and the minutes from the last meeting?"

"De minutes weren't sent oyt, oi only jist foun' oyt so they're gettin' copied as we spake," Treasa said as humbly as she could, and humility was not prominent in Treasa Doherty's backpack.

Alan tuttered "it doesn't matter" although it clearly did as he quickly added "why not?"

"Yiss brah'der George wus supposed ter 'av sent dem oyt an' on top av dat he didn't cum into work the-day an' de bus got stolen, it wus foun' in Fazacree."

"You mean Fazakerley, Treasa," Alan corrected.

Treasa was the only one who called Googie by his proper name and the emphasis she put on his name was decidedly accusatory implying that Alan had special responsibilities for his "brah'der" and should explain his unauthorised absence.

"He has some urgent domestic issues to deal with," Alan felt compelled to say. "He should be back tomorrow, and anyway the minutes should have been sent at least a week ago. Let's get to this agenda and see how we can cut it to the bone if we have to deal with it all," said Alan in a staccato voice.

"De bus 'ad a lorge dent on de front win'," Treasa insisted.

"Our Paul'll fix that," Alan said quickly. "He'll do it for a good price."

"Yer brah'der did not gie us a gran' price de last time, it verged on de extortionate" said Treasa pursing her lips.

The meeting started at five o'clock sharp in Treasa's small office.

The John Archer Youth Centre, situated on Park Way was part of a row of tall, bruised Victorian terraced houses. The building stood in between a small boarded up church with its roof missing that had ceased to be a church for nearly a generation and *Parker's Tools wholesale merchants (Established in 1894)*. The centre's brick façade held a sign proclaiming its name in bright red capitalised block letters; lounging youths usually decorated its stone steps and along its railings.

Alan Leung, Maureen Ajayi and Father Dominic were the founding members who had provided the impetus to get the project off the ground. The funds for the refurbishment of the Jaycee came from Ambrose Dickinson, the scion of a local rich and philanthropic shipping company Ambrose Dickinson also funded most of the centre's running costs. Central government agencies were not prepared to fund such a project as government urban funds were pointedly non-racial funds except for areas with substantial numbers of immigrants from the British Commonwealth, to help their assimilation into the general, meaning white, public. The premise for this approach was that the problems of deprivation and under-achievement faced by black communities had more to do with new immigrants finding it difficult to adapt culturally and linguistically to a new life in a new country. Once addressed these problems would eventually disappear as the indigenous community assimilated immigrants, went government thinking. Because Liverpool's black community was overwhelmingly locally-born, these special funds bypassed the city because the proportion of immigrants settled in the region fell below government levels at which urban funding could be triggered.

Local activists, principally among them Alan Leung and Maureen Ajayi, argued that the problems faced by black people were not to do with immigrants finding it difficult assimilating themselves into British society but white racism which oppressed black people. These arguments fell on deaf ears and the relatively small amounts of central government funding that came Liverpool's way went largely to first generation immigrants and ignored the needs of the majority of local black people.

Maureen Ajayi persuaded Ambrose Dickinson to step in and donate substantial sums and the John Archer Youth Centre was born, *'to engage in positive ways local youths at risk or involved with crime'*.

Alan had found the name *John Archer* when he was doing some research. John Archer was the first black man to become Mayor in Britain, back in 1913 in South London, and he was a Communist, which added to the attraction. Not that many Mayors in Britain's political history were Communist, let alone Black.

Ray Bootman dug out a photograph of John Archer from newspaper archives looking cocksure and handsome with a long curling moustache and fancy clothes. They had the photograph blown up, framed, and placed high on the wall at the entrance so everybody could see it when they came in to the building.

Alan Leung was the founding Chair of the organisation and the Chair still six years on, albeit by the skin of his teeth. Disaffection with his leadership was growing. He was increasingly being compared to an absentee landlord by some members of the committee. This was because he lived and worked in Teesside, hundred and fifty miles away from Liverpool. Alan vigorously defended himself whenever challenged as if his life depended on it, and nothing to do with safeguarding the mileage allowance he received from the Jaycee for attending meetings. Alan felt quite comfortable claiming out of pocket expenses as he worked a lot for the organisation. He was in daily contact with Treasa by telephone, he maintained (Treasa's eyes flickered in denial at that claim), and he visited the centre every month.

Alan felt quietly confident that he had an impregnable majority on the committee who would support him if one of the disgruntled, usually led by Norris Nobleman, moved against him. Always well prepared to defend attacks against his leadership, Alan reminded them of the Employment Tribunal case against the first Director that he had defended almost singlehandedly, briefing the lawyers, attending all those court appearances.

"Alan was the only member of the committee who has attended every single Management meeting in the past three years," said Ray Bootman, who was always spot on with statistics, and an unashamed Alan Leung supporter.

Alan was keen to remain Chair, mainly because the Jaycee was his baby, he had fought long and hard to get the project started, and he was not ready to let it go. The Jaycee also fulfilled a basic need to still be involved with the area and help assuage the guilt he felt about living in all-white suburbia all them miles away.

The committee trouped in to the main office, which was scarcely bigger than Treasa's cubbyhole, each quickly finding a chair. There were only eight chairs available (apparently a dozen chairs were stolen in broad daylight and everybody saw nothing) and the slow or late ones had to contend with sitting on top of a small metal filing cabinet, or on one of the three desks. Spaciously glamorous the Jaycee was not.

Keith Turner, the Council representative and a key member of the disgruntled, was the first in, followed by Father Dominic, a popular local priest and Norris Nobleman a small thin man with large glasses and a military bearing.

Keith Turner was supposed to ensure that the Council grant, which paid for a part-time project worker for the centre, was properly managed and accounted for.

Alan and some of the others referred to Keith Turner outside of his hearing as *The Council Spy*. Ben Miller was next in, a large elderly Jewish man with bushy hair, beard and moustache, sporting a '*Justice for Palestine*' badge on his lapel. Ben Miller's usual dishevelled dress suggested he had slept in his clothes every night in the past month without changing them. Ben had a shop on Lodge Lane where he had sold and repaired clocks and watches to three generations of Liverpooleighters. Ben was followed by Maxammed Adam, a Somali health worker; everybody called him Max except his compatriots who nicknamed him Madoowbe because of his dark complexion. Yvonne Khumalo-Birtwhistle, a Xhosa geography lecturer at the University, was the last one in. Norris Nobleman gave her his seat, the last available one, and sat on one of the desks.

Alan opened the meeting by welcoming everybody. He asked a volunteer to take the minutes in Googie's absence. Yvonne volunteered, but Alan said she always volunteered and that it would be nice if one of the men volunteered. Keith Turner gave his usual rejoinder in these circumstances about gladly taking the minutes, but his role as Liverpool City Council representative prevented him legally from doing so.

Alan then looked at Treasa with his eyebrows raised. Treasa protested about the difficulty of taking minutes and participating in the meeting but to no avail. Treasa reported that she was unable to reach Maureen and Nat Ajayi by telephone to inform them of the meeting.

"Maureen's first grandson got christened the-day, bless him, dey were proobably at de church," she said.

Alan announced in an irritable tone that the Minutes of the last meeting had not been sent out; then, as if rehearsed, Gary Clarke the YOP worker came sheepishly into the office carrying sheaths of paper in his arms.

Gary knew this was an important meeting and he had typed Googie's hand-written notes with great care. He was going to inform these important people, with some pride, that he had personally typed them, but he felt a little overawed by the occasion, keeping his eyes low, avoiding looking at anybody. He placed the papers neatly in the middle of the table leaving as inconspicuously as he had come in without uttering a word.

Treasa distributed the minutes. The list of names of those who were present at the last meeting or had given their apologies was on top of the page as usual but after each name were added comments.

Alan Leung Chairman of the Board, Leader of the Pack. The Cat got the Cream. Max Adam Muslim fanatic. Maureen Ajayi, the fattest woman in Liverpool 8. Nat Ajayi, the oldest man in Liverpool 8. Billy Brown, the laziest man ever, anywhere. Father (loves a tot or two of Scottish whisky)Dominic, the nicest white man in Liverpool 8. Yvonne Khumalo-Birtwhistle, Illegal immigrant, agent of BOSS, the South Afrikan secret service. Ben Miller, Treasurer/Book fiddler, undercover Mossad agent. Norris Nobleman, professional Uncle Tom. Gerry Thompson, trouble, trouble, trouble. Keith Turner the Council spy with a glass eye. Treasa Doherty (no Mother Teresa by any means), raving dyke and IRA terrorist

Pure Pressure

Keith Turner was the first to react, as he requested, indignantly, what was the meaning of these extraordinary comments and who had written "these disgraceful Minutes."

Treasa said her sexuality was her business and she was a sympathiser, not a terrorist.

Yvonne was outraged; she said she had never been so insulted in all her life, she, who has fought against apartheid all her life, a dedicated follower of the ANC, accused of being part of an organisation dedicated to subjugating her people.

Max took the word fanatic as a compliment. Ben Miller started by sniggering and then laughed aloud. Max looked suspiciously at Ben as if he had just had long-standing suspicions confirmed. Father Dominic smiled and said the writer should have specified Malt Whiskey. Treasa blamed Googie but Alan was adamant that his brother would not write such things.

Treasa called Gary Clarke, who was lurking in the hallway. Gary thought it was to receive congratulations for his good work. It took him two seconds to realise he had got the shitty end of the stick and six seconds to blare out that he only typed up what Googie had given him to write, before storming out of the room slamming the door behind him.

Alan broke the silence.

"There's clearly been some mix-up here and when we find the culprit we will deal with it appropriately. In the meantime, let's move on. Given the events of the past couple of days, I propose we shelve the agenda until a further date, like next Monday as I'm in Liverpool for another eight days and instead discuss the riots and the Centre's official response."

"I disagree," said Norris. "We should have the meeting as scheduled and discuss the . . . uprisings . . . after the meeting."

Norris's use of the word *uprisings* caught everybody by surprise. When recounting the meeting to Maureen Ajayi, Alan reckoned it was Norris's attempt to radicalise his reputation, to show that he was not an Uncle Tom, professional or otherwise.

It took half an hour for the meeting to vote for and agree Norris's proposal. The agenda was a routine one and Alan was whizzing through the agenda in record time when Gerry Thompson burst into the office.

Gerry Thompson was in his early twenties, a big man and an aggressive man. As a representative of users, he was a co-opted member of the committee with full voting rights. It was a right he had fought hard for before the committee agreed to change the Standing Orders. Yet, Gerry, in the nine months he had been on the committee, had never voted, not out of some principled ideology but because he seldom attended meetings and when he did he either came late or left early, every time.

"Is that all youze can do is sit around chin-wagging while de youfs are gettin' beat up by Babylon on yer doorstep? Are youze gonna do somefin or are youze gonna watch when de place gets burned down, cause de youfs are angry out dere an' wanna know who's on dere side, right." he bellowed, eyes and muscles bulging, fit to burst.

Dressed in dark loose clothes Gerry Thompson looked exactly like the numerous photos of *rioters* featured on the front pages of all the newspapers. The fact that he was not masked did not take away from the menace he was radiating.

Alan patiently calmed him down whilst the others stayed nervously silent. Alan reassured Gerry that a special spot had been set aside to discuss the issues that were worrying everybody. Keith Turner made to give Gerry his chair but Gerry just waved him away and plonked himself on top of the filing cabinet, quietly watching the proceedings his feet dangling the whole time as a reminder that he was still there. He did not contribute at all to the meeting even when asked direct questions.

"What do you think, Gerry, about Treasa's proposal to start a boxing club?" Alan asked him.

"Got noffin' t'say until we start talkin' 'bout de war," he replied defiantly.

"Gerry, do you think it's a good idea starting a women's keep-fit class?"

"Got noffin' t'say until we start talkin' 'bout de war, right."

The agenda item about changing the name from the John Archer Youth to the Ujaama Community Centre was dropped by Norris not only because there were more serious issues to discuss in Norris's humble opinion (he always called his opinions humble), but also his co-sponsor Nat Ajayi was not present.

With normal business finished, the *uprisings* item, as everybody had agreed by then to describe the events, except Keith Turner, who could not possibly lend the Council's approval of such a political, and in his view, an incendiary word given the circumstances. Keith Turner insisted the Minutes reflect his no comment on the use of the word and the reason for his no comment. Treasa grudgingly complied. She felt Keith Turner's insistence was negatively significant and that it could perhaps get the Centre closed down and her losing her job.

"Okidoke Gerry," said Alan. "Thanks for your patience. Over to you."

Gerry Thompson slid off the filing cabinet, and plonked himself in the middle of the room. "Dere's gonna be more trouble t'night, right? 'Eads're gonna get cracked and when one of the boys gets injured dere's nowhere for dem t'go, right? Dey can't get ambulances and dey can't walk to the 'ozzie coz Babylon will crack deir 'eads again, right? So, we want the Jaycee van to ferry the boys to ozzie, right. Googie'll drive, 'e's okay."

"George is nowha ter be seen at de moment, even if we agree," said Treasa unhappy about the van going missing again.

"This could be seen as helping criminals," ventured Yvonne.

"I can see you're no Mary Seacole," said Ben sardonically as he scratched his beard.

"Leave dat to de Charlie Wootton Centre, they 'av a minibus and they are more political than we are," said Treasa.

"I fink we should confine ourselves to issuing a press release condemning the violence but emphasising the context of past police brutality," said Alan by way of conclusion. "I'll draft something tonight and leave a copy in the office for people to make comments and we'll send it out tomorrow evening."

"I fought you had more balls dan dat Alan, what good's dat gonna do eggzacly, hey? And you, of all people, should know better," Gerry was pointing an angry finger at Alan. "But then you've never really been one of the boys, av yer? Sure you went to Granby Street School as yer so fond of remindin' us, but you haven't been one of us for a long time, if you ever were."

Gerry turned his back on the room and added as he walked through the door: "Me's resignin', lah. Me's resignin' from dis fuckin' committee as ov now."

Gerry slammed every door he passed on the way out of the building. Everybody turned to Alan to say something. It was apparent to all that Gerry had hit a sore nerve.

Alan hesitated, unsure what to say to regain the initiative.

The sound of heavy footsteps echoed in the corridor and the room door swung open. Gerry was back.

"One more fing," he said as all eyes turned towards him, "de Jaycee is probably de only black organisation in de country run by a white person. Wa' is wrong with us, don't youz feel embarrassed by dis. Is it ar' mentality in Liverpool that we need to 'ave white people runnin' ar' organisation? All she keeps going on about is fuckin Irishmun starv'n demselves to fuck'n death," Gerry reprised staring at Treasa who had thunder in her eyes and looked around the room in vain for vocal support.

"What's Ireland gorra do with us here," Gerry was shouting now, "when de youfs are being brutalised on de street n' burnin' de area to cinders ourra sheer frustration, and all she can go on about is fuck'n Long Kesh."

"That's a great cause they're dyin' for, they're dyin' for freedom," said Treasa, clearly outraged.

"But it's not our cause, we've got causes of our own" Gerry replied and turned around and headed back towards the door.

"One more fing," he said, "Don't be surprised if the Jaycee gets burned down tonight. Yerz'ev been warned."

"Gerry's a bit of a hot head," Alan said reassuringly once Gerry had left the building. "He talks before he thinks."

Then they all began to talk at once.

"He was threatening arson!"

"I'm sure he does not mean it."

"Report it to the police."

"Are you crazy, do you really want the building to be torched to the ground?"

"I think we should inform Ambrose Dickinson about what's going on."

"Take it easy," Alan said. "Let's not get carried away, rant is what Gerry Thompson does. To reassure everybody I will ensure there are responsible volunteers to stay in the building throughout the night until the uprisings and the police reprisals that will inevitably follow have ended. I have no fear that this building will not be threatened."

Alan was in full voice now.

"This building is their building, as small and under-resourced as it is, it is all the youth of Liverpool 8 have got. Please don't worry. If anybody wants to volunteer, Treasa will draw up a timetable for the next five nights and I will rustle up others. I'll personally check the. centre every coupla hours at night and make sure everyfin' is alright."

A few protested some more but Alan had taken control of the meeting again.

"Is there any other business," he asked Treasa with a look suggesting there should be none.

Treasa took a deep breath and said she wanted to bring an extraordinary item to the agenda. The issue of Irish nationalist prisoners starving themselves to death had been in the news for months, particularly since Bobby Sands' death and his subsequent election as a Member of Parliament. Treasa wanted permission to add the Centre's name to a petition signed by hundreds of organisations to give political prisoners political status in the UK.

"Foive people are dead already, a sixth, Joe McDonnell is expectin' ter die as we spake an' dare are dozens more who 'av begun de 'unger strike," she pleaded.

"Have you not been listening," said Ben Miller clearly irritated, "we are not in Belfast now, we are in Liverpool and there is a war going on out there on our very own doorstep, not overseas."

"We can't get involved in anything political, Treasa, we're a charity," said Alan shaking his head.

"Well oi tink tiz a cryin' shame dat yer cannot see de parallels between de Oirish struggle an' de black struggle 'ere in Englan', they are both aboyt a people fightin' discriminashun an' oppreshun an' they are both fightin' de seem oppressors. Can't yer see?" Treasa responded plainly incensed.

"Maybe she is an IRA terrorist," whispered Norris Nobleman to Max.

Max smiled and replied, "Maybe she's the other thing too."

They both tittered.

"Order please," ordered Alan as he closed the meeting.

Alan rubbed his face in an attempt to rid it of weariness.

Although it was a hot evening, Alan felt cooler out on the street as he locked the front door of the Centre. It was like a furnace inside that office in comparison. It had been a toss up between getting fans and air extractors installed and getting the minibus repaired and the minibus won. The upstairs lights were still on at the toolmakers' place next door.

Alan heard Gerry's voice before he saw him.

"You made a right cunt arra me in dere, so come on, let's 'avirout."

Gerry was standing less than six feet away from him. Alan watched as Gerry rose on his toes and squared his shoulders. Alan was sure Gerry was going to hit him so he instantly adopted a surrender posture by putting his hands up.

"I'm a poet not a soldier; I talk instead of fight," Alan pleaded. "What's yer problem, lah. You know my hands were tied in there; there's noffin I could do, you know that."

Gerry broke into a smile and gently nestled his fist on to Alan's chest.

"Gotcha dere, didn't I, you fought I was serious."

"D'yer like the line about the poet and the soldier," Alan rejoined having recovered quickly from the embarrassment.

"Yeah, man, cool," replied Gerry as he walked away. "Later."

"Later. You going de match on Sundee?"

"Yeah, man, see you dere."

Alan got into his car and drove off, stopping off at the off-license on Myrtle Parade for a bottle of Cognac before reaching Faulkner Square. It was eight fifteen and the sun was still shining.

He walked up to one of the large terraced 'Georgian' houses. Georgian was not strictly accurate. Imposing, as the buildings were in their Georgian-ness, they were not strictly speaking 'Georgian' although constructed in the Georgian style they were early Victorian.

Alan pressed the top bell. After a few seconds Lil Bob's voice inquired, "who's da?"

"Alan," he replied pressing his mouth close to the intercom.

."Come up, lah," Lil Bob said as he pressed his finger to open the door with a buzz.

Alan ran up to the fourth floor without stopping and was pleased that his breathing was unlaboured. Lil Bob opened the door to him, took the bottle of Cognac with a smile, and hugged Alan warmly, as if he had not seen him for years. They called him Little Bob (Lil for short, his real name was Robert Constantine) because he was less than five foot tall. Sometimes to tease him people would call him Little Cockney or Cockney Bob. Although he was born in Liverpool 8 and he had lived there most of his life, he had lived in London between the ages of 8 and 15, the legacy of which were traces of a London accent including never pronouncing his 'T's and Liverpudlians always did. To compensate for his Southern linguistic tendencies he frequently spoke the old slang to demonstrate his local credentials. He called every man 'lah' or 'cuz' and women behind their backs were always 'beefs'. The teasing, the endless Tommy Steele and Lonnie Donnegan jokes had stopped being jokes a long time ago for Lil Bob; he had to relearn Scouse by force.

Lil Bob had small locks growing all over his head. "It's not a religious statement it's a cultural statement, lah," he answered when asked if he had adopted Rastafarianism.

Alan caught the aroma of curry being cooked and complimented Lil Bob.

"It's not me who's cooking it's Pete," said Lil Bob.

"Pete Howard?"

"No, African Pete."

"Ya lie, African Pete can't cook," Alan replied closing the door behind him.

Lil Bob's place was the venue for the event, known as choir practice, held from 6ish to 10ish on Sunday nights. The Liverpool 8 intelligentsia was what those who had not been educated to undergraduate level called the group. A close shop for black and brown-skinned boozers said yellow-skinned teetotallers. Choir practice habitués had been hand-selected by Lil Bob; they were all men in their thirties who had something to say, and they did not wear socks summer or winter. Not wearing socks was not recognised by the members as a uniform, but because

Lil Bob said socks were unhygienic (and Lil Bob knew about these things), eventually everybody attending choir practice did not wear socks.

Choir practice had started informally with a few people going back to Lil Bob's flat for a chat a drink, a draw of weed and something to eat. Very soon, it became a ritual, an institution almost. Approximately 15 people attended on and off since choir practice began on Lil Bob's 35th birthday in December 1979, but mostly half a dozen people attended and not always the same ones. Peewee and Benji the self-employed electrician with a Mechanical Engineering diploma were the only constants because they were Lil Bob's best mates. The meetings were always held at Lil Bob's because his flat was the most sumptuous and crucially, he was the sole member of the group who lived alone.

Lil Bob rented a flat that took up the top floor of a large Georgian house in Falkner Square. The house was owned by Hassan Kassis, an Egyptian academic, who occupied the rest of the house with his partner Clinton, an architect, and their adopted child, the redoubtable Henrietta Kassis. Henrietta was spending the summer with her birth mother in darkest Norfolk and Hassan and Clinton were on a safari in Kenya.

Library pictures of Liverpool streets, blown up and framed in gilt hung from each wall. The open windows let in the sounds of the street thirty feet below.

Alan greeted each one with 'wapn' and exchanged handshakes. Peewee first, then Benji the electrician, he merely nodded to Bobo Jones the Project Worker at the Jaycee as he had seen him twice today, and a hug to Ray-*my-family's-been-here-since-1741*-Bootman as he had not seen him in months.

"Busy tonight," Alan said to Lil Bob.

"Special event tonight, we've got Lenny Roberts giving a lecture."

"Me Uncle Lenny?"

"The same one."

"What's the subject?"

"He didn' say. But you know him he can talk on any'in'. He's coming at eigh' o'clock. We'll ea' after tha'."

"We're in the middle of definitions of heaven and hell," said Lil Bob, as Alan sat down on one of the floor cushions. "We star'ed and we're halfway frew hell. We've had life without my kids," he said pointing to Ray Bootman "living on the dole till I die," pointing at Bobo Jones, "no women, from Peewee . . ."

"Have you heard about Peewee's hard on," Benji interrupted, "wait till he tells yer, it's wicked, man."

Alan looked at Peewee with a puzzled look.

"Tell yer later," said Peewee looking uncomfortable, his demeanour indicating he was not going to tell him later if he could help it.

"Benji here," Lil Bob persisted, "for 'im would be being the ugliest man in Liverpool. Peewee 'as a more universal vision than Benji's, 'is nah cure for Sickle Cell Anaemia is found. My own personal hell is being in total darkness with nah sound, nah smells, nah people, just you wi' your brain."

"I've changed me mind," said Bobo, "my hell would be being locked in a room with a band playing heavy metal music. That would be pure agony."

"Me say bein' on de dole for rest of me days is 'ell," said African Pete, carrying a tray of glasses and the bottle of Cognac, "me 'av anudder one, sitting and failing my accountancy exams until I die."

African Pete distributed the glasses, carefully opened the bottle and poured a small drop of the alcohol on the polished wooden floor.

"This is for our ancestors," he said grinning. "You can't open a new bottle without sharing it with our ancestors, right?"

"Right," everyone repeated, except Lil Bob who said "Righ'."

Peter Akinrinlola was a final exam or two short of being a certified accountant. Married with two young children, he liked to get away from his little responsibilities now and again and meet up with the boys. He lived way out in Kirkby and only came to the Southend to buy oxtails and ground food and on Choir Practice nights. He had gleefully volunteered to be the cook tonight.

"My heaven is 'aving the biggest cock in Liverpool," Benji announced mischievously.

"Dat dun mean nuttin', best have leekle wun that work an a big one dat don't; ain it, Peewee?" said African Pete smirking in Pee-Wee's direction.

Alan was intrigued about all these asides on Peewee's sex life.

They all looked at Benji a little bewildered by his frivolity. The look said these questions on heaven and hell were serious questions, intellectual questions that required intelligent answers, and that answer was not worthy of a choir practitioner.

Lil Bob had only allowed Benji into the sanctuary because he always brought some nice weed and because he was funny, sometimes.

"Bigger than Sweetness McKenzie's, coz he's got some weapon," said Bobo Jones

"How do you know Sweetness's got some weapon on him," Benji asked suggestively.

The line the conversation was taking did not amuse Lil Bob, particularly when Benji and Bobo started sniggering like school kids.

Peewee recounted his priapist ordeal while Alan's everyone sipped Cognac and Benji and Ray Bootman built a spliff.

"Wha' abou' you, Alan," asked Lil Bob, "what's your idea of hell?"

"Hell for me would be for the National Front to rule this country," Alan responded after a second's thought, "that would be hell for us all, not quite Nazi Germany but close."

"They already rule the country, man, they're everywhere man," said Ray Bootman, "in the present government now I could name you at least four cabinet ministers, including the Prime Minister that have identical beliefs to the NF and a whole heap of MPs. These NF are everywhere man, in the judiciary, in the police force, a whole heap o' dem dere." "Wha' abou' heaven, who wants to go firss," said Lil Bob.

"Heaven is right now," said Lil Bob firmly and the sniggering stopped. "Right now being 37 forever would be heaven for me."

"People would grow old around you; your kids would become older than you and die before you," said Alan, passing the spliff on without toking it.

Weed and tobacco had never really been Alan's thing.

"Never mind his kids," said Ray Bootman, "his great-great-great grandkids to the power of 100 would die before he did."

"That sounds more like hell to me rather than heaven, a bit like having the biggest cock in Liverpool," said Bobo Jones.

"You obsessed wid cocks or wha'," said Alan bursting in laughter.

"Yeah, well," Lil Bob persisted, trying to bring back some sanity into the conversation, "they would all have to stay the same age as me, and the ress of me fambo, and me mates, everybody in fac'."

"So heaven for you would be for everyfin to remain the same forever," said Alan, "that's a very establishment position to take, isn't it?"

The conversation moved to less controversial plane. They talked about the riots (Alan corrected them and said the uprisings) and how they started and how they would finish. They talked about the inconvenience caused, having to drive through debris and whole streets blocked off. Ray Bootman said there was nothing in black Liverpool's history to compare scale wise. The 1948 riots were skirmishes and the only people injured were black people. Even the awesome 1919 riots, he maintained, could not beat this, as if it was some competition of which were the best riots. Ray knew about these things, he was Black Liverpool aristocracy after all. His family had been in Liverpool since the 18th Century starting with Gwen who came as a free slave from Nassau. Everybody knew the Bootman family's story, self-published and dozens of copies sold.

Then they talked about the match on Sunday. African Pete said this could be Bonny Roberts' last season given his age, some agreed but Alan pointed to his cousin's legendary fitness adding, "he'll go on well into his forties."

Everybody agreed that Bombhead was the best goalkeeper in the league and Googie Roberts was the best player in the league.

"He should be playing in the 1st division," Alan added about his kid brother, but that was hyperbole, said Lil Bob.

They talked about death, about how many people they all knew had died in the last five years under the age of 45.

Back in 1976, Neil Wright and Bobby Jackson had died in the car crash on the motorway. They were on the way back from a blues party in Huddersfield in the early hours and Neil fell asleep at the wheel. Larry Smith, one of the most gifted footballers of his generation who had a trial with Oldham Athletic, was sleeping in the back seat. That saved his life but his left foot was crushed (the foot that could cushion a stray pass and volley it into the net in one fluid movement). Poor Larry, reduced to permanent lameness in his left leg and lameness in his brain as he took to drinking alcohol in a big way. At least he survived. Then One-Juke (so-called because he shook the dice once only before a throw), who died of cancer in his forties. They counted three more who had died of natural causes and two who died of gun shots in the last year alone.

"You just never know whose turn is going to be next," said Peewee gravely.

"Speak for yourself, lah," said Benji, "me ain't goin' nowhere for a long long time."

Lil Bob, who was well into electronics, put on a tape made up of the five best musical intros to a song as voted by the choir practitioners themselves. Everybody present except Alan had heard the tape several times, so Alan was tasked to guess which song the intro belonged to.

Alan knew by the first note to come out of the speakers that it was '*It's Growing*' by the Temptations, that piano clanking single notes was a dead giveaway.

The two note guitar lick of the second intro, the driving dark menacing beat embellished by brief organ flourishes could only be Bob Marley's '*Concrete Jungle*' and Alan said so loudly.

The third intro was more difficult. The opening violins made it sound like a fifties tune, Frank Sinatra or such like. Alan was going to skip that one then he heard the smooth dark chocolate sound of the trumpet that was unmistakeably Satchmo.

"'Summertime' by Louis Armstrong," Alan blurted out punching the air.

"Yeah, lah," replied Lil Bob, "but who does he duet with on this tune?"

Alan hesitated then ventured, "it's got to be Ella or Sarah. Ella Fitzgerald."

African Pete clapped from the kitchen.

The first few seconds of the electric piano of the next tune could only be *'What'd I say'* by Ray Charles, said Alan. So far so good.

"Hey, I should be on TV on that programme *'Name that Tune'*," said Alan feeling cocky. "I'd win it no problem."

The fifth tune had Alan stumped; space age guitar, crunchy bass and funky beat. Alan shook his head and turned down his mouth. He was never really into that disco sound.

"Bootsie Collins?" he guessed.

"Yes," replied Lil Bob to his surprise. "But name that tune."

Lil Bob played the intro again but Alan shook his head.

"*I'd rather be with you*," said Peewee with glee.

"I'd rather be with you, yeaaaah, yeah I'd rather be with you oohooooo," sang Bobo Jones.

The next one was easy, the Miracles' *'Tracks of my tears'*, Alan getting it inside three notes.

"Hey, that's six intros," Alan protested.

"We know, we juss couldn't leave out that one," said Benji smacking his lips. "It's more evocative than memorable, if you know what I mean, but we couldn't leave it out, it was the sound track to our love lives."

The best ending to a song ventured Bobo Jones (never one to let a conversation pass without showing off his soprano voice), was 'Purple Rain'.

"Oooh, oooh, oooh, ooh," he sang imitating Prince's high-pitched wail, "oooh, ooh, hoo-hoo-hoo."

Bobo Jones was still singing when Lenny Roberts arrived.

Lenny waved to everybody with his newspaper and sat down on the only armchair in the room.

"The last time I came here, that was over twelve months ago, I spoke on many things especially on the relationship between Irish people and black people in Liverpool, we also discussed the current problem in Northern Ireland and touched on its history and ended up with Castro's Cuba."

Lenny paused and rested his arms on his knees.

"I don't propose that the discussion today will be as extensive as then; I came here to talk about identity but having been overtaken by events I propose instead to talk about the troubles that have broken out and discuss why they happened, why now and where are they taking us. Feel free, by all means, to guide me in which direction you want to go."

He paused again. He had everyone's attention.

Lenny went on to describe a history of troubles within the black community, covering much of what Bobo Jones had said earlier but with more gravitas. Lenny could do gravitas very well. Bobo Jones challenged him on a few facts and Lenny indulged him.

"We have a historic situation where black people, young black people have had enough of harassment and casual violence from the police and they've hit back. This confrontational, potentially revolutionary challenge has shaken the establishment to its foundation. Liverpool we know is not an isolated case.

"In January this year, thirteen young black people died in an arson attack at a party in south London. Fifteen thousand people marched—the biggest black demo ever seen in Britain—to protest against police lack of action to investigate the fire thoroughly. *'Thirteen dead, nothing said,'* was their mantra.

"In March, that old reprobate Enoch Powell gets loads of media coverage—his lifeblood—by predicting racial civil war in Britain. As if on cue, a few days later, the police in London launch Operation Swamp 81 in Brixton. In six days, plain-clothes coppers stop over a thousand people most of them black, arresting less than one hundred. The word 'swamp' came from a remark from our Prime Minister, the Iron Lady herself Maggie Thatcher. You remember that quote about white people, though she didn't say white but that's what she meant, being swamped by people with a different culture, meaning black people, and that white people are afraid of it and may react with hostility. And we know all about that hostility, and we're not even immigrants.

"As sure as night follows day you had riots in Brixton and Bristol. Black kids had had enough and they fought back. Enoch Powell, that pernicious snake, rears his ugly head again and says 'you ain't seen nothing yet'. And he was right.

"Over the following weeks, black kids were confronting the police in ways they had never done before all over the country, including here in the Souffend, but it's seldom reported. The police haven't got a monopoly on group violence against black people, the National Front and other less organised racists pitch in as well. In the past five years, at least 30 black people have been victims of racist murders in Britain. It is against this background that you have to look at what is happening now. Add to it the class ingredients of poverty, bad housing, bad education and the wonder is that it hasn't happened earlier."

Lenny paused to pick up the glass of Cognac Lil Bob had placed near him. He took a sip and asked for a glass of water before resuming, his voice stronger now.

"They talk about a race war but that's been going on from time. Basically white people hate us and fear us, like you do a wild animal."

"It's not just us they hate," said Bobo Jones. "Look what they did to the Jews in Germany and Jews look white, they look just like Germans. Look at Slavery."

"The S word," sighed Lenny. "It always comes back to slavery; the refuge, the crutch for black weaknesses, the knowledge of the past to strengthen the future, the shame that feeds the anger. Of course we should never forget that fifty million black Africans were transported or killed by white people to be slaves on their plantations and elsewhere. Can you imagine how many people constitute 50 million? That's nearly the whole of the population in Britain today, at a time when the UK's population was less than 10 million. It's part of the same malaise—xenophobia," he continued. "The hatred of strangers, but just let's juss stick to black people for now. There's nothing they won't do to eliminate us. Look at the Tuskegee experiment in Alabama in the 1930s when the US U.S. Public Health Service let nearly 400 black men with syphilis die painful deaths without treatment but letting them think they were being treated. The experiment ended only 9 years ago when somebody blew the whistle on the whole fing. Pure evil these people I'm telling you. They enslaved us, then colonised us and then they had to invent a new word for a new form of exploitation called neo-colonialism. Now they just want us dead, pure and simple . . ."

"And we're fightin' back," said Lil Bob.

"Well, de youf dem are fight'n back," said Benji smiling.

"Not true," said Alan. "The kids might be fighting out there on the streets but we're fighting too in different ways, fighting for resources for the area, being politically engaged, voting, fighting to influence the political process. How many black people in this city actually vote? I'd be surprised if it was more than 20%."

"You can't say da'" said Bob spreading his arm around the room to emphasise his point. "Everybody in this room voted. That's 100% of those present."

"Ah, but we're the credit card revolutionaries and we're a small minority in this community," said Lenny grabbing back the spotlight. "Don't kid yerselves that what you do in getting peanuts off the Grand Master's table will change anything fast. Those kids out there," he added pointing to the open window, "they have terrified the establishment and that will be more likely to bring about change. Watch my words they'll pour money into this area. It'll be bonanza time for all you youth workers, community workers and whatever workers and the CRE. And as Linton says '*the CRE can't set we free*'"

"Which Linton's da'," asked Bob teasingly, "Linton Ferguson from the Falkner Estate?"

Louis Julienne

"Linton Kwesi Johnson," replied Lenny, "LKJ."

"Who's he when he's at home?" said Bob pretending he did not know of the dub poet.

"Never mind, you wouldn't get it," Lenny replied dismissively.

"I'm an accountant," African Pete protested, "it's no bonzana for me."

"It's bonanza, my friend," corrected Lenny him. "I'm sure you'll get your hands on some of that money, don't worry about that."

"In Africa," African Pete rejoined, miffed to be pulled up by black Englishmen about his pronunciations, "we call it bonzana," he said defiantly.

"You were saying about a race war," Alan interrupted attempting to depersonalise the debate.

"Yes, the race war," Lenny said and gulped a mouthful of water. "Yes, the race war," he repeated as he gathered his thoughts. "The race war, white against black, has been going on since we came here, since slavery and before. They had to demonise us in order to enslave us with a clear conscience."

Lenny unfolded his newspaper.

"Look at what the local paper is saying tonight in its editorial, praising the police, dissing the kids and asking for the police to be tougher," said Lenny reading out loud.

"The considerable courage of police officers ill-equipped to face such mob violence . . . The police policy has been one of containment; that must be abandoned in favour of a more positive approach.' And this is the editorial of our local newspaper urging the police to get their batons out and start beating heads, black heads; as if they haven't been doing that for years anyway."

Lenny carefully folded the newspaper.

"Look at the regimes this government support: South Africa, Rhodesia, Israel—white minority regimes that brutalise majorities black people and people of colour. Look at your own experiences, and not just the police," Lenny said looking directly at his nephew. "What we're seeing now is not a war, it's a battle and the kids are winning it. But, mark my words the authorities will win the second battle even if they have to bring in the army. They can then take the race war to a different level."

"Awesome," said Ray Bootman.

"Are you talking about the authorities," asked Bobo Jones, "or your everyday white person, because my mother's white and so is half my family; I'm half-cast."

"That's interesting as well as demeaning what you call yourself there brother," rebuked Lenny. "It implies you're not a whole person, when you should be calling yourself 'double-ethnic' if you want to reflect your two ethnic groups. It's also interesting because I thought half-cast was a description from people of my generation not yours and on that basis we don't seem to have progressed much. Don't get me wrong this is not a personal attack," Lenny added quickly to deflect Bobo Jones's frowned annoyance.

"Every generation seems to invent new terms for groups of people," Lenny continued, smiling for the first time. "For example, in my day we called Africans 'Afoes' and West-Indians 'Jamoes' and white people 'John Bulls'. They used to call Indian people Cha-Chas, short for Char Wallah, the name for the Indian men who ran little shops in the camps of British soldiers during the Burmese War. Now they call them Pakis. Every one of them terms was derogatory, including half-cast. You should call yourself double ethnic, it's a lot more positive; you're two instead of half. Or in our Alan's case it's treble ethnic as my grandfather and his great-grand father was Irish."

"They get everywhere dem Irish," said Bob. "We call ourselves British born blacks—BBBs—now."

"So what does that makes you a BBC," Bobo Jones said to Alan, "a British born Chinese, no sorry a B-B-B-C, a British born Black Chinese. Wow, that's a mouthful."

They all laughed.

"So what about this conundrum, how can we hate white people when they are an integral part of our community and have been for generations?" Ray persisted.

Lenny was incensed.

"What are you insinuating, that I hate white people," Lenny reproached wagging an accusing finger in Ray's direction. "I have fought with and on behalf of white people. I've demonstrated on many a picket line for the dockers, the miners, hospital workers, nurses, and the vast majority of them were white. I've spent more time sitting on white committees than all of you put together. I'm a member of the Communist Party's North West regional committee, and vice chair of their fundraising sub committee. I'm the secretary of my residents association, I run the Earl Road Allotment Holders Association. Also, for those of you who've got a short memory, might I remind you when the African Liberation Day was held in Liverpool back in the 1970s and the out-of-town organisers refused to let white people in, it was ME that led a walk out in protest. It was ME who told the organisers that Liverpool was different than Manchester and Nottingham and Birmingham and London. In Liverpool we stand together with white people so you can't have an all-Black

Liberation Day in Liverpool unless it's open to everybody in our community. As I said, my grandfather was Irish for goodness sake. He didn't hang around too long from what I gather, but I still carry his genes."

"Okay," conceded Ray, "but . . ."

"It's the young ones who feel it most, that's why they're rioting," said Alan changing the subject again to keep the peace, "especially those that haven't got a job, they've been miseducated."

"EDUCATION," Lenny exclaimed, "don't tell me about education. I hated school; or rather school hated me because I was too clever and too lazy, particularly Mr. Puddephatt, the Deputy Head in the seniors who doubled up as the Maths teacher. Mr. Puddephatt was an unreformed fascist at a time when it wasn't cool to be a fascist in Liverpool. And don't think because you've got a job or you've got a degree unemployment can't happen to you," said Lenny wagging a finger like a teacher.

"I should know," Lil Bob interjected, "I've been on the sick for donkey's years, lah, and believe me I know what pover'y is na."

Do you mean NOW," said Bobo Jones.

"Naa, that's what I said, naa," Lil Bob insisted.

"Naoow, not naa, there's a double-yew at the end of NOW," Bobo Jones laughed.

"You're just splitting hairs," Lil Bob replied shaking his head.

"Poverty? Are you saying you are poor?" asked Lenny looking around at the expensively furbished surroundings and back again at Lil Bob.

Lil Bob was one of life's chancers who lived off his wits. He ate well, dressed well and always had money in his pocket; granted he rode a bike but that was because he could not drive and wanted to lose weight anyway.

Ray Bootman reckoned Lil Bob was "giving one" to the landlord and getting looked after. Lil Bob gave him a sour look.

"None of us are safe," Lenny interrupted raising his voice and knotting his brow, indicating what he had to say next was important. "From getting arrested on trumped-up charges and found guilty by a compliant judiciary. Our Alan for one can testify to that. Whenever I hear that British justice is the best in the world, it just makes me fart. And for those of you who've got a job just remember that you're only one pay cheque away from unemployment and poverty."

"British justice is better than Nigerian justice," said Pete. "Nigerian justice is only good if you have money."

"No different than here and everywhere else," said Lil Bob.

"Awesome," said Ray for no particular reason, "awesome," he repeated.

Pure Pressure

"Don't tell me about the Norris Noblemans, Father Dominics, Nat Ajayis and Max Adams and all the so-called old-timers do-gooders of this world," Lenny reprised urgently. "Yes, they visit dying people in hospital and visit the riff-raff in prison and are at all the funerals basking in all the goodwill their GOOD DEEDS generate. Why do you think they are so old yet so sprightly, running here, running there," he continued, oblivious to the discomfort starting to generate around the room. "Because they suck the life blood of the people they are supposed to help and feed off it, prolonging their miserable selfish lives, all under cover of doing good."

"You're going a bit far there, Lenny. These are good people, and I can vouch for all of them anytime," Ray stressed. "Look at the work they've put in in getting the Jaycee up and running."

"The Jaycee," Lenny exclaimed, "what's happened to all the money it's received over the years? Hundreds of thousands of pounds have gone into that building and how much of that do you think went into the committee's pockets?"

"Come on now, you're out of order Uncle," said Alan indignantly.

"Maybe not in cash, I don't think you would actually steal money, but in expenses, you know what I'm talking about, you all do it," said Lenny firmly "The meals, the banquets, petrol in the car, trips to London and Brussels once I heard, on a conference or other—half the Jaycee management went, all expenses paid. I have a lot of respect for some of those who are truly committed to the cause, like our Alan and old Nat for example, I've known him since I was a lad, so we go back a long way. It is not him in particular but the so-called do-gooders in our community, that are doing it for themselves, they're getting somefin back."

Alan Leung shuffled uncomfortably in his chair. The spotlight had shone on his expenses too many times this evening.

"But juss for your information," Alan said, "the John Archer Youth Centre is the third largest employer of black people behind the Charles Wootton Centre which is second with 21 people, nearly twice as many black people as the whole of Liverpool Council, who only employ 12 black people out of a workforce of nearly 2,000 people. The Jaycee employs five and I'm not sure who comes fourth, but . . ."

"For others," Lenny interrupted, "being on committees is the only chance they are ever going to get of exercising some power, some influence on people who work there or people who use it. They do it for the prestige, to show the world and their God—and they've all got one, they're all holy-book-clutchers—what good people they are."

"There's noffin wrong in that, in fact there's everything right with that," said Ray, eagerly adding as if he had been waiting all evening to bring his guru in the conversation: "I believe that man's spirit can return to its source in heaven by performing good deeds on Earth. Abd-ru-shin says that in his Grail Message . . ."

"Don't tell me about religion," Lenny interrupted, salivating at the opportunity to expound on his favourite bête noire. "All the main religions support slavery," he said in a voice daring any one to dispute it. '*The servant will be severely punished, for though he knew his duty, he refused to do it,*' to quote the infamous Luke 12.47. In addition, Jesus says '*Slaves, obey your earthly masters with deep respect and fear. Serve them sincerely as you would serve Christ.*'

"Jesus never said that, he said servants," said Ray with a touch of indignity.

Lenny did not miss a beat.

"Slaves are invariably referred to in the Koran as '*possessions of the right hand*'. The Bible, old and new testaments, the Koran and the Tanakh all condoned slavery. Nearer to home, I've got two mates who have changed their names who were sound guys until religion discovered them. They've become Muslim and they're now sanctimonious bores. I've got a niece who literally believes God created the world in seven day and a sister who is completely round the twist who sleeps all day and sings all night, although to be fair it wasn't religion who turned her that way. Faith is based on hope not facts, and I believe in facts."

"And Liverpool is a God forsaken town," said Ray severely.

"Hardly," Lenny riposted. "At least as far as this area is concerned. Do you know there are more places of worship in Liverpool 8 than in any other district in the country?"

"Awesome," said Ray Bootman, "awesome."

"Having said that, religion has its place," Lenny continued mellowing his tone, "me, at least not yet, I'm not old enough. Maybe when I reach 80 and nearer to death, then I will keep my options open just in case there is a God who judges your every movement and rewards and punishes you accordingly after you die. As to which particular denomination I would choose, well Christianity has a lot going for it, although I've got huge problems with some of its imagery. Have you seen the portrait of Jesus Christ in the Methodist on Beaconsfield Street? It's a Scandinavian Jesus, with blond hair and blue eyes. Christian music, though, takes some beating. Gospel music is the music of angels and Mahalia Jackson its high priestess. That woman's voice alone could turn me into a Christian. Hinduism I found interesting for a very short while, when Ghandi was making the British shit their pants, and Islam always brought its own peculiar attractions, not least its holy book the Koran. I learnt a lot about myself reading that book. Voltaire, the

Pure Pressure

French philosopher, was a man after me own heart. On his death bed the priest came to give him the last rites. 'Repent your sins,' urged the priest, 'repent Satan.' 'My dear boy,' said Voltaire, 'now is not the time to be making enemies.'"

"Is it true that the Bible teaches that black people were cursed by God?" Peewee asked.

"The Curse of Ham," Lenny replied. "Also called the curse of Canaan and it refers to the curse that Ham's father Noah placed on his son Canaan. That's the propaganda spread by slave owners and their allies, including some members of Abrahamic religions, to justify racism and the enslavement of black people who were believed to be descendants of Ham." Lil Bob's shrill whistle startled everyone. It sounded like a referee blowing for a penalty.

"Rule number one at choir practice . . . no religion, righ'?" he said, frowning at Ray Bootman and Peewee for bringing the subject up. "You know that already Ray and Peewee, so you muss get taxed, you muss bring a bottle o' whiskey for next week, and none of your cheap supermarket brands either, righ'?"

"Hold on a minute, Bob," Lenny said, "it's not religion per se I want to discuss, but life and death."

"Go on, Lenny" said Peewee, hoping to get his 'tax' cancelled, "that's what I'm talking about as well, life and death."

"Human nature," said Lenny, brushing unseen specks from his trousers, "needs the carrot and stick of rewarding goodness and punishing badness, and that's what most religions teach us. However, what if there is nothing, as I believe, after you die? All your life is spent enduring an oppressive system that punishes you with impunity for being black, for being a woman, for being ill in mind or body, for being poor, for being ugly, for being unlucky, for being a communist, for being a conservative, for being different. For nothing because all this forced goodness to other human beings will have been wasted, because there is no heaven and there is no hell. You just die and that is the end of you, except for a few more years through your genes or through your personality. If you are a disadvantaged believer then it doesn't matter how hard and unjust life is because as a meek, in the kingdom of God, you shall inherit the earth when you die, so get on with it, endure it, in the scheme of things what's a human lifetime (70 or 80 years if you're lucky) compared to eternity. Don't live your life says religion as if what happens after life is all that matters, and religion is right in that aspect. Don't think in terms of you as an individual, which is what religion wants you to think, but think in terms of the legacy you leave your children, your neighbours, your friends and your family. Do you leave them a legacy that selfishness is the only way, look out for number one, or do you leave a legacy of loving, caring and sharing with your neighbour, your friend, your family as the only way to live a life regardless whether you get your reward in an after life or not. We are lovely people as a whole, the human race, of course some of us are evil, self serving and mean, and life is even more difficult when some of these people have direct power over our lives, but that should not deter you from doing the right thing and acting like a decent human being regardless of hereafter consequences. You should live your life without expectation of being rewarded or punished when it ends. You should go through life treating others as you would like to be treated and life will be sweet if you are lucky, because luck or lack of it is a major determinant of how smoothly your life develops, and you can't legislate against luck, good or bad."

Lil Bob clapped his hands and encouraged the others to do so.

Then turning to Lenny, Lil Bob said, "thank you Lenny. You wen' off on a tangen' a lil' bi' here and there, bu' anyway I think I speak for everybody when I say we found your talk quite stimula'in' and though'-provokin', righ'?"

"Right," they all repeated emphasising his missing 't'.

"I would describe it as a master class rather than a talk," Lenny replied grandly. "And on that note, I'll call it a day."

Lenny drained the rest of the Cognac in his glass in one gulp.

"Unless there're any more questions," Lenny added in a tone indicating he wanted no further questions.

Lil Bob did a whip round for Lenny and collected £11.

"Aren't you gonna stay for some scran," said Pete. "It's beef curry, Nigerian stylee."

Lenny declined politely, and left smiling his appreciation. Better than last time, he thought, as he swiftly counted the money on his way down the imposing stairwell.

Pete served the food in bowls and they all sat down and began eating.

"There's too much pepper in that," complained Peewee after his third mouthful, sweat drenching his forehead and streaming down the side of his face."

"Pepper's good for you, man," replied Pete. "And it is good for your libido."

"That's the last fing Peewee needs," laughed Lil Bob. "He's had enough hard-ons to last him till the end of the year."

"I think your hand might have slipped with the Scotch Bonnet," said Alan also sweating profusely.

"Faint hearts," mocked Pete, pouring hot pepper sauce on his food as if it was ketchup to prove his fortitude.

"Anybody else for some sauce?" he asked as a challenge.

Pure Pressure

None took up the offer.

"You are only one pay check away from the dole and poverty," said Bobo Jones in his best Lenny Roberts voice.

"Enoch Powell is the devil," said Peewee carrying on the skit.

"Hey, Enoch was a clever man," said Ray pointedly

"So is the devil," Peewee rejoined.

"Not all racists are stupid but all stupid people are racist," said Lil Bob sombrely.

"White people are devils!" rejoined Bobo Jones lifting his index finger.

Everybody laughed except Alan who merely grinned to show some semblance of solidarity with his mother's brother.

Crowd noises rose faintly through the open windows. Lil Bob and Bobo Jones rushed to the window.

"There's som'n goin' on, I can see smoke but I can't see any'in else," said Lil Bob peering through the night that had placed its dark blanket on the streets.

"Looks like trouble at t'ranch," Bobo Jones said wryly with a yokel accent.

"Let's go see," said Lil Bob slipping a black and white keffiyeh loosely around his neck.

"What's this," asked Ray pointing at Lil Bob's garb, "Yasser Arafat?"

"Bob's latest fashion statement," said Benji, "Sometimes he's worse than a beef over clobber."

As they all made to leave, Pete asked with a pained look in his eyes, "what about the scran, man, no one's finish it and dem plenty more left."

Pete was a nice man but cooking was not really his thing. Everybody knew that except him. Lil Bob made a mental note that it would be a long time before it was Pete's turn to cook again.

"Yes," said Lil Bob, "can youze clear up your plates and pu' them in the kitchen. The place is star' in' to look like a pigsty. Cheers."

In line they scraped the food off their plates into the bin and stacked them neatly on the kitchen top, they then all followed Lil Bob down the winding stairs.

As they hit the street walking towards the Jaycee, a few hundred yards away, a fire engine, gleaming bright red in the street lights, sped past them with lights flashing packed with grim-faced helmeted fire fighters heading in the direction of the centre.

They followed the vehicle, led by Alan who ran as a man demented fearing the Jaycee was on fire, with Lil Bob trotting way behind because of his small legs and the extra weight he had to carry, and of course not being of an athletic bent. The last time Lil Bob ran for any distance was during physical education at school, and he did not like it then.

Alan was greatly relieved the toolmakers' building next door was on fire rather than the Jaycee. The fire fighters were aiming streams of water trying to quell the flames that were licking the window frames on the ground floor windows. A petrol bomb exploded a few feet away from the fire fighters, followed by a volley of stones and bricks. The fire fighters fled, leaving their vehicle and pumps behind.

One of the missiles hit Peewee on the leg; he winced.

"What de fuck youze doin;" shouted Bobo Jones towards a group of hooded youths quickly advancing towards them with menacing intent.

"Don't come the hard knock with me, Harrison," said Ray to one youth he recognised despite the scarf half covering his face. "And you," he said pointing at a skinny youth. "You're Maureen Ajayi's lad, Dion isn't it?"

"I'm just watchin'" replied Dion bashfully.

"Does your mother know you're here, at this time?" Ray queried.

"Me grandad said I could stay out until ten o'clock," Dion said as politely as he could.

The Harrison youth who had thrown the petrol bomb hesitated then slowly melted back into the group.

Addressing himself to Larry, one of the Jaycee youths who appeared to be the ring leader, Alan asked: "What did you set the tools people's building on fire for?"

Larry replied simply: "All the years dey've been dere dey've never employed black people. It's revenge time."

Two lads ran out of the front door of the toolmakers' building carrying small cardboard boxes, dropping some on the road as they ran, but Alan was more concerned with the fire spreading to the Jaycee building. He grabbed one of the hoses gushing water into the road and guided the forceful stream back towards the fire. Ray picked up the second hose and followed Alan's lead.

Out of nowhere a camera crew arrived on the scene and began filming them.

"BBC," shouted the one holding the camera.

"British-born Chinese?" reposted Alan.

"Pardon?" asked the bemused cameraman.

"It's okay, private joke," said Alan returning his attention to the fire.

Dion Smith watched Alan and Ray in wonderment. Acting as firemen, there in front of him three feet away, they were realising his dream of fighting fires.

After a few minutes Dion welled up the courage to tap Ray on the shoulder.

"Can I have a go?" he asked him. "Please, I've always wanted to be a fireman?"

Ray looked at him, smiled and passed him the gushing hose.

"Try and aim at the base of the flames," Ray told him with an authority that suggested he had been putting fires out all his life.

The force of the water surprised Dion and nearly made him lose his grip on the hose as the stream headed towards the Jaycee building.

"Hey," Alan shouted good-naturedly to Dion, "it's the building with the fire that you're supposed to aim at."

"Awesome," said Ray to no one in particular.

It took twenty minutes to extinguish the flames, and as they did so, the Choir Practice gang celebrated noisily, jeering at the youths most of whom slunked away looking for excitement elsewhere.

"Fighting fires and saving lives," Dion repeated cheerily grinning from ear to ear.

With the youths dispersed and no missiles being thrown, the police came back with the firemen to help them recover their equipment.

"You did a fine job there kidder," said one of the firemen to Dion as he took the hose off him.

Dion was disappointed; he could have happily gone on flooding the smoking building all night. He watched the fireman get right up close to the building spraying into the smoke and then, unable to contain himself any longer, he ran excitedly all the way.

It took a further half-hour before the fire fighters were satisfied the fire was extinguished. Alan and Bobo Jones installed themselves in the front room of the Jaycee, Bobo Jones at his desk, rearranging papers and Alan on the phone.

The first call was to Eiddwen to tell her he would be staying the night at the Jaycee guarding the fort; the call lasted over an hour.

The gist of the conversation between them did not feel good to Alan. She had had enough of him and did not want to see him again. He was never there, always disappearing somewhere, particularly when they were in Liverpool and even in Newcastle it was always meetings in the evenings and weekend conferences.

Alan defended his time away valiantly, saying he was not paid that high a salary just for a simple 9-to-5 job, life was not like that. Besides, he insisted, she did not complain when that salary helped fund her lifestyle; and the school fees when Cardew's Dad missed the maintenance payments, which was often.

Eiddwen countered by citing that his mother detested Cardew and he, Alan, did not have the guts to stand up to her.

She had not found someone else, she assured him, but there was someone from work she liked, nothing more, they were just friends, nothing had happened, yet.

"What else is your problem other than Evil Lizzie," he asked her sarcastically.

"You don't love me," she said adamantly. "I know what it feels like to be loved and this was not it."

"It's not all one way," he asserted. "I've got real problems with you too; your addictions to exotic substances like cocaine, ecstasy and pep pills."

In turn, Eiddwen pointed to his less than perfect performances in bed. Sore point.

"You haven't made me come in two years," she said, "TWO years, for goodness sake. I'm a woman in my prime. What do you expect me to do if you can't satisfy me, scratch my arse? No thank you, I've had enough."

Eiddwen closed the conversation by instructing him when to collect his things and putting the phone down.

The front door bell rang. Alan looked out of the window. It was Gerry Thompson. The bell rang again then impatient knocks on the door.

"It's Tommo; go see what he wants," said Alan pulling rank.

Bobo Jones studied his paper work, like they were the most critical documents he had ever read. Bobo Jones was not a natural for taking orders, as Treasa Doherty could and often did testify; in fact she had disciplinary proceedings pending over him for, it was not hard to guess, persistently refusing to follow instructions.

"What the fuck does he want?" said Bobo Jones his eyes still glued to the documents in front of him.

"Go find out, there's a good lad," replied Alan more softly, but inwardly shaking his head about insubordinate staff.

Bobo Jones reluctantly dragged himself from his chair and headed towards the door. Gerry was being pursued by a police snatch squad, he said breathlessly, and would they let him out the back way. As Gerry climbed over the back wall, the police were ringing the front door bell. Bobo Jones waited until Gerry had disappeared over the wall before answering the door.

Six policemen barged past him as soon as Bobo Jones opened the door, despite his protestations. They searched the building and went out into the yard.

"Hev yee got keys tuh this van," the sergeant asked in a brusque Geordie accent pointing to the John Archer Youth Centre minibus.

"It's open," said Bobo Jones mimicking the sergeant's accent. "An' anywa, the lad went owor the waal an', befawa yee ax wor, ah don't knar whe he is."

Two of the policemen climbed over the wall whilst another climbed into the minibus.

"Don't try tuh be smart wid wor, sonny-boy," said the sergeant pointing his finger.

"He's not being smart as you put it," said Alan, "he's giving you a straight answer. As it happens you have no right being here. Have you got a warrant?"

"Don't neet one," replied the sergeant, "Wuh are porsuin a riotor."

Alan noticed that the uniformed policemen had covered their numbers on their epaulettes with black tape.

"I need your names and numbers; we will want to make a formal complaint. This building, as is the minibus, is a Council-supported youth facility and . . ."

"Yee knar wuh cud d'ya fo' harbourin' a criminal see dee yersel' a favoor," said the sergeant getting so close to Alan he could smell his sweat.

"Unlock this back door; yor mate, yor cousin, the lad neene iv yee hev ivvor seen befawa is probably lang gone cos iv you; remember that," the sergeant warned as he and his colleagues rushed into the night.

"I didn't know you could speak Geordie," Alan said with a grin as he locked the back door.

"Me Mam's Geordie," Bobo replied. "Broad Geordie n' all an' she's been here since she was eighteen. Did you see the pig's face drop when I put pure Geordie up 'is arse?"

Alan was no longer listening. He was too preoccupied where he was going to sleep tonight. He rang his mother and told her that Eiddwen had packed him in. He asked her if he could sleep at the house for the next few days until he got back to work.

"There's always a home for you here, son, whenever you want it," she replied predictably. "You can take Paul's room; he hardly ever sleeps in it. I'll get the room ready for you. I've got some pigtails and rice cooked; I can warm it up for you when you come in."

"Thanks Mam thanks," he said.

"You can do better than her, son, much better," Lizzie added, "nice girl as she is."

The added compliment, Alan noticed, had not bestowed on the previous exes she had inevitably dissed. That made the parting harder to take. She was worth keeping if his mother, the greatest of critics, thought Eiddwen was a nice girl. He could try to win her back, he had done it before, but it would come at a price, an offer of marriage, an engagement ring. He contemplated whether he really wanted her that badly, to marry her and to be insufferably bright Cardew's permanent step-dad.

Chapter 12

Stiff Necked Fool

2:15 pm Monday 6th July 1981

Lying on the unmade bed, Googie woke to the sound of rumbling thunder. He had not intended falling asleep, because although he had given up the idea of an immediate release, he was waiting for the door to be unlocked and informed that he had visitors.

The rumbling went on but it took him a while to realise the noise came from his belly. He was starving and had to eat, now. Immediately his eyes went to the food tray discarded earlier and shoved in the corner. He rose from his bed and began to examine the food. It was potatoes with a layer of dark brown meat with congealed running cheese stuck on top. He sniffed it and curled his lip. He was not *that* hungry. He scooped the few peas and carrots with his fingers and shoved them in his mouth, chewing slowly to make it last. The dessert was a small sponge cake with custard. He ate it heartily with a spoon that he carefully wiped on his shirt. He heard shuffling noises outside his cell. Visitors at last, he thought as he jumped up, spoon in hand, towards the door filled with anticipation.

There was a knock on his cell door. He looked from a distance to see if he could work out whom the eyeball belonged to that was leering through the spy-hole, where the glass had been previously removed or bashed as in his previous cell. He saw the man was white and it did not belong to The Face or his acolyte.

What do you want he asked, keeping himself at a safe distance from the cell door? Once bitten twice shy

"Get yer laughin' gear round dis," a Scouse voice invited. "Dere's a quarter ounce a' baccie in it for yer."

The eyeball disappeared then an erect penis jutted through the aperture. Instinctively, Googie threw the spoon at the pink object with great accuracy. The offending member was quickly withdrawn and the voice said more in pain than anger.

"I'll get yer fer dis, yer fuckin' paedo," said eyeball.

Googie listened for eyeball's footsteps as they walked away; he cautiously peeped through the hole and glimpsed a retreating figure carrying a chair. Googie felt his body shake with disgust. He brushed aside the tears that had swollen up in his eyes, looked up towards the blue sky through the small barred window, and gazed longingly at the sun's teasing bright shafts half-hidden behind the rooftops.

Googie thought nothing ever happened in this place to make one day any different from the previous, but so much had happened in such a short time that it was more as if everything had happened in this place.

There was numbness in his head that would not go away, that made thinking difficult and played tricks with his sense of time. Was it really only two days since this all began? Had it been weeks, months or years? Did all these things happen to him or someone else? Was he really Googie or was he someone else? Was he going to die in this cell?

Googie remembered reading somewhere that 2,973 people committed suicide whilst in penal custody throughout the world in 1980. That is maybe twice the total population of Risley Remand Centre. Googie knew what made that many people want to end their lives.

There was nowhere a place as evil and frightening as a cell. Locked up in a different world that may be only a few miles from where you live but may as well be on Mars. Totally cut off from the world that you know, from the people that you know, from people you love. Not knowing what is going on out there. Was his daughter safe; was his job safe, when would he get out of this place? He could be in here for weeks before somebody knew he was there. Risley Remand Centre, who would have heard of it, and who could find it hidden in the middle of all these fields cut off from humanity.

It was probable that all 2,973 hanged themselves. That was the easiest way of doing it as far as he could tell. He wondered what it felt like to hang yourself. Would it take long to die? Maybe, it would depend on how high you dropped and it would probably painful. The pain of living, he surmised, is worse and maybe his death would solve all the problems. Michelle would go and live with his mother and be brought up the same way he was. She will probably become a Rasta of her own volition.

He wondered what sistren Issachar was doing. Issachar was a real Jamaican gal who had lived in Huddersfield since she was 12. He met her at a reggae concert in Manchester in April. They spoke on the phone a few times and promised to meet at the Leeds carnival in August. Will he make it to the carnival, he wondered; and if Issachar had found other brethren, there would be plenty there to choose from at the Carnival. Rastas from all over the country went to the Leeds Carnival. No hassles, no fighting, just peace, tunes and ganja, and where was Norris Nobleman when you needed him?

What would Jah say? Googie sunk to the floor on his knees staring at the faraway shafts of sunlight and murmured.

Deliver I and I from the hands of our enemy, that I and I may prove fruitful in these Last Days, when our enemy have passed and decayed in the depths of the sea, in the depths of the earth, or in the belly of a beast. O give us a place in Thy Kingdom forever and ever, so we hail our God JAH. Who sitteth and reigneth in the heart of man and woman, hear us and bless us and sanctify us, and cause Thy loving Face to shine upon us thy children, that we may be saved, Selah.

He rose from the floor and sat on his bed waiting for deliverance, questions flooding his mind. How long would he stay in this place before he breathed free air again? What if he was to die in this place, who would miss him? Michelle, no doubt, but she would soon forget him; forget they were ever together except for the unreality of faded photographs. His Mother, brothers, and sisters would cry for him, particularly Doreen to whom he was the closest. Eventually their tears would dry up and his memory consigned to history. Gad and the rest of his posse would smoke some herb and finally knock down that Huskisson statue and replace it with that of Bob Marley in his memory. Every time they passed the statue, they would remember him, Googie Roberts, Rootsman, Rastaman, Brotherman Nyahbinghi man, and maybe remember him to their children and their children's children. He will surely meet Bob Marley. Jah's own minstrel had only died three months ago and would probably show him around Jah's kingdom and introduce him to Selassie I and Marcus Garvey and Abraham's descendents Moses, Jesus Christ and Muhammad, and the other prophets, Leonard Powell and Martin Luther King, and the princes and princesses. There would be other Issachars there, even more beautiful, even more serene.

He would tell them about his contributions. He would tell them how he had defended his community against white racists back in the 70s when still a youth. He would tell them how had helped build the street barriers that stopped the white thugs from preventing black families moving into the Falkner Estate; strictly hostile white territory in those days. Years later, Googie did not think the Falkner Estate was worth fighting for because of the dump it had become, but it was the principle of the thing—the right to live where you want without being harassed. He had been one of the lucky few without a criminal record, even among his brothers who both had form. Many of his brethren-soldiers (including Gad and Nya before they became Rastas) received their first criminal conviction because of the Falkner battle. The video of the *Listener* march he produced that was seen all over Merseyside. The Listener was a BBC magazine in which an article was published that said we were the products of black seamen and white prostitutes. He filmed the community's anger as they marched through town to the BBC offices; he recorded the voices of anger to the soundtrack of Linton Kwesi Johnson's *Five Nights of Bleeding—Madness tight on the heads of the rebels, the bitterness erupts like a heart blast, broke glass.*

He could have been a filmmaker, filming injustice, filming the truth. Jah knew he was a good man, a true Rastaman.

Googie swept the sheet from his bed and began biting at the material until he formed a small a hole in his white sheet. He manoeuvred his finger into the hole and pulled hard until it tore. The ripping noise was strangely satisfying, relieving, like an overdue piss. Then he gnawed at the sheet again to make a new hole and tore into the hole, then that ripping noise that seemed to echo inside his head.

He would probably be the 4,000th suicide in prison since last year if he chose to end his life here and now. He fashioned a knot with the sheet and wrapped the cloth around his neck.

He smiled. If he had a mirror, he was sure he would look like a priest with his righteous dog collar.

He tied the other end of the long strips of material around one of the bars at the window with a double knot, climbed up to the window lifting his feet tight to his body, and let his body fall towards the floor. His body dangled against the wall his feet a few inches from the floor. Googie felt as if his head was about to explode and began pulling at the material around his neck to release himself from the stranglehold. This was too damned painful, he thought as he struggled to free the pressure on his neck; there must be easier way to die. As his legs thrashed uselessly, he quickly slipped into unconsciousness.

The ritual noise of the prison filled the quiet cell; doors locked and unlocked, directives shouted, scraping of feet along the metal walkways. It was another day at Risley Remand Centre.

Chapter 13

Coming In From The Cold

8:30pm Monday 6th July 1981

The girls—Lizzie, Beryl and her twins—had finished a tuna and potato salad dinner prepared by Beryl. Lizzie was in the kitchen, a lit cigarette dangling from her mouth, washing dishes in the sink. The front door bell rang.

That moment, that precise moment when the bell rang and ash from her cigarette fell on the plate she was rinsing, that moment would stay with Lizzie until the day she died. She would remember the clothes she was wearing, her washed out yellow cardigan, that brown skirt she only wore at home, and the brown leather slippers Maggie had brought her back from somewhere foreign.

Lizzie was surprised, as she was not expecting visitors. Alan had taken Eiddwen out for dinner somewhere exotic he told Lizzie, and Lizzie was not expecting them round until late if at all.

Lizzie took the cigarette from her mouth, flicked the ash in the plughole and stuck the coffin stick (as Paul called them) back into her mouth.

"I'll get it Mam," she heard Beryl call out.

Maybe it was Bonny, he and Beryl had been spending a lot of time together these past few days.

"What's with you and Bonny," Lizzie had asked her earlier that day.

"Noffin Mam, he's good company," Beryl had replied guardedly.

"And I suppose he'd be useful to have around if that Greg shows his face," Lizzie had added watching closely her daughter's reaction.

"I hadn't thought of it that way, but he's more that just an athlete you know, he's quite sensitive, really upset about Valerie leaving and the kids."

"Have you two . . . you know . . . done anything. He is your first cousin; people will jangle because that's what idle people do."

Pure Pressure

"Mam," Beryl exclaimed indignantly. "You're as bad as our Paul. If anything . . . physical . . . develops I'll let you know, okay."

There were two uniformed police officers, one male, one female, on the doorstep. When Beryl saw them, she immediately assumed they had come to inform her that they had arrested Greg.

"Are you Mrs Elizabeth Leung?" asked the woman.

"No, that's me mother. What's it about?" Beryl asked knowing the answer would be bad news.

"Is Mrs Leung in, can we speak to her?"

Beryl called out to her mother.

"What is it?" Lizzie asked warily wiping her wet hands on her skirt and taking the cigarette out of her mouth

"It's the police, Mam. They want to talk to you."

"Are you Mrs Elizabeth Leung?" she repeated.

"Yes, what is it?" she replied but feared she already knew the answer.

Lizzie felt like it was déjà vu, when the police came to tell her that Kai died at work. She held on tight to the side of the door and braced herself.

"It's about your son George. I'm afraid we have some bad news, Mrs Leung. Your son is dead," she said gravely.

Lizzie opened her mouth wide and tried to scream but no sound came out. Beryl held her to prevent her from collapsing to the floor.

"No, no, no, no!" Lizzie screamed.

Her screams filled the house and the street and then turned to howls.

Lizzie, Beryl and the twins squeezed into an unmarked police car to the city morgue to identify Googie's body, the short journey completed in total silence.

The mortuary was eerily cold. An attendant pulled a leaver and out came a trolley on top of which was a body wrapped in a white cloth. The attendant lifted the top of the cloth.

Googie looked like he had fallen asleep, lying on the metal trolley. His eyes were shut, his face composed and his lips tightly closed. The faint mark around his neck was the only suggestion of abnormality.

"Oh my God," gasped Beryl putting her hand to her mouth.

Lizzie shouted his name, wanting him to wake up, to say he was all right, to wish her happy birthday. She reached out to him, touched his cheek, and let out a scream, almost one of surprise that Googie's skin was so cold. She wanted to take him out of that cold room and bring him home she pleaded to the disconcerted attendant.

Beryl formally identified him. Lizzie was speechless and only spoke when.

"Don't leave him there, I wanna take him home," she said, her voice barely audible in its hoarseness, as the attendant pushed the trolley back into the wall.

A police officer with silver pips on his shoulders told them that Googie was found dead in his cell; it was suspected that he had taken his own life. An inquest would be held to determine the cause of death, he explained. Googie had been arrested for public disorder offenses during which several police officers were assaulted resulting in injuries.

"That's not true," Lizzie pleaded. "My son is not violent, he has never been violent. He should never have been arrested and now you've killed him."

Lizzie wiped her eyes, grim-faced she said in a slow deliberate voice, "murderers, that's what you are, murderers."

The police offered to drive them back home but Beryl, her eyes and mouth spitting anger, refused her as she held her Mother tightly by the arm. They went into the waiting room for the twins and walked out of the morgue.

The walk back home was long and silent for Lizzie. She felt like a cursed woman. First, her daughters Lillian and Elizabeth, then her husband Kam and now Googie. How could there be a merciful God if he allowed all these tragedies to occur? What had she done in a previous life to deserve such misfortune?

Beryl was promising retribution but Lizzie was not listening.

Walking up the Hardman Street hill, a journey she undertook at least twice a week without strain, had become a strain, but a welcome strain; maybe the pains in her body will distract her from the pain in her soul.

The twins, who were walking ahead, had never been out that late before, despite the sadness of losing an uncle they scarcely knew, they wanted to marvel at the lights, point out the scantily dressed revelling crowds coming in and out of the bars and restaurants, and all the little English cars bunched up in the traffic jam. They just took the sights and sounds in, solemn faced as was expected, but could hardly wait to recount every detail to each other as soon as they could.

Beryl had rung a few taxi firms but they all said they were not travelling to Liverpool 8 because of the troubles. Beryl suggested they get a bus but Lizzie wanted to walk, a sort of penitence in the airless heat.

By midnight, the Leung household was full of friends and relatives who had come to lend support. Lizzie had grown weary repeating all she knew to each new arrival about Googie's death and the events leading up to it, and then the inevitable disbelief. Lizzie went to bed, not in her own room but Googie's bedroom.

Googie had not been in his room for days but his odour was strong; not just the burning bush, and that was quite overpowering, but the aroma of his pores, fresh and soft yet tangy. She looked at Googie's room as if for the first time.

Never again will Googie sleep in his bed or play his music as soon as he entered the room, never again will she hear him sing with his squeaky voice when he had the headphones on and he thought nobody could hear him.

She stared for a few seconds at the posters: a larger-than-life poster of Bob Marley smoking a Jamaican cigarette. A stern looking Marcus Garvey dressed for pomp, a drawing of Queen Nyahbinghi of Uganda.

She remembered how sad Googie had been when Bob Marley died, and that was only a few months ago but it seemed like centuries ago. Photographs of Googie's daughter nearly covered a whole wall. There was a recent close up of Googie and Michelle not looking at the camera but at each other. That must have been the very last picture ever taken of her beautiful son, an angel in looks and in nature; a kind and generous boy, an inquisitive boy who absolutely loved life. Why would he want to end his life, he had everything to live for. He had a good family around him, his daughter, a good job, his faith, his friends and his music; he had everything to live for. Everything.

The police killed her son, of that Lizzie was now convinced. If they did not kill him they drove him to kill himself, drove him to suicide. Everybody downstairs was of that opinion. Even Claudia Hamilton conceded it smelt fishy, and her fancy man was a policeman.

Lizzie tried to think of the last conversation she had with Googie or even the last words, but it would not come to her. Strange that, because she remembered Kai's last words, they were buried in her mind as was his face when he said them.

"Don't forget to pay the insurance man, and the pools man coz we're gonna win big, I feel it in me bones and fish and chips for tea tonight."

"It's Friday," she replied as he pecked her lips, "you know we always have fish on a Friday. What kind of woman do you think I am who would cook meat on a Friday for her family, hey?"

Lizzie watched her husband through the living-room window as Beryl pulled at her skirt demanding attention. She watched him walking up North Hill Street towards Park Road to catch the bus into town, with that stiff-back gait of his. That was the last time she saw him alive.

What had she done to deserve so much heartache? She wished God would take her too, to end the pain and reunite them. There were so many boys that deserved to die more than Googie, bad boys with malice in their eyes who spent their lives hanging around, thieving and cheating, worthless boys, Liverpool 8 was full of them.

"Googie's gone away with Elsie and Michelle away somewhere for the weekend," Paul had said.

Had Paul not lied, the lying, low-down hound, maybe Googie would be alive today.

Lizzie could see Paul's smug face as he mouthed those words. She should have looked at his eyes when he said that, they would have told her if he was telling the truth. It was her fault, nobody else's. She should have known that Googie would not go away on the weekend of her special birthday, he would want to be with all his family and he would have telephoned her. If Paul had not lied to her, Lizzie would know that Googie was missing and would have moved heaven and hell as far as they could be moved to find out what had happened to her baby boy.

Doreen is never off that phone, that's why poor Googie could not get through, the cow. Doreen thought she had a right to use the phone because she pays all her phone bills, but Lizzie did not ask her to pay her phone bills, she can afford to pay her bills. But saintly Doreen would not take no for an answer. She even insisted on paying Lizzie's heating bills as well, so Lizzie would never die of hypothermia.

"Dying of hypothermia my arse," Lizzie said to herself, "it just made her feel more righteous; the bloody hypocrite."

Lizzie blamed herself for not questioning Paul; she knew he told silly lies just to keep her quiet, she should have known he had not gone round there at all. She told Paul that in front of everyone and then started on Doreen, who was not even there, and that's when she decided to go to bed, away from all those people.

Lizzie slipped under Googie's bed cover and buried her head into his pillow trying to sniff out Googie's scent but the smell was of chemical freshness as she had only changed the bedding yesterday and her hand must have slipped when she put the conditioner in the machine. His dirty bedding was still in the machine waiting to be washed. She will put them back on his bed and wrap herself in his aroma and feel close to her baby again.

Lizzie did not sleep at all that night and neither did them lot downstairs. She heard them talking right through the night. By the time Lizzie came downstairs most people had gone.

She went to Bashir's store to get milk and things for the breakfast and found that Bashir's shop had been burned down; only the walls were still standing. The business and their home upstairs were gone, buried in the black ash you could see through the doorway and the windows. Lizzie walked the length of Granby Street and all the shops were closed, even those who would normally be open at this time. She was heading for the Dairy on Upper Parliament Street but she got frightened when she saw a dozen uniformed police officers with large shields sitting on the corner of Selbourne Street talking loud, so she made her way back home. She stopped everybody she met to enquire about Bashir and his family. It was Flossie Hawkins, who lived opposite Lizzie, who told her that the police had evacuated Bashir and his family in the middle of the night and firemen put the fire out. Flossie had to go all the way to Dingle to get her milk, and told Lizzie how shocking it all was. Lizzie told her about Googie and Flossie broke down in tears. Lizzie had no tears left so she could not join her.

Lizzie made an appointment that afternoon with Doctor Goldman and the pills he gave her lifted her out of reality for a whole week.

Chapter 14

Guiltiness

4pm Wednesday 15th July 1981

It was pure chaos at the John Archer Youth Centre, chaos like they had not seen since the after-game party when the Jaycee football team won the local league football championship and the cup. There was singing, drinking, dancing, fighting and shagging going on that day, oh yes, the football team was known for its partying, except now it was not a party there was no laughter just febrile activity.

The two phones were in constant use, Felicia Goolsby-Power-Wright was arranging transport to ferry people to Risley Remand Centre and various police stations to visit relatives, and Max Adam on the other phone arranging for lawyers to represent some of those arrested. In the lobby, Lenny Roberts was lecturing Ben Miller, Norris Nobleman and Yvonne Khumalo-Birtwhistle how the Liverpool riots were the beginnings of Engels' prediction of the abolishment of the state as a state. Ben Miller was nodding in agreement having had his shop looted and burned down with the police or fire fighters nowhere to be seen. Dutch television was interviewing Alan Leung and Maureen Ajayi in the yard with Swedish television next in line. Marianne was trying to talk sense and caution to a gang of angry young men on the front steps and Treasa was in the table-tennis room in the basement with some volunteers building placards for the demonstration against police brutality schedule for the next day.

In a corner of the main office, Beryl Leung was talking to Bonny's keen ears. They were not an item, Beryl told those bold enough to ask, "we're not girlfriend boyfriend, we're really good mates", was their mantra. There was a steady stream of people coming and going, the front door left open virtually day and night for the past week. Some were seeking advice or refuge, others to share in the limelight or the energy that the Jaycee was generating.

Pure Pressure

After the television interviews, Alan took a telephone call from a national newspaper.

"Are you Alan Leung," an unctuous voice asked.

"Yes," replied Alan, "what can I do for you?"

"Are you the Chairman of the John Archer Youth Centre?" the voice continued.

Alan was getting slightly annoyed by the tone of the caller, as if he was sneering at him.

"We understand," the mellow voice carried on, "you were convicted of living off immoral earnings in 1970 and sentenced to five years imprisonment?" the voice said cool as a block of ice. "Have you any comments to make, your side of the story perhaps?"

The sneer was out in the open now.

Alan felt the blood pumping furiously in his head. He gripped the telephone hard and swallowed hard on a mouth that had gone suddenly very dry. He had feared this phone call since he began that job in Middlesbrough, the phone call that would bring his life crashing down.

Alan's reply when it came was a feeble croak, "yes," he said. Then he recovered his voice and added, "and I was framed, convicted on trumped up charges. I was never guilty of those charges and one day I'll prove they were lying through their teef. That's all I've got to say. You can publish that as well."

The mellow sneering voice asked him for any other comments, Alan replied he had none and quickly put the phone down as if it was contaminated with something nasty.

Alan thought of his job. Middlesbrough Council would not want a convicted pimp as Senior Policy Adviser, that's for sure, that just would not do. He remembered Uncle Lenny's warning about only being one day away from poverty and sat down on the nearest chair, suddenly exhausted.

Bobo Jones asked him if he was okay, but Alan did not hear him, his mind was not in that room at that moment.

"Woman problem," thought Bobo Jones. "All them thirty-something have woman trouble."

"What did you say?" asked Alan.

"You okay?" Bobo repeated.

"You okay," Maureen joined in.

"Yeah, man, everything's cool," said Alan.

Alan hoped that perhaps they might not publish; perhaps his telling them that he was framed would scare them off. He smiled but his heart was not in it, he kept thinking of newspaper headlines with his name in it.

The next morning the newspaper published the article.

'*The House of Hate*' said the newspaper headline on page 4.

The article described the John Archer Youth Centre as an anti-police establishment that had harboured rioters and looters from justice and issued inflammatory statements to the media. It named Alan Kam Leung, aged 32, as a convicted criminal, found guilty in 1970 of living off immoral earnings and sentenced to five years imprisonment. It questioned the wisdom of the JAYC Management Committee for electing a convicted criminal to such a senior position and called on the City Council to withdraw its modest yearly grant.

Alan would not normally buy a right wing newspaper, but he was Bashir's first customer that morning. He read the article three times, with each reading his heart sank lower, and he could feel a nerve twitching irritatingly on his temple.

Alan was in his mother's front room and as soon as he put the paper down, not bothering to look at the sports page as he would normally, the telephone rang.

It was Eiddwen.

He had made it up with Eiddwen a few days before after a sumptuous meal at a posh Italian restaurant in Victoria Street and a marriage proposal. The wedding was set for next summer. She was back in Newcastle.

Eiddwen's first sentence was to the point and not unexpected,

"Is it true," she asked.

He explained how the police had framed him, that he was not guilty of the charges, and that the police evidence was pure fabrication.

He asked her what she was doing reading that right wing rag. She said her neighbour showed her the article.

"If it wasn't true, why didn't you tell me?"

"I was trying to put it behind me . . ." he tried to explain.

"And to think I've agreed to marry you. I'm sorry, Alan, but I've got to think of Cardew and my mother, she reads that paper religiously ever day, I'm surprised she hasn't called yet . . . she probably has there's messages on my phone . . ."

She began to cry.

"Look," he said, "believe me, I was set up."

"I'll call you back when I've thought about it," she said and put the phone down.

Alan rang her back but all he got was a busy signal. He tried a few more times and gave up.

Pure Pressure

So it is back to square one with Eiddwen, he thought. It might be for the best, he was no longer sure he would want to spend the rest of his life with her when she lets him down at the first hurdle.

At times like this, when he was in a jam, he would talk it over with his Mother. He decided against it, the last thing she needed was more bad news after Googie; he was thankful she only read the Daily Mirror.

Alan looked at his gleaming car parked outside the house through the curtained window and wondered how long it would be before he had to give it back. He had rang his boss last week (Derek Coulter with whom he got on quite well, regularly playing squash with him, having him for dinner) to ask for ten days paid leave because of Googie's death. Derek Coulter agreed five days as paid special leave but three days would have to come from his Annual Leave as, Derek Coulter pointedly reminded him, he had to prepare for the Government Minister's visit on the 16th July.

The phone rang again. Maybe this was Derek Coulter; he had his Mother's phone number.

The call was from Treasa. Her voice sounded different, like she was talking to a dead man. She asked him if he had read the paper, he said he had and was quick to tell her that he had been framed by the police. She said Keith Turner the Council man, had rung her and he was not happy. He was calling for an extraordinary meeting to discuss the implications of the revelations for the Jaycee. The meeting was scheduled for tomorrow night at 6pm.

As soon as Alan put the phone down it rang again. It was Maureen Ajayi and she had read the article.

"It's the friggin' cops who told the press, they're bastards," she said. "That monkey Keith Turner is after your head and stirring things up, he wants you out."

"I know," replied Alan wearily. "Treasa told me he's calling a meeting for tomorrow night."

"What about the people in Middlesbrough, have they been on to you?" she asked.

"Not yet, but I expect them to any minute."

"Anyway you should be okay your conviction is spent, I mean 1970 that was over eleven years ago."

"Eleven years, one month and five days to be precise, and any sentence of four years and over is never spent, ever."

"Doesn't time fly when you're having fun, hey? Chin up; don't let the bastards get you down. See you tomorrow night then."

"Yeah, catch yer later. And thanks Mo, you're a good skin."

"Whadya mean we've gorra stick together, lah. And leave me skin out of this."

Alan put the phone down, became contemplative and whisked himself back to 10 June 1970, as he had done countless times before.

It was the first time he had ever been inside St George's Hall, that monolithic building that even dwarfed Lime Street Railway Station opposite and that was a huge affair. The Hall's giant columns, the bronze doors, the statues of Victorian figures, the winged angels and stained glass window—all served only to intimidate him. The court room itself, tucked away in the Hall's labyrinthine bowels, was all polished old wood with a wigged, smooth-faced, stern-looking judge dressed like a malevolent bird and an all-white jury (shop-keepers and pen pushers from the white suburbs, Paul had warned him) who were his peers he was assured.

"Three upstanding and honest constables who had no reason to lie delivered their evidence," said the Judge in his summing up.

Detective Constables Halliday and Royce, and Detective-Sergeant Sands, names forever imprinted in Alan's memory, swore straight-faced on the Bible to tell the truth, the whole truth and nothing but the truth. Reading from identical notes, they word-for-word repeated that they had seen him, Alan Kam Leung, punch the woman in the face and the woman falling down to the floor. They said they saw Alan Kam Leung taking Bank of England notes from the woman's purse, and walk away saying 'you will have to get more money'.

The police said they then went to the woman's aid and asked her why she was putting up with this and she replied 'I have to otherwise he would throw me out, I would be homeless.'

The woman gave her name as Kathleen Grant (a name Alan had never heard of before or since).

"It's a fictitious name of a person who doesn't exist so they can't come to court," an old lag who had been round the block a few times would later tell him in Walton Prison. "It's a classic; the bizzies use it all the time, hearsay evidence from fictitious people."

On 11 September 1980 at 22.35, the trio said they saw a woman having sex in the back of a car in Back Saint Bride Street with a white male. They knew the woman as Doris Anderson.

"A woman with seven previous convictions as a common prostitute," the prosecuting barrister asserted, adding with a twinkle, "she has more form than the racehorse Arkle."

Pure Pressure

The white male gave Doris Anderson some Bank of England notes, the police testified.

"They have to say Bank of England notes," a recidivist pimp would later tell Alan in Wakefield Prison. "The law had a case thrown out once. They could not say whether what they thought was money being exchanged was not a love letter, which is what was put forward by the defence."

The police alleged they then followed Doris Anderson to the Somali Club on Upper Parliament Street and saw her giving Bank of England notes to the accused with which the accused bought drinks from the bar.

In the witness box the police looked so sincere that Alan began to believe them, thinking perhaps these events did take place, and they mistook him for someone else. However, they were all adamant that it was he, Alan Kam Leung, that they saw.

Then it slowly dawned on him that perhaps they were making it all up; but why and why him?

Doris Anderson was Alan's witness who said that Alan did not know she was a prostitute and he had never taken money off her.

The jury were out for two hours. Another old lag had told Alan that you always know which way a jury has gone when they walk back into the courtroom. If they look at you, it's a not guilty verdict and if they don't then you're going down.

None of the jury members so much as glanced at him.

Guilty on three counts of living off immoral earnings was their verdict.

The judge said that this type of offence was rife in the Liverpool 8 district and that the cry of the woman that she would be made homeless by the defendant if she did not carry on prostituting herself was a cry of help.

He sentenced Alan to 5 years on each of the three count of living off immoral earnings.

He heard his brother Paul shout "he's not guilty you bastards; I hope you all rot in fuckin' 'ell."

Alan had to hold on to the bar to stop collapsing to the floor. Fifteen years for crimes that he did not commit and for crimes that never happened.

Alan found out later that the sentences were concurrent not consecutive and was almost relieved, only five years not fifteen.

Alan spent three years nine months and fifteen days locked up in different jails. His appeal against conviction, with new lawyers, dismissed. On the eve of the Appeal Alan wrote a poem based on the Four Horses of the Apocalypse he had found in the prison library. He could still recite the poem word perfect.

Louis Julienne

I met perfidy today
He looked like Halliday
Very glib he seemed, yet grim
Seven police dogs followed him
All were fat, and so they might
Be in admirable plight
For one by one and two by two
Halliday tossed them black limbs to chew

Next came Royce, and he wore
All over his face, a huge sore
His big tears, for he wept well
Turned to millstones as they fell

The little black children who
Round his feet played to and fro
Thinking every tear a gem
Had their brains knocked out of them

Last came Sands, he rode
In a dark mini, splashed with blood
He was pale even to the lips
A liar to his finger tips

The vice squad like to dare
To ride among us there
Arrest and abuse and lie and jail
The black suspects without fail

With folded arms and steely eyes
Little fear and less surprise
Look upon them as they misinform
And bring disgrace to their uniform

So that they may return with shame
To hell from where they came
We shall all live more contented
With justice and truth we shall be treated

Alan tried to make the best of the ordeal. He studied for a MastersDegree in Social Policy at the Open University, although he never completed it, he played the game by expressing sorrow for his 'crimes' when in front of the Parole Board, but was still refused twice. He also read a lot.

Paul paid for subscriptions to saucy magazines and The Guardian. Beryl, recently immigrated to the United States, sent him historical and biographical novels. Maureen Ajayi sent him black consciousness books by James Baldwin, Eldridge Cleaver, Frantz Fanon, George Jackson, and Angela Davis and back copies of *Race Today*. Those books gave focus to his anger and bitterness. Alan knew who the enemy was now; it was white people.

The prison authorities at first refused to give him the black consciousness books, or the black power books as the prison censor called them, because they were "*eminently unsuitable*". Undeterred, Alan went to the prison library, discovered books by Enoch Powell, Adolf Hitler and Jack London, and quoted racist passages from each book in a letter of complaint to the prison Governor who eventually allowed him access to the books.

Uncle Lenny sent him a copy of the Robert Tressell's *The Ragged Trousered Philanthropists* when he started a painting and decorating course after being transferred to Kirkham Open Prison. That book helped Alan redefine his philosophy, it was not all about race, it was also about class.

His mother kept a cool distance apart from letters keeping him up to date with family developments. She did not believe the police had set him up, although she never said as much. Perhaps her belief in British justice and fair play was stronger than her belief in him. His Dad would have believed him if he was still alive, that's for sure, but he did not hold it against her, that was the way she was brought up and that's who she was—*Coronation Street*, *Double Your Money*, and the British flag, in that order.

Peach sent him a couple of letters but he never read them. He wrote her a short letter.

Dear Peach don't write to me again. Although it's not your fault that I was framed for a crime I did not commit, I would not be here, rotting away, if you had been a store assistant, an air hostess, a typist, a cleaner, anything except a prostitute. Goodbye, Alan

Doreen sent him 'spiritual' books, and a huge English Dictionary and a book of crosswords, "*so you can find peace, and keep your mind active,*" she wrote.

He learnt and tried to use a new word every day, not that he had much occasion to drop into conversations in the workshop or on the exercise yard the words **abnegate, abstemious, aegis or apogee**. Beryl was another who did not believe he was innocent, although she never actually said as much, not in so many words, but no smoke without fire was a favourite motto of hers.

The phone rang again; it was Lil Bob. After the ritual sympathies, Lil Bob came straight to the point.

"You should have changed your name when you came ou' o' the nick," he said. "You should have taken your mother's name, Alan Roberts, and nobody would have been any the wiser, lah. Look at Neville Keita, making a name for hisself in education somewhere in Lancashire, Senior Education Officer, not just an education officer but a SENIOR education officer. Da' means he's the bossman of all Education Officers, and he's one of the boys. I remember when I got done for shoplifting with him in Lewis's when we were sagging school. Years later, he got done for that van full of biscuits from outside Owens's bakery off Granby Street and even got jailed for 12 months for doing dem cheques. And you wanna know how he go' to be the boss of all these education officers somewhere in Lancashire, how this man can be in de higher echelons of socie'y although de man is a teef and a fraudster self?"

Neville Keita, Alan knew, had simply changed his name to Alan Keith and his criminal record disappeared with his African name.

"Well, I mean, he couldn't rely on the Rehabilitation of Ex-Offenders Act, now could he," Lil Bob continued. "Otherwise he'd be emptying bins, or stealing lead off some roofs or som'n. If you didn't tell lies about your past you didn't get a job, simple as da'. Bu' if you've gorra new name, you can star' again, like a clean shee'. Look at Basil Smith, he's working with handicapped kids in Old Swan, bu' he's not Basil Smith anymore is he, he's Arthur Basil now, the Smith has gone for ever from his documents, as if Basil Smith never existed."

"The horse has already bolted, Bob, it'd be a little late to lock the stable doors now, wouldn't it?" Alan replied wearily and hung up.

"Everyfin alright, Alan?"

It was his Mother, still dressed in her dressing gown. He assured her everything was fine given the circumstances.

"Any news on Googie," she asked.

This was the first time she had mentioned him by name since the day after he died, as if his name had become taboo; perhaps by not mentioning his name the pain would be less acute.

"He should be home early next week. Beryl's making all the arrangements," Alan replied hesitant still about using Googie's name in front of Lizzie.

"You know," she said with a thin smile, "I haven't smoked in days. Some good will come from all this."

Chapter 15

Redemption

11:50am Wednesday 29th July 1981

Alan Leung found the road almost deserted since leaving Middlesbrough, giving him plenty of time to think about what he was going to do next. Not having to worry about those bullying lorries launching themselves in front of you without warning or blocking you in to a slow crawl for mile after interminable mile.

Cars were scarce on the road this morning, a weekday, was because the heir to the British throne was marrying some aristocratic airhead and today, Wednesday, was decreed a Bank Holiday. Alan had chosen that day to travel for precisely that reason, suspecting the whole of Britain and much of the world would be watching the wedding and Alan Leung does not do royalty.

The route was a familiar one but one Alan normally undertook in the evening or early morning to avoid heavy and capricious traffic. This particular trip, he had finally decided last night after careful thought, would be the last one he made. No more monthly journeys between Middleborough and Newcastle to Liverpool, that part of his life was over. His job was over of that there was no doubt.

The meeting with Derek Coulter had not gone well. He was a friendly man but also a man who had been promoted beyond his capabilities. Rumour had it he got his job because he is the Chief Executive's second cousin.

"This authority cannot be seen to be employing a convicted pimp on its senior management team," Derek had told Alan with undisguised contempt.

Derek Coulter advised him to resign and he would provide a reference based solely on his work with the authority without mentioning his convictions; otherwise there would be no alternative than the sack for failure to divulge important details that had a bearing on his capacity to do the job. Alan protested that the police had framed him and he had tried to explain to Derek the details of the case. Derek began fiddling with his pencil, which he only did when he was not listening.

Alan refused to resign as he maintained he had done nothing wrong, besides he added, he was not asked on interview whether he had a criminal record. However, Derek suspended Alan on full pay until procedures for his dismissal were exhausted. Whilst Derek was still speaking, Alan got up and walked out slamming the door behind him. He drove straight to the home he shared with Eiddwen and put as much of his belongings as he could carry into a suitcase and two hold alls. Eiddwen and Cardew had gone to Whitney Bay further down the coast for a few days' beach and sun. She expected him to be gone by the time she got back.

The telephone rang. Alan let it ring until the answer-phone clicked in. It was Derek as Alan suspected asking for the immediate return of the car and keys. Alan had decided to keep the car for as long as he could get away with it that was why he had almost ran out of Derek's office so that he would not hear him asking for the car.

It was relief to Alan to read the road signs welcoming him to Liverpool. His watch told him it was just gone one o'clock. The fastest time he had ever achieved in the fifteen months he had been making the journey.

Meanwhile he was without a job, without a partner, soon without a car and with no savings to cushion his fall. Yet, despite this uncomfortable reality that was slapping his face quite hard, at the back of his mind was what he perceived to be the betrayal of a man he considered a friend. He had played squash with Derek twice a week for the past twelve months, gone out for a pint or two of Newcastle Brown Ale afterwards, had him round for dinner once, although, significantly now, had never been invited back to Derek's house. They had attended several football matches together at St James Park to watch Derek's beloved Newcastle United although Alan was no big football fan, although that Chris Waddle was useful, bound to go far. Alan had provided Derek with an alibi for his wife when he was shagging Irene from Parks and Recreation, and consoled him when Irene began shagging the Lothario from Probation Services. Being realistic, Alan expected Derek to sack him; his hands were tied but he expected more empathy from Derek, his reassurance that he believed Alan was set up. Instead Derek had stopped listening and the look on his face said that Alan was just another nigger who had got further than most and deserved to be knocked down to the gutter where he belonged.

On Alan's first day back at work after the article had been published it was obvious word had got out about his criminal record. Starting with Jenny, the normally jovially greeting receptionist, she gave him a perfunctory nod when he came in that morning punctually at nine o'clock. Eileen Bowles however, his scrupulously neat and ferociously ambitious deputy who he knew had been in the office since 7.30 as she often reminded every one and who bore him a lasting grudge for pipping her to the job in the final interview, pretended as if all was normal. With a neutral smile that suggested neither warmth nor frostiness, she handed him her expense form to approve and sign and asked him informed questions on a policy paper he had asked her to draft.

The office Alan worked in was open plan, a new concept *"to help create a work environment that offers more opportunities for observing and learning from others"* Derek Coulter had told him, probably quoting some management guru but claiming it as his own.

There were 22 people working in the office from the Director of Youth Services, Paul Hayward whose area was by far the largest and screened out of view, to the lowest notch on the totem pole, Jenny the receptionist at the front desk. Alan Leung, as Senior Policy Adviser was number four in the hierarchy with two subordinates: the aforementioned Eileen Bowles and the ebullient Helena Swift who was anything but. Helena seldom came into the office before ten, usually out of breath with having to carry around all that weight and the remnants of a hastily ate breakfast around her lips and down the front of her cardigan (Helen swift always wore a cardigan).

Alan sat at this desk and buried his eyes into the first report on top of his pile without reading it so that he did not have to look up at his colleagues as they came in to begin their day's work.

Helena came in at 10.30 apologising for her lateness twittering on about a burst pipe causing traffic congestion all along Russell Street, with yellow egg stains on her cardigan and toasted breadcrumbs around her mouth. Helena made Alan a cup of tea then asked him in a low almost conspiratory voice looking him straight in the eye: "Are you alright?"

He asked her what she meant.

"Yee knar, the newspaper article, the prison thing, yee knar, everybody's talkin' abeut it," she whispered.

"I was framed by the police," he said.

"It's in the past, yee served yee time, yee paid yee debt to society," she continued.

"I did not do what I was accused of," he insisted, his voice rising.

"Shshshsh," she cautioned. "People will hear yee."

"I've got noffin to hide Helena," his voice loud enough now for everyone in the open office to hear.

It was at that moment that Patricia Wren, Derek Coulter's personal assistant, came to summon him to the fateful meeting with Derek.

That is what troubled Alan more than losing his job, people's reaction, particularly people like Derek whose opinion he respected. It suited their stereotypes to believe that black males are pimps. Maybe Uncle Lenny was right; maybe they were white devils out to get us. Therefore, despite all the positive things he had done, that conviction on that overcast June day in 1970 looked like it would end up defining him.

As Alan steered his car around the mini-roundabout facing Princes Park Gates into Kingsley Road his thoughts reverted to his dead brother Googie. He stopped outside his mother's house and languorously rubbed his face with both hands as if to wipe away the sadness.

Paul Leung knew as soon he left the restaurant and he saw the O'Connor brothers across the street that someone was going to die.

At last the sky was crying its summer lament, short but fierce, drenching the streets in seconds, washing away the accumulated dust that had imperceptibly cloaked the city for the past three weeks. The sun had not appeared all day; the thick clouds saw to that, so when the rain finally came it was more what-took-you-so-long-you've-been-brewing-all-day than a surprise,

Paul Leung finished his meal, stretched his legs as far as they could go and burped very loudly. African Henry sucked his teeth at his companion's rudeness.

"Told ya it would rain, didn't I," Paul said to African Henry.

"I told YOU," African Henry answered back. "Me see it on de weather forecast. Do you have to burp like dat?"

"I don't need no weather fingy to know when it's gonna rain. Dem thingies, watcha call dem . . ."

"Weather forecasters?"

"Yeah, man, dem forecasters, it's pure guess-work with dem, dey get money for jam."

Paul started to dig deep into his molars with a toothpick and fished out bits of chewed food. If he liked the taste he would eat it and if not he would spit it out, like a bullet, anywhere, but he ate most of what he found, it was good stuff. It was always the same dish, Won-Tun Noodle soup; today it was with Char Sui, but sometimes with Roast Duck. He ate at the same restaurant six to eight times a month, usually after he had had a hard day at the garage, and today had been a hard day.

Paul's Jaguar car had been the main problem. It would not restart if the engine had been turned off for more than fifteen minutes. The problem seemed intractable, as all the parts appeared to be in good order. He put two new batteries in, pulled the car apart and put it back again. It took seven solid hours before it was solved, missing his lunch break in the process and Paul liked his food.

Paul had been a regular at Mabo's for nearly 10 years, a no-frills, no alcohol, Chinese restaurant in Chinatown. Mabo has served the best soup in town by a distance Paul told everybody as if he owned shares in the place. His cousin Colin Leung from over the water in Wallasey had taken him there five years ago, the day after the funeral of Uncle Kwok, Colin's father, to discuss some business. It was an impressive funeral with six limousines and enough flowers to open a florist's shop. Uncle Kwok was a freemason and the local lodge always gave their members a good send-off.

Paul and his Mother were the only ones representing his Dad's family. Paul's grandfather, Loh, and Uncle Kwok were brothers from Kowloon, had travelled the world as seamen and settled in Liverpool with Liverpool wives and children. Uncle Kwok's age was estimated at over 100, but he could have been anywhere between 90 and 110, nobody knew either his true age or Paul's grandfather's, although Loh Leung was years younger than Uncle Kwok, but then everybody was younger than Uncle Kwok.

Paul felt he had to apologise on behalf of the family for not keeping in touch with their Chinese side of the family. He assured Colin that they all loved his father, "particularly ar' Beryl, she adored him," he said, but she was in America and couldn't get over. Alan was in jail on a five-year stretch on some trumped-up charges. Doreen had moved down to London and was getting married to some preacher man. Aunty Maggie lives in Cardiff, had lived there for years. Aunty Esmee is away to the mixer as you know, and little Googie's camping in Colomendy with the school. As for Uncle Lenny he moves in mysterious ways—one minute he's here and then you don't see him for two years."

"I bet you thinking about your cousin Colin," said African Henry reaching to touch Paul's hand.

"How do you know dat?" said Paul pulling his hand away, not one for displaying affection in public.

"You always say when we come here '*I must ring our Colin*'"

Paul's laugh echoed in the empty restaurant.

"Muss be a thingy, you know,"

"Guilt trip," said African Henry, well used to filling in the word gaps.

As African Henry went to the toilets, Paul rose slowly from his seat and paid for the meals then pressed two pound coins in the hand of the middle-aged Chinese waitress like he always did, as if he was handing her the secret of life. And, as usual, he said: "That was an elegant dinner, Mrs Ching, thank you," in pure Cantonese.

He picked up the local Chinese Community newspaper on his way out and satisfyingly took in the damp warm night deep into his lungs. The neon lights reflected on Nelson Street's wet road and sidewalk and parked cars were glistening with moisture.

Twenty yards away he could see someone jumping on the bonnet of his car.

Paul adjusted his glasses, not quite believing what his eyes were telling him.

He recognised the man jumping on his car as Lecky O'Connor.

"Somebody's scratched yer car all down the side. You must have enemies, blue," said Bull O'Connor, appearing from the shadows like a bad dream.

Bull was holding some metallic implement in his hands with a nasty smirk across his face.

Paul looked across at his car, his shining pride that he had spent all day getting right was now battered and dented. His professional eye had automatically assessed the damage. Windscreen, two doors, roof panel, front and side panel, back panel and priced the whole job including the parts and how soon he could get them.

Paddy Dalton was leaning on the Mabo railings nearest to him; that made three of them. Paul quickly took out his Swiss Army knife that he always carried with him, from inside his trouser pocket just in case a situation like this arose.

Paul slowly and warily walked down the restaurant steps like a man walking to his doom. He could have dashed back into the restaurant and sought safety but that would have jeopardised Henry and he was a harmless soul. Paul felt confident that he would take at least one of them with him, maybe two. It would be a miracle if he could conquer all three of them.

Paul saw Paddy Dalton's clenched fist flying towards his face and pulled back to let it swoosh past his head and hit thin air.

Paul jabbed Paddy in the ribs with the knife and tried to block the blow from Bull's iron bar with his arm as it hurtled through the air towards head but the bar slammed against his temple sending millions of bright red hot stars shooting into his brain and his glasses flying into the night. Instinct made Paul throw a wild punch and it connected. Bull O'Connor fell to the floor and from the corner of his good eye, Paul could see Paddy Dalton was kneeling against the railing clutching his side with anguish.

Lecky lunged at Paul with a sword in his hand. Slowed down by his injuries Paul felt unable to avoid the blade as it sliced into his lip and nose. The blood gushed out of Paul's face but he still felt sufficiently in control to hit Lecky hard on the forehead sending him reeling sideways and down on one knee.

Bull recovered quickly and caught Paul flush on the jaw with the iron bar. Paul stumbled backward but his knees did not buckle. He knew he had to keep on his feet or he was a dead man. He had to escape; staying put and trying to fight his way out was a hopeless strategy. Paul attempted his getaway by backtracking away from his attackers and then running as fast as he could, avoiding a screeching taxi full of passengers in the process. All he could manage was a stumbling trot in a desperate attempt to reach Berry Street where there were people, where people could stop them from killing him.

As he was running Paul managed to dodge Bull's first blow altogether but only deflected the second blow onto his shoulder which knocked him off balance and he fell. Immediately, Paul bounced off the floor and fumbled to his knees, escape still a possibility. Another blow to the back of his head knocked him right back down to the pavement. Instinctively Paul rolled himself into a protective shell, his arms shielding his head as the blows rained relentlessly on his body; and then the pain disappeared. He saw himself in front of Harrington Board School, dressed in baggy grey trousers that reached to his knee and sturdy black boots that had a hole in the right toe where he played football constantly. He was standing outside of the boys' entrance in Mann Street then he saw himself walk to the girls' entrance on Caryl Street waiting for pony tailed Beryl and Doreen with their. Higson's brewery, across the road, disgorged clouds of a smelly cocktail of hops, ginger and soap. Ginger and soap the unmistakeable smells of his childhood.

Paul heard himself say "Gan", Cantonese for fuck, before everything went very dark.

The blows did not stop until a group of joyous revellers coming out of the restaurant a few doors away from Mabo's protested at the carnage. One of them shouted, "hey, leave him alone you fucking bullies!"

Paddy Dalton was already revving the engine of their car when the O'Connor brothers got in. The dark blue car drove off at high speed into the damp night.

African Henry rushed out of Mabo's to Paul's prostrate body. He was relieved when he realised that Paul was still breathing. The police arrived a few minutes later followed by an ambulance. He accompanied Paul in the ambulance to the hospital. The frantic ride with sirens ringing was mercifully less than a mile away. He was grateful for the speed and professionalism of the medics in getting Paul to the operating table. African Henry had to be told several times to wait outside in the corridor. He went to the payphone and rang Paul mother's phone hoping she did not pick up the phone. How can you tell a Mother whose son had recently died violently that another son had been badly beaten up and could die. The woman had had enough shocks without being told of another; it would kill her. Thankfully, Beryl answered the phone.

"This is Henry," he said to her.

"Oh, African Henry," Beryl replied. "You okay?"

African Henry hated that nickname but he told himself that now was not the time to make his feelings known.

"Me's at the Royal; your brudder Paul been badly beat up," he said as quickly as he could.

He heard Beryl gasp and then ask, "How badly, is he conscious?"

"No, he not conscious but dem said him gonna be alright," Henry replied.

The operation took more than six hours after which the doctors put him on the critical list before sending him for an x-ray to assess what bones had been fractured. They had drilled a hole in his skull to drain accumulated blood and sewn up his wounds.

"What do you mean by critical?" Paul's sister Doreen asked the nurse over the phone all the way from London the next morning.

"It is serious, he is very ill," was the blunt reply.

On the second day, with Alan, Beryl and Doreen Leung, Bonny Roberts and African Henry assembled, one of the doctor told them that Paul was in a coma, "a state of deep unarousable unconsciousness" the doctor said, which sounded worse.

On the third day, the doctors said there was little brain activity and major organs were failing. Machines were keeping him alive.

"Paul would love de idea of machines keepin' him goin'," African Henry said with an attempt at a smile. "'he love mechanics, all teengs mechanic 'e love."

On the fourth day, the waiting room had become a permanent packed meeting of Paul's nearest and dearest. The news of Paul Leung's attack had made the third page of the Liverpool Echo and broadcasted on Radio Merseyside News five times on the first day.

Lizzie was the only person in Liverpool 8 and beyond who did not know of son's condition. She was at home, mainly in Googie's room, wrapped in grief over one son's death. By common consent, she was not informed of Paul's death in case it sent her over the edge.

On the fifth day, there was talk of switching the machines off.

On the sixth day, Paul's brain activity soared.

Pure Pressure

On the seventh day, Paul opened his eyes.

"You can't tell me that wasn't a miracle," Doreen told anyone who would listen.

On the eighth day, Paul Leung died.

Beryl led her siblings to inform their mother about Paul's death. It was not easy.

"Why didn't you tell me; at least I could have seen him before he died," Lizzie howled.

She took her cigarettes and her Emecheta book from Googie's room and locked herself in her own bedroom. She stayed there for three days, apart from occasional trips to the bathroom, until her sister Maggie arrived from Cardiff.

"C'mon girl, get a grip," Maggie urged after they had both hugged tightly for several minutes and cried on each other's shoulder. "Is this the way your Googie and your Paul would like you to behave, to shut yourself off from the world and act like a hermit? Of course not and you know that. They both would have wanted you to be strong for the rest of the family. Show leadership; that's the Roberts way, you know that. I'm staying here until it is all done so you'd better arrange a bed for me otherwise we'll be sharing yours, like in the old days and I haven't changed, I still fart all night and it still stinks. First things first, you need a good pan of Scouse down yer; it looks like you haven't eaten for days. You get yourself dressed and I'll send one of the kids to the shop and get the stew started."

"I'm cursed," said Lizzie wiping the tears from her face, "my family is cursed. Lilian and Elizabeth dying in the fire and Kai died early not long afterwards, and now this, my youngest and oldest lads dead within weeks of each other. All of them have died a violent death. Paul was beaten to death, for Godsake! What have I ever done to deserve such punishments? There is no God and if there is he's not merciful, he's a bloody sadist!"

"Now now, come on sis, I know you've had it awful, you're not cursed, you're blessed. Sometimes God moves in mysterious ways."

Lizzie rose from her bed and took a cigarette out from the cabinet drawer.

"You don't know the half of it, girl," she said as she lit the cigarette. "My first ciggie in days," she said staring at the white cylinder as if it contained memories best left alone.

"I betrayed me own daughter," she added with a sour smile.

"What you talking about Lizzie, you haven't betrayed anybody, least of all your kids."

"Like I said you don't know the half of it," Lizzie continued ignoring Maggie's cajoling words. "Doreen's the one I betrayed."

In an even voice, as if she was reciting a story from a book, Lizzie reminded her when Doreen had her baby aged fourteen. The baby's father was not some young lad from Caryl Gardens as she had told everyone. George Small, Lizzie's partner, was the father of Doreen's child. She had caught them in bed together one afternoon when Doreen was supposed to be in school and Lizzie was not expected back until later that evening because Paul was supposed to be taking her to one of his car races in Bristol. The van they were driving in broke down half way there and she was fed up waiting for him to fix the van so she got a taxi to the nearest train station and returned home. Lizzie was four month pregnant to George at the time. She threw George and all his clothes out of her house. Lizzie was tempted to call the police on him to get him locked up but for Doreen's sake she decided it best not to, besides he left town shortly afterwards and went to live near Huddersfield she was told.

Doreen, she reminded Maggie, had her baby three months after Googie was born. Doreen was always with the baby; the baby never left her side despite Lizzie telling her that the baby would be put up for adoption.

Lizzie had made plans with Nora Philips to take the baby. Nora was a well-off woman, a light-skinned woman from Old Swan who could not have children. She was married to a Gambian sea-faring officer and wanted to pass the baby off as her and her husband's own.

Lizzie arranged a meeting with her near at the car park facing Sefton Park's boating lake. She got Doreen there under the pretext of taking the baby out for a walk. As Nora approached them, Lizzie quickly lifted the smiling baby out of the pram and handed it to Nora. Nora took the baby and drove off in her car. It happened so quickly it was over in seconds.

Nora had told Lizzie that she was emigrating to The Gambia so they would never see her or the baby again.

"Doreen screamed when she realised what had happened," said Lizzie her voice calm and even, only her hands twisting the corner of her bedcover betrayed any anguish.

"Doreen screamed *my baby*,' It was a horrible scream, a sound that came from deep inside her, a sound I had never heard before; it was horrible. I hear that scream every day of my life."

Lizzie sighed as if exhausted.

"God has punished me hard for my sins by taking my two sons away from me," Lizzie continued, slowly blowing the smoke from her mouth. "That's my final punishment—my sons dying a horrible death."

Chapter 16

Forever Loving Jah

10:30pm Sunday 16th August 1981

Lizzie's house was full of people—in every downstairs room, on the stairs, in the hallway and by the open front door, all coming to pay their respects. Lenny was trying to convince Lizzie to let him speak at the funeral service in the morning.

"I swear on everything that is dear to me, Liz, that I'll do them both proud."

Beryl was having none of it.

"There's too many people speaking already Uncle Lenny, it'll turn into a political meeting with speech after speech. Our Wayne and Bobo Jones are singing, and we've only got an hour and a half."

"It'll be short," pleaded Lenny.

"Give us a sample then," Maggie suggested not averse to liven things up on sombre occasions.

Lenny stood up immediately, eager to demonstrate his oratory skills. He elaborately brushed off imaginary specks from his canary yellow open-necked shirt and his tight beige trousers that emphasised his paunch. He paused for a few moments and looked around the room. There were no more than 25 people in Lizzie's back living-room compared with the 1,000 plus he had addressed at the Pier Head after the massive demonstration against the Chief Constable.

"Paul and Googie were good men who we will all miss," he began in a strong voice.

The room went quiet.

"If there is a heaven both of them will be there, big Paul fixing whatever needs fixing up there and Googie will be smoking spliffs and digging sounds with the angels."

The audience laughed, even Lizzie smiled. Lenny was off.

Louis Julienne

"If there is a thereafter it'll be mighty crowded up there. What if there is nothing, as I really believe, after you die? All your life is spent enduring an oppressive system that punishes you for being black, for being a woman, for being ill in mind or body, for being poor, for being ugly, for being unlucky, for being a communist, for being an artist, for being different. For nothing, because all this forced goodness to other human beings will have been wasted, because there is no heaven and there is no hell. You just die and that is the end of you except for a few more years through your genes or through your personality."

Lenny was losing his audience; his monologue was rapidly emptying the room. Maggie had stopped listening to Lenny and was saying to Lizzie what a marvellous job Bernadette Murphy had done of the front room.

"She's quite good like that," said Maggie. "She does abortions as well, or used to."

"The room is so peaceful and pure, it looks like heaven in there," Lizzie remarked, her face composed.

The Murphy clan were lined up outside the closed door of the front room where Googie and Paul's bodies lay, waiting in line to be confessed by Father Dominic.

Uncle Albert came out of the room looking chastened.

"What did he say?" Franna asked him.

"Seven Our Fathers, five Holy Marys and ten bob in the collection box."

"Ten bob! You mustave a lorra fuckin' sins den," said Bernadette.

Terry, Franna's 25-year-old son, was seeking advice from his Mother being the next in the queue for confession.

"Wha' should I tell de Priest, Ma, should I tell him about de parking ticket?"

"No," replied Franna authoritatively, "dat's too petty"

"Wharrabout de weed?"

"No son," she warned, "dat's illegal, yer've gorrenough on yer plate widout bringin' in de weed, yer can't mention de weed ting in a confession, God bless us, Jesus, Mary and Joseph," she added crossing herself.

"Dere's dat robbin' twat, Eric Wilson," said Bernadette, pointing at Eric standing alone in the lobby looking bashful. "I gave him 30 purple hearts for a gram of coke but the coke turned out t'be chalk grinded up, the robbin' bastard."

Lenny had fixed his attention on the handful of people still listening to him.

"I don't believe in God as we have come to know Him," he continued barely lowering the tone of his voice to suit his dwindling audience.

"You know, the old white man with hair all over his face. I see God more as a force that is beyond our comprehension and is not involved in our daily lives. Human nature, I say, needs the carrot and stick of rewarding goodness and punishing badness. However, if you are a disadvantaged believer then it doesn't matter how hard and unjust life is because as a disadvantaged, in the kingdom of God, you shall inherit the earth when you die, so get on with it, live your life on your terms. Religion says don't live your life as if what happens after life doesn't matter, and religion is right in that aspect. Think in terms of the legacy you leave your children, your neighbours, your friends and your family. Do you leave them a legacy of selfishness, looking out for number one, or do you leave a legacy of loving, caring and sharing with your neighbour, your friend, your family as the only way to live a life regardless whether you get your reward in an after life or not . . ."

"Give it a rest," Maggie says to Lenny. "Your mouth runs like a sick nigger's arse."

Lenny's command over the room had evaporated. Only African Henry and a young Rasta friend of Googie were listening but Lenny's skin was thick as a dictionary.

"We are lovely people as a whole, the human race, and my nephews, my dear departed nephews, were splendid examples of humanity."

Lenny was now talking only to African Henry who had the desperate look of a man wanting to be rescued. If only Paul was still alive he would have walked into the room like Alan Ladd in Shane, his favourite film character, and set African Henry free.

A middle-aged man came into the room carrying a small bouquet of flowers. Lenny called him over.

"Miguelito," Lenny greeted him, "I haven't seen you since the Sixties. Where you been hiding?"

Lenny and Miguelito were close friends at school and started work in a factory together—their first job.

Miguelito was not his real name, Lenny had given him that nickname because Michael St Clair (that was his real name) had a fascination with Latin America. Simon Bolivar was his hero and the Coasters' *Down in Mexico* was his favourite song. Back in the day he dressed like the Coasters' character with a red bandana, a black moustache, even the purple sash around his protruding waist, and he did used to play a cool honky-tonk piano.

"Wha' appen' cuz, yeah man, I'm still here, ho," Miguelito replied with a wide smile that shrank quickly, suddenly conscious of the solemnity of the occasion.

"Sorry to hear about your Paul," he said quickly, "and the young lad. I didn't know your Lizzie had another kid."

"Yeah, terrible," said Lenny. "I heard you moved out to the sticks years ago."

"It was 1962 and it was Skelmersdale we moved to," Miguelito replied referring to a suburb 13 miles away.

"The sticks, exactly," Lenny replied with a mock sneer. "No black people up there, I bet."

"There's a few of us," Miguelito said guardedly.

"No theatres, no arts, no culture, it's a desert up there man. Do you ever come back to civilisation, apart from funerals," Lenny persisted.

"Yeah, man" Miguelito replied indignantly. "Smally still cuts me 'air and I come down fer me yam, and me saltfish n' fings."

Beryl came to Miguelito's rescue. She remembered him in her youth when he used to dress like a Bolero dancer.

"Hello Mr. St Clair," she said petting him on both cheeks, "is Uncle Lenny giving you grief? Have you got a drink, there's teas and coffees or som'n stronger if you want, it's all in the kitchen."

"I'm really sorry to hear about your brothers," Miguelito said giving her the bunch of flowers he was carrying. "A tragedy it is, a real tragedy,"

"Thanks, I'll put them in the resting room," Beryl said as she turned away to see who else needed attention.

How's the fambo," Lenny asked Miguelito as they sipped tea in the kitchen, "I heard you had a bit of bother."

"A bit of bother, well," he started, "you know me beef Cindy ran away with one of the young Mackenzies, only a lad, she's old enough to be his mother . . ."

"I heard something like that, I'm sorry to hear that. Phil Mackenzie I heard it was, Phil's Bernie Mackenzie's lad."

"Phil, hey, is that the little get's name. I've a good mind to get our Marty to sort this young Mackenzie fella out. Marty's me elder lad, to Jean Coist, but he's moved to the States; he's been there five years now. She's left me with three kids to bring them up on me tod, you know. On me tod, and those kids are givin' me pure grief. At my age, I should be sitting pretty, like grandfathers should . . ."

Slim is sitting on the stairs with a cup of tea in his hands listening to Mally Gibson and Neville Keith

"I'm walkin' along Parliament Street, mindin' me own bizness when dis finger comes up to me and says fuck off back to Africa nigger," Neville says to Vinnie. "He was pissed of course, full of Dutch courage, he was. So I just slapped him on his cheek, not hard enough to knock him down but enough to sober the finger up a bit. This was in de middle of Parley. Can you imagine a black guy cursing a John Bull on Scottie Road; he'd be lynched for sure!"

"White drunks are all the same. They want to either kiss or hug you—the guilt of hating you; or they want to curse and fight you—the hatred," replied Neville Keith, or should that be Neville Keita. "Isn't that so Slim," he added slapping slip on the knee.

"Yeah, man" replied Slim.

Terry came out of confession. His mother asked him about his penance. Terry looked a little bewildered.

"He gave me 10 *Holy Marys* and 12 *Our Fathers*," Terry said. "Den I tought he was goin' to give me probation or a suspended sentence. He was like a magistrate, Mam. He didn't fine me dough, cos I told him I got me Giro robbed and de Sowsh won't replace it."

"Dat's a lie, you didn't get your Giro robbed, you blew it on ale," Franna scolded him. "What's the point a' goin' to confession if yer gonna tell lies to de bloody Priest, you soft bastard."

Father Dominic eventually emerged from the confession room, waving his hand gently like the Pope.

The Murphys gathered round Father Dominic, some holding his hands, extending their thanks.

"Tanks, father," said one.

"Tanks very much, father," said another.

It was not just the Murphys who ignored their aitches; they all did in the Nortend.

Beryl walked up to Bernadette.

"Fanks," she said to Bernadette as she hugged her. "You've made my brothers proud. Me Mam's asked me to ask you how much we need to give you," Beryl added lowering her voice.

Bernadette blushed.

"Notink, girl, I never charge fer dat. Yer can't make money off de dead can yer."

"Some do," said Beryl referring to Father Dominic's dog collar, but Bernadette thought Beryl was referring to her past as an illegal abortionist.

"Hey, I heard that," said Alan Leung, "Father Dominic is a good man."

"Hey," she protested. "I haven't done a fuckin' abortion since the sixties, and I paid me dues to society, twenty one fuckin' months in Styal."

Beryl quickly apologised.

"I'm sorry Bernadette; I didn't mean anyfin about you, honest."

"It's alright, girl, it's me who's just a bit touchy. Forgive me language in front of the dead."

They hugged again and Beryl opened the door into the *resting* room and slowly closed the door behind her.

The room was like a cocoon. White sheets completely covered the walls. The left side of the room was quite distinct from the right, garlanded with red, green and gold coloured streamers. The Ethiopian flag was draped around a coffin of shiny wood. A black and white portrait of Marcus Garvey in a fancy military hat hung high up on the wall. A life size picture of Paul in his hot-rod racing gear hung over his coffin.

Beryl's face hardened and tears filled her eyes.

It was the biggest funeral procession in Liverpool 8 since Sylvia Brownings's funeral back in the sixties, someone observed unchallenged. Two policemen on motorbikes slowly headed the cortege, followed by the carriage containing Paul's coffin pulled by four black horses. A confection of red and white flowers shaped like a racing car rested on the coffin.

Googie's coffin draped in the Ethiopian flag, was pulled by four white horses. Eight black limousines followed by and a line of cars stretching from the Upper Parliament Street end of Kingsley Road right down to Princes Avenue.

The tall trees, standing guard on the central reservation swayed gently by a warm breeze were at their most luscious, bright green bursting from every branch. The Boulevard had never seen anything like it since Prince Arthur and his seventy-seven carriage procession officially opened the Park on 20th May 1872.

As the cortege slowly snaked its way up the Boulevard, there were spectators lined on both sides of the road. Four ice-cream vans were making good business but kept their ear-piercing chimes reverently silent. The white background of all the street signs in the area were painted a Rasta red, green and gold

Seated in the first car after the coffins were Lizzie and the rest of her live children. Lizzie, who had been drinking Vodka with Maggie most of the previous night, snapped out her trance and tried to wind the window down as their car passed a policeman walking officiously along the cortege.

"You bloody killers," Lizzie shouted at him. "You should all hang for this. God forgive yers, cos I never will!" but the policeman did not hear her tirade because Lizzie could not get the window down.

"Come on Mam," Alan said pulling his mother away from the window. "Take it easy, please, for the boys' sake."

At the end of the boulevard where the stone statue of a toga clad William Huskisson MP (1770-1830) used to stand just a few days ago, was a statue of

Robert Nesta Marley (1945-1981), made of wood, wire and cloth. Around the statue and facing the procession were four Rastas beating drums ceremoniously. The head of the convoy drew level with the statue and stopped as instructed.

"Who's the statue supposed to be?" asked Doreen to no one in particular.

Lizzie and Beryl had their minds on other things.

"It's Bob Marley," replied Alan. "It's written on the front."

"Not exactly a role model for the youths with his having children by different women and his ostentatious ganja smoking," said Doreen with pursed lips.

These were the first words uttered by Doreen for three days so naturally everybody took notice.

"At least Bob had a Liverpool connection, his father was a Scouser," said Alan defensively. "Sure I'd prefer it if it was John Archer or even Muhammad Ali or maybe something celebrating the end of slavery, rather than Marley, but our Googie would have been sweetened by that statue, I'm tellin' yers."

"Why does it have to be a man? What about Angela Davis or Winnie Mandela?" Beryl said, dabbing her eyes, grateful for even a brief distraction away from her grief.

They were all silent for a few moments then Evelyn, Doreen's preacher husband, the sixth passenger, suggested a peace symbol instead and reignited the conversation.

"A statue of Googie himself," Doreen suggested.

"What about our Paul, he's dead too," said Beryl annoyed that Paul was being agnored."

Googie had always been Doreen's favourite, ever since he was born. It seemed to Beryl that Googie was the only one Doreen was grieving about.

Police motorcyclists blocked Upper Parliament Street to the traffic as the cortege drew past the Rialto's burnt out hulk and into Catharine Street, sidling along the sidewalk fronting St Philip Neri Church.

There were crowds of people milling outside the church, many had brought flowers and some took photographs.

Lizzie's eyes filled up but her will defied the laws of gravity and commanded the tears to stay where they were. She walked into that church like a Duchesse, head high, slow pace and solemn face, although she felt like screaming and running away. She would do her boys proud if it was the last thing she did.

A tape recording of John Holt singing *'Help Me Make It Through The Night'* played loudly as people began to sit down.

The handout for mourners was a printed and bound memorial booklet, the glossy cover of which featured a colour photograph of Paul and Googie taken three years before in the days when Googie had an Afro; they were posing outside Paul's garage on a sunny day and they were smiling at the camera. They looked happy.

There were a few comments among the congregation that the booklet was too flash and expensive. Someone even said the cost of the booklet would have kept him watered and fed for six months.

In truth, the Leungs had it printed by Mally Gibson, the revolutionary, who had a job with a printing firm. He worked for three nights in his own time producing the booklets and only charged for the paper and ink.

Bonny, who was in the fourth car, on entering the church spotted his mother sitting in one of the back rows. He was surprised, as he did not think she would come.

"I'll be at the church, don't worry about that," she had told him. "They're me nephews. I'll make my own way to the church it's only 'round the corner."

Bonny went over to her and urged her to sit nearer the front with the rest of the family.

"I'm alright where I am, stop making a fuss," she said firmly.

Agu, Googie's best friend, was impressed by the turnout.

"Everybody is here, Rasta," he said to Reuben. "It is like biblical times dem, hundreds of Rastas from all over. Rastas from Birmingham, Rastas from Sheffield, Rastas from Manchester, Rastas from Peckham, the Grove and Shepherd's Bush in London Town; Rastas from Reading, Rastas from Leeds, Rastas from Bristol. Dis brethren dere come all de way from out Glasgow Scotland way. See 'im dere wid 'im wife and five pickney-dem, dressed in the colours, see dem?"

"Yes, man, Lion," replied Reuben, "me can see," he said impatiently, irritated by Agu's habit of describing everything he sees, like you are blind and can't see it for yourself.

"We gather in the Church of St Philip Neri to honour Paul Leung and George Roberts. To remember them, to celebrate their life and say goodbye, entrusting them into the gentlest arms of Eternity," began Father Hughes, a forty-six year old Welshman with a mottled complexion and a mop of thick black hair ă la Beatles; the shadows on his cheeks suggested that Father Hughes had to shave twice a day.

"Today, we have a special ceremony, or rather two ceremonies," he continued. "On the one hand Paul will receive a traditional Catholic Service and on the other George will receive a Rastafarian service from the Nyahbinghi Order led by Ras Harding."

Ras Harding, wearing a wrap around his locks and a layered robe in Rasta colours [*Red for the blood that flowed. Yellow for the gold that they stole. Green for the land—Africa. Black for the people—beautiful*] with a black cross on the back, acknowledged the salutes from the Rasta contingent and stood next to Father Hughes, his equally colourfully attired preacher colleague.

"Did you hear about Arnie Williams from Stanhope Street," said Dolly Bootman to Betty Clarke. "He fell into a diabetic coma, he didn't know he was diabetic and neither did the 15 stone ambulance man who broke his ribs trying to resuscitate him when all Arnie needed was a Mars Bar. He's okay now. But he's on insulin for the rest of his life."

"Shshshsh," said Betty.

"Beryl Leung will recite from St John Chapter 14—1 to 6," said Father Hughes.

Dressed elegantly in black, Beryl made her way to the podium. She picked up a sheet of paper from the lectern and spoke in a voice that only the front rows could hear.

"Jesus said to his disciples, 'Do not let your hearts be troubled. Trust in God still, and trust in me. There are many rooms in my Father's house. I am now going to prepare a place for you, and after I have gone and prepared you a place, I shall return to take you with me, so that where I am you may be too.'"

"Speak up," came a voice from the congregation.

"I would like to say a few words about my brothers other than those scriptures," Beryl said raising her voice. "My baby brother Googie loved life because he had everything to live for. He had never been in trouble with the police; he was a gentle soul and would never hurt anyone. He got arrested, flung into jail on some trumped up charge and was not given the opportoon-erty to call his family or a lawyer."

"How long she been in the States," whispered Dolly to Betty. "Do you think she's putting it on to impress us like."

"Shshshsh," replied Betty.

"I don't believe he committed suicide," said Beryl, "me family doesn't believe he committed suicide either. We believe his death is suspicious and should be properly investigated," Beryl continued her voice rising.

Beryl felt tears stinging her eyes and blurring her vision.

"My brother Paul, my eldest brother who was also a father to me, to all of us after Dad died. He was generous and he was protective of all of us. Sometimes too protective, I had no chance of romance while he was around."

The mood lightened as quite a few people laughed.

Beryl smiled as she wiped her eyes.

"He was a bully," whispered Dolly. "Those who live by the fist die by the fist."

"Shshshsh," said Betty.

"My brother Paul was beaten to death in the street in the middle of Chinatown and nobody came to help him. Nobody raised a finger to help him."

African Henry felt as if the accusation was directed at him although he had given a sanitised version of his involvement, or rather his lack of involvement.

"He died for no reason," said Beryl, "and his killers are still running loose laughing at having got away with it. The police know who did it because we told them. The three people who killed my brother are Bull O'Connor, Derek O'Connor and Patrick Dalton. All three are walking the streets as free men. I can assure they won't get away with it; if they don't go to jail then we'll use our own methods. We want justice for Paul and Googie, that's all we're asking for . . ."

Beryl burst into tears and Bonny sitting in the front row went up to her and placed a consoling arm around her shoulders and led her back to her seat.

"They're an item them two you know," Dolly whispered, "first cousins an' all."

"Shshshsh," said Betty.

The church organ led into the hymn 'All Things Bright and Beautiful the Lord God Made Them All'

Bobo Jones, dressed like a penguin in a shiny black suit and white shirt, sang *'They're Not Heavy They're My Brothers'*" in a soft high-pitched voice without fluffing a note with the church organ providing very loud backing.

"Jimmy Jenkins died, only young, not even in his 60s," said Dolly. "Lung cancer, he didn't have a chance, he was gone in three months."

"Shshshsh," said Betty.

African Henry, dressed resplendently in white and green (fila cap, tight fitting buba, sokoto trousers and topped off with an agbada with bunched up long arms), walked up to the podium, his eyes moist but his head held high.

He took out a sheet of paper and began reading from it.

"Paul was my best friend for over 20 years, the best friend me ever have," he began solemnly. "He was my boss also, so he spent more time with me than with anybody else. He was a wise man and always give me good advice. Me don't always take it. He encourage me get engineering qualifications but me never did. He try to stop me drinking but I don't lissen. Me love that man, me love that man and he left a big hole in my life that will never be filled if me live 100 years old. An old Yoruba says how can man be remembered when the giant trees in the forest are soon forgotten, but Paul Leung will remain in my mind and in my heart. Me not a religious man but if there is a God please look after my man."

"What's he saying, that he and Paul were lovers," asked Dolly.

"Paul Leung a pouf, I don't think so," replied Betty remembering romps with him as teenagers.

Lenny Roberts rose from his seat and made to walk to the podium but the looks he received from the front row were so disapproving that despite having so many things and the thickest skin in the whole universe, he stopped and sat back down, his face set in disappointment.

Our Wayne sang '*Blue Moon*' accapella, one of Paul's favourite songs.

He began in a soft voice but on the second verse he turned the tune into a dirge, his voice agonising with angry passion, giving a deeper meaning to the words of Blue Moon, tearing the lyrics apart and taking them to a place they were never meant to go.

"*Once in a blue moon was when I saw you,*" he sang, "*no dream, no love, no one who really cared for me.*"

When Our Wayne finished to mixed applause, Lizzie rose from her seat and walked slowly to the lectern. Her eyes were bloodshot. Her appearance was not on the programme's schedule. This was unpredicted territory.

"Family and friends . . . thank you for your support . . ." she said in a faltering voice. "Thank you for supporting me and my family at this terrible time," she said her voice firmer now. "My sister Esmee is here and we've not spoken for years. I am so pleased that she's here and it would give me great pleasure if she could come up and sing a song for my boys"

Everybody turned towards where Lizzie was looking.

Esmee felt hot when seconds earlier she was cool. Everybody was looking at her, hundreds of eyes all scrutinising her. She should never have worn that suit it was too baggy. She had last worn it for Harry and Joan's funeral and she was much fleshier then. Her black hat with the veil mercifully covered her hair that had stubbornly refused to be tamed by brush or comb this morning.

"Come on Esmee, for my boys" Lizzie pleaded.

Esmee walked slowly up the aisle, one leg crossing the other like a model on a catwalk. That was how she was taught to walk by Mrs Benson at the base where she stayed for a few weeks with McCarthy Her feet were killing her; she had not worn shoes for years. It had taken her twenty minutes to walk to the church when in the good old days it would have taken her seven. She had taken her shoes off to search out a stone or whatever that was making walking so painful, not once but several times. Nobody took any notice of this old woman dressed in black walking like a very old woman, but now everybody was staring but Esmee was looking straight ahead to where Lizzie was standing, not seeing the faces which, if she had looked, would mostly be familiar to her.

How could Lizzie ask her to sing at a time like this, after all that had happened, and what would she sing? What could she sing? People will point at her, laugh at her and then she would go completely round the twist. It would be best if she refused, point to her throat like it was sore. She would go up there, hug her sister and sit back down again. That would be a nice gesture and no one could complain she had been disrespectful at her sister's children's funeral.

She saw a man walking towards her and he gently held her arm. It was Bonny; he was a good lad was Bonny, looked just like his Dad. Gloria joined them just before they reached the podium and held on to Esmee's other arm.

Lizzie and Esmee hugged and the congregation murmured its approval.

"What am I gonna sing?" Esmee asked Lizzie.

"Whatever you want to sing, Ez," replied Lizzie who had not used that name since they were children.

Esmee lowered her eyes as if she was looking inside herself for an appropriate song to sing.

"Thanks darling," Lizzie said softly and went to sit down.

Esmee shook her shoes off her feet, coughed a few times to clear her throat and found herself singing *I'm gonna take a sentimental journey, a sentimental journey back home* croakily at first then her contralto voice began to assert itself, deep and mournful.

I'm gonna take a sentimental journey back hoooome
To renew old memories
Never thought my heart could be so yearning why did I decide to roam
Gonna take a sentimental journey back home

One of the Rasta drummers joined her on the podium and caressed a rhythm out of the skins.

Esmee had long forgotten the rest of the words but stayed with the melody and delivered a masterclass in scatting.

Esmee stretched the notes like only a saxophone, until the original tune was barely recognisable but the beat constant. *Senti-boodi-pop-pop-boodi-ment-al, senti-boodi-pop-pop-boodi-ment-al, coo-doo-bee-doo-wee-pop-journey back boodi-boogi-shoo-boodi-back-hoooome.*

The audience began chanting *senti-ment-al* as a counterpoint and the organist joined in by counterpointing the chant.

Esmee received what would have passed as a standing ovation for a funeral when she sat down next to Lizzie. Maggie had made Uncle Frank give up his seat as he was no blood relation and had gate-crashed the front row anyway.

Father Hughes waited patiently until everyone was silent and then invited Ras Harding to the podium.

Ras Harding fingered his thick plaited beard that stretched to his midriff and spoke in a powerful voice that carried to every corner of the church.

"This part of the service is livicated ter the loife of George Googie Leung," Ras Harding announced in an incongruous Birmingham accent. "Bredrin and dawtas gather cya todic ter remember tew special people. It is fitting that Googie should be buroid on the 17th doy of August, the same date as Marcus Garvey's bufty. The righteous shall return ter Mount Zion on Haile Selassie's doy of judgement where they wull live forever in peace, love, and harmony. Moy their soul find contentment in the achievements of his loife and rejoice in the grace of Jah Rastafari."

"He wasn't such an Angel that Googie, you know," Dolly whispered to Betty. "I hear that he never gave money to keep that child that was singing earlier. The poor mother had to work all hours at a Binns Lane factory . . ."

"Shshshsh" said Betty, "for God's sake be quiet."

"Music 'as always been a central part of black people's lives," said Ras Harding. "The rhythms we 'ave played an' the words we 'ave sung summen our experience frum the percussions ter the story tellen of the aud continent. exported through tred, includen slavery ter all corners of the world, battered an' bruised, dignity an' pride suffocated, but always the rhythms remained, the passion, the sorroo, the anger, the pain, the poetry, the African birthright."

Ras Harding lifted his arm and chanted:

Ithiopia the lan' of ar faither
The lan' where Rastafari love ter be
As the swift clouds are suddenly gathered
Thy children are gathered to thee.
With ar Red Gold and Green floaten over I

"All I'm sayin' is he was not a saint, and neither was his brother. That's all," said Dolly.

"Shshshsh" said Betty.

With our Emperor to shield I from wrong. With I Jah and I future before I n I,

Louis Julienne

I n I 'ail and I shout and I chant.
Haile Selassie I is, I Negus, Negus high, Who keeps Ithiopia free,

Most of the Rastas in the congregation took up the Chorus:

To advance, to advance with truths and rights,
To advance, to advance with love and light.

By the time the sixth chorus was sung the Rasta drummers' sounds were bouncing off every wall and the place was rocking. Ras Harding and Father Hughes each gave a blessing and a tape recording of *Dreamland* played the congregation out.'

'*Surely we will never die*' sang Third World. '*Surely we will never die*'
As they walked back down the aisle, Dolly said hello to an old school friend.

"How are you, Stella, haven't seen you in years, how's the kids?" she asked her.

"They're hairy-arsed men now," replied Stella.

"That was one of the best services I've ever been to," said Dolly.

"How would you know, you talked right through it," replied Betty.

"Where are they having the do?" asked Dolly.

"Don't know," replied Betty. "We'll find out at the cemetery. It's bound to be a good one; the

Roberts have always been good at throwing parties."

"Betty," said Dolly feigning outrage. "How could you, this is a funeral."

The burial, in Sefton cemetery on Smithdown Road, was greeted with pouring rain; the first rain in weeks. Agu said it was a sure sign that Jah had given his blessing. A dozen white doves were released to the sky and everybody got mud on their shoes. While the older generations threw symbolic pieces of earth into the grave, careful not to strain their aging bodies lest they damaged a joint or got a stroke, the younger generations assiduously shovelled the earth on top of the coffins. While the grave was being filled, the quartet of Rasta drummers as well as beating their instruments sang a number of songs with militant titles like: '*If you burn we herb we burn your cane fields*'.

The post burial party was held at the Caribbean Centre. Dolly and Betty and two hundred other people were not disappointed. Lee from the Gladray had cooked the chicken, Jabby his noted speciality, fried fish and dumplings——and Felicia Goolsby-Power-Wright the rest. There was a free bar, ganja smoke hung heavy in the garden and Our Wayne was the deejay. Inconsolable African Henry got drunk and melancholic early on. Mad Danny Odegunji drove him home to sleep it off. The Roberts sure knew how to throw a party, Danny kept saying to him.

Chapter 17

So Much Things To Say

11:30 am Sunday 30th August 1981

Nathaniel Ajayi is living in hell. The last time he felt as miserable as this he was burying his wife. He remembered the promise he gave Elsie Murphy as they lowered her coffin into the ground. He would be a good father to Maureen in a way he had not been in the past and a good grandfather to her pickney, however many she had. Maureen was pregnant with Maxine at the time and Elsie would never live to see her. This was worse than then. He had purpose then and he had none now. He was an old man now and for the first time in his life he was alone and living in hell.

Warwick Close did not look like hell. It was what they call sheltered accommodation. He had a small bedsitter on the first floor of the building that looked out onto Warwick Street. Everybody there was old and everybody there was white. All 39 residents were white except him. He did not have a problem with white people, never had, people were people, but it would have been good if there had been at least one other black person living there. Not necessarily a West African like himself, any black person would have done.

Maureen came most evenings with a cooked meal and sometimes she sent Colin or Dion, never Maxine who was too busy with her own life. They talked to him like he was an old useless man, not Nathaniel Ajayi, the head of the family. They talked more slowly like he had gone deaf and daft in the space of a two weeks and when he talked, they never let him finish, taking words from his mouth before he had said them. Maureen would not look him in the eye so she talked to the curtains, the sofa, the small black and white television, the floor, the walls, the ceiling, anywhere but to his face. Nat saw the shame and embarrassment in her eyes every time she came. Only Dion listened and usually stayed the longest, he slept at the flat a couple of nights the second week. Nat's oldest friends came on

Pure Pressure

his third day with a bottle of whisky and they talked of old times and got drunk. They had not been since; they were too busy with their young wives and young children.

There was one person in the whole place that he knew, Rosie Mac. She was married to Okon but her mind had gone and she recognised no one and he heard she was to be transferred to what they called a care home but by the description was anything but a caring home. Olive O'Connor, whose sons beat Paul Leung to death, lived here also. He had seen her around but never spoken to her or even tried to acknowledge her. It was said she and her cousin, who also lived here, hated black people and both of them would give him bad looks whenever they passed him. Other than them, there was nobody from Liverpool 8 apart from Rosie Mac and that contributed to his depression. The person he disliked the most in Liverpool 8, Charlie the joiner, a man he had not spoken to in thirty years, a man who would beat his mother if he still had one, rob off his children and talk about his friends behind their backs. Even Charlie the joiner would be welcomed as a resident; it would be at least one person to share past memories with.

It had all happened so quickly.

Yvonne Khumalo-Birtwhistle gave him a lift in her car after a Jaycee meeting. The meeting had been a particularly bruising one as Alan Leung had not survived a vote of no confidence and had to resign from the Chair and committee. Maureen had fought hard against Alan's dismissal and was even tearful during the meeting but to no avail. Nat, of course, had supported Alan. A man should not be punished twice for the same crime he kept saying, particularly if he is not guilty of the crime. Father Dominic gave an impassioned defence as to why Alan should remain. Keith Turner had threatened withdrawal of Council funds if Alan remained and the rest followed his lead. They all expressed deep sympathy for the deaths of his two brothers. Maxammed Adam and Ben Miller, who were sitting on the fence, urged Alan to stand down from the committee for a period to allow himself time to grieve and to let the fuss over his conviction boil over. The contest was three votes for Alan's dismissal, three votes against and two abstentions. Yvonne Khumalo-Birtwhistle, who temporarily took the chair whilst Alan's fate was being decided, commandeered the chair's casting vote and voted Alan out.

Alan left the room looking like a defeated man. Maureen followed him in sympathy, leaving Nat to walk home, not that he minded, he liked to walk, to stretch his limbs. However, Yvonne insisted she drive him home oblivious to his protestations. For a moment Nat thought she was after his body, so persistent was her offer of a lift. Nat thought for a brief moment after she started the car that she was going to suggest to him some hanky-panky but he was being delusional. All

Yvonne wanted to do was to feel good for driving an old man home, although he lived less than half a mile away and it was a warm night.

Nat Ajayi relieved the next moment hundreds of times in the following weeks. He felt faint and slumped in his seat on his left side. Yvonne stopped the car and spoke to him but he did not seem to understand the words. She drove him to the Royal Hospital and within minutes, he had all manners of tubes plugged into his body. He had suffered a stroke and the whole of his left side was very weak. His words were slurred and he could not stand up or walk unaided. The doctors had told him he had suffered an injury to the right cerebral hemisphere, which had produced sensory and motor deficits on the left side of Nat's body. He was in hospital for two weeks by which time he had recuperated somewhat, but needed a walking stick and his speech was still slightly impaired, like he was chewing a sweet and trying to talk at the same time.

A few days after coming out of hospital, when the war between the kids and the police had all but ceased and anarchy seem no longer to be threatening, Nat was looking out of the front room window watching the police chasing after some boys. It was like something out of the television. The boys ran up the stairs of the walk-up flats opposite and dropped a fridge towards the police 40 feet below, barely missing them. The police chased the boys and they disappeared from view. Moments later, two of the boys came knocking on the door seeking refuge and Maureen let them in.

Nat told her that she was wrong in sheltering these hooligans, particularly in front of Maxine and Dion as it gave the impression that she condoned what they were doing. They could have killed one of the policemen and they had wives and children too, he said to her.

Colin agreed with him but did not say so; he just nodded discreetly to Nat. After the boys had gone, Maureen recited one of her angry discourses. She went on about how he, her own father who had fought against racism and oppression for so long, how he did not understand the pressures the police were putting on these kids. She then stormed up the stairs, stamping every step as a marching soldier and shut her bedroom door so hard the clock fell off the kitchen wall and broke.

Maureen did not come back down again until the following morning and before walking out to go to work she said to Nat, her eyes cold, her voice quiet and measured, that she needed to talk to him when she got back from work and that it was very important.

Nat was alone in the house everybody had gone out. Colin was back at work. Dion had gone fishing in Sefton Park with his friends. Colin had dropped in with two bottles of milk, as was his custom after Maureen had left and Nat asked him if he knew what it was that Maureen wanted to talk to him about, but Colin, who could not tell a lie with conviction, said he did not know.

The scene she had created the night before had caught him by surprise, all that stamping and slamming, not that he was ignorant of her temper, she was Elsie's daughter after all, but she had never been that disrespectful to him before. She had had rows with him granted, but never in front of the children. She had been acting strange in the past couple of weeks; even Colin noticed it and commented on it to him.

Nat went into the small kitchen that morning and cooked his last breakfast in the house that had been his home for over thirty years. Porridge with milk and water garnished with a banana, grapes and strawberries. If he had ate as healthily during his life as he was now, he mused, he would surely live to one hundred and make a point of sending the Queen's telegram back informing her that he was a Republican.

Nat teased a smile from his craggy features at the thought of him writing an indignant letter to the Queen of United Kingdom Great Britain and the British Commonwealth.

While waiting for Maureen to return he contemplated where he would go.

He could put his name down for Council accommodation but he would be dead for sure before somewhere suitable came up. Renting privately was not an option because it was too expensive.

Nat looked at the new clock Colin had bought hanging on the wall above the photograph of Malcolm X. Maureen would be home in one hour.

He hobbled about the kitchen, clearing and washing the bowl and cutlery and wiped the table collecting the crumbs into the palm of his hand. He did not want to give Maureen room for any criticism about his personal habits.

Maureen came in shortly before midday.

She came straight to the point and told him it would be best for him if he left. She had found him a place in sheltered accommodation off Warwick Street. It was a nice place, she assured him, clean and fully staffed. There were people of his age with whom he could make friends and the staff were trained to deal with his incontinence.

Nat protested that he had had an accident once only.

Maureen warned him as kindly as she could that the incontinence would probably be more frequent as he got older.

Maureen would take out a mortgage on the house, she continued in a controlled voice, and give him sufficient money to meet all his needs. She added that they were overcrowded and that it would save him the indignity of sleeping on the couch after he had given up his room.

"But this is me house," Nat protested raising his voice. "Furs you kick me out of me room to sleep on the couch like a dog and now you chase me out me own house, hah."

Maureen's look said 'it's not your house anymore'.

Nat gave up the fight at that moment. It was pointless reminding her that he had gifted the house to her and Colin on the understanding that he would spend the rest of his life there. Maureen would have ignored him anyway and pressed on with her plan; her mind was set.

He would move in on Wednesday, she informed him. That is how he became a resident of Warwick Close.

Tim, the warden, a nice but lazy man, knocked on the door to inform him lunch was ready downstairs.

"I'm not hungry," Nat shouted in Spanish.

He still had some of the cooked food his grandson had brought him yesterday.

Tim's father was Spanish and he learnt from young, therefore Nat only ever spoke to him in Spanish.

Nat was a naturally gifted linguist and it sprang from and was driven by a restless compulsion to talk. He could also listen and did it very well at times but only because your words became ammunition for the topics he chose to talk about.

At first Nat used to go to the lunches, not for the food (the only rice they ever served was rice pudding). He went for the company. Nat tried hard to eat the food, spreading Cayenne pepper he brought down from his flat all over the food to spike up the blandness. That food was beyond redemption; boiled so long everything tasted the same.

Nat only went to the lunches so he could talk to people but they did not want to speak with him except Tim, in Spanish. He stopped attending the luncheons and the bingo sessions.

At first Nat came close to hating Maureen for putting him in this predicament.

As the days wore on, he developed a different perspective and blamed himself for giving the house away. He should have guessed that as the family grew space would be at a premium. He knew that Maureen had a good heart; she was a giver by nature. The problem with Maureen as far as Nat could work out was that for her the bowl was of more concern to her than the soup. What was happening

Pure Pressure

outside in the community—the kids with no facilities, the police, and in the world, the freedom of Nelson Mandela and the Irish problem—were all more important than what was happening in her home, and of course, there was the gambling. She had nothing more to give when she was home. Nag poor Colin all day long, keep Dion prisoner and let her daughter get pregnant by some young half-cast boy who should be at school.

Foued, his great Moroccan friend, his mentor, who taught him all he knew about keeping a ship engine well-greased, and how to love people without being a fool to them.

'*Welcome everyone but stay alert to treachery,*' Foued warned him on many occasions, like a latter-day Machiavelli in the bowels of the ship.

"But how could I predict my own flesh and blood to betray me," he would have asked Foued, and Foued, would have repeated, Nat knew, '*stay alert to treachery, always*'.

If Elsie were still alive, she would never have allowed him to give the house up without a legally binding contract. As a businesswoman she knew and respected these matters. He did consult Elsie after she died before making the decision to hand the house over but he was not sure whether she was listening that day. Nat spoke to Elsie most days.

" . . . *Make them wait . . . 58 . . . Half a crown . . . two and six . . . Old age pension . . . 65 . . .*"

The booming voice of the bingo-caller rose up to Nat's flat from the hall.

Lunch was always followed by bingo on Sundays, a game Nat did not like very much. He had tried it a couple of times but the numbers were called so quickly that he always lagged a few numbers behind.

" . . . *Bobby Moore, number 4 . . . Downing street, number 10 . . . Your place or mine, 69 . . .*"

Nat hobbled on his stick over to the transistor radio on the window shelf and switched it on full blast to drown out the bingo-caller's explosive voice.

"*The Environment Secretary Michael Heseltine, appointed 'Minister for Liverpool' in the wake of the Toxteth riots said that no additional government money will be made available to the riot-hit areas . . . Prince Charles and Lady Diana are on their honeymoon on the royal yacht . . .*"

Nat changed channel and stopped the dial at a pop music station, listened for a few seconds and turned the set off.

" . . . *Dirty Gertie, number 30 . . . Bunch of fives, 55 . . . Sexy Kate—Is she in yet, number 8 . . .*"

This was how he would end his life; Nat despaired cooped up in a little bed-sitter amid strangers hostile to his culture.

He had not gone very far from the young teenager who came to England, little Nathaniel and his mother's brother, Isaac, not much older than he was, from Lagos to Liverpool on a ship laden with peanuts. They spent most of the time hidden, sometimes under a tarpaulin, in the darkest and coolest corners of the engine room, where it was still insufferably hot. Some of the kitchen crew knew they were there and fed them leftovers. They called him Jimi their mascot because they could not pronounce Ajayi. One of them was not a friend. Carby was the main cook and decided if Nat ate well or not at all. Nat had to be nice to Carby and he had to do things to him that he had never done to another human being, not even to himself. At first, it was just his hand until it became sodden with sticky stuff, then his mouth and that was worse.

"Lick it clean, boy, clean, clean, clean," Corby would say to him.

Those had been terrible times but worth enduring for the promises of a rich life in England, but he had ended up in Warwick Close, miserable and alone among strangers. Twenty years ago maybe he would have had the energy to mix in and organise things, but now all he wanted to do was sit down in this small place that was his prison. Maybe once he settled in he would get use to it, but probably, he contemplated, he would die before he settled.

The sound of a key turning in his lock startled Nat.

"It's only me," he heard Maureen say.

She kissed Nat on the cheek, gave him a brief hug and headed for the kitchen with a hot pan in her hands.

"Why don't you play bingo, Dad," she said. "Make friends, something to do. Shall I serve it now or will you have it later; it's Beef Stew with real Scotch Bonnet. Colin did it, I've tasted it and it is not bad, I think he's finally got the hang of it."

"He better cook dan you," Nat said without malice. "Leave it there to cool. Me yam later."

"And a couple of beers to wash it down," she added. "I'll put them in the fridge."

"Beer as well, you want me drunk," he grinned showing a gap-filled mouth.

Maureen sat down on a chair by the table.

Nat's grin collapsed; she was going to say something bad.

"I've got some news," she said.

"Is wha' 'appen?" he asked anxiously.

Maureen said Maxine had accepted an offer from a Housing Association for a two-bed maisonette in Canning Street; and was moving in over the weekend. Nat could have his old room back. He could move back in on Tuesday to give her time to get the room ready.

Nat's nose began to run and his eyes misted.

"I can't stay, Dad. I promised Dion to drive him to the football match. A benefit match for the Leung brothers in Sefton Park; the match kicks off at two."

They hugged.

"Wow, wooman," he said teasingly. "You smell garlic!"

"Come with us to the match. Dion would like that," Maureen suggested, "and so would I."

" . . . *Getting plenty, number 20 . . . Monkey on the tree, number 3 . . . HOUSE!*"

Sefton Park was windy and overcast but the grass was mercifully short. Scheduled to kick off at two o'clock, the game was held up because half the L8 Veterans All-Star team were still missing. Brian Mensah was not happy. He had organised the charity match to fund raise for the Leung family. The Jaycee boys, as expected, to a man were there by one thirty, the goal posts firmly planted, the nets secured, and they were dressed in their green and black kits and ready to go. The rest of the Vets were eventually rounded up and the kick off delayed until three o'clock.

The Veterans All-Stars team was a misnomer. They were veterans all right, but little more. Sure, they had Thommo and Ricky up front, Tony Wong in midfield, but Slim was their goalkeeper, and he was pushing fifty. In addition, they were cursed with a poor defence personified by Alan Leung and Peewee who had been hopeless even when they were in their prime.

This was going to be a disaster as a spectacle, thought Bonny, a mismatch.

Bonny suggested that some of the Jaycee veterans, those over thirty, should play for the All-Stars and whomever they replace, play for the Jaycee. Brian Mensah reluctantly agreed.

No goals at half time. The Jaycee had most of the possession, and the Veteran All-Stars did most of the fouling. One of the Veteran All-Stars, Derek Brown, was sent off for punching a spectator who called him a dirty player. Everybody thought Derek should have shaken the spectator's hand, because Derek normally prided himself on being a dirty player. The Vets conceded two penalties and Slim saved them both. One of the penalties hit his knee and the other, was a weak effort by Pete Howard; Slim fell on top of the ball only just stopping it from squirming under his body and over the line.

Not a game to regal the purists and there were many of them in the seventy odd crowd of spectators. The second half, though, began with a bang. Spot McKenzie dribbled past the whole defence leaving Slim on his backside as he slotted into an empty net. The crowd roared its approval. Spot's Dad, Ralph McKenzie, who was part of the crowd, was mobbed and congratulated on the touchline by all those near him as if he and not his son had danced through the Veteran's defence himself and scored the goal.

Beryl did not have the slightest interest in the game. Watching twenty-two men chasing a ball was not her idea of fun, she came mainly to show support for the venture being as it was a tribute to her dead brothers but also to show support for her man, Bonny Roberts. Bonny was the best man to have happened to her, she had decided. He was quiet like Greg, but there was a dignity and gentleness about him she found irresistible. Issues, however, still remained unresolved between them. He being close family seemed to be the biggest obstacle to a lot of people, but she had no intention of getting pregnant again, to Bonny or any other man (those days were gone forever as far as Beryl was concerned), so their blood ties did not concern her. His unemployment bothered her a great deal, although not as much as his lack of ambition to do anything about it.

"Wha' kinda fuck'n ref are you," a spectator shouted. "That was a free kick not a throw-in, stoopid."

"I don't get paid for this, y'know, so I can do without the aggravation, get me?" replied the referee.

On the plus side, people respected Bonny, he was not violent, at least not towards women, like some she could mention, and Alice and Alma really got on well with him and that was very important. He also appeared completely besotted with her and that went a long way towards her starting to feel the same for him.

There was an appreciative murmur from the crowd as Bonny made a scything tackle in the middle of the park and then sent a 30-yard pinpoint pass to the right wing; however, Titch's poor ball control brought gasps of exasperation from the crowd.

Beryl would have loved this relationship with Bonny 15 years ago when it was near impossible for black girls, even the lighter-skinned ones like her, to get a local black guy to take an interest in her. Beryl looked around the pitch at the girl friends and wives urging their men on and concluded that nothing much had changed. Apart from Felicia and Peewee, and he was not born here so he did not really count, and Beatrice with Eddie, all the locally born black men had white partners.

Maureen Ajayi waved to her from the other side of the pitch. Some of the women too went to the other side, thought Beryl as she waved back.

"Keep the ball moving, come on, attack for shitsake!" somebody shouted.

Beryl could still taste the disappointment, the humiliation, weekend after weekend preparing for the dances, hair done, make up on and lots of hope that things would be different that night, the Hope Hall was the place to go then. She had hoped for a long time of being noticed, of having a dance other than with one of her girl-friends. She dreamed of laughing and kissing and being fondled.

"Penalty ref! That was a clear penalty."

You could try to catch the eye of one of the lads' as they lurked around the toilet entrance door but they were not interested. They would let on to you out of courtesy but their eye was on some white bitch with dirty knickers or no knickers at all. They would rather dance with a white girl, any white girl, no matter how plain or bedraggled, rather than one of us.

"Man on, man on," the crowd shouted.

Every dance night was the same. Always the white girls were asked to dance and were walked home, whilst the black girls, with few exceptions, would stand there all night like lemons. After a while, Beryl stopped going out, stayed in for months on end and her brother Paul accused her of being a lesbian. She thought about that, being a lesbian, for a while but she did not know any black lesbians and dropped the idea.

The crowd roared as Bobby Gee scored a second goal for the Jaycee. Bonny looked dejected. Beryl waved her sympathy and he meekly waved back.

Beryl was pleased he was her man. He was spiritual without the baggage of religion and he loved his food; Beryl liked a man who loved his food.

The crowd booed. Devon Cornwall was lying immobile in the middle of the pitch. If it was air Devon needed he was not going to get much of it as two dozen people surrounded him at close quarters asking what the matter was. Somebody said he had swallowed his tongue and another said his leg was broken. It was neither it was concussion.

Brian Mensah had to bribe one of the spectators with a fiver to drive him to hospital and, more onerously, Brian had to take Devon's place as full back. Brian was fifty-one years of age, a fit sixty one year old but fifty-one nevertheless, so nobody expected him to overlap with the left-winger Josh Amos and make dashing runs down the wing followed by arrow-like crosses into the box and they did not get them. Beryl yawned.

The Jaycee team scored three goals inside three minutes. Slim's teammates berated him for his ineptness but Slim was having none of it.

Louis Julienne

"Me's a cricket man. I tell Brian me's a wicket-keeper not a goal—keeper but 'im nah lissen," he said picking the ball out of the net for a third time.

Beryl screamed at Alan, her own brother, when he deliberately tripped Bonny over and sent him clattering to the floor

"Send 'im off!" she said, getting into the lingo.

Bonny brushed himself off and was up and running in a second.

Beryl liked the shape of Bonny's legs with their defined musculature. She had seen more of his body in his football kit this afternoon than she had seen before, except when they were kids. She felt tightness between her legs and wanted Bonny inside her. There were practical difficulties, as they did not have a place of their own. Bonny was virtually homeless and her Mother would certainly not approve of Beryl and Bonny sharing a bed in her house. They could however go to Paul's garage he had a flat there, if she asked Paul nicely.

"Hello, Beryl; long time no see," said Peach, as she slid up to Beryl.

Beryl hated Peach, blaming her for Alan's incarceration, in fact, she hated her ever since Alan took up with her, but she had heard that Peach had fallen on hard times so she said hello back and asked how she was.

Beryl started concentrating on the game she barely understood as a diversion from hearing about Peach and the Social Services and the no-good men who fathered her children. Then she saw Robbo walking importantly around the pitch like the co-sponsor of the event that he was. She called after him, he came over and hugged her and asked her if she had heard that Cilla Jenkins had died. He was not sure what she died off but he suspected it was an overdose. They reminisced briefly about when they were at school with Cilla and everybody thought she was going to be an actress because her theatrics. Robbo said he would organise a collection to pay for the funeral because she had no family. Then the Jaycee scored another goal and he went off celebrating.

After he had gone, Peach said to Beryl, "he's a murderer that Robbo, and his side-kick JD. I saw them carrying a body a few weeks back."

"What you talking about," said Beryl both intrigued and disbelieving.

Peach told her in detail what she remembered of that night.

The crowd roared in expectation. Clancy for the Vets was through on goal. Clancy, however, hit the turf before he hit the ball and sent the ball 30 feet over the bar.

"Ar' Googie would have put that one in no problem," said Our Wayne shaking his head.

"I know, he's fuck'n useless that Clancy, no first touch at all," said Bobo Jones.

The final score was 10-1. The Veterans' consolation goal was a good one. Tony Wong tore down the field, beat two men and passed to Thommo who sent the ball screaming into the back of the net on the half volley. The Veterans celebrated as if it was they who had scored ten goals. Slim ran around his penalty area in celebration at the solitary goal, gesticulating like a lunatic.

The teams and their supporters went back to the Carousel pub on Myrtle Street. Sandwiches and Sandra's spicy chicken wings had been laid on. Alan gave a speech thanking the Carousel, the John Archer Youth Centre and Frederick Robinson who we all know as Robbo for sponsoring the event and helping raise the funds to launch the Paul and Googie Leung Challenge Trophy, to be played every year for the best football club in Liverpool 8. Alan choked with emotion when he said if Googie had been playing, the score would have been twenty instead of ten. Later on, some people got drunk and there was a fight but Bonny broke it up and made Beryl proud.

Beryl went to the pay phone at the side of the bar and rang African Henry's number. She could not hear herself talking for the raucousness of the crowd.

"I need access to Paul's flat, have you got the keys," she said as quietly as possible.

She had to repeat her request three times as quietly as possible so no one else would hear and get African Henry to repeat what he was saying at least three times before she could hear him promise to come round to the Carousel to give her the keys

"And be discreet about it," she told him, although she was not sure whether he heard her last comment.

Beryl walked over to where Bonny was standing by the pool table in the parlour listening to Ray Bootman telling how awesome the event had been. As she slid her hand into his Bonny looked slightly embarrassed but did not withdraw his hand as she thought he might in front of all his male friends. Instead, he surprised her as he squeezed her hand and brought it slowly up to his lips and kissed it gently all the while looking at her face.

"I thought you weren't romantic," she said in his ear.

"Only with you," he replied.

African Henry came in a few minutes later, when they went back into the bar, and shouted her name across the room waving the keys in his hand. The model of discretion is African Henry, even when he is sober.

Beryl was sure everybody in the pub had noticed. African Henry, she surmised, had not heard her last sentence. Beryl snatched the keys from him and thanked him with as much sarcasm as she could muster without attracting further unwanted attention and quickly dropped the keys in her bag. Beryl waited for a few long minutes before suggesting to Bonny that they should leave.

"Do you fancy a walk through the Cathedral cemetery," Bonny suggested to her as they left a heaving Carousel.

Beryl crunched her face suggesting she was not keen.

"Along the river then, it's a lovely evening for walking," said Bonny holding her hand.

Beryl was going to say it would be a better evening if they spent it shagging, now that they had somewhere private to go to, but she lost her nerve and nodded in agreement.

By the time they reached the Pier Head, Beryl had told him about how she often went to the docks with her friend Muriel just to look at the ships as they sailed away to faraway places. She wanted to see some of this world out there.

"From the time I was in my mid teens," she said to him, "I wanted to get out of Liverpool, to leave and go anywhere. I felt that as a black woman I wanted most of the time to be anonymous, invisible, because growing up as a young adult I felt that I had no value. As a young woman you want to date, you want to have fun. In school, I felt that that there were few black men who were interested in me, they were more interested in white women. After a while I shut myself in, never went anywhere, staying at home all the time. Then I made a conscious decision to look beyond local black men and as you know, that meant mainly seamen and GIs. Of course, I could have chosen local white men but that wasn't an option for me. I met Greg and we married and had Alma and Alice and, although ultimately it didn't work out, and I've got lots to hate him for, at least he made me feel valued as a black woman and I'm thankful for that. But I'm well rid of him now, he's probably back in the States getting high," she added sardonically.

Bonny wondered whether she suspected something about her husband. Maybe his Mother had told her or somebody else; enough people knew. Perhaps it would be best to tell her what happened; after all, it had been an accident and he had not shot him.

"Peach told me something really strange earlier," Beryl said looking pensive.

Beryl recounted what Peach had told her and she had slowly started putting things together.

"Paul said that he saw Greg with JD in a car. Paul went round the gambling house to see if he was there but Robbo told him he had been and gone. Then Peach says she saw JD and Robbo, and others she could not make out, carrying a body, a black man's body, she said. Greg has since disappeared from the face of the earth. Don't you think all this is more than coincidence?"

Before Bonny could respond, Beryl added, "were you there that night?"

"Yes," he replied firmly, a thin bead of sweat appearing on his top lip. "I was there that night. It was Ringer," he lied, "you know Ringer, a big Kru man who drives a Vauxhall. It was him that was carried out; he was blind drunk so we carried him to his house. He only lives at the back of Robbo's in Cairns Street. It was easier and more discreet carrying him through the back way than the front, if you know what I mean. Greg had well gone by the time I got there and it was still light when I got to Robbo's that night. I remember because it was the same day I found out Valerie and the kids had gone. Maybe she ran away with Greg," he said forcing a smile.

"Oh no, she didn't," Beryl snapped. "She ran away with Zacky Pong."

"Wha' d'yer mean she ran away with Zacky; wha' you on about?"

"I thought you knew; everybody knows."

Bonny stared at Beryl for a few seconds with a disbelieving look at first.

"It's starting to make sense now," said Bonny slowly shaking his head.

"This business with someone getting carried out in the middle of the night because they were drunk sounds strange to me," said Beryl.

"It's not strange and it's true," he said. "That bloody Zacky, I'll kill the little rat when I get me hands on him."

Beryl looked at him for a few seconds, rose from the bench they were sitting on and walked towards the river and then along the deserted docks, containerisation having turned them into ghost areas.

Bonny followed her ruminating whether to tell her the truth and concluding that he would probably lose her in the process. Whether he told her or not Bonny was convinced he could never keep a clever girl like Beryl anyway. It would not take her long to suss him out as a loser with nowhere to go.

He dared not tell her that he loved her in case he frightened her away. She liked him and told him so several times; they had kissed and fondled but no penetration.

"It's too early," she said resolutely, this after nearly six weeks of courtship.

He did not push it and let it drop, the argument that is.

As he caught up with her he heard himself say, as if the words were coming out of somebody else's mouth: "I've got something to tell you."

Beryl looked at Bonny with a look that pleaded 'don't tell me anything that is going to spoil what we have'.

Louis Julienne

"I'm scared to lose you. I'm in love with you and I don't want to lose you," he said to her after hesitating.

"I love you too and I don't want to lose you," Beryl said as she reached for his face and held his chin in her hand.

They watched the ferries chugging along the dark waters of the Mersey until the sun left the sky. She told him she wanted to spend the night with him. She kissed him full on the mouth and laced her arms around his neck.

Bonny said to her "better watch Nanny doesn't catch us," as if they were back in their grand mother's house.

Beryl talking about growing up had made him think about what it was like for him.

He remembered the jokes about his colour, not so much from white people but black people, and his own family including Beryl. Bonny had the darkest skin of all his family and the remarks he used to get hurt him deeply. Remarks like he was "*so black he's almost purple*" and "*black enough to go to a funeral naked*" and "*black enough to piss ink*". All these insults came from within his own family, but it was seen by everybody as a joke. "*Bonny's okay, he can take a joke,*" they would say because he grinned, but it was not a grin of pleasure it was a grin of embarrassment. Bonny Roberts had a repertoire of grins, each denoting a different emotion. His own Mother, who was not much lighter than he was but she often denigrated the nigger in him—the flat nose, the thick hair, the *titty* lips, even his athleticism, and the final warning "*don't marry someone darker than yourself or your kids will have no chance.*" These remarks, these insults, made him hate himself and his blackness throughout his youth. Bonny was happy now in his own skin, proud even, but it had been a long and painful process. His father was an American GI who he had never met, not even seen a photograph and who was never discussed, although his mother, ever the skin shade snob, told him his Father was as black as the proverbial ace of spades.

Bonny and Beryl did not realise how far they had walked when they reached Otterspool. The Otterspool car park brought back memories to Bonny of a different time. Aged 16, when 18-year-old Kipper, took him in her Dad's car to Otterspool car-park, known as Malibu beach, because it was a hundred yards from the waterfront with a narrow pebble and rock beach and a nice view of the gently undulating river.

Malibu was a favourite of couples because of its privacy. It would be all wet mouths and breast fondling because Kipper "I only give the top" Grimes would never allow a finger pie let alone a shag.

Bonny told Beryl of his attempts to get past Kipper's '*I only give the top*' edict.

Beryl laughed and then Bonny started laughing too and they laughed all the way to Paul's home off Windsor Street.

They embraced as soon as Bonny closed the flat door. They joined loose lips together, tentatively flicking their tongues into each other's mouths. Bonny caressed her back and her bare shoulders; Beryl pressed her chest against his, uncertain if the beating heart she could feel was hers or his.

The day had finally arrived; this is it thought Bonny. What will happen if things go wrong, what if he cannot perform, what if she changes her mind?

They undressed, scattering their clothes and lay on the couch their limbs intertwined. They kissed each other's mouths, neck and shoulders. Every part of Bonny's body that touched Beryl's mad it feel like it was on fire, not a burning painful fire but a passionate and sensual fire.

Slowly he entered her.

"Don't come inside me," she said breathlessly, "come on my belly."

Within seconds, Bonny withdrew and drenched her belly with his seed.

Beryl laughed.

"I didn't mean that quick," she said

Her laughter was not mocking but humorous.

"I didn't know you liked me that much," she said smiling at him.

Beryl closed her eyes and slowly, rubbed the viscous liquid all over the front of her body. She rubbed it into her breasts with the dark circled nipples and on her neck and shoulders like it was Dior body lotion, no, more than that, as if it had a life of its own.

"Beryl, I'm sorry," he muttered.

"You've noffin to feel sorry for," she said as she opened her eyes, looked directly into Bonny's face and licked her fingers, one at a time, as if laced with syrup.

"You muss come again," she said her smile widening.

Bonny laughed, Beryl laughed and they were still laughing when they showered together, making a mess of the floor and sending tidiness freak Paul spinning in his grave.

The electric heater on full blast illuminated the room with an orange glow, and they sat in front of it.

"Your lips encapsulate two continents, two cultures," she said to him feeling poetic."Your upper lip, thin, taut, guarded, and sinister even in its Europeaness; your lower lip thick, fleshy, generous, frivolous, and sensual even in its Africaness."

"Where d'you learn that," Bonny asked.

"I've just made it up," she replied.

She asked him where he thought the relationship was going and its future, how it would develop.

Bonny eulogised in his restrained way about a lovely future together full of happiness and passion and love and companionship. Beryl was a little more practical than that.

"Let's work out what we got going here. Imagine there are two sides to our relationship, the good things on one side," she said holding her right hand up, "and the not so good things," holding up the other. "First, on the bad side we're first cousins. It might be a problem to some people but it's not a problem to me."

"It's not a problem to me, I love you," Bonny said, his hand stroking her hair.

"We've known each other all our lives," she continued, "that's a good thing."

Beryl waited until Bonny made a suggestion but he seemed quite happy stroking her hair.

"We're both unemployed," she kept on, "that's a bad thing, but I'll get a job even if I have to live in London or somewhere. Skills wise, I'm good at dealing with the public, I can cook for a hundred people, I know how to run an office, I can type, I can do accounts, what about you?"

Beryl had been annoyed at his lack of activity outside of herself; it was very flattering having Bonny at her beck and call, but they could not live on fresh air.

Bonny hesitated, he did not like where this conversation was leading, and on their very first night together. "Other than being a good fighter and footballer, I can't think what other skills I've got; I've never had a proper job." he answered after what seemed an age.

"You do security work don't you? You could organise other bouncers and act as a kind of agent," she suggested.

"That's already been done. There are three main outfits that regulate most of the bouncers in the clubs in town and it's a closed shop, you would need an army to get the muscle out. And it's a risky business coz they carry shooters."

They abandoned the game when Bonny kissed her mouth, gently at first then with increasing passion.

Soon afterwards, Beryl rang her mother and asked her to mind the kids for the night. Lizzie did not need to ask what she was going to do and whom she was going to do it with.

"Goodnight God bless," Lizzie said to her.

Lizzie put the phone down and shouted up the stairs, "Have you done your teeth yet?"

She waited for the twins to reply before returning to the living room.

"That was our Beryl," she told Maggie. "She's not coming home tonight, staying at our Paul's with Bonny," she added meaningfully.

Maggie sipped at her cup of tea and cooed. "I think they make a lovely couple. And Beryl'd be the woman to sort him out."

Lizzie nodded in agreement.

"I hope they don't have children though, sharing the same blood you don't know what could happen," Maggie concluded.

Lizzie nodded in agreement and said as she lifted the cup to her mouth. "She's got plenty of kids already with them two little angels upstairs."

Alice and Alma came into the room dressed in their nightclothes.

"Granma, can we go to the front rum ter watch a movie. It's called *Chitty Chitty Bang Bang*. It's really neat Granma, can we watch it please?" Alma pleaded. "We both wanna watch it, don't we Alice?"

Alice acquiesced.

"Okay, okay," Lizzie said, "and then straight to bed. Mummy's staying out tonight, she won't be back till morning."

Then Maggie began talking. She talked of times gone by with Googie and Paul, she talked of her cruise, she talked about how she finished with Basil, she talked about settling down with her long-suffering cuckold husband Jim, now that the kids were all grown up and had flown the nest. Then she brought the conversation to life and death and what happens afterwards.

Lizzie was not really listening to Maggie; she was more caught up with her own memories. Like the time Kai returned from a long trip. Two Christmases he was away for, so this trip was special. He brought back dresses, scarves and stockings and underwear, all silk, for her and a watch, the same one she's wearing now, plus other jewellery that was still in the box upstairs along with the all the other jewellery he brought back from every trip. Paul loved the Chinese and Buckaroo outfits his Dad had brought him and slept in them for three nights. There were gifts for everybody; for his Uncle Hui, a length of fine wool material, for Billy his best mate who had not worked in donkey's years, he gave cash. He bought Esmee some carvings from West Africa and blues records from the States, and a real leather football for Bonny; and Timi Yuro records. Kai loved Timi Yuro nearly as much as he loved her. He also bought a small monkey. He had bought it from a man on the docks. Paul will love him, Kai assured her. Paul did not love the monkey, nobody loved the monkey. The beast was quiet and cuddly for only a few hours. Then it became playful and energetic. It broke the two side lamps, three light bulbs, and the coffee table's glass top, and it shit and pissed all over the house. Kai had to go looking for the man the next day to take the animal back.

"What's the point of living, where does it all lead, is there a heaven and hell?"

Maggie's questions were purely rhetorical so answers were neither required nor sought.

"The hardest thing in my life," Lizzie began looking into space as if she was talking to herself, "was not being told that two of my babies had perished in a fire and another who was badly burnt and would spends months in hospitals and clinics. It wasn't being told I had lost my Kai forever because some stupid man crushed him with a fork-lift truck, or seeing my little Googie's body laid out in a morgue looking like he was asleep . . ."

"Now, now girl," Maggie interrupted, "no need to bring all that up again, you'll only upset yourself again."

"Let me finish for God's sake," Lizzie shouted. "You've got me shouting like a mad woman and the kids in the next room."

Lizzie took a short sip from the lukewarm cup of tea.

"Let me finish what I want to say," she continued her voice back to normal. "The hardest thing in my life was not the shock of finding out that my Paul had 71 different injuries when they found his body in the gutter. The hardest thing I have had to put up with in my life is Doreen's scream when that woman walked away with her baby. I will never forget that scream, a scream that came from the very bottom of her soul. That sound has haunted me for 22 years, Mag; I will die hearing that sound, that sound has been hell to me and it's gotten worse as the years have gone by."

"I know girl, you've told me this before, you know," said Maggie. "Them kids should be ready for bed, yes."

Lizzie straightened up.

"Yes," Lizzie said rising from her seat. "I'll go see to them, they've probably fallen asleep; it's been a long week for them, same as all of us. Maggie, I've got to tell you this, I've never spoken about it to anyone since it happened. I'll be back in a minute."

Maggie was not looking forward to hearing about her sister's guilty secrets; Maggie had guilty secrets of her own. However, these were special times; she had to be indulgent and support her sister in her moment of need. Family and duty were tattooed on my heart, Maggie always said about herself.

Lizzie cried silently, dabbed at her eyes with her sleeve, and lit a cigarette, the first in days.

Maggie took the cigarette out of Lizzie's hand and crushed it in the pristine ashtray idling on the sideboard.

"I'm cursed Maggie," Lizzie said, "and I don't know why. I keep looking back in my life and ask myself what have I done to deserve this? I've done a few bad things in my life. In the thirties I remember throwing bricks at Mr. Rosenfeld's grocery store's windows off Mill Street along with a dozen other kids, just because he was a Jew. Word got back to Mam and she beat the shit out of me."

"Yeah," said Maggie, "I remember that, but we were only following the adults. Was that the secret you were gonna tell me about?"

"Do you remember what Mam said, apart from the fact that it was wrong to damage someone's property? Mam also said that Mr. Rosenfeld gave us credit for food and stuff and that we would go hungry without that man. She roared at me and beat me with her slipper so hard I couldn't sit for days."

"Not as hard as she hit me as the eldest. I remember those days very well," said Maggie keen to get on to lighter subjects. "Do you remember that time when . . ."

"If there is a heaven and hell," Lizzie interrupted, "then this is my hell, I'm living my hell right now. To tell you the truth I'd be quite happy to die and move on up to heaven."

"You morbid saddo," said Maggie shaking her head.

Chapter 18

Fancy Curls

10:45 am Monday 22nd September 1981

Alan Leung parked his car (or rather Middlesbrough Council's car as he was still obdurately refusing to hand the car back) outside his mother's house, burping from the full English breakfast he had eaten. He had been to an interview with an Italian television network to discuss '*the troubles*'. He had met them at Liverpool's poshest hotel, and, of course, they had breakfast. Alan got used to this interview lark, the words just oozing out of his mouth.

"The police in Liverpool 8 are noffin more than an army of occupation," he had repeated at every interview, including in the broken Spanish to a Spanish radio station he had picked up working in bars in Spain before he was put away. "And like any such army there is a resistance to that occupation. People of all ages, of all races, and mainly from the Liverpool 8 area [Alan Leung refused to yield to the media's new label for Liverpool 8, the archaic '*Toxteth*'], are defending themselves and their community from these oppressors, particularly those in uniforms. We want to be treated as white people are in this city and elsewhere, with respect and dignity and an equal chance to compete for resources particularly jobs, housing and education. This community wants no more and no less than what the vast majority of people in this city and elsewhere take for granted. Incidents like we have had in the past few weeks will persist and maybe get worse unless these issues are properly addressed."

Alan waved at Billygoat who beeped his horn at him as he drove past in his truck. Alan slotted the key in the front door and let himself in; he had taken over Paul's old.

Still no word from Middlesbrough Council about the disciplinary proceedings but Alan's union representative had told him that the likely scenario would take approximately eight weeks and lead inevitably to dismissal. Roger Rogers, the union official, had shown little sympathy, his face dissolving into sheer contempt at Alan's conviction.

"I didn't do it," Alan protested to Roger Rogers. "I was fitted up by the police."

However, in Roger Rogers's mind, as in many others, Alan Leung fitted the bill. A young black man, bold and full of chat, what else would he be but a pimp, living off white women, stands to reason, like a horse and cart, the two go together.

"You're late," Beryl told Alan firmly as he stepped into the hallway.

Beryl was standing by the front door with fire in her eyes.

"Sorry, sis," Alan replied meekly. "The press wanted their piece of flesh and wouldn't let go."

"Oh," she sang, "*Mister Big Stuff Who Do You Think You Are.*"

"Somebody's got to do it. Are yers ready then?" said Alan feigning impatience.

"The appointment was for ten thirty not midday," Beryl shot back.

"Okay, okay, it's only gone 10.30," said Alan putting his hands up defensively. "Take it easy, they're not going away, they'll still be there, keep your hair on or you'll have none left to get dressed"

"Mam," Beryl shouted. "Would you believe Alan's finally arrived? Come on let's go."

Alan dropped off Lizzie, Beryl and Doreen at the hairdresser's on High Park Street, relieved to get away from Beryl's instructions to drive faster.

"And don't forget to pick us up at twelve," Beryl reminded him for the third time.

It was Beryl who had talked Lizzie and Doreen into getting their hair done, to cheer themselves up a bit and do girly things away from the house.

Barbara Boualouache, the salon's owner, hugged Beryl as she entered. They had not seen each other since Beryl attended her wedding nearly 15 years ago. She was Barbara Lim then, the youngest daughter of a white mother and a Malaysian father. Her wedding to Samir Boualouache, an Algerian immigrant, had been like no other wedding Beryl had ever been to with its array of exotic foods, dazzling jewellery and bursts of colour and emotion.

The salon was packed with women of all ages, their chatter bouncing across the room full with smoke from cigarettes, singed hair and fumes the ubiquitous raucous hairdryers. Two older woman (contemporaries of Lizzie's, who she acknowledged and who in turn offered sincere condolences) were sitting next to each other close to the entrance waiting for their hair to dry. They were competing as to who could remember the most Liverpool 8 clubs they had known.

"Wilkie's on Parly," said Wendy Clements.

"The Palm Cove owned by Roy Stevens and opened in 1952 the year ar' Margie was born," said Judi Wallace, providing chapter and verse.

"The Nigerian, the Yoruba, the Somali, the Ibo, the Federal," said the other reeling off some of the African clubs.

"Gwen was here last week, she was asking about yer," Barbara shouted to Beryl above the noise from the raucous hairdryer blow-drying a victim.

"Yes," said Beryl, "I saw her yesterdee. Her hair looked nice. I want mine done like that. That short angular look is great. I want streaks in as well; I'm pushing the boat out."

"Joyce will look after you," said Barbara.

Doreen wanted her hair shampooed, trimmed, relaxed and set, nothing fancy she insisted. Lizzie was unsure and looked at some of the hairstyles illustrated on the walls with some interest but decided on the simplest option of shampoo and trim.

"The Pink Flamingo on Prinny Road . . ."

"The Beacon on Parly owned by Joe Bygraves, the boxer . . ."

Felicia Goolsby-Power-Wright emerged from the anonymity of a towel wrapped around her head.

"Hello Mrs. L.," she said to Lizzie, "I didn't see you come in."

"Hello girl," Lizzie replied. "How are you, and your Mum?"

"We're fine Mrs. L. I'm really sorry about your boys," Felicia added and hugged her warmly.

Barbara put money in her till from one of her customers, a young girl in a mini skirt with a brand new spiky haircut. The girl walked to where the coats were hanging picked one out and turned to leave. Before the girl opened the door, Barbara rushed towards her.

"Hey," Barbara said to her grabbing her by the shoulder, "that's not your jacket. You didn't come in with one."

The girl blushed and mumbled her apologies saying she had a coat exactly like it, but Barbara who was wise to these things told her not to come back again and closed the door sharply behind her.

"You have to have eyes behind yer 'ead," she said to the jacket's owner who was getting a manicure and was oblivious to everything except her nails.

As one person left another came in. Vinny Kitson, aka Shirley Bassey, came into the salon carrying a cardboard box. He shouted "hello everybody," and then grimaced pointing to the street. "I've juss saw a rat outside in the street."

"That muss be my fellar, don't mind 'im 'e likes it in the gutter," said a woman getting her hair trimmed.

"Hello Vinny, long time no see, how are you," said Beryl. "What happened to your eye?"

Vinny hugged and kissed Beryl and told her how it all was.

Vinny could have said Beryl's dear departed, homophobic, gay-as-Paree brother beat him up, but God had revenged him and it was best left alone, God bless his soul. He could tell her that when he waltzed into the Federal club with a new man, Paul Leung got jealous and beat him to a pulp. He could have told her that he had been Paul's lover on and off over the years, but, Vinny deep down was a compassionate individual. Of course, Vinny could be thoughtless and selfish and many people knew him that way. However, he had cried sincere tears in remembrance of times past at the funeral and bought flowers for the grave, and he was not going to cause Paul's family more pain by telling them what a bully he was; they probably knew that already, although Vinny was sure the family knew little about his sexuality.

"You wanna see the other guy," Vinny said defiantly, "his own Mother wouldn't recognise him. He kissed and hugged Beryl and Lizzie and turned to Barbara. "Babs darling, I need me wig washed and styled."

Vinny placed the box on the table next to the till. "Can you do it for me for tommora evenin' Babs darling, please?"

"The earliest I can do it is Wenzdee, first thing," said Barbara. "We've just introduced half price for Pensioners on Mondees and Tuesdees, it'll be worst tomorrow."

"Come on cuz," he pleaded. "I'm sure you can squeeze me in for tonight, pleeese."

"It'll cost yer," Barbara conceded.

"The Gladray, the Silver Sands and the Tudor run by Teresa and Dutch Eddie . . ."

"The West Indian Club on Montpelier Terrace but they knocked those beautiful big houses down in the seventies and built Falkner Estate instead, one of the worst estate we've ever had . . ."

"You still in Wavertree, Marilyn," Lizzie asked the latest customer after exchanging greetings.

"Been there three years now," Marilyn replied.

"Any black people in Wavertree," asked Beryl before disappearing under a hairdryer.

"We've got three families, so things're improving. If it goes on like this Wavertree'll become multi-cultural."

"And pigs'll fly," said one of Barbara's assistants as she coaxed the kinks out of Doreen's hair with electric tongs.

"The 101 Club, Johnson's on Grove Street and the Embassy that was owned by Roy Stevens as well . . ."

"The Bedford Club, the Polish Club on Catherine Street and Stanley House . . ."

"Stanley House doesn't count, that was a community centre not a drinking club . . ."

"The 68 Club on Prinny Road, the A&B Club on Devonshire Rd, opened by Pat Hamilton. You remember her, used to drive a big Jag."

"Are you two still going on about the clubs, you musta been right drinking girls in your time," Barbara said chewing gum ferociously as she douched Lizzie's hair through a showerhead.

Felicia emerged with a sober plain black hairstyle.

"What happened to your orange hair," someone asked.

"I've had enough of wild coloured hair," she replied loud enough for everyone to hear. "I have to start looking like a Mother now that I am pregnant."

The salon burst out in woops, congratulations and applause; Felicia Goolsby pregnant after all this time that was something to celebrate.

Barbara hugged Felicia and refused her money. "Dis one's on me luv, well done."

The baby was due in April and she was undecided about names.

At that moment, Chantelle walked into the salon pushing Cilla Jenkins, her mother, in her wheelchair.

Beryl was startled.

"I thought you was dead, Cilla," she said. "Your daughter told us you were dead and we made a big collection for you."

Cilla lowered her eyes.

"Well, I was nearly dead and I came back alive again" she said.

"You wanna gerroff that stuff you're on, Cilla," said Barbara.

"I can't Barb. I still like a drink but that smack just destroys yer, yer know warra mean, Barb," she said, as Chantelle manoeuvred the wheelchair inside the salon. "From the time I wake up I wanna score. I can't help it. I wanna do other things, I wanna live. I'll do anything, and I mean anything, for a charge. Although

I won't be ripped off and only use good stuff. But still it's breaking me up. I wanna do something else and I can't, I just can't . . ."

She then turned to Felicia.

"I heard that about you expectin' and lookin' for a name," Cilla said. "Chantelle's a nice name. All Chantelles are pretty."

"What can I do for you," asked Barbara pointedly.

Cilla was a huge pain in the arse, always cadging off her customers.

"I need me 'air tidied up," said Cilla, "the Duke of somebody is coming to the day centre tomorrow and I'm givin' 'im a bunch of flowers. The papers and the TV will all be there, so I've got to look me best."

"How many times have I told you to book in advance," Barbara replied standing guard over Cilla.

"Go on, Barb," Cilla pleaded.

Barbara hesitated then relented.

"Okay, Cilla, take a seat; and no cadgin' d'yer hear me."

Cilla wet her finger and traced a cross on her throat. "Stand on me girl," she said.

"So, wharrabarit," Cilla said to Felicia, "are you gonna call your baby Chantelle?"

Felicia wrinkled her nose. "I'm not sure," she said politely.

"Don't call it Summer Aurora," said the old girl with the white hair and pink scalp, "that's what one of me neighbours called her baby. Can you imagine when the kids're playin' out and she shouts: *'come in fer yer tea Summer Aurora!'*

"Talk about ridiculous names," said Doreen, "what about Eiddwen and it's spelled with two dees and a double-u."

"My daughter's mate called her daughter Guinevere. Guinevere, where's your knight in shining armour."

"Well, the funniest name I've ever come across was in the States, and there are some strange names in the South, was Merryleebelle," said Beryl.

They were still exchanging names when Alan Leung beeped his horn impatiently.

It was twelve o'clock and Alan's car was parked outside *Barbara's Hairdressing Salon* as arranged. Bonny Roberts sat in the passenger seat.

Bonny was in love. He knew he was in love because every time someone mentioned Beryl's name he would smirk inanely and every time he saw her, he felt inexplicably happy, no matter what his prior mood. It had never been that way with Valerie. Bonny still thought of his children, every day, but Valerie, well, they were better off apart. She would find someone and he will have Beryl. Beryl was good for him. She had plans for herself, getting a degree and a good job, and she made him plan for his future. He was going to join a foundation course for a year at the Charles Wootton Centre, studying English, Mathematics and Sociology. Then he would do a two-year Diploma in Youth and Community and get himself a job as a Youth and Community Worker. Bonny had never planned that far in his life. His life had been worrying about today because tomorrow would look after him. Somehow, Lady Luck would select him out of the millions of people in the world and carry him to a better life. He had stopped gambling, other than the daily flutter on the horses. He did not hang around the bookies anymore. He went in, put his bet on and walked out, merely waving as he left at those who virtually lived in the place, rather than stay to discuss form and chew the fat. He had not been to a gambling house since the night of the shooting. He did not have the time anymore. He lived with his mother now. Well he slept there because most of his waking hours he spent with Beryl and the twins. Aunty Lizzie had welcomed him like a son. Most of his meals were at Aunty Lizzie's house. She approved of Beryl and Bonnie, not in so many words, but by her manner, the way she looked at them.

"Go in and see how long they're gonna be," Alan said to Bonny looking at his watch.

"I don't like going in there," Bonny replied bashfully. "It's full of women, yer know warra mean."

"Don't be stupid, they won't bite yer, go on," said Alan smiling.

Reluctantly Bonny walked into the shop that men never enter.

Bonny was surprised to see it was so like the barbershops he went to, pictures of good-looking people showing off intricate hairstyles, Radio Merseyside on the radio and everybody talking at once. The difference was that the place was full of women and they all looked at him as if he had come direct from outer space. It felt like he had walked in to a women's toilets for a second and he was about to walk back out again when Doreen came up to him.

"Me and me Mother are ready now but Beryl's gonna be a bit longer, she's getting her nails done as well" Doreen said to him. "Stay and keep her company, she's over there."

Doreen was pointing at a body wrapped in white towels with its head under a gigantic helmet that looked like a space ship.

"Go on, she won't mind, you can walk back with her."

As Lizzie and Doreen left the Salon, Bonny felt desperately alone and exposed standing in the middle of the room like a schoolboy caught in a strip tease club.

Beryl looked delightful with her new shorter hairstyle with a quiff at the front. "Well," she said twirling round so that Bonny could have a better look, "Was it worth the wait, or have I just wasted my money."

"It's nice, really nice," Bonny answered staring at her, "really really nice," he added hesitantly, not used to being extravagant in his praise

"Flattery will get you everything," she laughed as she grabbed his arm and guided him towards the door.

The weather was still damp from the previous day's outpourings but warm.

"It's a lovely day," she said taking a deep breath. "Fancy a meal in Chinatown, we'll walk."

Beryl saw Bonny's embarrassment and quickly added: "It's okay, my treat."

As they cut through a side street to get to Park Road, a dark blue car was half parked on the pavement. Three white men were sitting inside the car as clouds of ganja smoke bellowed out of the open windows.

"That's Bull O'Connor's car" said Bonny.

"Are you sure," Beryl asked.

Bonny nodded.

"It's his car," he affirmed.

As they got nearer the car Bull O'Connor's bald head leaned out of the car as he spat on the floor. Beryl ran the few yards to the car awkwardly on her impossibly high heels and went to grab Bull's head but he pulled it quickly out of her reach. "You're a murderer!" Beryl screamed at him.

Bull O'Connor got out of the car followed by his two acolytes. He ignored Beryl and walked up to Bonny.

"I dunno oo the fuck you are but you'd better tell yer Judy ter keep 'er fuck'n mout' shut udderwise she's gonna get seriously hurt," said Bull O'Connor looking directly, provocatively into Bonny's eyes.

"I don' fink so," replied Bonny coolly.

"Oh, yeah," said Bull. "And who's gonna stop us, you?"

"Maybe," said Bonny grinning.

"You and whose army?" said Bull.

Bull looked with focused eyes at Bonny standing in front of him, quite relaxed, with a grin on his face. He aimed to wipe that grin off Bonny's gob and threw a punch towards Bonny's head. Bonny avoided the punch with a dip of his shoulder straight out of Unity boxing club and hit Bull with his forehead with such force it made a snapping sound, like a branch broken off a tree by a strong wind. Bull's legs crumpled under him and he lay flat on his back oozing blood from a cut on his eyebrow. Bonny turned to the other two who stood there without reacting. Bonny grabbed the one nearest to him by the front of his shirt, slapped him across the face and asked him his name.

"Phil, Phil Mallory," he said.

"I know you're Lecky O'Connor," he said, then to the second man. "But you, are you sure you're not Paddy Dalton, you look like him," Bonny said holding him tighter.

"Paddy Dalton's got fair hair and mine's black," the second man replied.

"Well give that to Paddy when you see him," Bonny said as he butted him on the bridge of his nose and watched him fall against the car.

"He's running away," shouted Beryl after Lecky. "Don't let him gerraway."

Bonny watched Beryl taking a shoe off, lifting it high in the air and strike the steel-tipped heel deep in Bull's face as he lay on the ground barely conscious. She wrenched the heel out of his face ripping the flesh as she did so, leaving behind a gaping hole in his cheek, like a second mouth with a bloody grimace through which some of Bull's teeth were visible. She then lifted the bloodied shoe aiming for Bull's eye but Bonny grabbed her arm and dragged her away.

"You'd better gerroff, get a taxi home. I'm going after the other guy," he said and ran off towards Lecky O'Connor who had a hundred yards on him.

The pursuit led down Park Road, where an ambulance with flashing blue lights missed Lecky by inches. Bonny thought of giving up the chase, not that he was tired, he was known on the football field as having a good engine who could run all day. What kept him going was Beryl, he could not return to say that the man got away. This was the least he could do for her for making him a changed man. Bonny was now signing on the dole, he had registered with the doctor and his first visit to a dentist in nearly 25 years had resulted in five fillings.

Bonny nearly caught up with Lecky by 'The Blackie' (the grandiose black church converted into a community centre, so named more because of the black grime it was covered in than the colour of the people who used it) on Great George Street. However, a police car cruised past and both stopped running until it had gone, then they started running again but Lecky must have got a second wind and by the time they reached Berry Street the distance between them had widened to more than twenty yards.

Lecky whistled for a taxi outside the rapidly expanding hardware store on Renshawe Street, but he could not get in it in time so carried on running. Bonny was content to keep within a short distance from Lecky until they came to a more deserted area and then he would pounce on him and leave him with something to remember. They jogged right across town, Lecky cautiously staying on the main thoroughfares where there were more people and Bonny dogged in the

Pure Pressure

pursuit. They were now on Netherfield Road. Bonny was mindful that he was in unfamiliar territory. If he held off any longer, he would be deep into the North End where black people were at best a peered-at rarity, so he decided to catch up with Lecky, give him one blow and then get away. He sprinted towards Lecky on tiptoes and, catching him by surprise, grabbed his shoulder and shoved him in a shop doorway.

"Look, it wasn't me," said Lecky breathlessly, his eyes wide with panic and his face drenched with strong-smelling sweat. "It was our kid, it was our Bull, honest ter God, on me Ma's life, it wasn't me. I wasn't even there. It was our Bull, Paddy Dalton and Phil Mallory, I swear. I was nowhere near. I wouldn't do som'n like dat. Dat wuz bad, lah, I swear . . ."

Bonny butted Lecky on the forehead and Lecky fell forward.

Bonny had been aware of the beating of a drum in the distance but had paid it no mind, then he saw a lone uniformed policeman walking in the middle of the street a few yards away followed by a lone drummer and dozens of people dressed in paramilitary uniforms and carrying musical instruments.

The Orange Lodge, Bonny grinned. Of course, it was the marching season. Bonny loved the Orange Lodge as a child. His mother used to take him and his sister Gloria. He would march with them to Southport and back every year; make a full day of it with cold flasks and soggy sandwiches. He remembered Beryl and Doreen coming with them a couple of times.

After the blow on his head, barely conscious Lecky fell in Bonny's arms. Bonny draped one of Lecky's arms around his neck and propped him up against a shop window as the Lodge marched past.

The St George flags were fluttering in the breeze, humourless-looking men in black bow ties and short-sleeves were marching as one to a solitary drum beat, then the music kicked in with big drums, little drums, flutes, accordions and bells.

A young girl dressed as a man with thigh-high black shiny boots, black hat with a purple ribbon, fancy curled blonde wig, braided blue jacket, orange sash across her chest was holding a sword like she was about to hurt somebody. King William the Second of Scotland, King William the third of England and William the Third of Ireland, from the House of Orange-Nassau, and conqueror of James II at the Battle of the Boyne in 1690. Bonny knew his Orange history.

Another King William marched up with a large black hat with a flourishing white feather, holding the hand of his bride dressed in white with a long train carried by children dressed in pink fluffy dresses as if to a real wedding.

There were a dozen bagpipers dressed in tartan and wearing skirts, old men with purple sashes across their chest marched under an Everton Protestant Boys banner

The whole procession had an air of carnival but with menace attached.

"Fuck-off off our streets, proddy bastards," shouted a man with a large gut hanging over his belt.

"Go on piss off, you Fenian twat," a man shouted back, dressed like a traditional Scotsman, twirling round a long wooden stick in his hand.

"Ay know oo yer are. Ay know where youz live," said the large gutted man wagging his finger sinisterly.

"'Ey, we don't want youz around e'yer," shouted a middle-aged woman in weary autumn clothes.

"Shut yer gob, Papist!" responded a stocky steward with an orange sash across his barrel-like chest.

Bonny felt Lecky fidget; he was coming round.

"Ay told yer, lah, ay wuz not involved at all, ay wouldn't do dat," Lecky pleaded his eyes still groggy and a red lump glowing on his forehead.

"Shut yer mouf, Lecky," said Bonny in a low voice, concerned that Lecky was bringing attention to both of them. "If you don't shut it I'll break yer arm," he said grapping Lecky's arm.

Lecky stopped pleading.

It was twenty minutes before the march had passed and the crowds with them heading south towards the city centre.

Bonny told Lecky they were going to find a phone and he was going to ring somebody to find out what he should do with him.

He frogmarched Lecky to a street phone box on Moss Street. Bonny asked him for change.

Lecky fumbled into his pocket and took out a large wad of notes and some coins. Bonny took the lot and dialled a number. Doreen answered and recognised his voice.

"Do you want Beryl?"

When Beryl came on the phone Bonny told her he had Lecky with him. She asked if he had injured him and he told her about the lump in the middle of his head.

"Break his arm, break his leg, I dunno, torture the white bastard," she said angrily. "Ring me back when you've finished with that piece of shit," she added then put the phone down.

He should have guessed Beryl's reaction recalling a recent conversation.

You know why I hate white people," she had told him, "because they hate me, no other reason. They hate us, they hate you, they hate me; they hate everybody who doesn't look like them. I've known that since I was small. Deep down, where it really matters, they think we're inferior to them. We come from monkeys and they're created in God's image.

"Come on Beryl, you're getting carried away with yourself," Bonny had protested, "not all white people hate us, you can't believe that. The O'Connors are not typical of white people; they're scum of the earth, the lowest of the low. What about Aunty Hilda, she's white, she used to spoil us as kids, and everybody loved her, even you."

"You believe what you want to believe, Bonny, but how do you explain my baby brother found hanged in a white man's jail. Tell me how a young lad, who wouldn't hurt a fly, who had everything going for him, how can he willingly take his life? He was murdered, Bonny, just like Paul was murdered."

Then there was a long period of silence, as Bonny did not have an answer for her grief and rage.

Bonny did not know whether Lecky had heard Beryl's suggestions about breaking his limbs, but maybe he had heard and that had been his spur for trying to get away. Lecky struggled out of Bonny's reach and ran out of the phone box into the road. There was a piercing screech of tyres and the 17 bus going to Kirkby knocked him down and crushed his head with its back wheels.

"His brains were scattered everywhere," Bonny told Beryl later to placate her.

"I always thought God was slow but sure," said Maggie. "But He can be quick too."

10.45am Tuesday 29th September 1981

The first thing Nat noticed as he walked back in to his old house on Crown Street (the first time in weeks), was the Bessie Braddock photograph. It was back on the sideboard, next to his wedding photograph, which had previously been in his bedroom. Other than that, all was as it had been. His bedroom had changed though, a new green carpet to go with the pale green newly painted walls. It felt good to sit on the familiar double bed with the carved wooden headboard and the soft mattress. The kids had taken all his clothes back and hung them neatly in the wardrobe. Maxine helped also, which amazed him, as they had not been close in the last few years. Everyone was helpful and made him feel important. He had to blow his nose several times to hide his emotions. The stairs were a bit difficult for him now that he had problems walking but it was worth it to be back to like it

Louis Julienne

was; he insisted on walking up unaided. It was only a few weeks ago when he did not care if he lived or died and now he felt ready to live for another twenty years peacefully in his own home with his family. Bliss man, bliss.

The front door bell rang shrilly.

Maybe it was for him, Josiah Ankrah or Kojo come to celebrate his homecoming. He listened to the voices downstairs and it was not for him. It was Alan Leung who had come to see Maureen.

Maureen assumed that Alan had come to catch up on the news on the Jaycee. He often popped around for a chat now that he was unemployed and not involved in any projects. Maureen knew he took his situation hard. The gutter press celebrated Alan's resignation from the Jaycee.

"I've been invited by the taxi drivers to speak at a meeting; it starts at one," he said to Maureen. "I don't fancy it on me own, will you come with me?"

Alan warned Maureen that it was a hostile meeting called to discuss boycotting the South End because two drivers were in intensive care after being attacked in the area, they say by black youths.

"Bonny has agreed to come in case there's any lumber," Alan added.

"Never mind Bonny Roberts, we're gonna need an army by the sounds of it," Maureen smiled.

Maureen needed some excitement as it had passed her by completely since she gave up gambling. Colin could not believe she had given up after all these years. It was more than two months now and Colin was counting the days before she went back to her old ways. Maureen, however, was determined she would never gamble again Shep-from-Ohio had seen to that. Of course, she had withdrawal symptoms, but distractions were the key, keep busy and the taxi drivers' meeting was what she needed, it would get the adrenalin pumping again.

"We'll have to go in your car," Alan said to Maureen.

"Where's your car," she asked.

"I had to give it back cos they wouldn't pay me me wages until I'd returned the car and me bank manager is giving me pure pressure. I was going to borrow one of our Paul's car but African Henry is not answering his phone and the garage is closed."

"Well that's a first, Alan Leung finally using the legs God gave him."

After they had gone and Nat was alone, he came downstairs into the living room; it took him nearly five minutes to conquer 16 stairs. He sank on to the sofa and took deep breaths. Doctor Goldman had referred him to a specialist, who recommended a hip replacement operation, but the waiting list was two years and he may well be dead before then. He stretched out languidly on the sofa that used to be his bed for so many humiliating months and slipped into his past when everything seemed less complicated.

Part II
1991

Chapter 19

No More Trouble

7:15pm Monday 7th October 1991

The oak-panelled room is grey with cigarette smoke. Around the large polished oak table, sit nine people, some more bored than others and showing it. The Council's Housing Sub-Committee meeting has gone on for four hours now and everybody is tired except its Chairman, Councillor Will Grimshaw OBE, and prospective Member of Parliament for the recently vacated Toxteth and Granby constituency, who is talking at length about why houses off Granby Street need to be demolished and replaced with new dwellings. He has been at it, hammering the point at great length, for over forty-five minutes. Whenever one of his colleagues dare interrupt to speak in favour of refurbishing the houses he reposts in flowery language, as is his way.

"The area in question is known as the Granby Triangle but it should be known as the Black Triangle," said Grimshaw.

Maureen Ajayi was quick to intervene.

"*Black Triangle*, Councillor, what do you mean by that? Is it because that's where the majority of Liverpool's black community lives? I'm waiting for an explanation and an apology Councillor Grimshaw," Maureen said in a tone seldom used against Will Grimshaw by members from his own party.

Will had always considered Maureen a loose canon.

"Now, now, Maureen," he said. "I meant no such thing and you know I did not imply race, gender, religion, belief, disability or sexual persuasion by my remark. I mean the Black Triangle, in the sense that it is a bleak area with a community that is economically dying, sinking into a dark hole, a black hole. It is therefore I who seek the apology for implying that I made an improper, inappropriate or derogatory remark. Come on Maureen, nobody wants more than I do see that area flowering, booming, alive with trade and prosperity like it once did when

Louis Julienne

I was a lad. I was brought up off Granby Street. I don't have any relatives left there but my soul and that of my parents, God bless them, belongs there. I am a Liverpooleighter to my fingertips, to my very essence Maureen, you know that and you know I would never betray my roots, the community in which I spent the best years of my childhood, the community that defines me still. I'm a Granby Street kid, for goodness sake. I was born in Beaconsfield Street two doors away from the Methodist Church. I was a pupil at Granby Street School. That area means everything to me; it is stuck deeply, very deeply, in my heart. Comrades, believe me, nobody wants to live there, in those wretched, crumbling houses. Look what we have done with most of the streets already. We knocked the houses down and replaced them with modern, central heated houses, some large enough to accommodate extended Somali families. We are talking here about three streets left to demolish—Cairns Street, Jermyn Street and Ducie Street. Half of these decrepit dwellings in those streets are empty, abandoned, boarded-up, and rat-infested. Only old people occupy the few inhabited houses, and these people would be gloriously happy rehoused in new, clean, efficiently heated homes with gardens instead of yards and the area spruced up. We need to regenerate the whole area and there are generous central government grants available to do so. We could revitalise the community, make it a more vibrant, viable community and lifting it out of its velleity, returning the area back to the multi-cultural, thriving neighbourhood it once was."

Councillor Will Grimshaw OBE, known by the local media as the dandy politician, always available to provide a colourful quote, always ready to blow the Grimshaw trumpet, takes a breath. He wears a rose in the buttonhole of the right lapel of his jacket, and the jacket always matches the trousers. Nobody could ever recall seeing him wearing anything else but a well-cut suit with a rose in the buttonhole, ever since he became one of the youngest Liverpool Councillors in the City's history.

"Can we agree comrades on the way forward on this issue?" he asks the meeting, although the tone of his voice suggests the question is more a directive to agree with him.

Heather Clarkson, the Deputy Chairman of the Housing Sub-Committee, raises her hand to speak. She has been silent for the past hour and most present thought she had fallen asleep. However, Heather Clarkson takes her cue and pronounces in a low-pitched carefully enunciated and cadenced voice, preceded by a polite cough.

"Mister Chairman," she begins, "I am not convinced a case has been made this evening for this sub-committee to make a recommendation either way to the main committee about the way forward for Cairns, Jermyn and Ducie Street, an issue which has been protractively debated this evening. We have established that rehabilitation of the buildings would be substantially more expensive than building new, and I am not convinced about demolishing homes many of whom are in reasonable condition, nor am I convinced that people would want to live or continue living in that area."

"I think we should canvass local residents," says Maureen shifting on her chair. "Let the people decide."

Maureen, of course, would prefer if the houses were left as they were. She did not want Shep-from-Ohio's grave disturbed.

"Might I remind you of the historical significance to the Party of Jermyn Street," Heather reprises, "the Toxteth and Granby Labour Constituency Party's first offices were located at number 5 Ducie Street and also that Percy Langstaffe, probably the greatest Socialist Liverpool has ever known, lived at number 17 Jermyn Street before the First World War."

She pauses for a very short time as she notices that Will Grimshaw is about to launch another diatribe as he has been doing all evening.

"May I propose, therefore," she continues without catching breath, "that we instruct officers to commission a research study into the popularity of the Granby Triangle to gauge whether demolition or rehabilitation would be the best course of action from the residents' perspective."

"Here, here," say the majority of voices relieved that the meeting may finally end.

Contradictions do not sit well with Will Grimshaw. He gives first Heather Clarkson then the rest of the members around the table who nod in agreement with her, a withering look as if they had collectively farted very loudly.

"Very well then," he says reluctantly, gathering the papers in front of him into a neat pile with the air of a spoilt boy wanting to take his ball home because everybody says his goal was offside.

"Is everybody agreed," Grimshaw says slowly and deliberately not as a question but as a threat.

Everybody is agreed and anxious to get home. They all leave hurriedly except Maureen Ajayi, sitting directly opposite Will Grimshaw, and eying him suspiciously.

"Yes Maureen, what can I do for you?"

"You know I'm putting my name forward tomorrow for the vacant MP post," she said looking him fixedly in the eye.

Will Grimshaw is not amused. As if a child has just kicked him in the shins and though he would love to give the blighter the back of his hand across his cheek, he cannot, so he smiles.

"I think you're wasting everybody's time Maureen; you have as much chance of being nominated as winning a beauty contest. All it will do is delay the process and why would you want to do that, Maureen?"

"You weren't saying that when you had your sweaty hands clasped on me minge at the Northern College conference party, were you?" says Maureen her eyes narrowing.

Will looks quickly towards the door to ensure it remains closed to eager ears.

"No one would believe you, you silly woman," he says witheringly.

"We'll see," Maureen replies nodding her head auspiciously.

"Look Maureen . . ."

"Yes, Will."

Will Grimshaw suddenly feels uncomfortable and starts wriggling in his chair.

"Look, I've always liked you," he says.

Maureen can feel the bribe coming up.

"I think you have a formidable political brain and are a great asset to the party, I really do. I was thinking of making you my agent when I'm selected as MP. You know, arrange my office, deputise for me, that sort of thing. In addition, there's also a jolly good salary and quite generous expenses. Think about it Maureen, just think about it. Give me a ring later this evening and we can discuss it. I'll be in after nine; I've got one more meeting to attend, I'm late already," he says looking at his watch and getting to his feet.

It is Maureen's turn to smile but she does so with amusement not charm. "You can stick your poxy job and expenses up your poxy arse Will, as far as you can get them," she says as she gathers her papers, stuffs them in her large shoulder bag and glides out of the room without looking back.

8:50pm Monday 7th October 1991

Doris 'Peach' Anderson is wondering what to do next. It is clear the man is dead. He is not breathing and she cannot find a pulse. She tries mouth-to-mouth resuscitation, breaking a trade tenet never to kiss clients on the lips. Well, she was not kissing him exactly, merely trying to blow some air into his body. He did not respond; he just lay there on his back totally still.

Although he is slumped in the back seat of the car in darkness, a beam shines from the flickering glow of the streetlight directly on to his limp penis, mischievously illuminating the instrument of his death. In his frenzy, the man had succumbed to a heart attack, gripping him like a vice precisely at the moment of orgasm. At least he got his money's worth, she thinks, looking down at the wet condom hanging from the tip of his penis.

She wonders why complications attracted themselves to her life like insects to bright lights. Peach looks furtively around the street and, satisfied it is deserted, she reaches for the door handle to make a quick exit but changes her mind. The man may have some money in his pockets, recompense for her ordeal. She riffles through the dead man's pockets, all the while repeating the Our Father prayer under her breath as penance for the desecration of the corpse. She notices that the man's moustache, a bushy brown affair, is askew across his mouth. The dummy moustache does not surprise her; Peach has encountered all manners of idiosyncratic clients over the years. She could write a book about it all. That would be some book, particularly if she could name names. Like Tony, the philosophy professor, who liked her to be a dog to his cat. Scratches and bumps everywhere, but he paid well; or Red Bill, the scaffolder who drives a red car, who just wants you to be his Mummy and scold him and beat him with a bamboo cane.

Peach once was a good Presbyterian girl, going to church twice a week, brought up in a posh part of Newton-le-Willows, after her Mother Carol Smith died. She was six when adopted into the large religious family where only the boys were abused. The small, industrious Lancashire town was only fifteen miles away from Liverpool and Manchester's respective black communities but Newton-le-Willows may as well have been fifteen hundred miles away it was such a different world.

Peach was the only black person in Newton-le-Willows and probably the only one that had ever lived there judging from the curious, mocking and sometime hostile stares she attracted every time she went outside the house. As soon as she met Arnold (a local beatnik five years her senior who could recite without prompting all the words to all Bob Dylan's songs) and alcohol, after finishing her exams, she was gone forever from the whitest town in the universe. From the age of sixteen, after gaining a lorry full of qualifications, Peach lived intermittently between Manchester's Moss Side and Liverpool 8, the cities' black neighbourhoods, suffocating in both on roots that were not really hers.

Arnold was soon gone out of her life but alcohol never quite gave her up. Her striking good looks and posh upbringing were not enough to prevent her going sliding headfirst into prostitution. She had three children by three different men, none of them any good, the men that is. The children do not live with her because deep down she knows she not is equipped to bring them up and care for them. No earth mother is Peach Anderson. Too many other things on her mind to concentrate on children. Her children were all anonymously adopted, the best thing for them and her she knows. Signing that form giving Robert away forever hurt the most, more than the first or second time. Peach loves the kids, but in her Newton-le-Willows kind of way, distantly, like they are not really her own.

Peach tugs at the dead man's trousers, carefully avoiding his nether regions as if she had never had contact with them before and would cringe if she did. She could deal with live ones, in fact, she was an expert at it, but a dead one was something different.

Peach extricates a wallet from his back trouser pocket and takes out a small wad of banknotes, fumbling in the restricted space trying to stuff the notes down her underwear and avoiding dead man's nethers at the same time. Peach's outer clothes tended to verge on the mundane, but her underwear was always top class. She did not have to dress up for these monkeys, she did it for herself, it gave her pride and control somehow. The mushes just liked her pretty face and her legs when she opened them.

Peach saunters down Hope Street with a little smile on her face and well she might. The money she took from the wallet was a good bonus. She would have to work right through three nights until the early hours to earn that kind of money and in the process having to put up with the unpredictability of drunks stumbling out of the pubs and clubs looking for a bit of fun before they went home to their sleeping wives and girlfriends. She hops into a taxi and directs it to the Nigerian Club, *Special Brew* celebrations on her mind.

6:52 am Tuesday 8th October 1991

The telephone is ringing incessantly. For a while, Maureen incorporates the sound in her dream, but the ring eventually wakes her up. She looks at her bedside digital clock. Seven o'clock in the morning, she curses, "who the frigging hell was ringing at that hour of the morning?"

It is Heather Clarkson.

"Will Grimshaw is dead," Heather says in her train announcer's voice. "They found his body in his car in Liverpool 8." The emphasis Heather put on *Liverpool 8* was akin to saying Will Grimshaw was found in a sewer. "The police think he had a heart attack but are waiting for an autopsy."

Maureen takes a few seconds to digest the news and then wonders why Heather has rang her, it is not as if they are bosom buddies. She soon finds out.

"I know it is indecently soon to be talking about this," Heather Clarkson says in a manner that tells you she cares not a banana whether it is indecent or not, she is going to say what she wants to say.

"You know that Will was a shoo-in for the nomination, but now that he's gone . . . well . . . the field is open . . ."

Heather pauses for a moment, and while she does, Maureen smiles the smile of someone who knows what is going to be said next.

"Will you support my candidacy for the nomination Maureen?" Heather asks. "I think I've already got an excellent chance of getting the nomination," letting Maureen know she is not scraping the barrel.

Maureen mischievously hesitates before responding.

"I think I will be getting widespread support from both the committee and the membership," Heather continues a little nervously, "and of course with regard for both the public interest and party fealty I think I would be the best MP."

"You really have swallowed a dictionary, Heather," says Maureen. "What the friggin' hell does 'fealty' mean?"

"The party faithful," replies Heather in a tone suggesting everyone should know what fealty means.

"So why don't you friggin' say party faithful rather than some archaic name like FEALTY. Friggin' hell, Heather, gerra grip and get to the point," says Maureen, teasing her.

"Will you support my nomination, Maureen?" Heather asks, without a hint of the impatience building up inside her.

Maureen hesitates some more, enjoying the game, then she bluntly asks Heather "that's not the point I was hoping for, Heather. What's in it for us, the black community, for you to get my support?"

"I would certainly use my influence to attract more funding to the voluntary groups you support and ensure central government initiatives take into account the special circumstances of Liverpool's black community, you would certainly get my support for Deputy Leader of the Council. You could also be my agent, with a lot of personal influence and access to all sorts of new contacts, and still remain Deputy Leader and eventually Leader of the City Council; the City Council's first black leader."

"You wouldn't be the first woman to be a Liverpool MP," says Maureen slowly, teasing still, "but these are serious considerations, Heather, very serious indeed. I'll give it a good think and consult some of my people. When d'you wanna know by?"

"A week on Thursday," says Heather sensing support.

Maureen says she will think about it, thanks her and puts the phone down.

Maureen immediately rings Robbo.

Robbo had not heard about Will Grimshaw's death. "Good," he says simply. Robbo is not a sentimental man.

Robbo no longer runs a gambling house. He is a legitimate businessman now, Currently importing yams and cassava from Ghana and exporting second-hand Lada cars to Jamaica to use as taxies.

Frederick Robinson is also the Secretary of the Toxteth Constituency Labour Party.

Peewee and his wife Felicia, Ray Bootman, Bobo Jones, Jazz Singh and Lil Bob are also members.

Peewee works as a Design Engineer, clocking up nearly 10 years with Cammel-Lairds, the ship-builders, and Felicia is still flogging the dead horse Spices restaurant has become. They have two children, Martin aged 10 and babes-in-arm Adonis. Bobo Jones is a Youth Worker for Barnados and Jazz Singh runs Apna Ghar Housing Association in Manchester as well as an elected Councillor, the first Asian Councillor in Liverpool apparently. Lil Bob no longer claims State Benefits and has become an expert adviser on Immigration Law, running a private practice from home.

As a group and with other locals specifically recruited, they normally constitute 25% of those present at most meetings and can muster nearly half the votes at general meetings. Their agenda is clear: jobs for local people and then there will no more trouble. Everything will be fine, people will be working with money to spend and that spending power will give the group added political leverage as they would be more likely to vote. That was the group's vision. A lot of work needed to be done to get to that stage, as *'the community'* was coming from a long way back. There were still no black people working in shops in town except shorthaired black-clad bouncers. Hell, even the McDonald's branches in Liverpool had all white staff; probably the only McDonald branches that did not employ black people. Peewee had seen black people working in McDonald's in Cornwall, for heaven's sake, where virtually no black people lived and the five that did live in Cornwall probably all worked in McDonalds. Liverpool was not the same as anywhere else as far as excluding black people was concerned, the City had centuries of practice, ask Norris Nobleman and Ray Bootman, between them they could give a historical chapter and verse.

Robbo listens patiently as Maureen outlines her plan to become MP and the support she needs.

"Go for it, Mo, go for it girl," Robbo urges her; "you'll have to talk to Jazz though. You know he's an ambitious bastard. Every time I see him he tells me how he's built another 100 homes, or units as he calls them. Fuckin' empire builder, the way he talks you'd think he'd built the units himself. He's only a bureaucrat."

Maureen rang Jazz at home and at work but he was in meetings. Friggin' hell, she thought, only tycoons and bureaucrats have meetings at 8 o'clock in the morning.

She waits until after nine o'clock and rings Detective Inspector Evans. He knows all the gossip.

"Hello Clifford, how are you," she begins, "What's new?"

"We've got another black sergeant, our second," he announces brightly.

"When you've got a black person at your grade then you can start congratulating yourself, Clifford. Anyway, what's this about Will Grimshaw?"

"I've only just heard myself. A suspected heart attack but he must have died on the job because he was lying on the back seat with his trousers down to his ankles and a used Rubber Johnny on his cock."

They both laugh, Maureen hysterically.

"I'm waiting for some photographs from me mate and then I'll know if he shot his load or whether the Johnny was bone dry. I didn't like the pompous bastard much but I do hope he came, for his sake," Clifford says and laughs again.

7pm Tuesday 8th October 1991

Lizzie Leung is sitting in her chair in the back room drinking coffee.

Alice, her granddaughter, is visiting. She has come up with her boyfriend Sven, the blondest man Lizzie had ever seen. His hair was so blond it was white, like an Albino. Alice is doing a Masters Degree in Macrobiotics at Manchester University

"Alice could not have a chosen a whiter man than Sven if she had tried," Beryl had said to Lizzie.

They had rented a flat together on the other side of Manchester for nearly a year after Alice graduated. Beryl hoped it was a passing phase between them and that Alice would come to her senses and start going out with a nice respectable black man.

Lizzie liked Sven. She described him as a gentleman and was sure he would make Alice happy, and that was all that mattered.

"As long as Alice's happy," Lizzie told Beryl, "that's all that matters whether he be pink, blue or tangerine. Don't forget your great grand father was a white man; he didn't have white hair until he was old but he was as white as pure snow, as white as Sven. Don't forget that."

Nobody could be whiter than Sven, of that Beryl was certain. His face looked like it had never seen the sun and he would probably shrivel up if it did, and Alice loved the sun. These were not thoughts Beryl shared with her Mother or Bonny or anybody else, let alone Alice. Alma, Alice's twin sister, was living in Tenerife working in a bar; she had been there for two years without a thought of coming home.

Alma had been Beryl's hell on earth. She was sneaking out at 15 to go to all-night clubs and parties, always leaving Alice behind, thank God. From then on, it had been all down hill. Truancy, getting expelled from school, shop lifting, boys. At 16, she ran away from home for three months with a married man with earrings hanging from his nose. Alma was a free spirit and so was Alice, ending up with the whitest man she could find to challenge her mother, of that Beryl was certain.

Beryl noticed a change in her mother since she got married. Lizzie was a woman of the world now, like her sister Maggie. The kids had clubbed together to buy a time share in Tenerife on her 75th birthday, for her to use, which she did twice a year. She had taken Alma there on holiday and Alma stayed on when she fell for a Bristol man, who deejayed in one of the bars.

Lizzie now embraced all her ancestors' diversity, not just African and the Caribbean, but also, Irish, Manx, and English. She had lately taken to speaking well of the Monarchy. The Queen Mother, a hitherto reviled figure, had almost become a role model.

Beryl had never been the right-on Mother, like some she met at work. As kids, the twins never went out unaccompanied. No unsupervised Youth Club children for her, thank you very much The twins went to acting and dancing classes on Saturday, all day. Tuesdays they went to Karate. The Deforo brothers ran a Karate and Kick-Boxing Club off Earl Road, only five minutes in the car. Wednesdays, she, Bonny and the girls would go swimming at Lodge Lane baths. Thursdays was Athletics night with the school. They would be in their bedroom by 8.30, 9.30 on Fridays and Saturdays when there was no school the next day. She took the twins to Church on Sundays and made sure they spent the rest of the day doing their homework or reading a book. Although when Beryl was out, Lizzie would let them stay up until late watching TV, there was always a scary film on.

She had brought her daughters up the proper way and it had paid off, well as far as Alice was concerned. No problems with Alice who was everything you hoped for in a daughter, but that regimented upbringing did not make a dent on Alma who always did the opposite of what was expected.

"She takes after her father," Lizzie said about Alice to Beryl, "a bloody head."

Beryl had recently bought a car in the auction. A big Vauxhall kept in pristine condition; she had the car sprayed a swanky yellow by African Henry and it made her feel like a star.

"Are Alice and Sven staying for dinner?" Beryl asks her mother.

Lizzie looks up from her glasses and shakes her head.

"I'll leave them somefin in the oven just in case."

Lizzie is quite happy Beryl and Bonny live in the house now as man and wife, well *de facto* man and wife as they are not married. Bonny gives Beryl all his wages and helps about the house and that is good enough for Lizzie. They do not pay rent but they pay all the bills. Besides, they are out all day at work and Bonny sometimes does not come in until after the late news. He says he is working late, but Lizzie knows that he still gambles on the side, according to Billygoat; she has not told Beryl and will not tell her until it becomes a problem.

Beryl is Deputy Manager at a hostel for homeless youths with six staff to supervise. Bonny is apparently doing all right in the security business guarding building sites and factories for his brother in law, Eric. Our Wayne also works with them, in between his gigs.

Doreen and Evelyn are divorced. As soon as her youngest left home to go to university, Doreen left Evelyn and her job at the nursery, declared herself an artist and went to live in Trinidad with Donacienne, a sculptor she had met in art class. Doreen painted landscapes, which Lizzie thought were beautiful and made her very proud, although she openly disapproved of Donacienne.

Lizzie glances at the latest post-card from Doreen angled against a pottery figure of a dancing jet-black woman with a headdress that were once fashionable. In the postcard Doreen promises to visit over Christmas and signed it from Doreen, Donacienne and Plum, their dog.

Beryl is keen on a house they want to buy off Ullet Road, 3 bedrooms and a nice garden. Lizzie discussed with her husband what they were going to do when Beryl and Bonny move out. Oh yes, Lizzie is a married woman again, eight years this November.

Agreeing to the marriage proposal had been the easiest part. Beryl, Doreen and Alan were encouraging. Kai also approved, as he never had over George. She

Louis Julienne

often spoke to Kai even in his death. He had good instincts did Kai. Sharing her bedroom and her bed took some getting use to. Sex was a carefully choreographed business, at least the preparations were and usually on Tuesday evenings when they had the house to themselves. Bonny trained his football team and Beryl went to keep-fit classes.

The oven alarm pings loudly from the kitchen. Lizzie walks into the hallway and shouts upstairs: "Dinner's ready darlin'." Lizzie smiles; she had not called a man darling for such a long time that the word tasted sweet whenever she said it. Darling. Darling. It reminds her of the sound of song birds in spring.

She slips on her oven gloves, takes out a Pyrex dish, carries it out to the back room, and places in on a metal mat. Curried Scouse is on the menu; there would be enough left over for Alma and Sven when they come back from the pictures. One-pot dishes was what she mainly cooked these days. Put everything in the dish—meat, vegetables and seasoning—and plonk it in the oven, time it then serve. No fuss.

Lizzie hears the sound of the stair-lift and Nat Ajayi walks wrapped in a thick robe, hobbling and leaning on his walking stick, his face still damp from the bath.

Nat goes to lift the lid from the dish but quickly withdraws it.

"Dis hot, is wha' it is Liz, beef or lamb?" he asks.

"Wait and see," she says gathering the plates.

"Billygoat died yesterday," she says pointing to the newspaper on her armchair. "It was in tonight's Echo."

"Seventy-two," she says before he asks.

"That's young," they both say.

"When de funeral?"

"It didn't say; Bonny will know. That's five deaths this year, and eight deaths last year," says Lizzie who keeps a body count. "There's still a few weeks to go before the end of the year so more might die. It's awful the amount of family and friends dying these days, I reckon the hospital are killing a lot of them off. They don't like black people much in this city."

"Maybe is because we gettin' old, Lizzie," says Nat running his hand along her back.

"There's only me and Esmee left."

Esmee lives with Gloria now and minds her grandkids while Gloria goes to work. Lenny was the first to go; he had what Lenny called a Humanist funeral and got himself cremated. The first in the family to be cremated. All the Union bigwigs were there."

"Me know Lizzie, Me was dere," Nat says gently.

"Maggie was next, and she came home to get buried. Half of Cardiff came to the funeral. Maggie lived with Fokou, a Cape Verdean man, after Jim died."

Nat had heard all this before and besides, he had other things in mind other than talking about the dead, that Chinese Brush was starting to take effect.

"It's funny how we both started with marrying opposites to us race-wise, but ended up with our own," Maggie said to Lizzie when she married Nat.

Lizzie had to explain to Maggie that Kai was more one of her own than Nat. She and Kai grew up in the same area, spoke the same language; the fact that Kai was of Chinese origins was secondary to both of them being a Liverpoolieghters. Jim, bless his soul (as he had only recently died when Lizzie and Maggie had this conversation), was a White Cardiffean, he was not even from Tiger Bay. Nat has a different culture than Lizzie. Although he has spent most of his life in Liverpool, he will always be a Nigerian in the same way as Lizzie will always be a Liverpooleighter, and Fokou could not speak English properly, unlike Nat. Maggie got quite defensive at that point so Lizzie apologised.

Maggie and Lizzie counted the number of languages Fokou and Nat spoke and it came to a kind of draw at five each because Maggie insisted on counting the African languages as one. It was not languages they were counting, Lizzie said reproachfully, but European languages.

Maggie was buried not far from Kai and the kids' grave.

Lizzie and Nat eat their dinner in silence; Nat is brushing her leg with his big toe but she does not seem to notice. Nat had wondered how Kojo kept his wife happy being thirty years older than she was.

"Chinee Brush," Kojo had confided. "It works every time."

Nat had heard of Chinese Brush and its aphrodisiac qualities, but had never needed it until now.

Their last '*session*', he told Kojo, had not been good. His wood was dead, no lead to prop it up. Kojo gave him a sample and, after getting out of the bath, Nat rubbed the solution of garro wood, bezoar, ginseng, clove and cinnamon on his genitals.

He strokes Lizzie's leg again. She looks up at him and knows by the glint in his eyes what he has in mind.

The front door bell rings. It is Maureen carrying a bunch of leaflets.

Councillor Maureen Ajayi for the Granby Ward, the first black councillor in Liverpool, Maureen looks as much as she ever did—plump, bad skin still—but she has dumped the wigs and wears her hair short, close to her scalp. The '81 uprisings made Maureen reassess her strategy. The closing down of the Jaycee after Ambrose Dickinson and the council withdrew their funding was one of the catalysts for change. There were plenty of others; Maureen had never been short of catalysts. Colin left her for a woman in his office after he was promoted to manager at the reconstructed and expanded dairy. He now lives in Islington with her, wears a beard and drives a car. Dion is a Lance-Bombardier in the Army oppressing and killing Irish people (Maureen has refused to speak to him until he leaves the Army). Maxine (who now calls herself Akili) has four kids, become a Rastafarian and lives in a commune near Addis Ababa in Ethiopia. Maureen lives alone and has no one in her romantic life. She gave that up after she humiliated herself with Alan Leung who obviously prefers white girls and she will probably end up with a white guy, another Colin probably.

Maureen fishes out some forms from her voluminous bag. "I've brought that Care Allowance form," she says to Lizzie.

"Do you want some dinner, we're juss starting," Lizzie says.

Maureen nods.

"Wha' matta?" Nat asks noticing the edginess in his daughter's manner.

"Oh, it's noffin," replies Maureen in a voice that suggests that was a lot the matter.

Nat has to ask three times before Maureen concedes. "Someone's written '*MOWEY AJAYI IS A TRAITOR*' in big friggin' letters on a wall in Selbourne Street," she answers bitterly. "You can't miss it; it's painted in big white letters right against the wall where everybody and their dog can see it."

"Don't pay them no mind, girl," says Lizzie putting the stew on the plates. "They're only jealous, that's all."

"Who do dis, ha?" Nat spat "is sick people."

"Here girl, help yourself. Any idea who could have done it?" says Lizzie.

"I've got my suspicions," Maureen replies reaching for the dish. "It's your Alan's mob."

Lizzie is not shocked but pretends as if she is.

"My Alan wouldn't do that, he's not like that. How can you say such a thing," she fires back defensively her eyes swinging to Nat for his support.

Nat buries his eyes on his plate as eats. Not getting involved in this one, he says to himself, as he chews loudly to demonstrate his whole attention is geared to eating his food. After a while, Nat looks up from his plate and suggests, "yu muss get it clean up."

"I'll ring the Corpy to wash it all off. Bloody graffiti that's all it is," Maureen says firmly, "I'll ring them first thing. They attacked the police station in Admiral Street," she says, mopping the brown sauce from her plate with a piece of bread.

"The Chief Constable is going absolutely berserk, it's gonna be a long night. The Leader rang me and he wasn't happy cos' I said the kids were right in fighting against police brutality. I reminded him that that was exactly what Bernie Grant, a Member of Parliament, no less, had said about the Haringey uprisings. Nobody else was fighting police brutality, I reminded him; neither the law, the press or bleeding society who don't give a frig. The Leader was talking about getting me thrown off the Party, the spineless get."

Lizzie nods her sympathy. "They should congratulate you for being the first black woman to be a Councillor in Liverpool, not be writing that kind of nonsense; they make you sick those people," she says, "they're sick."

Nat warns her not to be a hothead as she would be more useful to the community inside than outside the system, an aside he also directs to Lizzie with a quick glance as a reference to her son Alan.

Alan was a troublemaker, of that Nat was sure. Nat remembered Alan as a man in control, always smart, with a big job and a big car. Now the man had no job so all the time in the world to be mischievous. Just like his uncle Lenny who was full of mischief until the day he died.

Maureen stays a while longer and kisses them both before leaving.

Lizzie feels Nat's toe brushing her leg under table again. "What's the matter with you, you trying to catch flies down there or som'n," she says.

"You comin' up, I feel tired," he says as he lifts himself up from the chair with his cane and looks down at himself. "I think we can make somtin' happen tonight," he thinks. "The night is full of promise."

Chapter 20

Still Waiting

1:20pm Monday 4th November 1991

For Felicia this is the worst moment of the day. Cooking and dishing out food, and feeding Adonis at the same time. It is against all the health and safety regulations. Needs must however, as there are four main meals to dish out and Adonis started crying the cry of the hungry and you cannot ignore a seven-month old child crying at the top of his voice for too long in your place of work, it disturbs the customers. Adonis is resting on Felicia's hip, his pursed lips sucking hungrily at her breast, whilst with her free hand she spoons steaming white rice onto four separate plates. She sways her hips a few moments to *Feeling Hot, Hot, Hot* blasting out of the speakers, but her heart is not in it. She spoons the Jerk Chicken on top of the rice but spills some of the sauce, scalds her wrist, prevents herself from screaming and nearly drops the baby who squeezes her nipple with his two teeth so as to not grip and this time she screams Hot, hot, hot in time to the music no one notices.

From the time Adonis wakes up around lunchtime, he will feed then stay demandingly awake for the rest of the afternoon. There would be no peace until her daughter Marty came straight from school after four o'clock, have her dinner at the restaurant and take Adonis home. out front taking order in the empty restaurant, watching him grabbing with his pursed lips, squeezing and hurting. Feeding like a starved child as if this was his first drink of the day rather than his fifth. She had to take Adonis to the restaurant because she could no longer afford the nursery fees. She told Peewee she did not want to put Adonis in the nursery because he needed breastfeeding. The reality is Felicia could not afford the fees and she wanted to hide from Peewee the loss she was making on the restaurant. The proprietor was on the point of sending in the bailiffs for rent arrears until she persuaded her mother to pay him off without telling her father.

"Ye makin' rod fe ye back," Felicia's mother warned her. "Gi' up de place."

Peewee had given up on her "over-protective" manner of bringing up their two children; "wrapping them up in cotton-wool" is how he had put it this morning, his mouth full of cornflakes, because she did not want to enrol Marty in the Girl Guides. She needed Marty to help her in the shop.

"I'm not having my daughter indoctrinated by sub-paramilitary organisations," she told him defiantly.

Lunch had been and gone and only six customers, two of whom were for takeaways.

"Cut your losses and sell up, nah gal," was the last sentence she remembered her father saying to her before he died last month.

"She won't, Dad, your daughter is a stubborn woman," Peewee had replied with well-rehearsed exasperation.

Felicia knows Spices is in the wrong place. Granby Street had become a deserted dump, haunted by people with no money, just like Peewee and her dad had warned her. Her beloved Granby Street is well gone, buried in faltering memories. The picture house where she had her first date; the school where she spent the whole of her school years; the thriving, pulsating Granby Street with its chemists, greengrocers, fishmongers, hairdressers, Greek chippie, supermarkets, clothes shop, dry cleaners, watch repair shop, ironmongers, chain store and sweet shop, that made it Liverpool 8's main shopping street. All of it gone with the majority of shops boarded up, making the place look like a ghost town. The place had deteriorated rapidly since the riots with investments to pretty up shop fronts happening elsewhere, like Lodge Lane and Dingle. She had sought alternative premises. She was gazumped for a shop on Myrtle Parade; it would have been ideal just facing the University and near the town centre. Another good spot was Upper Stanhope Street near the Rialto and the bank and passing trade, but the deposit and the rent were far more than she could have convinced her mother to lend her. There was nothing wrong with the food she cooked, she was convinced, it was by all accounts tasty and good value for money and certainly much better than Chelly's on Lodge Lane who served Caribbean food as well. Yet Chelly was doing better business and Felicia was deeply resentful. Felicia considered setting fire to Chelly's place. She even went so far as to drive there one night, out of sheer desperation, with a can of petrol and a large box of Swan Vestas. Chelly had had brand new steel shutters fitted so Felicia abandoned that idea.

One evening she went to see Miss Marjorie. Miss Marjorie was the Obeah woman who specialised in manufacturing medicinal remedies, love potions and bad luck concoctions. Felicia tried to figure out how to get Chelly to drink the liquid. She found the perfect opportunity at Adonis's Christening party to which she invited him. She poured it in his Mauby and watched him drink it. Six months later and there was no sign of Chelly's business failing. Felicia went back to Miss Marjorie to ask how long it would take the concoction to start working, as it appeared to be having the opposite effect. Miss Marjorie suggested she prepare another batch but was resolutely uncommitted on timescales. Felicia slipped the liquid into Chelly's rum and coke at the Caribbean Centre during the Jamaica Independence Day celebrations and saw him drink it. Since then, Chelly had opened a grocery store next door to the café and both were doing well. However, his wife was in a car accident and nearly died and his cousin from Jamaica who was working for him in the grocery store was repatriated for possessing forged documents.

Adonis stops sucking and his eyes slowly begin to droop. Felicia rocks him gently. She waits for him to burp and the sound when it comes is like an anthem to relief. She carefully places Adonis in his carrycot on top of the table, but as soon as she attempts to pull the blanket gently over him, he starts to bawl and Felicia has to take him out of the carrycot again.

Two more orders quickly follow, which she has to service with Adonis stuck to her back in the bag her mother put together to enable Felicia to carry the baby and still have both hands free. They are the last two customers until Martin comes home from school just after four o'clock.

As Felicia faces another dismal day for business, Eric Wilson ambles in, seating himself at his favoured spot by the window on the bench meant for two. Eric dresses like kids a third of his age. Baggy trousers to his knees and a basketball shirt with stars and stripes motifs that looks like a tent in which all the customers Felicia had served today could comfortably fit.

"Good day today, honey?" he asks her.

"Not bad," Felicia answers, aware that single-handed Eric could turn her dismal day into a not so bad day, depending on how much he orders.

"How was your holidays?" she asks him.

"'Olidays, ain't bee on no 'oliday, honey," he replied.

"Somebody said you had and you hadn't been in for weeks, so I thought . . ."

"Nah, it's my man Rodney, a new man, he's been doing the orders and he went to Chelly's instead," he said. "It was ok for a change as well, you know."

A two-ton weight dropped from Felicia's throat to her stomach and back again.

He had switched his allegiance to Chelly! What kind of bad luck lotion was that when Chelly steals her best customer?

Pure Pressure

Eric usually came to Spices most weekdays at lunchtime to pick up the food ordered for his staff at Panthers Security. Three weeks ago, the orders stopped coming and she worried until Bonny Roberts told her Eric was on holiday. Felicia knew she should not trust what Bonny Roberts says, he makes things up for no reason.

"Don't you like my food so much now, Eric?" she asks as nonchalantly as she can.

"It's not that darlin', it's just a change. I'm back now, don't fret yerself."

True enough, Eric orders five main meals with side orders to take away and a large soup to ravage now, because that is what Eric Wilson did when he ate, ravage.

It could be that Eric stopped coming because she give him too much food, Felicia reckoned, too many calories.

Spices does have a few good regulars like Mally Gibson who still passes by most days for his Jamaican Patties, ordering two dozen once for a special lunch at the printing firm where he works and is *"making good money"*.

As Eric Wilson was by far her best customer (the money she made from him alone almost covered the rent and rates), she treated him almost like royalty. She did everything except bow and walk backwards in his presence.

"Your order will be ready in forty minutes or so," she says her smile broadening.

"How's the baby, must be distractin' yer?"

"Well customers are certainly not distracting me," she thought, "they are not enough of them."

"Wharrever 'appened to yer 'elper, Solly, dun see 'im no more."

"He lives in Mary Seacole House now," Felicia replies. "He doesn't come out much these days and I don't get much time to visit him."

"Bess make it a big soup; yer can't keep a big man 'ungry for so long, and the usual dessert, not had that for a ling time," he says eagerly

Big was the operative word for the man, Eric was over twenty stone and it seemed to Felicia getting bigger every year.

It all began when Muscley Eric with a girl's waist frequented her restaurant once a week, and now, 11 years on, he comes in most days, and his portions have increased, transforming him into a beast of a man with layers of fat where his muscles used to be.

She realised after a few months that Eric was addicted to her food, so pandering to his tastes became a priority. She began increasing the portions of rice and peas to the point that they were now twice the size of standard. She doled out his soups in a large mixing bowl with extra dumplings. She encouraged him to have ackee salt fish as a starter instead of a main meal because it was more expensive than the soup. She did soak the cod numerous times to get the last bit of salt out, she suspected that dish was a hindrance to heath recovery for a man in his condition; it was the trained nurse in her. However, she had to flatter and fatten the golden goose; it was the only way to remain this side of solvency.

Slowly over the years, Eric's six-pack melted into a blob that grew to an incredible girth right in front of your eyes. His pectorals morphed into double 'J' cups effortlessly and his thighs and calves, once as firm as girders and sculpted like a Michelangelo masterpiece, flopped sideways with every step. Consecutive chins developed until they became one with his neck. The athletic step became heavy; he rolled rather than walked.

One day, she decided she was not going to feed him to death and would re-educate his palate and belly. She stopped putting meat in his soup, now it was a purely vegetarian soup. She also noticed that he never ate the vegetables she served with his main courses, or the salad, so she shredded greens and thickened her sauces with them. She substituted beef for lamb one day to a next and Eric did not notice the difference. She steamed his fish dishes and roasted rather than fried his Jerk Chicken.

The only thing she had found difficult to make headway with him was the dessert. Eric always had the same dessert; the Eric Special, she calls it. She invented it especially for him. Fruitcake doused in rum, two scoops each of vanilla and strawberry ice cream and topped up with double cream and three cherries on top. There is more calories in the dessert than in the rest of the meal.

Felicia wonders whether she could face prosecution for manslaughter for misfeeding him all these years if he died of a heart attack, right there in her restaurant.

"I've made a special soup today, Eric, with green bananas, yam, dumplings and sweet potato, no expense spared but I'll have to charge you a little extra."

"No meat," he asks eyebrows raised.

"No meat," says Felicia shaking her head.

"No problem, that sounds like juss what I need," he replies shifting on his seat.

She serves him the soup in the mixing bowl and watches for a few mesmerised seconds as he immediately begins to scoop up the food one rapid spoonful after another.

"Take yer time, Eric, let the food digest, you'll do yerself a mischief one of these days," she warns.

"I like me soup hot, man. I dun like to give it time to go cold," he replies without breaking the frenetic rhythm of spoon, mixing bowl to mouth, spoon, mixing bowl to mouth.

Bonny Roberts, Eric's right hand man at Panthers Security, comes into the restaurant, dressed in black as usual, as if he was on his way to a funeral.

"You been running?" Eric asks him.

"I've juss run all the way from the Dock Road site yet, non-stop and I'm barely out of breath," Bonny says puffing out his chest.

Ever the athlete, Bonny was the oldest registered footballer playing in the Merseyside Football league when he quit last year.

He greets Felicia coolly.

They have history those two, ever since Bonny caught food poisoning after eating at Spices. Felicia denied it of course and got very defensive and then offensive, telling Bonny he got sick for eating Beryl Leung's food not hers. That was five years ago and Bonny only came to speak to Eric. She suspected Bonny of spreading bad rumours in the community about her food.

"There's trouble at t' ranch," he says to Eric.

Felicia quickly scurries back to the kitchen, not wanting to overhear about what were probably criminal activities.

After a few moments, Eric calls for Felicia.

Whatever news Bonny has brought, Felicia hopes it does not involve cancelling the order—a £35 order

"Everyfin' okay," she asks.

"Well," says Eric, "probably only need three rather than five."

Felicia's heart sinks.

"No," says Eric firmly, "we can give the other portions to the dogs, four pit bulls and they eat like horses. Yeah?" he asks Bonny.

"The dogs'll love it," Bonny replies, adding for Felicia's benefit, "they'll eat anyfin."

"What about your dessert?"

"Yeah, I'll still have that. Done, den," says Eric.

"Done," replies Felicia, clearly relieved but miffed at Bonny's sarcasm.

"Get 'old o' dat DI Hawkins," says Eric to Bonny, "an' tell 'im to sort it out. Wha' the fuck am I payin' dis cunt for if 'e can't sort out one of my best worker's immigration status. Tell me why?"

Felicia cuts a less than generous slice of cake than she would normally have done, and places it in the centre of one of her distinctive plates, the ones with the bold pattern of flowers she reserves for special occasions.

She adds two scoops of lemon sorbet (which is less fattening than ice cream, even the low fat ice cream she had started to buy to help salve her conscious), sprays the sorbet with fat-free frothy cream from an aerosol can, and sprinkles the dish with the last of the cherries. She takes the dish to him and says "enjoy" with a smile.

"Yeah man, respect to de sistah," he beams smiling at Bonny first, then at Felicia. "Youze a good gal, always treat me nice."

"You havin' some?" she asks Bonny.

Bonny taps his belly, shakes his head and grimaces, intimating that he has not got a flat belly by accident but that it stays flat because he does not eat calorie laden poisonous shit like she was serving.

Felicia ignores the silent insult and places the plate in front of Eric.

"Can I use your bog?" Bonny asks Felicia.

"Number ones or number twos, cos I'm running out of paper"

"Number twos," Bonny replies, clearly embarrassed.

She shakes her head in acquiesce and Bonny walks towards the back of the shop.

Eric plunges a podgy finger into the white froth and licks the finger with relish.

Outside in the timid autumn sun a motor cycle stops outside the restaurant with two helmeted men astride the noisy machine. The passenger glides off his seat and heads towards the front door.

"Customers," Felicia thinks with a twinkle in her eye, "and probably take away, so no dirty plates and maybe a multiple order."

Felicia's welcoming smile freezes when she sees the gun in the motorcyclist's hand, which he raises quickly raised and aims at Eric's head. The first bullet hits Eric in the jaw and pushes his face sideways into the Eric Special. Eric slowly lifts his face now covered with white foam sliding on one sides of his face and the piece of cake covering his nose giving him a clownish appearance, except Eric was not laughing. The second bullet hit Eric's cheek and he falls heavily to the floor. Felicia would swear afterwards that Eric's body bounced off the floor like a rubber ball. The gunman turns round and walks out of the shop, climbs on the back of the motorbike and disappears within seconds, leaving behind a cloud of dark smoke. Felicia strides over to the telephone to call the emergency services but lifts a dead phone; she had not paid the last bill.

"The phone's been cut off," she says aloud.

Bonny comes out of the toilet his fly wide open spraying piss down his trousers as he races towards Eric's prostate body.

Pure Pressure

There was no doubt Eric Wilson was dead. The one eye not covered with cream was half open but lifeless, like nobody was home.

"Where's the nearest phone," Bonny says checking the pulse on Eric's neck.

"On the corner of Granby by the Avenue," she replies.

Bonny tells her to go ring the police and an ambulance. Felicia hesitates a moment about leaving the shop but Bonny's determined air does not brook argument.

As soon as Felicia leaves the shop, Bonny rifles Eric's pockets and draws out a wad of bank notes that he stuffs inside his jacket.

When Felicia returns, Bonny asks her if she recognised the gunman.

"One of the Okwuosa brothers," Felicia replies quickly, "I recognised the eyes, a brown so light they look yellow. It was probably Okon cos' he's the shorter of the two, but I couldn't be sure."

"Don't tell the Bizzies it was them or the Okwuosas will come after you. Tell them you didn't recognise who it was."

The police came and took Felicia and Bonny to the police station for questioning. They released Felicia without charge shortly afterwards but questioned Bonny well into the evening, taking his fingerprints and DNA and eventually releasing him on police bail while further inquiries were made. When Bonny returned to the police station two weeks later to surrender his bail, the Police dropped the charge for lack of evidence.

Spices restaurant died that day along with Eric as it stayed shut the next day and never opened again. *Spices* became another boarded up shop on Granby Street.

Chapter 21

Stir It Up

4pm Monday 7th October 1991

Beryl Roberts is incensed. Tony, the thinks-he's-cool five-foot-nothing 16 year old, needs senior management disciplining for his lack of respect towards staff.

She grabs Tony by his lapels bring his face close up to hers and shouts, "don't you ever talk to me like that again, d'you understand Master Tony who thinks he's being cool by stirring things up between the staff."

Tony tries to struggle free from Beryl's grasp but she is bigger and stronger than he is. Tony is more concerned with the barrage of wet missiles coming from Beryl's mouth and landing all over his face.

"Okay, okay, take it easy," says Roy Denny the hostel's manager, as he prises Tony away from Beryl's grip.

Beryl lets him go and Tony dashes off down the stairs. All the residents have come to watch the commotion each, it seems, providing comments.

"Slap him one, because he's too cheeky," says Janet, the oldest of the residents at 18 and known as a staff favourite by other residents.

"You can't do that, that's child abuse," says Brian, one of the hotheads.

"Beat him," urged one, "throw him out," urged another, "call Mr. Denny," cautioned Rose, the youngest of the residents.

Roy Denny calls Beryl into the office and slams the office door behind him.

"What possessed you Beryl, have you gone out of your mind," he says in a low but aggressive voice. "That scene outside there, you holding that boy in that manner amounts to serious assault, let alone threatening behaviour, and that is gross misconduct for which I could sack you instantly, without recourse to management."

"I'm sorry, Roy," Beryl says meekly. "I lost it . . . I . . ."

"You can't afford to lose it in a job like this. You, as my deputy, as the Deputy Manager of this establishment, you above all should know better. You should never assault a resident except in self-defence. I'm afraid this did not look like self defence to me, it was sheer aggression."

Roy Denny goes on in that vein for ten minutes and, by then, Beryl knows she would not get sacked because his voice has softened.

"Beryl, I'm really disappointed in you. I'm sure this won't happen again. Call Tony to one side, apologise and everything should be okay," he adds as prepares to leave for the cash-and-carry for supplies.

Beryl thanks Roy for his understanding and assures him that nothing like this would ever happen again. After Roy has gone, Beryl walks down the stairs to look for Tony. However, Tony finds her as he rushes towards her holding a large kitchen knife in his hand. Before Beryl has a chance to react, the tip of the knife is pressing against her throat. Tony's eyes are bulging with rage and his mouth is wickedly contorted.

The wrong word or a false move could result in that blade killing her, Beryl thinks, as she stands quite still her eyes locked in his.

"Calm down, Tony," she says. "Do you really want to kill me, Tony? Do you want to be covered in my blood? Have my blood all over the floor and the walls?"

Tony did not release the pressure on the knife and was still angry, but he thought of the spittle from Beryl's mouth that he had had to wash off his face to get rid of all the germs, and concluded that he did not fancy having Mrs. Roberts' blood all over him as well.

He pulls the knife away and lets it drop to the floor. Beryl picks up the knife with one hand, takes hold of Tony's shoulder with the other and gently guides him up the stairs to the office. She sits him down and apologises for losing her temper with him. Tony begins to sob, hiding his face in his hands, a picture of contrition.

As soon as Tony leaves, Beryl starts to cry silently, conscious of the residents' voices chattering outside the office door. She sits down at her desk, wipes the tears from her eyes and face, and takes deep breaths to release the tension that has built up inside her. The thought that she could have died on that stairwell makes her shiver.

As shaken as she is by the incident, Beryl does not dwell too long on it because she has bigger fish to fry.

Beryl is at least four months pregnant and nobody knows. She has not dared tell anyone—not her mother and certainly not Bonny, her partner of ten years.

Pregnant at 44 years of age, a time when thoughts turn not to motherhood but grandchildren; pregnant, to a man she still loves in many ways but with whom she is no longer in love with. His lack of ambition is a huge problem. He is quite content working for his brother in law for cash in hand and she wants more than that. She wants more than Liverpool 8 offers. She wants to live in Allerton in a semi-detached house with a garden. Less than ten minutes drive from the city centre but simply a world away from where she was brought up. The mortgage people say her salary alone is insufficient to buy what she wants where she wants it. Bonny's earnings cannot be included as they are undeclared. Eric Wilson, Bonny's boss, says he has never paid tax in his life and he is not about to start paying it now. It was cash in hand or he would employ someone else. Besides, the fact that they are first cousins complicates everything. What if the child is mentally or physically damaged—Down's syndrome or some other unspeakable?

Bonny, she knows, would be surprised and pleased that she is pregnant. Surprised as he is convinced he cannot make babies after finding out that both Valerie's children were not his but Zacky Pong's. He would be pleased because he would love to be a biological father. Beryl knows he would be impervious to accusations of incest and would dismiss fears of genetic defects. Beryl's mother would be distraught and probably worry herself sick until the baby was born. Worse, though, every finger in the neighbourhood would be pointing at her deformed baby.

"What did she expect," they would say. "That's what happens with incest."

Beryl should have guessed as soon as she missed her first period, or maybe she did not want to guess. She has arranged to get an abortion. She is too far gone to get a legal abortion, even privately, the people at the clinic on Gambier Terrace informed her. Bernadette Murphy has agreed to do it for tomorrow. It would be the first time Beryl had ever thought of aborting a child, but then she had only been pregnant once before and she had loved Greg at the time; he was her husband and she thought they were the golden couple.

Beryl reverted to her maiden name once the divorce from Greg was finalised. It took a long time, longer than originally anticipated, for her to regain her single status, given that Greg had simply disappeared. All her attempts to track him down, if only to try and give her daughters answers, resulted merely in establishing that he had travelled with a US airline from New York landing at Heathrow airport on 3rd July 1981. Since then he had simply vanished from the face of the earth without a trace.

Beryl puts her head in her hands pondering her faith. What if the abortion goes wrong and it kills her?

Roy Denny comes back into the office, sees how distraught Beryl is and sends her home. She is not due back into work for another three days as she was taking annual leave to give her some time to recuperate from the operation.

The fateful day has arrived. Beryl sets off to meet Bernadette Dempsey, née Murphy. She takes a taxi as Bernadette had cautioned her that she might not be in a condition to drive home after the operation.

Bernadette lives in a maisonette on Radcliffe Walk, one of the few families left on the estate waiting to move before demolition. Bernadette is standing firm, she is not moving.

"I'm a Nortender, trew n' trew and I'm stayin' in de Nortend," she told the shocked Housing Officer, "you can stick your fuckin' West Derby, Huyton and Bootle up your fuckin' arse."

Bernadette Murphy's home is immaculately clean; the living room is decorated in bold colours with stuffy armchairs and sofa with framed family photographs everywhere. A colour television sits in the corner of the living room with the sound turned off and pictures showing the horseracing at Chepstow.

Bernadette gives Beryl a hug and makes her a cup of very sweet tea.

"You'll need the fuckin' energy, darlin'," Bernadette says, "so drink it all up."

"Will it hurt," Beryl asks.

"There's no pain, darlin', you'll hardly feel a ting," Bernadette says, "it'll take 'bout ten, fifteen minutes, tops. The pains won't start until afterwards, when the baby's flushed out. It'll be like goin' through a live birth, you'll go into labour. Don't worry, you can stay here all day. I've arranged for our Billy to stay at our Franna's, so you won't be disturbed and you'll be able to get your feet up for a few hours."

"Is this gonna to be safe," Beryl asks, adding, "I don't want to die," with a weak attempt at humour to lighten the mood.

"I haven't done one for at least 15 years, girl," Bernadette says, "but it's like ridin' a fuckin' bike, you never forget. Don't worry, girl, everytin' will be fine."

Bernadette goes into the kitchen and re-emerges with a large bowl of steaming water with a large lump of brown carbolic soap.

"Everytin's got to be sterilised," Bernadette says, placing the bowl on the floor in front of Beryl.

"Take all your clothes off and put on this old nightie. Don't worry about stainin' it, I'll throw it away when you've finished."

Beryl quickly takes all her clothes off and slips on the garment. Bernadette returns to the kitchen and comes out with a rubber ball the size of a large fist attached at two ends with a long plastic tube. She submerges the rubber ball into the hot water and pumps water into it until it is full of water.

""Dis end o' the tube goes inside you after I've filled the ball with water," says Bernadette, "making sure there's no air bubbles left, cos' if any air bubbles goes inside you, dat's it, you're a goner, girl. Okay, here we go, lie down here on the couch and spread your legs as wide as you can."

Beryl cringes as Bernadette inserts the tube six inches inside her and begins to pump the water. Watching Bernadette pumping away made her think she was playing an accordion. Any minute now, Beryl expected a French man to come out dancing the polka to Bernadette's accordion dressed in bell-bottom trousers and striped tee shirt with a cigarette dangling from the corner of his mouth.

"Most operations I've done have been because the girl's pregnant to their fella's best mate or their fella's brother. Not long now girl."

Bernadette keeps pumping the water methodically, as she and Beryl watch for any deadly bubbles.

"I had an abortion once," Bernadette says. "It was in prison down South. Pregnant t'me fella's best mate, I was. Had no fuckin' option, had to do it, otherwise I'd 'ave been brown bread, no question."

Bernadette is largely talking to herself because Beryl's mind is too preoccupied looking for deadly air bubbles. Several interminable minutes pass before Bernadette finally stops pumping.

"You can relax for now, girl; the worst is yet to come," Bernadette says as she slips the tube out of Beryl and begins putting the paraphernalia away and taking it into the kitchen.

"What now," Beryl croaks.

The pain when it comes is as Bernadette described it, though worse than when she had the twins, much worse. Beryl screams for what seems like hours trying to push this thing out of her, thoughts of dancing Frenchmen long gone.

Beryl did not dare look at the fleshy lumps that came out of her because she knew the sight would stay with her forever, a visual reminder of her guilt and shame.

"Fuckin' hell, girl, it's a boy," exclaims Bernadette, "d'you wanna take a gander b'fore I flush it down de lav?"

"Juss give me a cup of tea, please," says Beryl, sweating and exhausted, "very sweet please."

Beryl falls asleep before she finishes her drink and when she wakes, it is past midnight. Bernadette rings a taxi.

While Bernadette goes to answer the door to the car beep, Beryl puts a bundle of notes on Bernadette's dresser before leaving and thanking Bernadette.

There are 345 taxi drivers in Liverpool and six of them are black. Out of all these drivers, the one who answered the call is Beryl's brother Alan.

"Hello sis, nice surprise. What you doing down here," he says.

"Me mate, Bernadette Murphy," she stammers.

"Yeah, I know the Murphys; but didn't know you were mates with them. Bad people some of those Murphys and racist as well."

"Bernadette's alright," Beryl says, thinking what she is going to say to Alan next so he does not get suspicious, "how long you been minicabbing?"

Tonight is Alan's second night as a taxi driver. Alan had put his hands to many things. He was selling advertisement on commission for Mally Gibson's Links magazine. That worked for a few months then the adverts dried up. He pitched himself as a fundraiser for voluntary organisations and that paid his bills for a few months. Working for private enterprise was more rewarding but shorter-lived when Big Ben (who employed him to courier cash to and from a bent moneychanger) was arrested with the largest haul of Jamaican cannabis seized that year in the North West.

Alan sold insurance door-to-door next but that did not last too long either, not only because he did not sell much insurance but also because of the number of snarling dogs he encountered on his rounds and Alan always hated dogs. Then he got in tremendous debt running up credit card bills up ended up bankrupt at Liverpool County Court. The double hex of ex-con and bankrupt meant that job opportunities were fewer.

Alan got a job in Nottingham as a Project Manager, all the time looking over his shoulder wondering if they were going to find out about his criminal record. He was in the job three months when his employers, Nottinghamshire County Council, found out about his conviction and sacked him on the spot because he was still in his probationary period.

Taxi driving was rewarding if you put the hours in, his colleagues told him, so he did. He had slept no more than six hours in the last forty-eight.

Over the years, with all that spare time, Alan had cultivated his interest in radical politics. He is the chairman of the North-West branch of the Socialist Workers Alliance Party and was defeated as Councillor for the Granby Ward by Maureen Ajayi. They had not been friends for years and moved in circles antagonistic to each other. Alan canvassed hard prior to the election for Granby's black vote but was bulldozed by the Labour Party machine. He was less active politically of late, although he still gave talks at SWAP meetings most weekends around the country and passed the hat round "for the cause" the way his Uncle Lenny used to.

"Come and sit in the front," Alan says to Beryl.

"I'm more comfy in the back," Beryl replies stretching her legs along the seat.

"You alright," he asks her.

By the time they reach Madeleine Street, where Alan lives, Beryl has told him about the abortion, adding that she did it because she feared a deformed baby; she has not told anybody and wants it kept a secret. Alan suggests she stay at his house for the night and tell Bonny and their mother than he took sick or he is suicidal and she is looking after him, or something.

"You were my last call," he says as they pull outside his rented little two-up-two-down terraced house, "so nobody'll see me out, I need to catch up on me sleep, I'm back out again tomorrow lunchtime.

"There's no central heating," he adds as they walk in the narrow lobby, "but I've got an electric fire and spare duvets. No telly, though, only the radio and some CDs"

Beryl rings home. Her mother answers, Bonny is working late. Lizzie is suspicious as is her wont, but Beryl gives nothing away. Beryl goes straight to the spare bedroom and falls into a deep sleep. She wakes a few hours later sweating heavily despite the room being cold; she thought she heard a baby crying.

There are 58 members and 23 observers present who are eligible to vote at the Toxteth Constituency Labour Party meeting to select the person who was going to stand for MP for the constituency. Nobody knows who the observers are and Robbo does not like it. He whispers his misgivings to the Chairman, Kenneth Dovedale, sitting next to him at the head table. Also at the table is Felicia Goolsby-Power-Wright, Deputy Secretary, having barely recovered from the murder at *Spices* a few days ago, also Bill Miller the Treasurer, still sporting his '*Justice for Palestine*' badge on his lapel, looking relaxed, his elbows spread on the table and finally a representative from headquarters who does not look old enough to vote. Kerry McDonough says he has a first class Oxford degree and is destined for big things in the party, maybe even a future Prime Minister. That explains why Kerry, a union representative, is sitting so close to him at the end of the table, their thighs virtually touching.

Pure Pressure

Maureen Ajayi and Heather Clarkson are sitting on a table apart. They are bidding to be the candidates for what would have been the late Will Grimshaw's seat.

Heather Clarkson is dressed to impress. Heather Clarkson always dresses to impress, only this time she has pushed the boat out. She is wearing an expensive looking black suit that has never had a crease that was not intended, tight at the waist and broad in the shoulders, as the fashion dictated for important women of a certain age. The crisp white cotton blouse with the ever so slightly turned up collar, demurely buttoned up to the throat; her porky pink face hidden with discreetly layered foundation to make her skin less shiny.

Maureen Ajayi thought long and hard before discarding the long dress with African motifs considering it too African. She did not want to throw her blackness in their faces. She opted for a simple, inexpensive navy and white dress with long sleeves, which Beryl Leung had helped her to choose from Blackler's store in town. The dress revealed more of her cleavage than she cared for, but Beryl was persuasive. She wore a trace of rouge on both cheeks and on her lips, and her eyelashes had just a hint of mascara. The last time Maureen's eyelashes had been mascaraed was in 1963, on her first date with Colin, but Beryl was most insistent it would make a difference, emphasising her eyes, her best feature.

"It's not what I look like it's what I say that's important," Maureen protested.

"First impressions make a big difference," Beryl persisted, "don't forget, you're gonna lose ten points for being a black woman, so you need to pick up some first impression points by the way you look."

Maureen had not worn a wig since that night in Robbo's gambling house. Look at him, she thought, seated there like a VIP. Where's your mother to see you now Mr. Robinson, and Maureen's mother too come to that, she would be so proud to see her daughter now, This evening, Maureen wears a short and straight haired black wig that softens her face. Again, it was Beryl's suggestion but Maureen liked the wig as well and agreed it made her look less threatening.

She had beaten the odds to get to this position and not only because she was black. She had not helped herself with her tongue. She was widely condemned for her speech to the Liverpool Black People's Organisation. Although it was a closed meeting and only black people attended, the media quoted the speech within days.

"I don't like to talk bad of the dead," Maureen's speech began "but the shame Will Grimshaw brought on his family, to his colleagues and comrades in the Labour Party and to his constituents, and that poor woman was one of his constituents, cannot and should not be ignored. She was a poor desperate woman who had her kids taken off her because she had to sell her body to feed them. He wasn't Councillor Will frigging Grimshaw the designate local MP then was he, with his neat suit and fresh flower in his buttonhole, denouncing thugs, druggies and prostitutes that supposedly plague Liverpool 8. He was a friggin' pervert who used low-income women for his own gratifications."

Maureen and her supporters strongly denied she had said any of the words quoted but then says on the radio as an apology for Will Grimshaw that there ought to be space in our society for the seedier side of life.

The furore only died down when one of the three original candidates, Theo O'Malley, a strong Union man and the favourite for the nomination, was caught shoplifting in a city centre store.

Heather cites the women who inspired her. Eleanor Rathbone, described as a Member of Parliament, the first female Councillor in Liverpool and the godmother of family allowances. Battling Bessie Braddock, Liverpool MP and a committed Socialist, and Kitty Wilkinson, who pioneered public washhouses in Liverpool.

Maureen, who speaks after Heather, conscious of how well Heather's inspirators went down with the audience, decides to improvise. Her inspiration was her mother, Agnes Murphy, brought up in terrible poverty in the North End, became a well known trade unionist and provided a moral compass that included fighting injustice and caring for people. She also name checked Angela Davis, US political activist and Winnie Mandela, South African freedom fighter.

Both candidates adequately deal with the questions from the floor, pledging support and commitment to local constituents, condemning the government's policies, avoiding controversy—all routine stuff, but oratory alone will not get the votes tonight.

Just before the vote was to take place, a group of a dozen men burst into the room, shouting, carrying banners and distributing leaflets. Led by Alan Leung, these were members of the Socialist Workers Alliance Party

The police were called, the SWAP people were evicted from the meeting and order was restored. It took over one hour to get them all out and finally the voting took place.

Maureen won the vote by 30 against 28. She would be the Labour Party candidate for the Toxteth and Granby constituency. The proverbial donkey, even a black donkey, in Labour Party colours was a shoo-in for the Granby and Toxteth Constituency.

They celebrated all night at Lizzie's house. Nat Ajayi kept repeating it eyes wide with wonder, "Maureen Ajayi, my dauta, is Member o' Parliamen'. Maureen Ajayi, my dauta is Member o' Parliamen'."

Chapter 22

Babylon System

1 NOVEMBER 1991

Bonny Roberts is on the bus to Fazakerley. He is on his way to a work experience. "To get you in the habit of getting up every day and attending a place of work," the man at the Dole had assured him.

Bonny Roberts had been on the Dole for eight weeks now, courtesy of his partner of ten years, Beryl Leung. Beryl had quite simply nagged him into signing on as the first step into getting him into employment.

Not that Bonny was lazy or did not provide. He had a job of sorts, mainly night work, with Eric Gibson, his brother-in-law. Eric ran a security firm responsible for night and weekend security at some of the building sites that were popping up all over the city. Bonny was in charge of making sure the security men were not falling asleep on the job or didn't go home early; it was cash in hand but the work did not pay too well, or rather there was too little work. Sometimes he would go weeks without any work, but lately Bonny has been working nearly most nights and some days, because there was trouble at the ranch. The Okwuosa brothers had begun muscling in on Eric by beating up two of his men and wrecking one of the sites. Eric could not handle the pressure and paid Bonny to relieve it.

Bonny met with the brothers and they wanted at least half the security contracts that came up in the area otherwise they were going to war. These young punks were serious. There was a purpose in their manner that unsettled Bonny and Bonny was not easily unsettled. Bonny told Eric of the meeting and Eric flew into a rage.

"The fuckin' upstarts," he spat, "they're getting' fuck all off me. I'll show them."

Bonny is not looking forward to this 'work experience' lark, what with the security work, he'll just have time to eat and sleep.

Pure Pressure

Victor Mandacos comes on the bus two stops later. He spots Bonny sitting alone on the crowded bus, the only vacant seat left.

"Wha' 'appen?" they say to each other.

Victor and Bonny were gambling acquaintances, going back to the early Turkey days.

"These people would rather stand than sit next to us," Victor says pointing at the white passengers.

"I'm not complaining," Bonny replies, "more space for me."

"Where you off?" Victor asks him.

"I've just started work," said Bonny guardedly.

"Who for?"

"Some engineering firm in Fazakerley," Bonny replies scratching the back of his head although it did not itch, "What about you?"

"A big printing firm, only been there a week, that's in Fazakerley as well," says Victor, "the pay's alright but I don't like it much and they don't much like me. Fazakerley seems the place to be, though, businesses everywhere."

They reminisce about the old days for the rest of the journey, talking in backslang, so no one would understand. Victor gets off at the stop before Bonny, promising "to catch up and go out for a jar or two."

Bonny feels like he is in a foreign country, having never been before to Fazakerley. It is like being outside your comfort zone. Not that Fazakerley is any different to other Liverpool suburbs he knew. Same shops, the traffic is no different, busy and loud.

Beryl was so pleased when he left this morning just after 8 0'clock. She prepared and packed an egg sandwich, with the crusty ends of the loaf, which Bonny preferred, with English mustard and chopped onions inside.

"This is not a proper job," he warned her, trying to lower her expectations; "it's a pre-job, to prepare me for a regular job."

"You've got to start somewhere," she said, "it's a new beginning."

"We'll see," he cautioned. "I could be there for months before a proper job comes up, that's what they told me at the Dole."

Bonny gets off the bus and, after getting directions from a passerby, Bonny reaches a single-storey building in its own grounds, looking a bit like the dinner centres he remembered from his youth. There are no signs to identify the building except a small Department of Employment plaque stuck to the fence. The barbed wire on top of the fence surrounding the grounds makes the place look like a prison, getting Bonny to think that the security features was there to keep people in rather than keeping people out. Bonny opens a metal gate, closes it behind him and heads for the nearest door. He rings the bell and a man about his age opens the door.

"Come in," the man says with a neutral face.

Bonny walks into a large room that looks like a workshop with benches and tools. There are approximately 15 white men and one black.

It's Victor Mandacos.

They both walk towards each smiling the smile of the relieved that they are both in the same boat and start laughing.

"An engineering firm, hey," Victor says extending his hand.

"A printing firm, hey," Bonny replies smiling.

The work was monotonous, or rather, the routine was monotonous because it was not work, as Bonny understood work to be. A bit of messing about with woodwork, a bit of messing about with metalwork, testing this and testing that, it was all a droning blur. Bonny paid little attention to his tasks and spent most of his conscious time talking to Victor and daydreaming.

Bonny had to get a proper job because Beryl's whining was getting him down. She wanted him to learn a trade, an electrician, joiner, plumber, plasterer, bricklayer, any skill that would get him a regular well-paid job, and bouncer or security guard or part time football coach did not do except as pin money, she warned.

At the end of the fifth day at the Centre, Bonny does not think he will last another week let alone four weeks and that was the minimum period expected. It could last three months if you did not "progress" and you could have your Dole money docked.

Normally, Victor would be with him at the bus stop talking about the odd characters they 'worked' with, but he did not turn up today. It is a wet and an unusually cold day, the worst weather of the week, which always seems to begin on a Friday before the weekend. Bonny did not know about this general longing for Friday by nine-to-fivers, because Bonny had never worked a nine-to-five, but he was now beginning to understand.

He joins the queue at the bus stop and spots Zacky Pong coming out of the bank fifty yards from the bus stop. Zacky Pong. Zacky Pong the traitor, the adulterator, Judas Iscariot, the sneaky snake, the cunning fox, the two-faced piece of shit.

Bonny grins and as he strides briskly towards Zacky who is walking away his back to him. Bonny nods his head at the Anglican Cathedral silhouetted on the horizon, as if it has ordained this moment he had been waiting for for so long.

Pure Pressure

As soon as Zacky Pong feels the strong grip at the back of his neck, he knows it is Bonny Roberts. Alternatively, maybe it was the police feeling his collar for some crime or other committed in his distant past. No, it is Bonny Roberts. Destiny has caught up with him.

Zacky had been dreading this moment ever since Valerie and the kids—his kids—joined him in Scotland. It did not take him long to find somewhere for them all to live after he got the job as a cook on a rig in the middle of the North Sea, over hundred miles from Aberdeen. He rented a fully furnished four-bedroom house in west end Aberdeen. They lived there for nearly a year but rent levels nearly doubled in that time as the North Sea oil boom attracted thousands of workers from all over the country. As his shift was two weeks on and two weeks off, they could move anywhere. They chose Pollockshields, a multi-ethnic suburb of Glasgow, where Zack's Malaysian origins helped him to blend in. The children loved it there and were now fully-fledged Glaswegians. Valerie was in the final year of a teacher's qualification.

He had often talked about Bonny to Valerie, about how difficult it had been, how scared he was of Bonny's anger if he had told him he had been seeing Valerie behind his back all those years. It was just a bit of fun to begin with. Subsequently, she got serious and wanted to end it with Bonny. For three years, Zacky persuaded Valerie to keep their relationship secret, even after Mark was born. The second pregnancy was the catalyst. They would leave town, the further the better and soon. This soon turned out to be shortly after Melody's first birthday. Zacky had made dozens of application for jobs without getting anywhere, with Valerie pushing him on. He was a trained chef but had little experience, not having done anything other than hustle shortly after qualifying. It started well this hustling lark—gambling, dealing stolen goods, that sort of thing—then it became less lucrative but a way of life from which it was difficult to break away. There were some interviews but either he or the job was never quite right. The job on the rigs was a gift from the gods. The money was incredible and it was the furthest he could get from Liverpool without leaving the country. They could start a new, well-rewarded and open life.

Zacky curses his bad luck, as he used to curse it in the gambling houses when the run of cards went against him, or his horse just failed to win or the dice would not roll for him. This was bad luck of the highest order because he had only visited Liverpool twice to in more than 10 years. This was not even Liverpool proper. This was Fazakerley, way out of Bonny's beaten track. What was Bonny Roberts doing in this anonymous suburb when he never leaves the Southend?

Louis Julienne

Zacky had hailed a taxi from the station straight to the address where he was selling some bent jewellery to a fence he met on the rigs who happened to live in Fazakerley; Zacky always kept an eye out for opportunities. Zacky collected the cash, put it in the nearest bank for safety so that he did not have to carry it all the way back home, and was looking for a taxi straight back to Lime Street Station.

"Only mountains don't meet," says Bonny into Zacky's ear. "I wanna word with you Zacky," Zacky turns and faces him. Bonny is grinning while Zacky's face is as miserable as a lamb in an abattoir.

"Me and you are going round the corner where it's nice and quiet cos we have private business to settle," Bonny says as he grips Zacky's arm and propels towards a side street. Zacky does not bother struggling, there was no point as the grip was like a vice.

"We don't want to be arguing in front of all those white people now, do we? We need somewhere quiet, right?" Bonny says still grinning.

Zacky know that the beating of his life is about to begin and he is scared. Bonny might break his teeth, his white film-star teeth, the teeth that dazzled dozens of women over the years when he was a player. Although Zacky knew Bonny would not use a weapon to beat him, he did not need to; he could inflict terrible damage without a weapon, Zacky had seen him do it.

"Look Bonny," cries Zacky as they turn into a small deserted street, "I fell in love with her; I've never felt that way before. I was besotted. I didn't know how to tell you."

"For years it was going on, you lyin' little bastard."

"What you talking about, Bonny, it only happened four weeks before she left."

"People are saying you're the father of my kids."

"No, no, that's nonsense Bonny. It happened all suddenly, I swear Bonny, ask Valerie."

"Don't you mention her name to me you little piece of shit," said Bonny gripping Zacky's shoulder and pointing an accusing finger close to his eyes. "You're gonna die today you two-faced little fart."

"Look Bonny, please," Zacky pleads. The dam that had been filling up right to the brim finally burst from his eyes and nose. The resulting emulsion of snot and tears as Zacky tried to wipe it away with his sleeve drew a white streak right across his face.

"Don't 'look' me," says Bonny wrapping his hands around Zacky Pong's throat, "you're gonna die right now."

"Please . . . lissen . . . please . . . I swear . . ." Zacky croaks.

Bonny looks at Zacky, pathetically submissive, and his anger, his need for revenge evaporates somehow. Zacky sees the change in Bonny and seizes the moment.

"I loved you Bonny, you were the best friend I ever had," Zacky says wiping his face as Bonny releases his grip. "I've wanted so much to meet you and explain. I know we could never be like we were but . . ."

Zacky's legendary gift of talking himself out of trouble is in full on mode. Zacky persuades Bonny to join him for a drink at a nearby worker's café. During his persuasive monologue, Zacky concedes Mark and Melody are his children and that he and Valerie are happy together. They were laughing about the time when Zacky sold a boxed television set to a bouncer that contained a pile of neatly piled bricks when Bonny's eye spots an *Echo* headline over another customer's shoulder.

'*Body found buried in Toxteth*' it reads

Bonny tries to read the story over the man's shoulder but the man gets annoyed and tells him to buy his own bloody paper.

"I'd better get off," Bonny says to Zacky, "Beryl's on earlies and tea'll be nearly ready."

Zacky is the happiest person in Fazakerley as he shakes Bonny's hands with great vigour.

Bonny reads the story three times when he finally buys a newspaper. It is as he feared; they had found Greg's body, unless, coincidences of coincidences, another body had been buried in the same street.

The police had cordoned off Ducie Cairns Street and Jermyn Street and the talk was that more bodies lay buried there. When Bonny arrives home the whole house is talking about nothing else. Beryl looks at Bonny in a strange way, in a '*chicken have come home to roost*' way. She never mentioned the body or her suspicions when they were in bed alone that night, but made a point of sleeping on the edge of the bed so that they did not touch and she kept the routine up for days afterwards.

On the following Thursday, during the lunch break, the police come to the Rehabilitation Centre in Fazakerley and arrest Bonny on suspicion of murder. The police had found a set of keys near Greg's remains with Bonny's DNA all over them.

Chapter 23

Time Will Tell

December 1991

It is a peculiar thing about time; it goes so quickly, particularly when you are enjoying how you are spending that time. Life has gone too quickly, not the seconds and minutes so much, nor the days or even the months, but the years. So quickly have these years passed, and there are fewer years left to live, that you start resenting the wasted time, the time doing nothing, except wasting time. Sleep, for a start, is a main culprit. Eight hours sleep a day every day. That is a third of your life gone in a click of the tongue. Therefore, by the time you reach 60 you have slept for 20 years. Twenty years, SLEEPING! That is too long a time. Sleeping four hours a night should be sufficient and it would bring a bonus worth at least 10 years. Oh, but the pleasures in sleep are irresistible. The cold mornings under the warm blankets, when you could go back to sleep for two, three or even four hours more and feel none of that time has been wasted, in fact it had been blissful. After a long day, when much work has been done, eight hours is sometimes not enough. Maybe there is not a lot of time to be trimmed from sleeping after all. Maybe time is not wasted, except when sitting watching television for hours on end. It was not time wasted that mattered then, but how time was spent because there was so little of it to spare.

These are the thoughts of Alan Leung and he is trying to convey them to Lil Bob. It is late in the afternoon, they have been smoking ganja since lunchtime, and both are feeling heavy but talking shit. They had a drink earlier in the *Alex* on Hill Street, then a fight broke out and it became quite rowdy, so they left and went to another pub, *Cavanagh's* on Egerton Street, where the atmosphere is more serene.

After sitting down with their drinks Lil Bob finally brings up why he went looking for Alan in the first place.

Pure Pressure

"Lissen, lah," Lil Bob begins, "we've gorra suppor' Maureen. She's under pure pressure and we need to suppor' her. You need to talk your kid out of giving evidence against her. Anuvafin', you're a so called communi'y leader according to the press and any'in' you say to the press they prin'. If the press wanna quo' from black people they always go to you. Like i' or no' I' tha' the way i'is, andtha' reali'y means responsibili'y."

"Why should I," Alan counters straightening his shoulders, "She's noffin to me and I don't need her."

"Yes, she is," Lil Bob says, "she's your step sisser, but you were best friends years before tha'. Tha''s no' the poin' anyway lah, iss no' abou' personali'ics; iss abou'the firss black MP in Liverpool; a black MP who is radical and on our side. We could not have imagined twenty years ago, or even ten years ago tha' we would elec' a black MP. If she doesn' ge' through this and is sacked as an MP it'll pu' us back another twenny years before we can think of elec'ing another black MP."

There is a long silence between them while Alan thinks over what Lil Bob is requesting, the habitual background patter at Cavanagh's at lunchtime on a weekday percolates around the room.

"I've just finished directing a promo for British Gas and I'm looking for finance to do a short film."

"What's it about Ken?"

"The time Adolph Hitler stayed in Stanhope Street in Liverpool, before he became famous. It's a comedy, Charlie Chaplin type but more subtle. I've written the script already. Large rum n' black for me Deirdre and John's having a pint of bitter. It is a pint of bitter, isn't it John? Yes, bitter for John and rum n' black for me."

"Of course they're knock-off, how else you gonna get this quality merchandise at that price. Do you want them or don't ya?"

"But is it real gold?"

"Real gold! Look at the hallmarks, man, look at the hallmarks."

"Well he took off with one of his students, less than half his age. He bought me out of my share of the house, so now he and his little scheming floozy are living large in my house, while the kids and I are living in a small terraced house in Dingle. It's not fair."

"I didn't think he would do that, Audrey, not to you and the kids. He's a wicked man."

"Another riot, what good did the last one do? Half the area was destroyed. They built a garden festival e costing millions of pounds, creating 150 jobs, but only one black person recruited to work there and she was so light-skinned they probably couldn't tell."

"The way things are going if we don't do som'n abourrit, we'll end up as a community wid less than we've got now, so we may as well riot. We've got noffin' to lose."

"I fink fings are getting better not worse. A black MP for Liverpool, can you imagine? A black MP for Liverpool, who'd have thought it!"

"Okay," says Alan at last, "I'll go visit our Bonny and ask him to withdraw his statement against Maureen and I swear I won't backchat her to the media. I can see where you're coming from and maybe I should be going there as well."

Lil Bob smiles at Alan's cooperation and suggests they go back to his place as he only lived around the corner. The old choir practice place.

"So you fink she'll set us all free den?" Alan asks sarcastically

"She can' do I' alone, but time will tell, brudder-man, time will tell," Lil Bob replies as he dials for home-delivery pizza.

Chapter 24

Dreamland

11 May 2001

Lizzie did not see much of her funeral, but she knew the moment she died. It was like no other event in her long life, as one would expect given the nature of the event. She gasped for breath that was not there, trying hard not to let go as she felt she was being pushed away to die.

She was vaguely aware of people around her. Beryl and Bonny, Alan, Alice, Our Wayne, Michelle, Googie's daughter and some people all dressed in white, fussing around her, asking questions she could not answer. Lizzie knew she was at the Royal hospital, the bright lights and that familiar public-place disinfectant smell told her that.

Father Dominic had been brought out of retirement to give her the last rites. Alan would not have any other priest.

Lizzie knew when the ambulance came that it would be the last time she ever saw the home again. A lovely place the Steve Biko Sheltered Accommodation, she knew most people there, at least those that had survived. It was like going back in time—Phyllis, Roy, Ben, Miriam, Hilda, Scots Annie and her husband, Winnie Smith, the Grants, Sheila McKenzie, Lorraine Wilkinson—so many from her past life. She had been well looked after there, like a Queen Mother. She had her own flat and a tiny little garden. She would get herself wheeled out on to the patio and sit there in the sun listening to the birds and letting her mind wander to the good times and the bad times. Her mind often recalled the fire as the beginning of the bad luck in her life.

Lizzie left home at eight o'clock that warm September night in 1952, all dolled up for work behind the bar at Wilkie's place. Lizzie needed the money; Kai was a saver and kept her allowance to the strictest minimum. It was only when he came home from his long trips that the Leung household flourished. There was no rationing for them then—bacon, eggs, sugar, soap and sweets for the kids and stockings for the missus.

It was good to get away from the house and the kids as well as earning extra cash. It was like being a single woman again, flirting with the customers and enjoying a dance or two. It never went further than that, of course, although she had plenty of offers; Lizzie was not that kind of woman.

Esmee would come over with her kids and stay the weekend. A single mother, Esmee was pleased to get away from the four walls of her one bedroom room rented flat, and Lizzie always fed and watered them well.

That night, before she went out, Lizzie had bought a bottle of Sherry and encouraged Esmee to have a drink with her. Esmee did not normally drink but she was obliging by nature that is why she had two children by two different men.

While Lizzie was out Esmee had drunk most of the contents of the Sherry bottle and all the lemonade. Esmee lit a cigarette and fell asleep in the armchair. When she woke up a couple of hours later, Esmee did not notice the smoke slowly and inexorably released from the bowels of the armchair. She staggered upstairs straight to bed unaccustomed to the feeling in her head, which was sending the walls spinning around her; she fell on top of the bed fully dressed and slept.

Esmee woke up in hospital a few hours later being treated for smoke inhalation. The flames had been ruthless. Bonny, escaped virtually unhurt after his sister had dropped him out of the bathroom window into a neighbour's arm. Beryl was next out of the bathroom window, followed by a badly burned Doreen. The rest did not make it, sacrificed to a duty that dictated the younger ones took preference out first. Harry and Joan, Esmee's precious little angels, were dead. Lillian and Elizabeth, Lizzie's heaven on earth were dead also.

Esmee had miraculously survived virtually and shamefully, unscathed. Emotionally though, Esmee may as well have died that night. Depression from then on became an eccentric companion.

Kai Leung flew over from Mexico eight days later just in time for the funerals. Lizzie had only seen him for seven days in the past fifteen months. Kai never went back to sea after that. He managed against bitter opposition to get a job on the docks in Liverpool. Kai Leung was the first locally born Chinese to work on a permanent contract on Liverpool docks and quite an oddity he became. Predictably, he had been nicknamed Chinky by the less sensitive and Can-Can by those who thought themselves more liberal. All Dockers had nicknames; colleagues assured him it was part of the tradition. Kai had a thick skin so the insults did not make a dent.

Lizzie did not look at Esmee for over twenty years after the fire let alone speak to her, and that was at their mother's funeral when they hugged each other at Maggie's behest and they cried together.

Lizzie might not remember what had happened last Tuesday or even this morning but she remembered times long past. Terrible times, good times, she recalled them all in detail. Now she was dead.

Well, her body was dead but her spirit was very much alive. This was not a dream, not heaven nor hell—that judgement had yet to be made. This was purgatory, Lizzie instinctively knew, waiting in transition. Lizzie was in no hurry for that appointment so she just hung around her body, like a faithful dog to its owner.

Lizzie hovered over her body as it was getting 'dressed' at the funeral parlour. Disgusting to look at and the end results were so bizarre. The mouth, which stood gaping revealing eight gnarled teeth (four on the top and four on the bottom), had its jaws broken, then stuffed with paper to puff up the sunken cheeks. The lips had been stitched tight so the mouth remained firmly closed. A clean white shroud covered the length of her body. The make-up powder that covered her face and hands, and rouge dabbed on both cheeks, made Lizzie Roberts-Leung look like an old "oower" from Selbourne Street.

Lizzie referred to her corpse as the body, because it was not Lizzie anymore; Lizzie was floating above the body looking down at it. This was a deliberate choice, hanging around. She could have gone straight on to judgement and if heaven was chosen, well she could lose out on the deal because heaven was better than keeping a narcissistic eye on her remains. On the other hand, if she was going to Hell then it was time well spent. You had that choice, to hang around for a while, to give you chance to recollect and maybe repent or go straight to the next stage. There must be billions of people who exhausted their time repenting as much as possible and then drifting in to hear their fate, to find out whether the ultimate prize had been earned or not. Others would go straight for the Judgement, conscience crystal clear, banging on the door almost, but most just floated away buying time.

Lizzie stayed for her funeral, a splendid affair with four white horses pulling the hearse, a packed congregation and Father Dominic. He gave a fine sermon, as usual, but in a faltering voice—age had caught up with him. At the graveside, taped music of Nat King Cole songs played on a portable music machine. Twelve fluttering white doves were released to the grey skies, and some people cried—the usual suspects—but most people sang and clapped hands.

Lizzie had weighed the balance of good deeds and bad deeds in her life countless times before this moment. At her worst, she had given her grandchild away against the wishes of her daughter. At her best, she had brought up a family with selfless love and devotion. Other than that, she had led a blameless life she had always convinced herself. Now, in front of Judgement Day, she was not so sure.

She feared that God may be white and biased against black people like back on earth. She feared that racism was not just an earthly, human phenomenon, but a celestial one also. What will be her fate if the man at the gate is a Boer from the veldt, a redneck from Alabama or a yob from Huyton? What would he make of a Liverpool mongrel who had given her grandchild away, like in some Greek tragedy?

Imagine Lizzie's absolute delight to find out that God was black. Not light brown or dark brown or this brown and that brown, but jet-black. At first It was just a plain black face without characteristics, but gradually features developed so that by the end of the process God looked just like Lizzie did the day she met Kai. No sermon was given, no words were exchanged, but Lizzie knew she was going to heaven now, although she did not always deserve it, she knew then, at the very moment that face was revealed, that she always was one of God's children.

She felt her spirit soar into a blinding light and that was the last Lizzie Roberts-Leung was able to communicate after her death. Her message that God was you and me and everybody, floated in the ether for a few years; only three people during that time in the whole world picked the message up about what happened after you die (one of her great granddaughters, a medicine man in South Africa, and a pickpocket in Peru). Her great granddaughter Carlene (Alma's daughter) was the first to receive the message one frosty morning when she was picking firewood in the woods near a cottage she rented in the Lake District. The following week she laid a bouquet of flowers on Lizzie's grave and talked to her for hours. Unfortunately, Lizzie could not hear her as she was already in Heaven and incommunicado.

The Zulu medicine man in South Africa was the second recipient as he lay meditating in his compound and shortly afterwards immigrated to Sheffield, England and became a wealthy Evangelist. The last was a professional pickpocket in Peru, who gave pickpockting up as a career and became a medium.